The fiery brilliance of the Zebra Hologram Heart which you see on the cover is created by "laser holography." This is the revolutionary process in which a powerful laser beam records light waves in diamond-like facets so tiny that 9,000,000 fit in a square inch. No print or photograph can match the vibrant colors and radiant glow of a hologram.

So look for the Zebra Hologram Heart whenever you buy a historical romance. It is a shimmering reflection of our guarantee that you'll find consistent quality between the covers!

ECSTASY'S SPELL

"Josie, please, we have to talk. I want you to listen to what I have to say." He continued to coax her, his attention equally divided between her wide, green eyes and her soft, inviting lips. "You must give me a chance to explain. I had my reasons for what I did, foolish though they might seem."

Josie's mouth opened, an angry response ready on her lips. But before she could speak, Nathan's mouth came crashing down on hers to claim it with a bold, soul-shattering kiss, and all traces of coherent thought slowly slipped away. It was as if he'd cast some mysterious spell over her. Never had she known such a need to return a kiss and explore it for all it could offer.

Finally, after several mind-reeling moments, Nathan gently pulled away from her. Too spellbound to move, Josie gazed once again into his glimmering eyes. When he spoke, his voice was a whisper. "Please stay . . . stay with me. . . ."

EXHILARATING ROMANCE
From Zebra Books

GOLDEN PARADISE   (2007, $3.95)
by Constance O'Banyon
Desperate for money, the beautiful and innocent Valentina Barrett finds
work as a veiled dancer, "Jordanna," at San Francisco's notorious Crystal
Palace. There she falls in love with handsome, wealthy Marquis Vin-
cente—a man she knew she could never trust as Valentina — but who Jordanna can't resist making her lover and reveling in love's GOLDEN
PARADISE.

SAVAGE SPLENDOR   (1855, $3.95)
by Constance O'Banyon
By day Mara questioned her decision to remain in her husband's world.
But by night, when Tajarez crushed her in his strong, muscular arms, taking her to the peaks of rapture, she knew she could never live without
him.

TEXAS TRIUMPH   (2009, $3.95)
by Victoria Thompson
Nothing is more important to the determined Rachel McKinsey than the
Circle M — and if it meant marrying her foreman to scare off rustlers,
she would do it. Yet the gorgeous rancher feels a secret thrill that the towering Cole Elliot is to be her man — and despite her plan that they be
business partners, all she truly desires is a glorious consummation of their
vows.

KIMBERLY'S KISS   (2184, $3.95)
by Kathleen Drymon
As a girl, Kimberly Davonwoods had spent her days racing her horse, per-
fecting her fencing, and roaming London's byways disguised as a boy.
Then at nineteen the raven-haired beauty was forced to marry a complete
stranger. Though the hot-tempered adventuress vowed to escape her new
husband, she never dreamed that he would use the sweet chains of ecstasy
to keep her from ever wanting to leave his side!

FOREVER FANCY   (2185, $3.95)
by Jean Haught
After she killed a man in self-defense, alluring Fancy Broussard had no
choice but to flee Clarence, Missouri. She sneaked aboard a private rail-
car, plotting to distract its owner with her womanly charms. Then the
dashing Rafe Taggart strode into his compartment . . . and the frightened
girl was swept up in a whirlwind of passion that flared into an undeniable, unstoppable prelude to ecstasy!

*Available wherever paperbacks are sold, or order direct from the
Publisher. Send cover price plus 50¢ per copy for mailing and
handling to Zebra Books, Dept. 2812, 475 Park Avenue South,
New York, N.Y. 10016. Residents of New York, New Jersey and
Pennsylvania must include sales tax. DO NOT SEND CASH.*

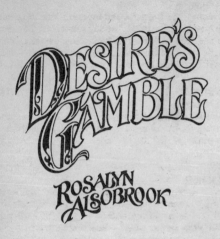

DESIRE'S GAMBLE

ROSALYN ALSOBROOK

ZEBRA BOOKS
KENSINGTON PUBLISHING CORP.

ZEBRA BOOKS

are published by

Kensington Publishing Corp.
475 Park Avenue South
New York, NY 10016

Copyright © 1989 by Rosalyn Alsobrook

All rights reserved. No part of this book may be repro-
duced in any form or by any means without the prior
written consent of the Publisher, excepting brief quotes
used in reviews.

First printing: November, 1989

Printed in the United States of America

In loving memory of a truly *great* man.
Lowell Edison Rutledge, MD
Dec. 17, 1920 — March 30, 1988
"My Dad."

Prologue

March 29, 1875

Nathaniel Garrett set his father's letter down on top of the attorney's desk and frowned, perplexed by what he'd just read.

"Do I understand this right? My entire inheritance rests on the whims of this one little girl?" he asked, his voice appropriately deep from a man so powerfully built.

"I'm afraid so," Jason Haught said with a short, confirming nod, and leaned forward in his chair. His narrow face remained expressionless while he stared through round-rimmed spectacles at the concerned young man who sat before him dressed in a fitted three-piece cutaway.

Nathaniel glanced back over the first page of the three-page letter until he located the girl's name again. He raked his hand through his thick brown hair as he studied it, then narrowed his pale-blue eyes when he looked back at the attorney. "You mean to tell me that if this little Josephine Leigh takes a notion not to cooperate with us in this matter, I'll end up with absolutely nothing. But if she does agree to cooperate, I'll get at least half of everything my father owned?"

"Exactly half of everything. And she will get the other half," Jason verified with another brisk nod. "If you both cooperate in fulfilling your father's last requests, you will both be well rewarded for your efforts, I assure you. I don't have to remind you that Oakhaven alone is worth a small fortune. And your father's art collection has to be worth almost twice that. There are paintings in that house he refused to sell for any amount, one in particular. But then, any of his paintings are going to bring quite a price back East, especially now."

"You mean now that he is dead," Nathan said, his tone laced with bitterness.

"I know it seems cruel, but, yes. Once a famous artist dies, his artwork becomes even more valuable. So, as you can clearly see, the amount you two stand to inherit is quite considerable. There's no doubt in my mind you will both be financially stable for life when this is all over. But if either of you defaults, for whatever reason, neither of you will inherit a cent. I know it seems a little strange and probably very unfair. But, because I was your father's personal friend as well as his attorney, I can assure you this is the way he wanted it."

"So, I'm to put up with the little girl for three months," he sighed heavily. "And where do I find this Josephine Leigh?" Nathan asked, still frowning. His pale eyes glittered with annoyance as he slowly refolded the letter, then tucked it carefully inside his coat pocket.

"Last your father knew, the girl was living with an aunt and uncle over in Louisiana, in a small town called Cypress Mill. I've investigated the different modes of travel to the area and suggest you take the train east as far as Alexandria. There you can probably rent a horse, or maybe you can hire a rig of some sort to take you the final distance, which I understand is another seven miles toward the south."

"Has the girl been notified about any of this?"

Jason tilted his head to one side. The sunlight from a nearby window caught the silvery highlights of his gray hair. "No, not yet. I wanted to wait until I had a chance to talk with you first. I wanted to explain to you that I do have a potential buyer for the house, and I also know of several other people who are interested in your father's paintings. I felt you should be fully aware of the opportunities here."

"I appreciate your consideration." Nathan pressed his lips together for a moment while he considered what action he should take next. Though he did not like the idea of leaving his own place to the management of others, it looked as if he had no other choice. If he wanted his share of the inheritance, he would have to play by his father's rules, strange as they were.

"First, I'll need to go back home to Quail Run and pack enough of my belongings to see me through this. I also want to be sure that everything there will be run properly in my absence. Randall Clifton, my foreman, will want to know exactly how long I might have to be away, as well as when and where he can reach me if he needs to. I'll have to give him your address, since that would be the easiest way to get in touch with me. If that's all right with you, that is."

James nodded that it was indeed all right with him. "I'll pass along any messages I get."

"I'd appreciate it. I guess after that, I'll bring most of my things on by here, or maybe I'll go ahead and carry them on out to Oakhaven. Then I should be on my way to Louisiana to see if I can find this Josephine Leigh and her aunt and uncle." Nathan stood, then smoothed his thick, unruly brown hair back with his fingers before replacing his hat. "I'll send word to you as soon as I get back from Cypress Mill. Or should I say, as soon as *we* get back."

"I'll be waiting to hear," Jason said, rising to accompany Nathan to the door. "And until you do return, I'll keep the place padlocked and continue having a man ride out daily to check on the stock. Come by here for the key before going out to leave off any of your things . . . When do you expect to leave for Cypress Mill? I'll try to have a letter prepared for you to take with you that should explain to Miss Leigh exactly what is at

9

stake here."

"It'll take me a week or so to get my own affairs settled enough so that I can leave with a clear conscience. But I fully understand that the sooner I find Miss Josie Leigh, the sooner I can speak with her and her guardians, and get everything settled — and the sooner we can get the provisions of that will under way." He paused. "Father's letter said she lives with her aunt and uncle. Do you happen to have their names?"

"Edward and Nadine Hammet. Josephine also has an older cousin, named Trey Hammet, who I understand owns a saloon there in Cypress Mill. But that's about all I know. I'm afraid the details your father gave me were a little sketchy. But then, I don't think he was planning to die so soon."

"Hammet." Nathan repeated the name aloud, committing it to memory, then reached out to shake the older man's hand. "Thank you for all your help. I only hope this Mr. and Mrs. Hammet prove to be as helpful as you have been."

"For the amount their niece stands to inherit, surely they will be."

"Oh, well, if they prove too uncooperative, I'll just kidnap the child and be done with it," Nathan said jokingly, and for the first time since he learned of his father's death, he smiled.

Chapter One

April 10, 1875

"Read them and weep, gents," Josie Leigh said just before she laid her five cards on the table, faceup. A triumphant smile played at her lips. "A pair of sixes and a pair of threes."

"You weren't kiddin' when you said you felt lucky today," Sirus Gordy muttered, tossing his own five cards on the table, facedown, then puckering his grizzled face into a childlike pout. As he leaned forward, he shoved a fist up under his whiskered chin and watched while Josie gathered her poker winnings from the center of the small wooden table. "That's four hands in a row for you. Why don't you ever give the rest of us a chance at winnin'?"

"Oh? You want another chance at winning, do you?" Josie asked. Her huge green eyes glittered with meaningful delight and her smile deepened until tiny dimples formed at the outer corners of her mouth. Tinges of pink highlighted her cheeks. "Shall I deal another hand then?"

"Dern right you shall. I gotta win back some of my money," Sirus replied. His bushy white brows dipped low while he continued to rest his chin heavily on top of his knobby fist, his elbow propped against the table. "Don't you feel even a little bit guilty when you win so much of our money in one whack?"

"Awe, hush up your belly-aching, Sirus," Lloyd Taylor scolded, frowning at his best friend while he handed his cards back to Josie. Being four months older than Sirus had always made Lloyd feel he should be the one in authority, though Sirus did not usually see it that way. "Miss Josie didn't force you to bet all that money. As I recall, it was *your* idea to hike the pot that last five dollars."

"Besides," Josie said, laughing, fully aware that Sirus's sudden display of ill temper was more show than anything else, "I can use the money. I'm still trying to save enough to get my own place. Though I do appreciate my cousin's hospitality here at the Dogwood, and I love being so near my friends, I'm a little tired of having to live in one of Trey's spare storage rooms upstairs."

Her smile grew wistful as she visualized the small house at the far end of Elm Street that was still for sale. Granted, the house was in dire need of painting and the yard was overgrown with every kind of weed imaginable, but the place had definite possibilities. "I do so want a real house—a house all my own—with a pretty little garden to grow flowers and a fluffy white cat sitting on the porch patiently waiting for me whenever I come home."

"You wouldn't know what to do with a real house if you had one," Sirus grumbled. "Quit your jawin' and deal those cards. Sometimes you can be slower than a one-legged turtle."

"Would you like to deal the next hand?" Josie asked and offered him the cards, knowing he would never take them.

"You know nobody trusts me enough to let me deal," Sirus muttered, and his scowl darkened. Slowly, his gaze fell across the others at the table while he chewed on something imaginary. "They'd all have a red-eyed fit if'n I was to try and deal."

Voncille Sobey laughed good-naturedly. Leaning back, he took a long draw of his beer. After he wiped the excess off his upper lip with his shirt-sleeve, he said, nodding agreeably, "That's true enough. Can't trust that old codger when it comes to poker." Then he looked from Sirus to the other two men with a raised brow and a huge grin. "As usual, Miss Josie, you're the *only* trustworthy person at this entire table."

"In this entire saloon," Frank Pyle added. Laughing along with the rest, he gave the people milling about a quick once-over.

"So, hush up and deal!" Sirus grumbled as he reached for his whiskey glass and gulped down the last of the fiery liquid before signaling for more. Though Sirus was one of the oldest patrons in Trey Hammet's saloon, he had the uncanny knack of putting away more whiskey than any of the younger men, and in far less time. Yet he rarely showed any of the usual effects. "I didn't come here to talk about what a noble person Miss Josie is. I came to play cards. So start dealing."

Still smiling, Josie placed the twenty-five discards into a small stack in front of her, then dealt a second round from the unused portion of the deck. Because Sirus and Lloyd preferred to play Texas sweat, in which everyone got all five of their cards at once, all dealt facedown, there was always a short pause to study the cards before any betting started.

It took Josie only a few seconds to put her cards in the order she wanted. While the others moaned and groaned, studied, and rearranged the cards they'd been handed, Josie took a moment to open her lightweight ebony fan and put it to good use. Because very little breeze stirred through the three open windows or around the undersized saloon doors, the room felt stuffy, despite the moderate spring temperature outside.

While the men continued to mull over their cards, Josie continued to work her fan with short, rapid movements, glad she had taken the time to pull her heavy brown hair up into a stylish array of curls, which kept it from trapping her own body heat against her neck and shoulders. Absently, she let her gaze sweep the small, familiar room with its gay colors and shiny overhead mirrors. Due to the early hour—barely four o'clock—there were very few patrons in the saloon at the moment, mostly the town regulars, or farmers and plantation owners in town to conduct their weekly business.

But, later, because it was a Saturday and payday for most folks, the room would soon be filled with boisterous laughter, clinking glasses, and blending voices. For the most part, the voices would be loud, booming male voices, though the three young women who worked for her cousin would certainly add their fair share of girlish laughter. Josie, too, would add a goodly portion of laughter to the noisy din, for Saturday nights were always full of fun and surprises. Her blood stirred at the thought of all the excitement sure to come, certain tonight would prove to be no exception.

Aware Sirus and Lloyd were not yet satisfied with the arrangement of the cards in their hands, still hoping to find better possibilities, Josie continued to look about the room. Eventually her gaze wandered to the only other female in the saloon.

At such an early hour, only one girl was needed to see to the customers, and today that was Carla. Josie watched while the girl quickly cleared several empty glasses from a nearby table while smiling to herself over some private thought. Josie smiled, too.

Carla Porterfield was the oldest of the three young women who presently worked for her cousin, and very skilled in the mysterious ways of feminine flirtation. Josie was fascinated by the way men reacted to Carla's womanly charms. Carla had an uncanny way of turning even the most sophisticated gent into a bumbling, money-spending schoolboy in a matter of minutes. Her ability to get the customers to drink up and enjoy themselves was well worth the eighteen dollars Trey paid her each week, though he knew that was more

14

than some ranch hands made in the same week's time. But it was those high wages that kept Carla from having to supplement her income with prostitution. Trey was smart enough to know that once Carla or any of the other girls felt it necessary to turn to prostitution, they would lose a lot of their special appeal. And it was that appeal, that these women were not easily conquered, that brought the customers in time and time again.

Dressed in a bright-red, low-cut satin dress that hugged all the right curves and was adorned with fluffy blue-and-white feathers and bright silver sequins, Carla was very appealing to the men who patronized Trey's saloon. Men of all ages flocked around her like addle-brained geese. Though Josie knew Carla was barely twenty years old—a full three years younger than herself—the dark face-colors the girl wore made her look much older. And with such a winning smile, well-rounded bosom, and quick wit, Carla was clearly the favorite of Trey's customers. Even old Sirus had a hard time keeping his eyes off her.

Josie shook her head in wonder. She could never be like Carla. Though Josie felt pretty enough and popular enough, she just did not have whatever it took to be an attraction like Carla.

Indeed, Josie was easily set apart from the other girls. Attired in a mint-green, fashionably cut dress of Swiss muslin with a wide, flounced overskirt and a moderately cut, heart-shaped neckline, and wearing an elegant emerald-and-diamond choker at her slender throat, it was obvious Josie was not there to tempt or taunt, or to encourage the customers to drink. Though she did occasionally help behind the bar when her cousin needed her, and she truly enjoyed visiting with her many friends, Josie's real interest at the Dogwood Saloon was the gambling tables. Not only did she love a lively game of cards, it was how she made her living. Though she hated the term, in actuality she was a professional gambler.

"Whose turn is it to start?" Sirus asked, after having finally arranged his cards to his satisfaction.

"Yours, you forgetful old coot," Voncille answered, glancing up from his cards just long enough to be sure Sirus had heard him and reacted accordingly.

"That's what I thought," Sirus responded with a sinister smile, his gaze intense. "So I'll just start things rolling by tossin' out the first three dollars."

"Suits me," Lloyd said with a sly nod, cutting his gaze around the table. "I'm in for three."

By the time the betting reached Josie, she felt certain her pair of kings would not hold up against the others. Both Sirus and Lloyd had been a little too eager to let go of their money.

"I'm out," she stated simply, and placed her cards on the table in front of her, facedown.

"Now, that ain't fair!" Sirus said, narrowing his greygreen eyes until they were two small slits beneath his bushy white brows. Again his whiskered jaw worked furiously, as if chewing on something made of hard rubber.

"Oh, hush up, Sirus, and play. The rest of us are still in," Lloyd told him, then ran his tongue over his own sun-weathered lips in keen anticipation of the eventual outcome. His foot tapped impatiently on the wooden floor.

Josie leaned back in her chair and watched. Because gambling was her livelihood, she took every game seriously and was not about to take a chance on a questionable hand—unless she happened to be in a situation where she felt she could run a bluff. But bluffing Sirus did not come easy, since it usually didn't matter to the old man if the others had something worth betting on or not. If he thought he had anything at all, he played the hand out to the end, which accounted for the amount of money he usually lost every Saturday afternoon.

And at the moment, Sirus thought he had something. Josie knew by the sparkle in his eye and the twitch at the corner of his mouth. She wondered if it was enough to beat whatever the others had.

While Sirus dug deeper into his shirt pocket to find another dollar, Josie noticed a movement out of the corner of her eye and glanced toward the door, more out of habit than anything else.

Far more curious to see how the game would come out than in who might have entered the saloon — especially after the other four players had all stayed in and bet so heavily — she had intended to give the newcomer nothing more than a passing glance. Just enough to see if it was someone she knew and should wave to.

But when she caught sight of the man who stepped through the door, she found he rated far more than a passing glance. He was both tall and handsome, and probably only a half dozen years older than she. Enchanted, she watched while he turned a powerful left shoulder toward her, then moved further into the room.

The game continued without her notice. She was mesmerized by the man's smooth, lithe movements when he casually sauntered toward the bar and rested a well-stitched black boot on the footrail. With his knee slightly bent, he leaned forward on one muscular leg and spoke with Pete Moon, the bartender. Being only five foot eight, Pete was dwarfed by the man's size.

Staring at the powerful lines of his body and wondering what he did to keep himself so fit, Josie suddenly found it increasingly difficult to catch her breath. The muscles in her throat tightened and her blood stirred into hard, rapid motion while she instinctively fought to fill her lungs with fresh air. Although many a handsome man had entered her cousin's saloon through the years, none had strode in with quite the same air of confidence and purpose as this man.

There was just something about him that not only commanded her attention, but the attention of everyone else in the room as well. She wondered who he was and why he had come to Cypress Mill. Next, she wondered how long he intended to stay, and if he was by any chance unmarried, though she could not fathom why that should matter to her at all. She certainly had no intention of getting to know the man, or did she? She fought the urge to laugh at such a silly notion, though she continued to watch him from across the room, trying to decide who he was and what business he could possibly have in Cypress Mill.

Judging by the quality of his clothes, he was not a poor man. He wore a pair of dark-blue duck trousers that fit him perfectly, as did his spotless pale-blue pleated shirt and his dark-blue summerweight coat. Clearly, his clothing was tailor-made, and she wondered brazenly what it would be like to take a measuring tape across those broad, masculine shoulders. For the first time, she decided sewing might have at least one worthy aspect.

Wanting to continue her perusal of the handsome man without being caught doing so, Josie turned her head slightly away from him. She hoped to make it appear she'd resumed her interest in the card game while, in truth, she continued to observe the perfection of the newcomer's profile out of the very corner of her eye while he continued to speak with Pete. She felt her pulses race with alarming speed when, moments later, he shifted to an angle which allowed her a three-quarter view of his face.

She could now see how very strong his facial features were and how undeniably attractive he was. Everything about him was appealing, even the way he moved his mouth when he spoke. She decided God must have been at his finest the day he created such a man, for he was without a doubt the most magnificent human being she had ever seen. There was such a strong sense of self-assurance and powerful masculinity about him that it sent shivers of awareness cascading down her spine and settling all the way into her toes.

Then suddenly he smiled at something Pete had said and Josie feared her heart might do permanent damage to the inner lining of her chest. She abandoned all hope for normal breath when long, narrow dimples formed along his lean cheeks and his smile parted to reveal his white teeth. His mouth was incredibly appealing. *He* was incredibly appealing. Again, she wondered who he was and why he was there.

"You goin' to deal another hand or not?" Sirus's voice jabbed into her thoughts, startling her.

"Oh, yes. Of — of course," she stammered, suddenly embarrassed that she'd allowed herself to be so easily distracted by a total stranger. Wanting to return her attention to the game, she tried to shake the strange, fluttery feelings that had so quickly consumed her. It was not at all like her to let such wanton thoughts take over. She needed to get her emotions back in control before she ended up making a complete fool of herself.

To her growing bewilderment, her hands felt heavy and her arms weak when she reached out to accept the last of the playing cards from Sirus. How odd. She'd felt perfectly fine just moments ago.

Trying to concentrate on her own actions instead of any movements coming from the direction of the bar, she hurriedly divided the cards into two equal sections. She watched herself as if from afar as she attempted to shuffle the two stacks into one, only to see most of the cards scatter haphazardly across the table. Embarrassed, she felt her cheeks stain with color while she hurriedly gathered the stray cards back into one stack to try again.

"Sorry. I guess my hands slipped," she apologized feebly while her fingers again worked to divide the cards into two equal parts. Dismally, she wondered if the handsome stranger had witnessed her blunder, when secretly she'd hoped to impress him with her mastery of cards. Then it occurred to her that he may have somehow linked her sudden clumsy behavior to himself. Fervently, she prayed he had not turned around in time to see the incident, but she didn't dare chance as much as a quick glance in his direction to find out.

Pressing her lips together with determination, she bent the two stacks of cards. This time, they fell properly into place, coming together in one neat pile beneath her cupped hands. After repeating the process successfully twice more, she decided not to press her luck and immediately began dealing the cards.

"Hey, you forgot to have someone cut the deck," Sirus complained in a loud, gruff voice which Josie felt certain had carried across the room and into the next state.

Growing more flustered by the moment, she took back the cards in the order she had dealt them and promptly handed the deck to Sirus. "I'm sorry. I forgot. Here, cut them."

"What's the matter with you? It's Voncille's turn to cut the cards, not mine," Sirus muttered, and passed them on to the man at his left. "I cut 'em last time."

Josie closed her eyes for a moment, hoping to regain even a small portion of her equilibrium as she considered Sirus's question. What *was* the matter with her? It wasn't like her to let anyone or anything rattle her like that, especially not during a card game. She had never allowed herself to be distracted from her cards. Never. Yet, even after Voncille had handed the cards back to her and she'd hurriedly begun to deal them again, it remained impossible for her to concentrate on what she was doing. She came very close to handing everyone six cards instead of five.

Angry with herself for having let the mere presence of a total stranger shake her concentration, she took a deep, determined breath, then tried once again to return her attention to the game. But her efforts were useless. She was simply too aware of the man still standing at the bar.

Even after he'd turned his back to the bar and began to casually scan the room, she couldn't keep her gaze off him for long. The thought of what he might think of her if he happened to catch her staring at him horrified her, yet her eyes refused to remain on her cards and kept darting away to snatch tiny glimpses of him. Each time she did, her heart missed another beat and her throat slowly tightened until she could barely swallow.

Drawn to the way his fascinating blue eyes reflected the bright glow of the candelabras poised high overhead, she was well aware his casual search of the room had ended — the moment he caught sight of her. Suddenly, she could not breathe, nor could she look away. His brow arched with momentary surprise, then promptly lowered while he studied her from across the room. Carefully, he watched her every move.

A warm, uncomfortable feeling spread through Josie's entire body, rising slowly up her neck to her cheeks. She wished she had the courage to reach for her fan, but was afraid he would realize her sudden need for such cooling comfort was a direct result of his own close scrutiny — and that would never do. She would have to tolerate the prickling heat.

But the longer he stared at her from across the room, the more uncomfortably warm she felt. His lips pursed thoughtfully to one side while he continued to study her, as if trying to form an opinion of her. Afraid he might think her far too bold for returning his gaze, she finally found the strength to look away. She fastened her gaze on Sirus, who she realized had just spoken to her.

"You in for two dollars or not?" Sirus asked, frowning.

Although Josie had no idea what cards were in her hand, she quickly reached into her stack of money and placed two dollars into the pile. She certainly didn't want the stranger to think she'd become so addled she'd forgotten to look at her own cards. "Of course I'm in."

Sirus smiled and licked his lips with eager anticipation, but Josie never noticed.

Though she pretended to have her mind back on the game, her attention remained focused on the man now leaning casually against the bar, his boot-heel hooked over the footrail behind him. Aware the man continued to watch her closely, she felt too self-conscious to notice that the telltale glimmer had returned to Sirus's blue-green eyes. He raised the pot twice before claiming his victory.

"Hot damn!" he cried out with glee when Josie revealed her cards. "My three nines sure beats that measly pair of fours. I win. I win. Two hands in a row! Hot damn! I'm on a roll."

Josie frowned, staring dumbfounded at her cards. Why did she play with such a flimsy hand? Why didn't she fold? What on earth was wrong with her? It wasn't as if she'd never had a stranger stare at her with such obvious interest before, since a woman gambling in a saloon was quite a novelty. So why was she so deeply affected by this particular stranger's attention?

Tossing her shoulders back in a willful gesture, she turned in her chair so she would not be tempted to glance up at the man again. She had to get her head back into the game before she lost more money than she could afford to lose.

With her concentration finally back where it belonged, on the cards and not on a pair of astonishing blue eyes, she won the next two hands with relative ease. Sirus was back to muttering to himself, and Voncille was back to teasing him about it. With a little of her confidence returned to her, and her heartbeat settled to a more normal beat, she decided the crisis caused by the stranger was over—until, suddenly, he appeared at their table.

"Is there room for one more?" he asked in a smooth, deep voice.

Josie felt her eyes grow as round as dinner plates

when she looked up to find that the source of all her earlier unrest now stood only a few feet away. Her eyes grew wider still when she discovered that, unbelievably, the man was even more attractive than she had at first realized. Now that he was closer, she could better see the long, inward curve of his cheeks and how extremely thick and silky his eyelashes were—eyelashes that were as dark brown in color as the lightly curling hair that ducked out from beneath his wide-brimmed hat. Again she became mesmerized by the liquid blue of his eyes—even when they boldly dipped downward to take in the modest cut of her neckline and the curve of the material below.

The strange warmth that had assaulted her earlier returned, centering this time in her cheeks, forcing her to look away. Self-consciously, she gathered the last of the cards and carefully shuffled them, determined he not know how truly disturbing she found his close scrutiny. She refused to chance glancing in his direction again, but she felt his gaze continue to rake over her, as if mentally he undressed her. The rogue! How dare he be so bold! The exposed skin along her neck and collarbone prickled with a keen sense of awareness.

"Let's see your money, stranger," Sirus remarked, pushing his hat back and eyeing the young man suspiciously. Sirus was never one to trust strangers, even well-dressed strangers like this man.

Josie hoped Sirus would send the man away. Bravely, she glanced up from the cards to see if that would happen but noticed how the man continued to regard her with a look that seemed to devour her while, casually, he reached inside his upper coat pocket and removed his wallet.

With deft fingers, he opened the wallet one-handed, revealing quite a hefty stack of greenbacks. "This enough?" he calmly asked.

Sirus's eyes widened at the sight of all that money.

"Sure is," he answered quickly, taking off his battered

hat for the first time since he had entered the saloon. Eagerly, he wet his lips with his tongue and pressed his battered hat against his heart, for if there was anything that commanded Sirus's complete respect, it was money. "Pull up a chair, mister. Lloyd, Voncille, move apart there to make room for the gentleman. Looks like we got us some new blood in this game."

Instantly, Lloyd and Voncille's chairs scraped across the wood floor, making room for another chair at the small table.

Josie wanted to protest, but found herself at an uncharacteristic loss for words. Her heartbeat increased tenfold and her throat constricted until she had to forget swallowing.

Though her brain frantically sought the words needed to express her disapproval, all she could think about at that particular moment was the brazen way he continued to stare at her while he placed a chair in the space the others had so quickly provided. His slow, deliberate actions reminded her of a hungry cat eager to sample some tasty morsel. Apparently, he thought she was simply another one of Trey's saloon girls, put there for the sole purpose of being ogled. She felt herself slowly grow angry.

"Got a name, stranger?" Sirus asked, as soon as the man had taken off his lightweight coat, draped it casually over the back of his chair, then hooked his wide, ranch-style hat over one corner. Everyone watched while he settled in and immediately made himself comfortable by unbuttoning the top two buttons of his pale-blue cotton shirt.

Josie bit her lip and refused to be affected by the deeply tanned skin and the dark, springy hair his open shirt revealed or by the way the soft material strained against the muscular movements of his wide shoulders when he casually leaned forward and rested his hands on the table.

"The name's Nathaniel Garrett," he supplied, glanc-

24

ing again at Josie with a peculiar expression, as if he felt she should recognize the name. "My friends call me Nathan. Just don't make the mistake of calling me Nate."

"But you wouldn't mind if we were all to call you Nathan, would you?" Sirus wanted to know. "I like thinkin' I'm on friendly terms with whoever I play cards with."

Clearly, the name had meant nothing to Sirus. Josie hoped that galled Mr. Garrett, since he obviously thought so very highly of himself. For the first time since she had watched him enter the saloon, she smiled. Her throat relaxed a degree and she finally managed to speak.

"Welcome, Mr. Garrett," she said, stressing the word "mister" to let him know she had no intention of being on friendly terms with him. Self-consciously, she reached up to touch her emerald-studded choker with the tips of her fingers. "I'm Josie Leigh. And these two older gents are Sirus Gordy and Lloyd Taylor. The younger two are Voncille Sobey and Frank Pyle."

Each man tipped his hat or touched his forehead in turn to let him know which was which.

"We were just about to play another hand of Texas sweat," Josie went on to explain. "That's where each player gets five cards, all dealt facedown. Is that agreeable with you?"

"I know the game. And since what's played is usually the dealer's choice, I have no complaints," he said with a slight nod and a dazzling smile.

Josie's breath held while she carefully placed the cards in the center of the table, but she tried not to let the sudden burst of inner turmoil enter her voice when she spoke again. "Newcomer cuts the cards."

Nathan's eyes never left hers while he reached out his right hand and lifted a portion of the cards off the top then, in one smooth movement, quickly ducked them underneath.

Wordlessly, Josie picked up the cards and began to deal.

"What brings you to Cypress Mill, Nathan?" Sirus asked while he picked up his cards one at a time the moment they were dealt. He appeared almost as eager to know more about the man who had joined them as he was to see his own cards.

Josie tried to appear disinterested in the man's answer, but listened carefully while she casually arranged her five cards, pitiful though they were.

"I'm in town on business," Nathan responded, glancing up at Josie yet again. No matter who spoke to him, he always answered as if speaking only to her.

Looking away, feeling more flustered than ever, Josie wondered what sort of business the man could possibly have in a town as small as Cypress Mill. She wished Sirus would think to ask him; but the old man picked that particular moment to be uncharacteristically silent. Josie's eyebrows notched with frustration. None of the men wanted to question him further about his business. They seemed more interested in how long he had been in town.

Curious to know more about the man's business, Josie tried to figure out a way to encourage one of the others to ask him the questions she wanted answered without seeming too obvious. She was not about to ask such questions herself, not and chance the man thinking her interests ran deeper than they actually did. He looked like the type of man who was all too used to women being openly curious about him, and she certainly didn't want him to think she was just another in the long line of many such mindless ninnies, especially when his opinion of her was already so clearly low. Why else would he continue to be so brazen?

"Newcomer opens," she said, when it appeared everyone was ready to play. She did what she could to remain calm.

When she glanced at him then, she expected to find

26

him busy studying his cards, but instead discovered he was still staring at her. His brashness was becoming more and more offensive. Again she looked away.

She tried her best to concentrate on her cards and not on the way the man continued to watch her every move. But the longer he stared at her, the more removed she felt from the game, until it seemed as if she was nothing more than an observer—not a real participant. Yet it was her money that partially filled the pot.

To her dismay, Nathan won the first hand with nothing more than a pair of jacks.

"Beginner's luck, I guess," he said as he gathered the money he'd just won and placed it in a neat pile before him.

"I hope so," Sirus muttered, narrowing his eyes suspiciously before he glanced across at Josie. "Deal up another hand."

Out of the next four rounds Nathan won one more, then lost three. Meanwhile, he continued to watch Josie's every move, nodding his head speculatively from time to time until he finally asked, "Why is it Miss Leigh is the only one who ever deals the cards? It is *Miss* Leigh, isn't it?"

"Yes, it is Miss Leigh. I'm not married." She felt irritated with herself for having supplied him with the very information he'd so obviously sought.

"Well, that's certainly good to know. I'd hate to think some man had already laid claim to you before I ever got a chance."

Josie bristled at the way he'd made it sound like a landowner staking out new property. Not wanting to create a scene in her cousin's saloon, she pressed her tongue against the top of her mouth to keep from telling him exactly what she thought of him.

"So, tell me, Miss Leigh," he went on to say. "Why is it they let you deal the cards every time, instead of allowing the honor to be passed around the table?" Again his gaze dipped boldly to assess the charms that

27

clearly marked her a woman.

Josie lifted her chin in an unconscious gesture of defiance, aware he was chiding her for having had the misfortune of being born of the female species—just like so many other such arrogant men had done in the past. She came very close to speaking out in her own defense, but decided to remain silent rather than chance sounding waspish, which would only give him something else to ridicule. She felt deeply grateful when Sirus decided to come to her defense.

"We prefer to have Miss Josie deal the cards. Everyone around here knows what an honest person she is. And, because she is so honest, we all trust her completely. By letting her deal out every hand, we avoid a lot of arguments over whether or not someone cheated. Even when she doesn't feel like actually playing with us, we still try to get her to at least deal the cards for us," Sirus told him. "But if you'd feel better about the game if you was allowed to deal some of the hands, that'd be fine with me. What about the rest of you?"

Now that Nathan had lost three hands in a row, Sirus felt much better about having him in the game and clearly wanted to keep him there.

"Fine with me," Lloyd put in, and the others quickly agreed.

Nathan glanced from Sirus to the other men, then returned his gaze to Josie. After a long, speculative moment, he shook his head and shrugged. "No, if you men believe she is so trustworthy, I guess it's all right to leave things the way they are. It's just that I'm not used to having a woman sit in on a card game like this, much less be the only dealer." He tilted his head while he studied her cool expression. "It takes a little getting used to. You understand."

"Of course," Josie responded politely, biting back the rest of what she would like to say to him. She understood all right, too well, and the man's cocky attitude irritated her even more.

In an effort to keep control of her rising temper, she gripped the cards with such force, her knuckles turned white. "We understand fully, Mr. Garrett. You have obviously found it a little difficult to cope with the fact that a woman has dared to participate in what to your point of view should strictly be a man's game."

"Oh, I can cope with that well enough. It's the fact that I will be taking her money away from her that I think bothers me the most."

"Don't be too sure of yourself," she responded with a meaningful arch of her brow. Her green eyes sparkled with challenge. "It could be your own money that is in danger here. It's not often I lose."

His resulting smile unnerved her. "Feeling lucky, are you?" Then, as if his words held some secret meaning, his smile widened into one of pure contentment. "I'm feeling pretty lucky myself. It'll be interesting to see whose luck holds out the longest."

Chapter Two

Angered by Nathan Garrett's arrogant manner and by the bold, suggestive, and at times almost lurid comments he continuously tossed at her, Josie played with pure determination.

She wanted not just to win but to beat the man so badly he would be forced to leave the table disgraced. She would then humble him further by demanding a public apology for having displayed such unforgivable behavior toward her. Oh, how she yearned to make him finally admit to everyone that a woman was just as competent as any man when it came to such things as playing poker—maybe more competent in some ways. And to prove it, she played with all the cunning and skill she had. But to her growing frustration, they did not always prove to be enough.

As the afternoon turned into evening and the evening into a typically boisterous Saturday night, the winning hand traveled back and forth between Josie and Nathan, with an occasional hand won by either Sirus or Lloyd.

By the time darkness had firmly settled over the small river town of Cypress Mill, most of the money on the table was in the possession of either Josie or Nathan.

One by one, the other players dropped out of the game and eventually left the saloon. Two other men had ventured to take their place at the table, only to find their money quickly gone. No one else dared sit in on the game, seeing how serious the play had become. Only Sirus remained seated at the table with them, but he had barely enough money to last one more hand. After that was gone, he would be forced to quit the game and become a part of the large group of spectators that surrounded the table.

In all, during the five hours of play, Josie had won far more games than Nathan, though he seemed to lose less money on a bad hand than she did. Still, she managed to stay just enough ahead to feel good about the game—and about the eventual outcome. She felt certain it was only a matter of time.

"Well, I know when I'm licked," Sirus said, sounding disgruntled when he tossed his final cards onto the table. "I'm out. Looks like it's between the two of you now."

Josie glanced at Sirus, and smiled gently. Even as ornery as Sirus usually was, he was still her friend, someone she could count on in times of trouble. She did not want him to leave the game feeling defeated. "You certainly had a run of bad cards. Maybe next week you'll do a little better and will be able to win some of your money back."

"I fully intend to," he replied with a tired laugh, then shook his head dismally and rubbed his whiskered jaw with a heavy hand. "I should have had the good sense to quit sooner. Tonight was just not my night. Lady Luck is with the two of you. It's sure goin' to be interestin' to see which of you two she ends up favorin' the most. I'm curious as all get-out to see who finally leaves this table the big winner." Then, rather than get up and stretch his legs like the others, Sirus signaled for Carla to bring him another drink, then slumped further into his chair, ready to stick it out until the end.

Nathan glanced up at the many set of eyes watching them. Though the faces changed from time to time, the number of people interested in the eventual outcome of the game had remained about the same. The table was

31

constantly surrounded by curious onlookers, most of whom chose to stand. No on had dared sit in any of the recently vacated chairs—even to watch.

"Anyone else interested in joining us?" he asked casually, indicating one of the empty chairs with a slight wave of his hand.

Everyone shook their head immediately. A few stepped back to indicate exactly how they felt about such a ludicrous suggestion. Only Carla had a comment to make.

"Not for poker," she said, her voice teasing, her lips turned up into a playful smile.

For some reason, Carla's flirtatious comment annoyed Josie more than it should have.

"I'm afraid poker is all that I'm interested in at the moment," Nathan replied, laughing when Carla's face turned into a pretty pout. He winked playfully, then returned his attention to Josie. "Well, it looks like it's down to just you and me," he said, eyeing her thoughtfully. "I hope it doesn't bother you to play one on one."

"Not at all," she assured him just before she reached out to place the cards she'd just shuffled before him. In all honesty, she preferred to play him one on one. She wouldn't have to worry about taking any more of her friends' hard-earned money during her attempt to bring this obstinate man to his knees. To beat her friends out of their spending money was one thing, but when they started to dip into the money they needed to live on, it bothered her. Usually she'd leave the game before allowing one of them to risk his grocery money or the money she knew needed to be put aside for the rent or family necessities. "Cut the cards."

Again, without bothering to take his gaze off her, he reached out a well-muscled hand and lifted the top layer of cards before smoothly tucking it underneath. Then, rather than wait until she reached over to pick up the cards, he curled his fingers around the deck and held it out to her.

When she stretched her hand forward to accept them, the side of his hand brushed her palm, sending a fiery jolt through her that caused her to gasp aloud. His eyebrow shot up at such a noticeable reaction.

Furious to know he had done that on purpose, obviously hoping to distract her with what he clearly felt was an overwhelming male charm, Josie worked the delicate muscle at the back of her jaw. Unwilling to react in the manner he wanted, she held her anger back while slowly she dealt the cards. She understood the importance of remaining emotionally calm and as level-headed as possible. If she truly wanted to break him, the game needed her full attention.

"Hey, Jo'," she heard moments after she had set the spare cards aside and before she could reach down to pick up her own. She glanced back over her shoulder and saw her cousin Trey working his way through the crowded room to get to her.

Nathan watched with keen interest.

"Jo', can I ask a special favor of you?" Trey said, his voice pleading as he knelt beside her and took one of her delicate hands in his. His thick mustache twitched back and forth beneath a well-shaped nose while he eagerly awaited her response.

Nathan frowned at the familiar way the man held her hand and at the eager way he gazed into her eyes.

"What sort of favor?" she asked suspiciously, knowing Trey all too well. She reached out her free hand to push back his thick brown hair, wanting to get a better look at his hazel-colored eyes, knowing they were the mirrors to Trey's every thought.

Trey's eyebrow rose a degree while he considered the best way to go about approaching her. "How well do you love me?"

Josie hesitated to answer that. "That depends on what it is you want me to do."

Everyone in the room laughed—except Nathan, who leaned forward in his chair and propped his elbows on the table while he continued to study the familiarity between the two.

Trey released her hand and reached up to delicately touch her cheek, smiling timidly when he did, almost blushing. "I know when I asked you to stay so late last night, I promised I would not ask it of you again, but tonight is really special."

"How special?" Josie continued to be suspicious.

A broad smile lit Trey's face, stretching his mouth wide. Even with such a heavy mustache shadowing his lips, his grin appeared boyish. "Jane has agreed to go on a moonlight ride with me tonight if I'll promise to go to church with her tomorrow. Please, Jo', you've just got to lock up for me again tonight. Pleeease."

Josie tried to look truly put out with her older cousin, but knowing how head over heels in love he was with Jane Holt, she could only shake her head and smile. "Sure, Trey. Anything to get you in church."

Everyone laughed again while Trey quickly stood and rubbed his hands together with eager anticipation.

"You won't regret it, cousin. I'll make it up to you, I swear," he said as he bent forward and placed a brief kiss on her cheek.

"I know, I know," Josie said, laughing with the others, aware some of the tension that had held her in its grip for the last several hours was slowly slipping away. Laughter had always been like a soothing balm to her. "Just leave the key in the money drawer this time so I don't have to go looking for it."

Trey rushed over to make certain the key was in its proper place, then bounded from the room, eager to get to the livery before they closed for the night.

When Josie returned her attention to Nathan and to the cards she had yet to pick up, her smile lingered.

"I gather that was your cousin," Nathan said offhandedly while he waited for an indication she was ready to play. His gaze settled on her smile for a moment, then lifted back to her sparkling green eyes. Again, he had the strangest sensation he had seen her before, and that made him as uncomfortable as it had to discover she was no small child, but instead a grown, extremely attractive young woman.

"Yes, that was Trey. He owns this place," she answered, avoiding his studious gaze by looking down to arrange her five cards into perfect order.

Though her insides were already a boiling cauldron of electrified emotions before she ever touched her cards, her heart shot skyward in a wild burst of excitement when she saw exactly what she had—a full house. The three of a kind were jacks. Hoping her sudden elation had not shown on her face, she continued to rearrange her cards and study them, as if undecided how she should play them. She pretended to be not at all pleased with her choices.

Nathan glanced away only long enough to arrange his own cards into their best order. "And does he live here?"

"Who?" she asked, so stunned by her good fortune that she had lost grasp of the conversation.

"Your cousin, Trey. Does he live here?"

"You mean in the saloon?" she asked, trying to keep up with what he was saying, yet at the same time deciding how much money to lead with. "No, Trey lives in his parents' old house."

"Old?" he asked, appearing only casually interested while he divided his attention between his cards and what she was saying.

"They died several years ago."

"And do you live there, too? In their old house?"

Josie frowned when she suddenly realized what all his questions were leading to. He was trying to find out where she lived and if she lived alone. Men could be so obvious at times.

"No," she answered simply, not about to supply him with any more information. She then fell purposely silent.

"Miss Josie lives right upstairs," Sirus quickly supplied as he shifted forward toward the table and rested his whiskered chin on top of his folded arms.

Josie felt like strangling the old man. Didn't Sirus see what Mr. Garrett was attempting to do?

"Upstairs?" Nathan asked, also leaning forward. Sirus had suddenly piqued his interest. "You mean *here*, at the Dogwood?"

"Yeah, but don't go gettin' the wrong idea like some of the womenfolk around here did there for a while. Miss Josie moved in upstairs because she didn't think it looked too proper for her to go on livin' in the same house with Trey after his parents died, even though the two of them is first cousins, and almost like brother and sister. So, the two of them cleared out one of the storage rooms upstairs where she'd have a decent place to stay that wouldn't cost her nothin'. It's real nice, too."

Knowing he would get far more information out of Sirus than Josie, Nathan temporarily turned his full attention to the older man. "You've been up there?"

"Oh, sure, I helped Trey carry some of her belongings up when she first moved in. They've got it fixed up real nice. They wallpapered the walls, put rugs on the floor, duded it up until it looks like a real bedroom with a small sitting area on one side. All pretty and yellow."

Josie glared at Sirus. A strange turbulence twisted deep in the very pit of her stomach at hearing her bedroom described for everyone. She decided they had discussed her and her living quarters long enough. "I believe it is my turn to open, Mr. Garrett. I'll start out with three dollars."

To her relief, everyone's attention returned immediately to the game—which she easily won.

Another two hours passed, and in that time the victories continued to pass back and forth between the two, until it appeared neither would ever come away the true winner. Finally, Nathan leaned back in his chair and glanced at the thinning crowd of spectators, then at the huge clock nailed high on the wall near the bar and frowned.

"It's past eleven o'clock. We've been at this for over seven hours now. I don't like to complain, but I'm growing extremely tired of the game the way it's going now. No real progress is being made," he said as he reached up to release yet another button of his shirt, then arched his back to stretch his sore neck and shoulder muscles.

Instantly the pale-blue material pulled apart to reveal a better view of the dark hair that grew in soft, distinct patterns across his tanned chest. The muscles in his neck pulled taut with each movement, then relaxed. "To tell you the truth, I'm starting to get bored. I'm beginning to find myself more interested in what is happening in the room around me than I am in our card game."

"Are you quitting, Mr. Garrett?" Josie asked, wetting her lips and wondering if that was what she wanted. She had hoped that when he left the table it would be because he was defeated, but she was just as eager to get away from him and from the strain his constant scrutiny caused her. Having had her fill of his rude behavior and of the way he couldn't seem to keep his eyes off the places no real gentleman would dare pay heed to, she held back any words that might encourage him to stay.

"No, of course not," he assured her. "I merely want to suggest we raise the stakes to make the game a little more interesting."

A low murmur rose from those who had stayed to watch. Even the customers who had not been keeping a close eye on the proceedings suddenly turned their attention to what was being said between Josie and the handsome stranger.

"And how much do you think we should raise the stakes?" she asked, feeling suddenly apprehensive about the whole thing.

"I suggest we play with no limits at all," he responded a little too quickly. "And I also suggest we both put up twenty dollars before each hand is ever dealt. And, although I don't mind playing *Texas sweat,* which leaves not even a hint to what the other fellow might have, I think it would be far more interesting to start the betting as soon as the second cards are dealt, like we would if we were playing stud. *That* should get things moving along at a better pace."

The low murmur around them rose several degrees. Clearly, everyone else was as eager as he to see higher stakes wagered, and at much higher risks. Several people moved closer.

"A twenty-dollar ante?" Josie felt Nathan's eyes on her again, carefully watching her, but she did not bother to meet his gaze. Instead, she lifted her hand, absently tracing the outline of her emerald-studded choker while she mentally counted the money on the table. Clearly, she had the advantage moneywise at the moment. But with the no limits on the game, that could change instantly.

Still, she decided to chance it.

"All right," she responded with a slow smile, remembering she'd won far more games than she'd lost. She had no reason to think that should not continue. With all limits off, the chances were he would begin to take higher risks. Men always did when the stakes were high.

If she played very carefully, she might be able to take all his money and put him out of the game in a very few hands. Not only would she finally be rid of him, she would have defeated him in the process. How sweet it would be to bring the scoundrel down a peg or two.

Her smile broadened as she placed her twenty-dollar ante in the center of the table, then laid the cards she'd just shuffled directly in front of him. "Cut them."

With her blood racing wildly, driven by both her fear and anticipation, she dealt them each their first two

38

cards, then set the deck aside. She took a quick glance at her own cards and could hardly believe the pair of queens staring back at her.

"Your turn to open," she said with far more calm than she felt.

Nathan laid his two cards back down, then rested his hands over them. "Let's get serious about this, and start with each of us adding fifty dollars to the pot."

Josie's stomach knotted. Queens or no queens, she hated to have to bet when she had no way to know what her other three cards would be. It was why she hated to play stud. But, as she thought it over, she decided the pair of queens was worthy of meeting his initial bet.

"Fifty dollars it is," she stated evenly while she counted out the money and placed it in the center of the table beside the fifty dollars he had just laid there. Then, without another word, she placed her two cards back down and calmly lifted the deck and dealt them each a third card.

Nathan had already picked up his latest card and added it to the other two before Josie had time to set the main deck aside again. Quickly, she peeked at her card.

Another queen! Her pulses raced with eager anticipation.

"If you are still so eager to play a serious game of poker, I think another fifty dollars would be appropriate," she stated calmly, careful to keep any excitement from her voice. With an amazingly steady hand, she counted out the second fifty and placed it beside the rest. She waited until Nathan had done the same before she dealt the fourth cards.

Josie quickly glanced at her newest card. It was a jack.

"You in for fifty more?" he asked just before he laid the appropriate amount where it belonged.

Despite her three queens, Josie felt a renewed twinge of doubt when it came to meeting that last fifty-dollar raise. He appeared far too casual about such large amounts of money. She paused to consider that by adding fifty dollars more, she would have one hundred and seventy dollars involved in the one wager. That was a lot of money to have riding on one single poker hand, but she knew the alternative would be to fold and automatically lose the one hundred and twenty she had invested thus far. Finally, her gambler's heart won out and she counted out fifty more dollars, placing the bills on top of the rest of the money, and prayed her three queens would bring her a royal win.

Her heart continued to hammer violently against the hard wall of her chest while she dealt the final two cards. Slowly, she placed the spare cards to one side and picked up her fifth card to examine it. When she discovered it was another jack, her stomach knotted with such a strong surge of excitement, she could barely breathe. A full house in a game of sweat was a hard thing to beat, but a full house made up entirely of face cards was practically impossible. She felt her heart leap skyward, aware everything she'd really wanted was about to come true.

Josie tried not to reveal her sudden good fortune as she considered her situation. Not only was she in a position to force the man out of the game at long last; in the process, she could end up with enough cash to buy that house she wanted. There was well over eight hundred dollars on the table, of which three hundred and forty had already been committed. And because she had more money on the table to work with than he did, she could easily match whatever bets were made. There was no chance of having to lose by forfeit. Already, she tasted the sweetness of her victory. It took all the restraint she had to keep a sober expression.

Her blood continued to pound frantically through her entire body causing her to tingle all over, yet she managed to keep even a glimmer of that eager anticipation out of her huge green eyes when she looked at the man.

"It's your bet," she said, trying to sound more nervous than excited.

Holding his cards low, almost to his waist, Nathan glanced at them again briefly, then at her, as if trying to gauge her reaction. Rather than look away as she had previously done whenever she discovered those pale-blue eyes upon her, she tilted her head innocently to the right and met his gaze.

"My bet? I thought it was yours. But, no matter. I figure we should each raise the pot at least one hundred more dollars," he stated, then calmly added the amount he'd called out to the rest. Nothing in his demeanor let her know if he was truly feeling that confident with his cards, or if he was merely running a bluff.

Josie tried to appear dismayed instead of thrilled. "One hundred dollars more? When you said you wanted to make the game interesting, you certainly meant it."

"Are you still in?" he asked as he neatly placed his cards face down on the table, then folded his hands protectively over them. "Or do you forfeit your one hundred and seventy dollars?"

"No, I plan to keep my one hundred and seventy dollars, and take whatever else I can in the process," she stated boldly while she, too, counted out one hundred dollars and placed it where it belonged. "In fact, I think I'll raise you another hundred dollars, just to show you I'm not in the least bit afraid of losing." Wanting him to believe her boldness was an attempt to bluff, she hesitated to release the money before she slowly returned her hand to her lap.

Nathan's face continued to reveal nothing of his thoughts while he quickly counted out yet another hundred and added it to the rest. Finally, while he carefully studied her expression, then the expressions of those who stood behind her and might have gotten a glimpse of her cards, he showed his first sign of concern. His teeth tugged absently at the inside of his lower lip. Josie felt it was a good sign and decided he must be having second thoughts.

"Well, now," he paused, glancing down at his remaining money. "It's my turn to do something here, and I think I'll take this opportunity to raise . . ." He paused while he counted out his money.

Josie waited eagerly to see if he would voluntarily bet the rest. If he did not, she would gladly force him to. Since there was now no limit to the number of raises or the amount of money involved, she would see to it every cent was at risk. She might even have him bet his hat to meet her last twenty dollars. That should bring him down off his high horse with a crashing jolt. Men always took deep pride in their hats, and his looked as if it might be brand-new.

Nathan's gaze rose again to meet hers. "Let's see just how bold you really are. I call for a raise of five hundred dollars."

Josie sat dumbfounded for several seconds. "Five hundred dollars? How can you? You only have about forty-five dollars there."

Nathan turned in his chair and slipped his hand into his coat pocket. When he turned back around he had a second, though much smaller, wallet in his hands. Slowly, he opened it and counted out five hundred more dollars, then placed it on the table aside from the rest. "Count it if you'd like."

"That's not fair!"

"What's not fair about it? You didn't ask for a showdown, you raised. That left me free to call your raise and raise again, which I did."

"But *five hundred dollars?*" Josie felt the blood drain from her face when she glanced down at what money she had left. Barely seventy dollars left uncommitted. She tried to swallow back the sudden feeling of helplessness. No matter how wonderful her cards were, if she could not come up with enough money to cover her part of the bet, she would automatically lose everything to that insufferable clod—including her own tender pride. She needed four hundred and thirty dollars more to stay in the game.

Frantically, she glanced at Sirus, who looked as dumbfounded as she. "Sirus, do you have any money left that I can borrow? I'll pay it back, and with an added bonus. I promise."

"Ah, Miss Josie, I wish I did, but you know I never bring more money than I can afford to lose. When I dropped out of the game, I only had six dollars left, and I've spent almost a dollar of that on the drinks I've had since." Frowning over the fact that he could not be of more help, he reached into his shirt pocket. "But you are plenty welcome to the five dollars I got left."

Josie did not refuse the paltry sum. She was desperate. Every bit would help. Placing a protective hand over her cards, she turned to see who else might have money to loan her. So involved in the game, she was unaware of the late hour, and was surprised to discover so few people remained in the room. Her gaze immediately fastened on Andy and Tony Andcreek, brothers she had known for as long as she'd lived in Cypress Mill. Their grandfather usually kept them supplied with plenty of spending money.

"What about you two? Do you have any money you could loan me?" she asked.

Andy and Tony immediately searched their pockets, dumping out everything from ivory-handled folding knives to a silver belt buckle with an angry bull's head engraved on it, but were only able to pool together another nineteen dollars for Josie.

Not yet willing to accept defeat, she quickly approached other friends only to discover most of them had already spent what little they had come with. Finally, she thought of the cash drawer. The Dogwood might have enough to cover the bet.

"Where's Trey?" she asked the bartender, forgetting her cousin had left hours earlier. She held on to her last

43

dangling thread of hope while she glanced around the room for him and waited for Pete's reply.

"He still ain't back yet," Pete answered, pausing just long enough in pouring a customer's drink to glance at the clock. "Besides, I thought you planned to lock up tonight."

Josie felt suddenly ill, but refused to give up. "How much money is in the cash drawer? I'm sure Trey wouldn't mind if I borrowed the money I need to finish this game from him. He knows I'll pay it back."

Pete stepped over to the small metal drawer built into the elaborate counter along the far wall and quickly pulled it out. After fingering the money inside for a few moments, he announced, "There's only about thirty dollars here. Trey must have took most of it with him so he wouldn't have to worry about no one stealing it again. But you can have what's here, if you want. I know Trey wouldn't mind."

Josie felt a growing sense of panic. Trey was off on a moonlight ride with his girl. There was no way to know exactly where they had gone or if he had the money with him or put away somewhere. In ten minutes' time, she'd only been able to come up with a little over fifty dollars. She decided to offer the remainder on a promissory note. "Pete, bring me what money there is, and also a pen, ink, and a clean piece of paper."

"Why do you need a pen and paper?" Nathan wanted to know, sitting back and clasping his hands together at the edge of the table while he patiently waited for her to somehow match his bet.

"I only have one hundred and twenty-four dollars in ready cash. I'll have to write you a note for the other three hundred and seventy-six," she explained while she waited for Pete to bring her the things she had asked for.

"Do you have enough money to cover such a note?" Nathan asked with a curious lift of his brow.

"No, not personally, but I'm quite certain I could

raise it if I had to. In fact, I know Trey will loan me whatever money I need to pay back the note. And I assure you, what he doesn't have in ready cash, he can get from the bank first thing Monday morning."

"And what if he can't? No, I'm afraid I can't take that chance," he replied, his tone deadly serious. "Besides, if you'll look at the clock, you'll see that it is now past midnight."

"So?"

"So, that makes it Sunday and banks don't believe in cashing promissory notes written on Sunday, not in this state. So, either match the bet with something far more tangible than an illegally dated promissory note or forfeit the game."

Blinking back tears of frustration, Josie hesitated only a moment before reaching up to undo her prized emerald-and-diamond choker. Though she hated to part with it, it was the only thing of real value she owned.

"What are you doing?" he asked, watching while she fumbled with the delicate clasp at the back of her neck.

"I plan to meet your bet with my necklace. I assure you it is worth well more than six hundred dollars."

"I don't want your necklace. I have no use for such trinkets," he stated evenly.

"B-but I have nothing else to offer," she protested, angry that he considered her beautiful choker a mere trinket.

"Oh, but I think you do."

"I do?" she asked, and glanced down, unable to fathom what that might be. Her dress was hardly worth that much money. Nor was her mother's ring. "What do I have that might be worth that much to you?"

"You," he stated simply.

"What?!"

"Simply put, to match my bet, all you need to do is offer yourself as a part of the wager," he explained calmly.

45

"That's ridiculous," she shouted, enraged that he could even consider such a thing. The audacity of the man.

"Ridiculous or not, it's either that or forfeit the three hundred and seventy dollars you've bet thus far."

Josie glanced down at where her cards still lay, remembering the three queens and two jacks with stark clarity, then glanced at all the money she had already invested in that one wager, which was certainly a lot to lose.

Finally, she lifted her gaze to the man's cocky expression and glared at him, wishing she could reach over and slap that arrogant smile right off his disgustingly handsome face.

After another moment of glaring at him, she looked back down at her cards. She felt sick inside. With a poker hand like that, she couldn't lose, but still—the thought of putting herself up as part of the wager was unthinkable.

Growing impatient, Nathan leaned back in his chair and eyed her speculatively for a long moment before clarifying the bet further. "It seems simple enough. If I win, I take all the money—and you—for three months."

Josie jerked her angry gaze back to meet his. "And just what do you plan to do with me in those three months?"

She noticed the immediate murmuring of voices behind her, but did not let her eyes stray from his.

A deliberately slow smile spread across Nathan's face until it formed a fascinating little dimple in his left cheek. "In those three months, I will gladly provide you with room and board, and you will in turn provide me with certain services."

Josie felt her neck grow hot. "How dare you! I'll have you know, the *only* services I would ever be willing to offer a man like you are purely domestic," she retorted through clenched teeth. "The *most* I'd ever agree to is maybe cleaning your house or possibly cooking your

46

meals. And I'd be very reluctant do either of those."

"Do you know how to cook or clean a house?" he asked, clearly doubtful.

"Of course I do," she lied, but with enough indignation to make it sound like the truth.

"Then that will do. If I win, you will go with me to clean my house and cook my meals for three full months, that time starting upon your arrival at the house. If you win, you get everything that's on the table. Is it a bet?"

Running her tongue over the inner edges of her compressed teeth, Josie glanced down at her cards again while she further considered her options. How she hated the thought of losing all that money to the likes of him—especially when she had one of the best poker hands she'd ever seen. And what made the situation worse was the fact that, in among her three queens was the queen of hearts—her lucky card. The chances of losing with that hand were almost nonexistent. But to risk three months of her life in the hands of a man like Nathan Garrett was far too reckless a notion to even consider.

Nathan leaned forward. His blue eyes glimmered as if to emphasize the challenge he'd made.

Finally, the fact that she had such an outstanding poker hand won over her reluctance. "All right, Mr. Garrett. It's a bet."

"You agree to the three months, which will mean leaving with me tomorrow afternoon?" he asked, wanting clarification.

Josie nodded.

"Are you willing to state as much on paper?"

By now Pete had arrived with the thirty dollars as well as the pen, ink, and paper she had requested moments earlier.

Again Josie nodded and took the paper from the wide-eyed bartender and set it on the table before her.

Carefully, she unstoppered the small bottle of ink, then dipped her pen and began to write, wording the agreement as carefully as she knew how.

Sirus, who was extremely intrigued by this turn of events, agreed to witness the document and signed his name just below hers, then handed the paper to Nathan.

After a momentary perusal, he nodded and smiled. "Since it is clear enough you don't have any more money, I call. Let's see what your cards are."

Too flustered to realize it was her turn to either call or raise, Josie took a long breath and held it deep while she slowly turned her cards over, one at a time, to reveal first her two jacks, then her three queens.

"A full house!" Sirus exclaimed, clapping his hand together with obvious glee. "And damn if it isn't ladies over jacks. What a hand! No wonder you were so willin' to sign that agreement."

Josie offered her friend a trembling smile and was finally able to release the breath she'd held. She swallowed weakly before looking at Nathan expectantly.

"He's right. That is quite a hand," Nathan stated with an appreciative nod, then tilted his head to one side while he studied her cards a moment longer. Slowly, he lifted his gaze to meet with hers, effectively holding her attention. Then, wordlessly, he began to turn his own cards over, one at a time. His face remained devoid of all emotion.

Chapter Three

Josie watched with horrified disbelief when Nathan Garrett revealed his cards — three kings and two aces.

"By golly, he's got her beat!" Sirus said, reaching out a stubby finger to touch the smooth faces of the cards, clearly in awe.

"I don't believe it," Josie said, staring at the cards, her voice wavering.

"You want a closer look?," Nathan responded lightly as he pushed the cards toward her. His lips stretched into a contented smile when he leaned forward to rake in his winnings. "Might as well face it, mine is clearly the winning hand."

Josie's stomach felt like cold lead. She watched, too numb to respond, while he carefully sorted the money into orderly stacks. Her misery was overwhelming. All hope of buying that little house at the far end of Elm Street was gone. And along with it went her only chance to put this arrogant man in his rightful place. But the worst of it was she had just lost three long months of her life to him.

A knot of apprehension formed at the base of her throat while she watched him pluck up their handwritten agreement and fold it until it fit neatly into his shirt pocket. She was made painfully aware, by his determined movements, that he had every intention of holding her to that agreement.

"About that paper . . ." she began not really sure what she intended to say, but eager to do something to

49

clarify her feelings.

"Ah, yes, our agreement," he responded, patting his shirt pocket soundly. "Tell you what, since it is so late, and you look tired—why don't we wait until midmorning to finalize our plans. That way we can both get a good night's sleep."

Hoping to discover some way out of the agreement in that time, Josie quickly agreed. "You're right, I am very tired. I could certainly use a good night's sleep. What time do you suggest we meet to discuss this further?"

"I'll come by for you around nine. We can discuss our plans over a late breakfast in that restaurant next to the hotel." His expression became thoughtful. "Since it will be Sunday and the Dogwood will surely be closed, should I call for you at the front door or would the back door be better for you?"

"There's a narrow set of stairs in the alleyway, along the east side of the building. My room is at the top of those stairs. You may call for me there."

"Fine," Nathan said, with a gallant nod of his head, as he tucked the last of his winnings into his bulging coat pockets. "I'll see you in the morning then." He paused long enough to give her a look of clear warning, as if he thought she might try to steal away into the night. Then, without further word, he picked up the last of his belongings, and left.

A cold mist clung to the early-morning air, causing the streetlamps to cast an eerie glow, while Josie quickly made her way along the shadowy street toward the far end of town. Though she was terrified to be out alone after dark, at the moment she saw no other recourse. She had to speak with Trey right away. He would know what she should do.

Due to the early hour, nothing stirred along the darkened street except the whispering leaves of the huge oak trees. No lights were visible in the neighborhood windows. Cypress Mill was asleep.

Pulling her cloak tighter around her shoulders, Josie shuddered at the thought of who or what might be lurking in the nearby shadows, but tried to push such foolish notions aside as she hurried her footsteps along the cobblestone walkway. Soon, she was at her cousin's front door, knocking sharply, hoping he would wake up immediately.

It was several minutes before she finally heard any movement within the small, two-story frame house. It was the same house that had been built by her uncle's own hands and to her aunt's personal specifications. It was simple in structure. The only real distinction between it and so many others like it was the wide, ornately designed entrance veranda that extended beyond the normal lines of the otherwise rectangular house and gave it a welcoming effect. It was on that exceptionally wide veranda that she stood now, hopefully hidden from the dim glow of the nearest streetlamp by the shadows created from the overhang, and knocked boldly on the door.

"Who is it?" Trey mumbled as he hurriedly approached the front door in total darkness. Suddenly there was a thud, followed by a sharp oath. "Confounded table! Who the hell's out there at such an hour?"

A dog started barking somewhere in the distance.

"It's me, Josie," she responded in a strident whisper, not wanting to alert the entire neighborhood of her late-night visit for fear of what loose tongues might make of it.

"Jo'?" he asked, his voice filled with curiosity. "Just a minute."

A soft light appeared through the double-lace curtains. Moments later, she heard the heavy iron bolt finally slip out of place, then the sharp click of the lock.

"What on earth brings you here at this hour?" he

wanted to know, even before he had the door fully open.

"I need to talk to you," she answered, stepping quickly inside. Immediately, she pulled her wide skirts clear of the doorway.

"You're alone? Was there trouble at the saloon?" he asked, deeply concerned. Hurriedly, he closed the door and secured it by slamming the bolt back into place, then turned to face her again.

"Yes," she answered, but then, realizing the panic that would cause in him, she quickly added, "But the trouble is mine, not yours."

Trey was noticeably relieved when he lifted the small lamp from the table that stood near the front door and indicated they should move into the main parlor. "What sort of trouble this time?"

The chilling dampness from outside had penetrated the tall, multipaned windows that ran along two sides of the room. Josie decided to keep her cloak as she made herself comfortable on the familiar three-tone velour sofa facing a darkened fireplace.

She waited until Trey had settled into his favorite leather-upholstered reading chair, with one bared foot resting protectively over the other, before she started to explain her problem to him, careful to leave nothing of importance out.

Trey rubbed his stubbled chin thoughtfully for several minutes before he finally spoke. "The only way I see for you to get out of this ridiculous agreement is to come up with enough money to compensate the man for the amount that was still left to match that bet. How much did you say you were short before he suddenly came up with the idea of having you bet yourself in order to make up the difference?"

"Three hundred and seventy-six dollars," she told him, her voice filled with misery, still unable to fathom how she could have let such a thing happen. It was not like her to be so reckless, especially when it came to poker.

"Tell you what," Trey said, still stroking the coarse stubbles along his chin while he thought the situation through as best he could in his sleep-addled state of mind. "Why don't I loan you four hundred dollars. Use it to try to buy back that agreement."

"Buy it back?"

"Yes, first offer him only the three hundred and seventy-six you were originally short, he may let it go for that. But if he insists on some sort of added compensation for his trouble, offer him the full four hundred. If the man has any sense at all, he'd much rather have the cash in hand than you cleaning his house for three months. Good Lord, girl, you don't even know *how* to clean a house. Mother certainly never made you do that sort of thing around here, and neither did your parents before that. And with good reason, as I recall."

"I keep my own place clean enough," Josie stated in her own defense.

"Oh, sure. You dust a little now and then; and, on a rare occasion, you might even sweep the floor," Trey quickly stated. "And I'll admit you keep things pretty much put away so that the room looks orderly enough, but that's not all that is expected of someone who keeps a man's house. I just can't see you down on your hands and knees once every week, scrubbing and polishing someone's floors or even bending over for hours on end, polishing his furniture, much less washing his clothes every other day and cooking all his regular meals. Oh, and what if there should be mending to be done?"

"I get your point," Josie grumbled, not wanting to be reminded of the time she tried to mend a tear in one of her own sleeves, only to discover when she was finished that she had sewn the entire armhole together.

"I'll get your money —" he laughed, pushing himself up out of the chair. " — as much for his sake as for yours. I'll be right back."

"Trey?" she called out just before he disappeared into

the darkness of the hallway, causing him to turn back toward her expectantly. "Trey, are you sure he'll be willing to take the money instead of me?"

Trey laughed reassuringly. "Give the man credit for having some sense, Jo'. For three hundred and seventy-six dollars, the man could hire himself three live-in housekeepers to keep his house clean for a full year and still have money left over. Of course he'll accept the money in place of that ridiculous agreement. I imagine that's why he wanted to give you until morning before discussing it. He wanted you to have a little more time to get the money together. By what you've told me, the man's no fool."

Josie breathed a slow sigh of relief, watching while Trey padded out of the room in his bare feet, his knobby knees visible beneath the narrow hem of his nightshirt. She felt much better about her situation now that she'd spoken with Trey. But, wanting to make sure Trey understood the money was strictly a loan, she raised both hands and carefully untied her choker. She planned to leave her necklace as collateral until she could pay back the money in full. She refused to leave the house with the money until he had agreed to hold the necklace for her.

That next morning, having been unable to sleep after finding it impossible to push aside the recurring images of the rakishly handsome, woefully arrogant man she was now so ridiculously indebted to, Josie was up early, trying to decide which dress to wear for their meeting. She wanted to choose something pretty, yet not too frilly — something that flattered her, but not outrageously. The intention was to be pleasing to the eye, but not in a way that might tempt him to force her to go with him.

As the hour of nine grew near, she finally made her decision and hurriedly dressed in a cream-colored percale walking suit with dark, rose-colored trimmings along the fitted bodice and the wide hemline. She took special care to shape her long brown hair into a sensible, twisted braid, adorned with only the two silver-tipped combs she needed to anchor it at the back of her head. Due to her cousin's generous loan and reassuring words, she felt very light of heart. She could hardly wait to meet with Mr. Garrett, pay him his money, and be done with it.

Though she knew it would take years to repay Trey such a large amount, she would much rather be indebted to Trey than to someone like Nathaniel Garrett. It felt as if a great weight had been lifted.

At precisely nine o'clock, Josie heard heavy, booted footsteps on the wooden stairs outside her room and knew the moment of reckoning had finally come. Though tempted to peek out between the tiny gap in her curtains and catch a quick glimpse of him, she remained seated on the edge of her bed until she had clearly heard his knock.

"Coming," she called out. To be absolutely certain the money was still safely tucked away inside her handbag, she paused to check for what had to be the sixth time before rising to answer the door.

"Good morning, Mr. Garrett," she greeted him with a cheerful smile as she stepped out onto the narrow landing and quickly closed the door, aware her rose-tipped skirts had brushed across the gleaming surface of his boots when she did.

Though the contact had not been in any way physical, she felt herself blush at the prospect of having allowed any contact at all. She wished she had the room to take a step away from him, but she was already up against the railing as it was.

"Good morning," Nathan responded, clearly surprised at her easy manner and delighted by the high color in her cheeks. "Did you rest well?"

"To tell you the truth, I did not sleep at all last night," she responded lightly. "I had quite a lot to think about, quite a lot to get done. But I imagine you slept very well. I understand the Cypress Hotel's accommodations are some of the finest."

Nathan made no responding comment, not wanting to admit he had tossed and turned until his bed was nothing but a twisted mass of sheets and blankets. Instead, he turned to face the stairs as he offered her the support of his arm. "Shall we go across the street to have our breakfast now?"

Josie's insides tightened at the thought of having to take the man's arm, but she didn't want to chance insulting him by refusing his offer of assistance. She wanted to keep him in an agreeable frame of mind until after they discussed the possibility of her buying back that paper she'd so foolishly signed. Forcing a pretty smile to remain at her lips, she gently slipped her arm in place. "Let's go, I'm famished."

The result of the simple action was like a thunderbolt to her senses. Her breath caught just as her heart slammed hard against her breastbone, paused, and then began to hammer at a dangerous rate, sending her blood racing through all parts of her body. Knowing it was a ridiculous response to his mere touch, she decided the strange, fluttery reaction was caused more by the ordeal that still lay ahead. She still must find some way to convince him to sell her agreement back to her for the amount of money in her purse.

With her smile wavering only slightly, she did what she could not to let her strange, turbulent feelings show, afraid that if he somehow realized just how eager she was to have possession of that agreement, he might demand more than four hundred dollars.

Moments later, when they entered the small restaurant that adjoined the town's only hotel, Josie took advantage of the situation and finally pulled away from Nathan's disturbing touch, only to discover her arm suddenly felt cold—which was absurd in a room so warm. Again she attributed the strange reaction to the fact she was still very nervous about the confrontation to come.

"May I seat you?" the hostess asked as she approached Josie and Nathan with two sets of freshly laundered napkins, clean tableware, and handwritten menus.

"Yes, please," Nathan said with a charming smile that caused their young hostess to smile shyly in return.

Josie found the flirtatious exchange between Nathan Garrett and the hotel owner's oldest daughter a little revolting, but said nothing while she followed Beth Walls across the room to a small table near a side-street window. By the time Josie had set her handbag on the corner of the table and had taken the seat their hostess had indicated, she had gotten back in full control of her senses. The odd, fluttery feeling she had suffered earlier was gone.

But when Nathan helped scoot her chair forward toward the table, then rested his hand lightly on her shoulder while waiting for Beth Walls to finish arranging their tableware, the strange, fluttery feeling returned full force. Again Josie felt it hard to concentrate on anything but the tingling warmth of his touch. She frowned, knowing there was absolutely no logic in such a reaction.

"I hope they have ham," Nathan said as soon as the hostess had left. Finally, he moved toward his own chair. As he settled in, he lifted his napkin and placed it across his right thigh. "I'm in the mood for a large plate, piled high with scrambled eggs and ham."

Pleased to note he at least had the manners to put his napkin away, Josie responded with a smile. "They usually give you your choice of a large slice of ham or beef here."

"I gather you've eaten here before," he commented as he quickly took up the menu the hostess had left for him.

"On occasion," Josie responded, not about to admit she ate there almost daily because she did not cook and the Cypress House had the best food of the three restaurants in town.

Josie waited until they had placed their orders and Nathan Garrett had begun to apply a generous helping of butter on one of the biscuits that had been left for them; then she broached the subject she wanted to discuss the most.

"As you know, I've had plenty of time to think about our agreement," she began, hoping to sound less concerned than she really was. She paused to consider exactly how she should word her proposal.

"And?" he prodded, dipping the end of his butter knife toward her with encouragement to continue.

"And I think it was really a ridiculous thing for us to do."

"And?" His eyes darkened while he waited for her next response.

"And I think it would be grossly unfair to both of us if we decided to actually go through with it. First, I don't think it is at all fair to expect me to give up three months of my life just because of some poker game. And at the same time, I don't think it is fair that you should have to be out the three hundred and seventy-six dollars that agreement supposedly took the place of." She reached for her handbag and moved directly in front of her. "Therefore, I have brought you the money. All three hundred and seventy-six dollars of it. Neither of us needs to come out with the short end of this situation."

"Your cousin loaned it to you?" he asked, his curiosity just as aroused as his anger.

"Yes, I put up my emerald necklace for collateral," she explained as she brought her gaze up to meet his. "Trey understands the value of such things. He was there the day I won it. And because he does understand just how much the jewels are worth, he was very willing to loan me the money against it."

"What an inconvenience for you both. But maybe

58

you'll have time to take the money back to him and reexchange it for your necklace before we leave." He resumed buttering his biscuit as if the matter was now closed.

"What do you mean, before we leave?" she asked. A heavy feeling settled across her stomach.

"I thought I made myself clear last night. We will have to leave here this very afternoon. We have to be in Alexandria by 5:15 to meet the train. That means we'll have to leave Cypress Mill by at least three o'clock." He took a sampling bite of his biscuit, nodded appreciatively, then laid it aside and lifted his amber-glass water goblet.

"Leave here? But I thought—" She glanced helplessly at her handbag. He hadn't even let her show him the money.

Nathan took a long sip from his water glass. "We really do need to be on our way by three," he restated firmly. "I've already hired a buggy and a driver to take us, since I knew you'd probably want to take a few items with you. I figured you would be more comfortable riding in a buggy than on horseback. The driver I hired seemed to know you and promised to be outside your door at precisely two o'clock so he can start loading your things just as soon as you are finished packing."

He paused to take another long sip of water before continuing. "I'm afraid there won't be much room, though. It's a small rig, but it was all the livery had available. You'll have to keep what you decide to take, down to one trunk and possibly a small valise. We might even be able to squeeze on an extra hat box or two."

"But I'm not going," Josie tried to explain, only to have her words cut short.

"Don't tell me you intend to go back on your word," he said, suddenly frowning and slamming his glass down angrily. Water sloshed out onto the white tablecloth unnoticed. "I may have misjudged you in a number of ways last night, but I was absolutely certain you would prove to be the type of person who honors her word no matter the consequences."

"I am. But I hoped after I'd offered you the money in exchange for the agreement, you'd be willing to let me out of it." Suddenly she felt an icy chill crawl up her backbone. Tiny bumps of apprehension formed beneath her skin.

"Well, you thought wrong. I have no intention of letting you out of that agreement. In fact, I have every intention of seeing the agreement through to the end."

"But why, when you could hire *three* live-in housekeepers to work a whole year for that amount?" she asked, echoing Trey's logic, hoping to reason with him but at the same time knowing he'd gone beyond all reasoning on the matter.

"An agreement is an agreement," he answered simply, then casually dabbed at the spilled water with his napkin. When he decided his efforts were useless, he looked up at her, his expression harsh. "Do you plan to keep your part of our agreement or not?"

"What if I offered you four hundred dollars? After all, I'm a sensible person. I know you should receive some sort of atonement for your trouble." She reached for the opening of her handbag hoping to retrieve the money.

"Frankly, I don't care if you offer me one thousand dollars. I don't intend to let you out of the agreement. You promised me three months of your labor and I intend to have all three months, even if I have to carry you out of this town kicking and screaming over my shoulder." His expression remained deadly serious.

"You can't do that," she challenged, hoping to run a bluff. It was her last hope.

"Can't I?"

"That would be the same as kidnapping. Sheriff Butler wouldn't let you get away with such a thing."

"Wouldn't he? Are you forgetting the piece of paper you signed for me last night? It clearly states that you agree to go with me; and if you have agreed to go, it is not kidnapping." Though his narrowed eyes revealed the force of his anger, his voice remained deadly calm.

"But that paper can't really be legal. And even if it is, I can't believe you'd actually try to hold me to it, especially after I've managed to come up with more than enough money to repay you." She narrowed her own eyes, to let him know she was becoming just as angry as he.

"And I can't believe you are actually trying to worm your way out of it," he stated coolly. He stared at her for a long moment before leaning forward and resting his elbows on the edge of the table. "The agreement was for you to leave with me today. Let me think, how did you word it?" He paused to try to remember the exact words she'd written. "For the sole purpose of cleaning my house and cooking my meals for the term of three full months. So, tell me, are you a woman of your word or not?"

When he put it like that, what could she say? "Of course I'm a woman of my word."

"Good, then it's settled." His voice was cold as polished steel and his eyes glinted with pure determination. "As soon as we've finished eating, you can go back to your room and pack what you think you might need. If you want help getting your things together in such short time, I can come and assist you in whatever way you want after I've checked out of the hotel. Just keep in mind I intend to be on my way by three o'clock. I will not miss that train."

Josie's anger continued to eat away at her. It felt like someone had spilled a vial of burning acid into her bloodstream. "May I at least know where we are going?"

"Ever hear of Silver Springs, Texas?"

"No."

"Well, you soon will" was his only comment before lifting his hand up to signal the waitress that he had spilled his water and would like a fresh tablecloth.

Damn that Nathan Garrett, Josie cursed silently for what had to be the twentieth time, while she flung her clothing into the large, open trunk with the fury of a madwoman. How dare he hold her to such a ridiculous agreement! How dare he not accept the generous amount she'd offered him in an effort to buy back that piece of paper! How dare he treat her like a small child, telling her what to do and when to be ready.

Angrily, she punctuated each occurring thought with another loud cry of outrage. All the while, she jerked her clothing off the tiny pegs inside her armoire and out of haphazardly opened drawers, then slung the items as hard as she could into a rumpled pile at the bottom of her trunk.

What did she care what her clothing looked like when she arrived in Silver Springs, Texas? For the next three months, she might as well be wearing a prison uniform. That was what she would in all honesty be—Nathan Garrett's personal prisoner, sentenced to three months' hard labor by her own hand.

Damn that Nathan Garrett!

And damn her own recklessness, and especially her foolish sense of honor, for that was all that kept her from simply stealing away before he ever came for her, then returning only after she was certain he had long since gone from Cypress Mill. But, then again, knowing the type of man Nathan Garrett was, he would come looking for her, never giving up until he found her. No, she was doomed. There was no getting out of the three months of pure drudgery ahead.

Overcome by her own anger and frustration, Josie finally collapsed onto the unmade bed and buried her face deep into her favorite pillow. She gave no thought to her dress or her hair while she lay there, drawing in several long, deep breaths — something her mother had taught her to do back when she was a child and found her temper had the better of her. Slowly, some of the anger subsided and she rolled over onto her back to consider her situation more logically.

For the next three months she would be at the beck and call of one overly arrogant Nathaniel Garrett. There was nothing else she could think to do that might let her out of it. And, finally having come to accept that fact, she began to wonder what else lay ahead for her. She wondered first what his house might be like and how much trouble it would be to keep clean.

Her stomach folded into a tight knot when she then wondered if she would be expected to live in the same house with him. What if he lived alone?

Suddenly her blood charged through her body at a frantic pace. Why hadn't she thought to ask him if he lived alone before she ever signed that foolish agreement? She tried to recall their past conversations. He had yet to mention a wife, or any servants already in his employ. In fact, she knew absolutely nothing about him. Josie's eyes grew wide.

"Ah, me," she moaned aloud. What would she do if he did indeed live alone? The mere thought of it made her insides flounder and twitch. She pressed her eyes closed. What *could* she do? She had promised to be his full-time housekeeper for three months. Full-time usually meant living on the premises.

But whether or not he lived alone should have been discussed before she'd made the bet. It was too late to worry about it now. A tight pain developed in her chest at the realization. Her word had been given. She would have to keep it. Again she cursed her own foolish sense of honor.

Aware valuable time was slipping away, Josie roused herself from the bed and reluctantly returned to her packing. Having refused the man's offer to help, she would have to finish the task herself. And quickly, if she wanted time enough to pen Trey a brief note, explaining why she was going and where in her room she planned to hide his money, worded in a way only he would understand. That way he could retrieve his money after he discovered she had gone and then replace it with her necklace. She also wanted to be sure he remembered to keep her room locked until her return. She didn't want anyone slipping upstairs and going through her things while she was gone.

Absently, she reached up to touch her bare throat as she glanced worriedly at the clock. She had less than two hours. She needed to hurry.

By the time the driver arrived at her door, Josie was almost ready to leave. She'd convinced herself to see the agreement through, but only because of that damnable sense of honor she'd been born with. She refused to believe anything else could have swayed her decision.

She also refused to link the stirring little responses her body experienced whenever she thought of what the next three months would be like to the fact the man was so undeniably attractive. Nor would she admit that she found his smile woefully intriguing — nor, even to herself, would she admit that she had truly admired the cool manner in which he had played that winning hand.

Instead, she attributed the strange feelings to the dark uncertainty that came from having no way to know what lay ahead for her. She clearly did not want to go. She did not want to leave her cousin Trey or her only friends. It saddened her to think of the poker game proceeding next Saturday without her.

"I'm coming," she called to the driver as she pushed her sad thoughts aside and hurried to the door. She hadn't even left her room yet and already she was homesick.

"I'm here for your things, ma'am," Sam Johnson told her, pushing his rumpled hat to the back of his head as he looked around the cluttered room for a glimpse of her baggage. His eyes widened at the way drawers had been left dangling at random angles and at the way the armoire doors stood wide open, rumpled clothing spilling forth. "Eager to be on your way, I see."

Josie tried to swallow back the emotion that gripped her throat, because *eager* was a far cry from what she really felt. "I'm not quite ready to close the valise yet. I'd like to take one last look around to make sure I'm not forgetting anything important. But you may take the trunk on downstairs. It's locked and ready to go."

Forlornly, she watched Sam heave the heavy trunk onto his broad right shoulder and head for the stairs just outside her door. As he disappeared from her sight, she knew there would be no turning back. She would see the agreement through, if for no other reason than she had given her word. For the next three long months of her life, she would do her best to clean Nathan Garrett's house and cook his meals—but she would *not* associate with him in any way other than as an employee would her employer. Then, remembering the sort of meals the man could expect from her, she smiled, and for the first time found an odd pleasure in the fact she did not know how to cook anything more elaborate than cinnamon-sprinkled oatmeal and hard-boiled eggs.

Her smile broadened when she thought of the man's reaction when he discovered exactly what sort of house servant he'd won. He clearly had no idea what he was getting himself into. If she hadn't found such pleasure in the prospect of being able to ruin his life, at least temporarily she might actually feel sorry for the poor man.

Chapter Four

During the hour-and-a-half buggy ride to Alexandria, Josie all but ignored Nathan Garrett, though at times it was impossible to do, especially in the close confines of the rig he had hired. Whenever they bumped across an exceptionally deep chug-hole or tossed into a sun hardened wheel-rut, the resulting jolt of the high-springed buggy sent Josie's shoulder slamming hard into the side of Nathan's solid arm. Each time, Josie's heart jumped with sudden awareness, making her wish there was some way to put a sturdy wall between them.

Even after they'd finally arrived at the depot and had sent the driver on his way, Josie did little to acknowledge Nathan's presence other than to nod briskly or shake her head, whichever seemed the appropriate response to his questions. Even when he asked her things that could not be answered with a simple yes to no, she kept her replies to single-word responses.

Finally, Nathan had enough.

"You know you could try to be just a little more on the friendly side," he stated in a barely controlled voice after she had carefully set her valise on the narrow benchseat beside her in an obvious attempt to prevent him from sitting there.

Turning in the seat and presenting a stiff shoulder to him, she responded without bothering to take her gaze off the many people who milled about the depot, "Friendship was not one of the terms of our agreement,

Mr. Garrett."

Nathan flattened his lips into a grim line as he considered what a grave oversight that had been on his part. He ran his hand along the jutting curve of his chin while he thought more about it.

"That may be true, but if we are to have any sort of relationship at all, it would help if you at least *tried* to be a little friendlier." He reached for the handle of the valise, intent on moving it so he could have a place to sit beside her until their train finally arrived, only to have his hand spatted as if he were some small child.

Josie wanted to chuckle aloud at how quickly he had jerked his hand away, but kept her face very sober when she finally bothered to glance up at him. When she did, she felt a perplexing leap of her senses. She had not taken time to notice how handsome he looked in his dark-blue, three-piece traveling suit; but then she had been very careful to avoid looking at him at all during the short buggy trip, intent on causing him as much aggravation as possible.

In an attempt to calm her unexpected reaction, she forced out her chin to a haughty angle and stated in a cool even voice, "Mr. Garrett, I think I need to make it perfectly clear from the very outset of our three months together, the *only* sort of relationship we will share is a strict employer-employee relationship. There is to be no friendliness between us, nor is there to be any casual familiarity."

Nathan ran his hand over his face while he considered his response. Finally he tossed his hands into the air. "All right, have it your way, Miss Leigh. At the moment, I'm far too tired to argue with you. I've had a long and trying day."

Spotting a vacant seat on an identical bench across the harshly lit room, he turned his back to her and stomped away.

Though it was just the sort of reaction she'd hoped for, Josie felt unaccountably displeased over his willingness to give up so easily. Fuming because he had not attempted to press the matter further, she waited until he'd settled onto the narrow seat across the way before triumphantly reaching over and removing the valise from its place beside her, then casually setting it onto the floor—where it should have been placed to being with. Almost immediately an elderly gentleman noticed the vacant spot and sat down.

Nathan's response was to fold his arms and glower at her.

Josie's response was to jut out her chin and glower back.

By the time the two had boarded the small westbound train in cold silence and had dutifully taken their assigned places—sitting side by side, but purposely staring in opposite directions—Nathan had started to wonder if his half of Oakhaven was really worth the aggravation he was having to suffer. True, the estate had to be worth more than a hundred thousand dollars, maybe twice that, but wasn't his sanity worth something? How could he tolerate three months of being so blatantly scorned by Annabelle Garrett's only granddaughter?

Grimly, he questioned the sanity of the entire situation while staring quietly at the flickering glow of one of the overhead lamps that had been lit an hour after their late departure.

Why had his father made such a strange stipulation in his will? Why had the man been so adamant the two of them spend three months there, together, at Oakhaven before the will could even be read? He thought that perhaps the old man had hoped that through forcing the two of them to live there for three entire months, one of them might grow to love the place as much as he had and might be willing to stay on and take care of it rather than sell everything to strangers.

Nathan felt that was hardly likely to happen, though, for he already had a place of his own that he was very proud of, one he had reluctantly left in Randall Clifton's care. And Josie Leigh hardly seemed the type to want a permanent home, especially not one so far removed from everything and everyone. Nor did *he* for that matter. He liked having neighbors close by, sharing in each other's troubles, and he liked having a town within an hour's ride. Oakhaven had neither. It was about as isolated as a place could get and still be in civilized territory. No, his only intention was to meet the strange provision his father had made, and see to it that Josie also met it. That was the only way they could ever gain ownership of the place, and the only way they would ever be free to sell it to that buyer his father's attorney had already located.

Glancing at Josie as she sat ever so primly at his side, staring intently at the many rows of passengers in front of her, Nathan felt a sudden stab of guilt for having kept secret the fact he had gone to Cypress Mill with the sole intention of finding her. The real reason he'd manipulated her into making that bet had nothing to do with needing a housekeeper. It had simply been a convenient way to make her go back with him.

The stab of guilt grew stronger as the attorney's letter weighed heavily in his pocket — though, in truth, it was addressed to Josie's guardians and not to Josie herself. How could he deliver a letter to a dead couple? Still, he knew he should have told her about the letter, or at least about its contents. She should have been allowed to make her own decision. But what if she had decided not to come?

He released a heavy sigh as he thought more about his deception. How much easier it would have been if she had simply been the child he had thought her to be, instead of such a strong-willed, stubborn-hearted young woman, who had taken such an immediate and obvious dislike to him.

69

His frown deepened when he considered what her reaction might be if she somehow discovered the true reason he had tricked her into going with him back to Oakhaven—or what her reaction would be if she learned that the contract she'd signed was in fact invalid, that any contract signed on a Sunday was worthless. She would be furious, without a doubt; but would she be furious enough to turn her back on the chance to inherit her half of a small fortune? He sighed again, certain she would. It bothered him that there could be no second chances. Either they fulfilled the stipulation during their first attempt at cohabitation or forever lost any claim to Oakhaven. He wondered what would happen to the place then.

"Must you continued to stare at me?" she asked, breaking immediately into his rambling thoughts.

When she faced him, she revealed such an expression of annoyance, he felt oddly obliged to deny her accusation.

"I wasn't staring at you," he answered quickly, then to cover the lie, he added, "I was merely looking out through the window there." He nodded toward the thick square of beveled glass just at the other side of her.

"At what, Mr. Garrett?" she asked accusingly. "It's far too dark outside to see anything."

She spoke the truth. All that could be seen in the large single-paned window at Josie's side was their reflection.

Nathan tried not to reveal his own annoyance, which was close to being stretched to its limit. "I do wish you would quit calling me Mr. Garrett. I've already told you, my friends all call me Nathan."

"And, as I have already told you, we are not going to become friends in this three-month little venture of ours. I am to be your employee and you are to be my employer, and I think it would be highly improper for one of your employees to call you by your first name."

Nathan sighed, exasperated.

"What if I *order* you to call me by my first name?" he asked, his eyes widening, thinking he'd struck upon the perfect way around her stubbornness at last. "What if I made it an employer's demand that you call me by my first name?"

"Won't do. My sole responsibilities, as stated in our agreement, are to clean your house and cook your meals. Nothing more. So, unless your orders have something to do with either of those two chores, I am not obligated to obey," she stated with a haughty shake of her head, which caused the delicate feathers on her small rose-colored hat to flutter back and forth, temporarily distracting him.

Tapping his forefinger to his pursed lips, Nathan carefully considered his next response.

"Well, then, whenever you are cleaning my house or cooking my meals, I insist you refer to me as Nathan, or at least Nathaniel, and not Mr. Garrett," he stated triumphantly.

Josie glowered at him. "As you wish, but until we arrive at your house and I officially begin my duties as your housekeeper, I will continue to call you Mr. Garrett" — she paused for effect — "among *other* things."

Nathan laughed, breaking the tension that had been steadily building inside him. "I've probably been called worse."

"I doubt it," she said, tilting her head to study the fascinating curves that had suddenly sprung to his cheeks. The response she felt was infuriating. She actually wanted to laugh with him, but having dedicated herself to his misery, she refused to allow it. Even so, her angry glower slowly lifted until it was nothing more than an expression that displayed mere caution.

Nathan was pleased to see progress had been made, however small. "I know you are angry with me for having forced you to keep your agreement, but I wish you would try to make the best of it. After all, three months is not a lifetime."

71

"Maybe it isn't a lifetime, but it sure does seem like it," she muttered, unwilling to give up any of the resentment she felt toward him, then lapsed again into silence as she crossed her arms and stared determinedly toward the front of the railroad car.

After an hour of listening to nothing more than the continuous chugging of the engine and the metallic clattering of the iron wheels on the molded steel tracks, Nathan decided it was time to try once more to encourage her to talk. Clearing his throat loudly in an effort to regain her attention, he decided to start by asking her a few questions about herself. He knew so very little about her and found he was truly eager to know more. "So tell me, Miss Leigh, how long have you lived in Cypress Mill?"

Josie brought her head around with a snap, startled from her thoughts. "Were you speaking to me?"

"Yes, I was just curious to know how long you have lived in Cypress Mill. I gathered from the way everyone acted so friendly toward you that you've lived there for quite some time."

She looked at him, her brow raised with immediate suspicion. "Why do you want to know?"

"I thought, since we will be living together for the next three months, that I might try to learn a little more about you."

The words "living together" struck Josie hard. It was the one thing she had tried her best not to think about all afternoon — and it was one thing she'd really prefer not to think about now.

Looking away, she finally answered his question, seeing no real reason not to. "I've lived in Cypress Mill for about seven years."

"With your aunt and uncle?" He wanted to know more.

"Yes, until they died." She felt a sudden lump of suppressed emotion form in her throat. How dearly she had loved her aunt Nadine and uncle Edward, who had

72

been generous enough to not only welcome her into their own home so shortly after her mother's death but into their hearts as well. They had cared enough about her to give her the freedom to be herself, and she would be forever grateful to them for that. Her mother had been very restrictive with her, always afraid she would give in to her capricious ways and end up with more trouble than she could handle. *How right her mother had been.*

"But now you live alone?" he asked, interrupting her thoughts after only a moment.

Josie cut her gaze back toward him. Her green eyes narrowed while she compressed her lips into a tight frown. "No, now it seems I live with you."

Nathan grinned, cocking his mouth into an off-center smile. Though he knew she saw no humor in the situation, he couldn't help wanting to laugh. "I see. And do you have other family?"

"Only Trey. My parents are both dead."

That was the first piece of information she had voluntarily given. He could sense she was starting to loosen the tight barriers she had put up around herself. "And your grandparents? What of them?"

"They are all dead, too." She closed her eyes briefly. When she opened them again, she was no longer looking at him.

She appeared so sad, Nathan's heart went immediately out to her. "I'm sorry. You must miss them very much."

Josie turned her gaze to the darkened window. "I hardly knew them. My father's parents died when I was still a baby. All I really know about them is that they owned a mercantile of some sort in St. Louis that did quite well. My other grandfather," she paused to consider the best way to phrase it, *"died* when I was barely seven. I can still remember a few things about him, but not much."

Nathan noticed Josie had only mentioned three of

her grandparents. "And what of your other grand-mother—your mother's mother?"

Josie shrugged, still staring at the window, as though she could suddenly see through the reflection there. "I hear she died about eight years ago."

Nathan had detected a sharp undertone of resent-ment in Josie's voice. He studied her reflection on the dark window glass. "But you never knew her?"

"She never wanted to know me," Josie replied, then closed her eyes again to help shut out the resulting pain.

Nathan felt it would be better to change the subject, at least for now. "I wonder what your cousin will think when he opens up his saloon tomorrow and discovers you have gone. Or did you have time to go over and say goodbye."

"I barely had enough time to write him a letter. And he'll probably think I'm a fool for having actually kept that ridiculous agreement." She looked back at Nathan then with her brow raised, eager to catch his response.

"At least it will comfort him to know what an honest person you are, having kept your word despite all the inconvenience it will cause."

Inconvenience? she wondered, thinking it an absurd description for everything she had since suffered—and all she had yet to suffer. "Trey already knows how I feel about honesty. He knows I hate dishonesty in anyone." She thrust her chin out proudly.

Nathan felt compelled to look away. After all, he was not being exactly honest with her himself. "I see," he said, stroking his chin self-consciously. "Honesty means a lot to you then?"

"You sure do ask a lot of questions," she finally said in exasperation. "Yes, honesty means a lot to me. So does my privacy."

Lifting his brows at the intended insult, Nathan crossed his arms and fell silent again. He wondered just how long it would take her to find out the real reason he had gone to Cypress Mill, and what her reaction would be when she realized she had been purposely manipulated into going back with him. He should have approached her with the truth right from the beginning and hope for the best. But now that he'd had a chance to see firsthand the way she felt about her grandmother, and knowing how she also felt about him, he decided it was probably for the best that he'd chosen to handle the situation in the way he did—without giving her the option of making up her own mind.

His only hope now was to keep her from discovering the real reason he'd gone to Cypress Mill, which also meant keeping her from finding out about the will and its strange provisions, at least until after the three months were up. It was the only way he could be sure she would not consciously do anything to ruin their chances of inheriting his father's fortune.

Throughout the remainder of the trip, Josie and Nathan said very little to each other. Each was lost in separate thoughts about what the future might hold in store. Though Josie wondered about Nathan, and tried to guess what sort of home he might have, she refused to let him know she was in any way curious about him and kept her questions to herself. Still, she couldn't help wondering what the answers might be, and tried to figure him out on her own, only to find it impossible to do so.

Judging by the manner in which he dressed and the way he talked, he was neither poor nor uneducated; yet his hands were covered with healed-over scars and thick calluses. And even through his fine, tailored clothing, it was easy to tell that the muscles along his arms, back, and thighs were strong and powerful. He was clearly a hard-working man, and it seemed obvious by the darkened tone of the skin along his neck and hands that he did much of that hard work out of doors. It puzzled Josie that he dressed so well, yet could not afford to have others do his work for him.

It puzzled her even more to discover, once they finally reached Silver Springs early that following morning, that no one there seemed to know him. Though several women turned their heads to gaze at him, most of the townspeople passed by them as if they were both strangers to the area. Only a very few offered either of them as much as a cursory nod.

By the time he had stopped by the livery to hire yet another buggy when she had truly expected there to be a carriage of some sort waiting for them, Josie had started to form grave suspicions about the man. And when he then made a stop by the local mercantile to stock up on supplies, she was bursting to know why.

Finally, she could stand her curiosity no longer and broke her personal vow not to ask any questions. She had to know why everyone seemed not to know him, and why there had been no buggy waiting for them. She also wanted to know why he should have to stop for such a common stock of supplies, like flour, coffee, and sugar.

She waited until he had loaded all the supplies into the rented buggy before finally asking the questions topmost in her mind.

"Why didn't you simply think to wire ahead and have someone make these purchases for you ahead of time? That same person could then have waited here to meet you when you got off the train," she asked, standing beside him and watching while he readjusted the load in the back of the buggy to better accommodate both their baggage and the newly purchased supplies. "Wouldn't that have been much easier than having to rent someone else's buggy like this and then having to make the purchases yourself?"

"Had no one to send the wire to," he answered simply as he moved toward the front of the buggy and held out his hand to help her up.

Josie's hand froze in midair as his words sunk in. It suddenly felt as if the air had been sucked right out of

76

her. Her heart quit beating, slowing her blood to a cold stop. Weakly, she asked the question she feared the most. "You live alone?"

Nathan grinned, still waiting with his hand out-stretched to help her up onto the seat. "Not anymore I don't."

Josie swallowed audibly, but said nothing more while she allowed him to assist her onto the high-springed black leather seat. His warm touch caused her senses to jump, but she did not withdraw her hand from his until she was safely in the buggy and holding on to the upholstered armrest as if it were to be her last link with life. Quickly, Nathan swung onto the seat beside her in one easy movement and took up the reins, still grinning.

They traveled for almost half an hour before Josie found the courage to ask him any more questions. "How much longer until we reach your house?"

"We have quite a way to go yet. Oakhaven, which is the name of the place, is in a very remote part of the country."

Remote? she wondered, her stomach tightening until it was rock-hard. *As in "quite distant, and far removed?"* She shuddered, glad her mother could not know the mess her reckless daughter had gotten herself into this time. If her mother had not already died of more natural causes, Josie was quite certain this most recent impropriety would send the poor woman directly to her grave. When would she ever learn?

Having sensed her uneasy reaction, Nathan reached over to pat her arm, partly to reassure her and partly because he simply liked touching her. It stimulated him to know he could reach over whenever he wanted and touch such an intriguingly beautiful young woman — even if she did resist his every attempt. "It's almost a two-hour buggy ride from Silver Springs to the main house at Oakhaven. On horseback, though, the trip can be made in a little over an hour and a half. I guess it's about a six-mile trip."

Josie was not sure she wanted to hear any more, but still she had to ask. "Just how remote is Oakhaven? Are there no neighbors?"

"Not close neighbors, like you might expect. You mentioned earlier that your privacy meant a lot to you; well, Oakhaven was built for privacy. There's only one other house on the estate, and it's about a mile and a half from the main house. And other than that one house, the nearest neighbor is well over two miles away."

Estate? The nearest neighbor about a mile and a half away, yet still on the same estate? Just how large was Oakhaven? She turned to look at Nathan with renewed curiosity. Just how wealthy was this man? And if he was so wealthy, why were there no servants living there to help take care of the place? Why did his hands look so work-worn?

She gazed out at the passing countryside while she tried to make sense of it all and found she was very pleased with what she saw. For some reason, she had not expected East Texas to look so much like Central Louisiana. Though the cypress trees were noticeably absent, in their place was a predominant number of tall, stately pine trees, blended in with a great assortment of broadleaf trees, their spreading boughs already heavy with bright-green foliage. Dogwoods bloomed in the distance — explosions of white and pink against a dark backdrop of green.

Along the roadway itself grew a wide variety of trees with huge branches that loomed high overhead, forming an almost constant arch of shade for the dusty lane. Bright green pastures and rich, cultivated farmland appeared on either side of them, but it was the grassy, rolling pastures that attracted Josie the most.

Having lived in an area where mostly sugar cane was grown, and an occasional planting of cotton could be found, it seemed a little strange to have wide open fields with little more than thick blankets of green grass growing across them. Narrow streams trickling with water wove their way through the vast oceans of green, and pretty little blue and gold wildflowers dotted the fields in places, making the scene before her seem almost fairylike.

Unaware Nathan watched her with intent curiosity, she smiled in response while she studied her surroundings but said nothing. Instead, she stared off at the large, wooded hills that lay beyond the wide, grassy fields. The earth, where it could be seen, was a deep, rich reddish-brown; and not at all dry like she'd expected. As she studied her surroundings further, she realized she had been too quick to accept the many stories she'd heard about Texas being nothing but vast, empty rolling plains, almost desertlike. She was surprised and very pleased to see that the area was so plush and green.

Occasionally, as they traveled along the rutted dirt and gravel road, they passed large fenced-in areas, which she found reassuring. Fences meant the people who owned the land planned to stay. The area was indeed settled, something else she had not been too sure of. The thought of Indians had crossed her mind several times.

Shaking that thought, she noticed that most of the fences were modern in design, made of posts and long strands of sturdy wire. But occasionally an old-fashioned wooden fence sprang up along the winding roadside, which let her know some of the people had resided there for quite some time. Another reassuring thought.

"More and more people have taken to fencing in their property," Nathan told her when he noticed what had her attention — anything to break the monotonous silence that had fallen between them. "The ranchers don't like their cattle roaming loose anymore and the farmers certainly don't like finding their neighbors' cattle stomping around in their carefully tended fields."

"And which do you have to protect, cattle or farmland?" she asked, glancing at him.

"At Oakhaven, there's not much of either. Oakhaven has more or less been kept in its natural state. The cattle it does have roam the acreage at will, finding enough substance in the grassy clearings and in among the woodlands to keep strong and healthy during the summer. In the winter, extra hay and grain usually have to be provided, because what little winter growth there is, is quickly eaten."

Josie's dread began to melt away as she learned more about this Oakhaven. "How much farther?"

"When we pass through the large gate just around that next bend, we will be on Oakhaven land. But it is still a twenty-minute ride on to the main house."

The large gate he'd mentioned turned out to be a massive artwork of ornamental iron painted stark white. In the center of the curving, forty-foot masterpiece was a perfect circle with the design of a huge oak tree in the center of it.

"Impressive," she stated aloud, though she had not intended to.

"Yes, I guess it is," Nathan said in an off-hand manner as he, too, stared at the elaborate gate his father had designed, and probably built himself.

Josie's eyebrows lifted. How could Nathan seem so casual about such obvious wealth? Eagerly she looked ahead along the shaded lane for her first sight of this main house he kept referring to.

The next twenty minutes seemed to go by at a snail's pace while they made their way through the rich, parklike woodlands that covered much of the estate's grounds. At each bend in the road, Josie again strained to see what lay ahead, wanting to catch her first glimpse of Nathan's house, the house she would soon have to live in and keep clean. She shuddered at the thought of the work ahead of her, now certain the house would prove to be a massive structure indeed.

Swallowing back her sudden apprehension, she wondered if the house was nestled in among all these trees, or if it was perhaps perched along some high hill overlooking the beautiful woodlands. She was soon to discover neither to be the case, because when the wooded area gradually parted to reveal a natural clearing with a large, partially shaded lake, she finally caught her first glimpse of the main house — which was indeed very large and very stately. The view surrounding it was breathtaking.

"Why, it's as large as a hotel," she remarked, as much in awe as concern. She tightened her grip on the thin strings of her handbag. How could she ever hope to keep such a huge house clean all by herself? Surely there were other servants. Suddenly it occurred to her that he must have lied to her. Not only were there to be other servants, there were probably other household members as well. There had to be fifteen or twenty rooms in that house. She wondered then if one of those household members would prove to be a wife. She could just imagine the reception she would receive if he indeed was married.

"My father built it" was all Nathan had to say about the house. "As you can see, *he* also valued his privacy."

"No doubt," Josie said, nodding apprehensively, still staring in amazement at the house and its picturesque surroundings, unaware she now clutched her handbag against her knotted stomach in a wadded heap.

The house itself was glorious. It was a two-story country mansion of English Gothic design, facing north, made of smooth Portland stone, with tall gables ornamented by handsomely cut verge-boards and handcarved finials. Across the front were tall, latticed windows and a wide, stylish veranda that ran the full width of the house.

Above the veranda was an equally sized open balcony designed to be enjoyed from the front bedrooms along the second floor. Elegant bay windows made of dark, leaded glass projected from the lower floor on both the east and the west sides, and clusters of rounded chimneys rose proudly from the steep roof in several different places.

The house and most of the half dozen outbuildings sat along a small tree-shrouded rise just the other side of the lake, the reflection mirrored picture perfect on the unblemished surface of the dark-blue water. Yellow flowers grew everywhere. Birds sang merrily from the treetops as a slight breeze rustled their surrounding branches. A narrow, graveled carriage drive curved gracefully along the far edge of lake and approached the house from the west side.

"Well, there you have it. Oakhaven," Nathan said, as if it needed verification.

"And you expect me to believe that you live there all alone," she said, pursing her lips into a narrow, flat line. "What sort of fool do you take me for?"

"A most beautiful fool," he remarked, producing a wide, crooked smile, not having taken her question at all seriously. "And a very suspicious one."

Josie glanced heavenward, as if hoping for some sort of divine assistance in handling this man. "I want to know who else lives here."

"No one else, at the moment. After you've gone inside, you will find that the house has not been in use recently, which is why I am in such dire need of a housekeeper. Most of the furniture is draped with sheets, which will need laundering, and I imagine you'll find a thick layer of dust over everything. I guess I should have warned you sooner—you definitely have your work cut out for you."

"And you expect me to clean that entire house alone?" she asked, glancing back at the huge house, disbelieving anyone could be that cruel or demanding. But then again, knowing what she did of him thus far, there was no real reason even to suspect he had a heart hidden away inside that broad but obviously vacant chest of his. "That entire house?"

"Well, you did agree to do just that," he reminded her, grinning that infuriatingly crooked grin of his yet again. His cheek dimpled when he thought more about it. "But I don't expect you to have that entire house clean again overnight. I guess the most sensible thing to do would be to begin with the rooms I'll be using the most." He paused, his grin stretching wider, causing his dimple to form a tiny crescent. "A really good place to start might be my bedroom."

Josie swallowed hard, then shifted nervously in her seat.

Chapter Five

If not for the sobering knowledge she would be the one responsible for cleaning the place, Josie might have been in pure awe of both the size and the true elegance of Oakhaven when she first entered Nathan's house.

The wide, double doors had swung open to reveal a large vestibule with a high ceiling. The floor was laid with polished stone of dark but natural earth tones, and the walls were partially paneled with rosewood—from the intricately carved chair railing to the floor—and covered with smooth white stucco from the top of the chair railing to the elaborately designed cover moldings. A narrow picture molding, also made from rosewood, ran the distance of both walls at a level about twelve inches below the hand-carved white plaster ceilings.

On either entrance wall, directly across from each other, hung two huge dome-shaped mirrors in massive rosewood frames. Below the dust-coated mirrors stood several narrow, sheet-draped pieces of furniture which Josie guessed to be matching entrance tables with courtesy side chairs on which those who came calling had to wait before being presented to the master of the house.

Just beyond the two tables and the side chairs, also directly opposing each other, were two large archways, each with huge double doors thrown wide. Both offered light to the otherwise darkened hallway. And though the left wall dropped away not thirty feet beyond that first archway, the right wall proceeded on to the back of

84

the house and included yet another grand archway with yet another double door thrown wide.

At the far end of this magnificent hallway began an angular-shaped staircase with two wide, platform landings. A waist-high, spindled rosewood banister ran along the outer edge. On the furthermost wall, in direct accordance with the gently rising slope of the stairs, were several linen-draped wall ornaments. Judging by their shapes, Josie guessed the wall hangings to be picture frames. She wondered if the paintings would prove to be family portraits or landscapes, or possibly a combination of both.

"How do you like it?" Nathan asked shortly, after he'd entered behind her, carrying only her valise which he set down just inside the doorway. Without waiting for her response, he walked past her and quickly jerked one of the sheets off the narrow, claw-footed entrance table to his left, then snatched the sheet that had been tossed over one of the courtesy chairs at its side.

A resulting cloud of dust rose high into the air, forcing Nathan to turn his face away as it billowed toward him and caused Josie to sneeze in a far less than ladylike manner. Nathan's brow notched when he turned to look at her then, his eyes wide with repressed comment.

"I—I—choo—wish you wouldn't do that," she said, sneezing again, then again. "I think it would be better for all concerned if we took the linens off gently so they can be carried outside into the open air and the dust carefully shaken off them out there."

She felt moisture collecting at the tip of her nose and tried to sniff it back quietly while she reached into her handbag to find her handkerchief. Before she could locate it, Nathan had produced his own from an inner coat pocket and gallantly offered it to her.

"Thank you," she said, embarrassed that she would have to soil his handkerchief in such an indelicate manner as she lifted the small square of white cloth to her nose. Turning away to gently dab at the moisture, she found the masculine scent which clung to the small cloth very disturbing, but breathed deeply the spicy fragrance nonetheless. It made her senses tingle.

Rather than hand the spoiled cloth back to him, she chose to slip it into one of the pockets hidden within the folds of her skirt.

"I'll return it after I've had a chance to clean it," she explained, afraid he'd wonder about her decision to keep the thing. She hoped she wouldn't ruin the lovely garment in her attempt to wash it. After all, it felt as if it might be made of fine silk, and her limited experience with laundering left a great deal to be desired.

"No hurry, I have others," he said, unconcerned, as he dropped the sheets he'd been holding onto the floor in a single heap, causing another smaller cloud of dust to billow into the air before he quickly stepped back.

Brushing his hands together to remove the thin layer of dust clinging to his fingers, he glanced farther into the house, toward the stairs at the opposite end of the hall. "I guess the first thing we should do is get you settled into your own room. Then I'd better get those boxes of supplies unloaded so you can cook up something for lunch. That breakfast they served on the train did very little to satisfy me. I'm already hungry again."

Josie was, too. Suddenly, she wished she knew how to cook something more substantial than oatmeal and boiled eggs — not necessarily for his sake, but for her own. If she had only paid closer attention to some of the things her aunt had done in the kitchen whenever it came time to prepare the family meals!

"Follow me," Nathan said enthusiastically, turning back just long enough to snatch up the valise he'd left near the front door. "I'll show you to your bedroom. It's the third door on the left once you've reached the top of the stairs, right across the hallway from my bedroom."

Josie's eyes widened at the thought of their sleeping quarters being so close. "But don't you think it would be far more appropriate for me to stay in a room downstairs? After all, I am merely a housekeeper here. Upstairs bedrooms should be reserved for your special guests."

"The servants' quarters at the back of the house are not as large, nor are they nearly as comfortable as the rooms upstairs." Nathan hurriedly sought to change her mind. As an equal heir, she had every right to the same comfort that he did.

"As a servant, I wouldn't expect much comfort," she responded, swallowing hard. "Show me to these servants' quarters."

Having taken the time to investigate his father's house during his visit earlier that week — the afternoon he'd brought his own things over — Nathan knew exactly which room would change her mind. Though two of the servants' quarters he'd found were indeed very nice and would no doubt prove comfortable enough to suit her needs, there was one small room near the back of the house that had obviously not been used in quite some time other than to store several unwanted items. The floor of the tiny room had suffered a large degree of water damage, sagging in one corner, and the walls stank of mildew.

"As you wish," he said agreeably, feeling no guilt for what he was about to do. After all, what was one more minor deception?

Smiling congenially, he turned and led her through what was obviously the grand dining room, then through a very modernly equipped kitchen. After entering the kitchen, he chose the narrower of two hallways that led away from the main house. They passed a large pantry and a laundry room before they entered into a tiny hallway. The first door down the hall led to the cellar. Then finally, as they neared the very end of the narrow corridor, they arrived in the tiny room that housed little more than broken pieces of furniture and a huge wooden box of empty glass jars and assorted metal lids.

"I realize there is no bed in here at the moment, but I can bring one down from the attic," he said, quickly lighting the only lamp in the room, which was attached precariously to a loose wallboard just inside the door.

"There's no bed?" she asked, stepping hesitantly into the tiny room. Her lips pursed into a sickly grimace, which indicated the repulsion she felt.

"And no window," he pointed out, giving the room a wide sweep of his arm.

Josie's nose wrinkled the moment the musty smell reached her nose, so pungent it made her eyes water. Her expression clearly marked her disapproval. The room was beyond hope. Even after a good hard scrubbing with lye soap and turpentine, with no window to bring in a daily supply of fresh air, the room would always smell damp and moldy.

When she reached out to touch the bent and broken furniture, she found it encrusted with ages of dust. She began to have serious second thoughts about having refused the offer of an upstairs bedroom. Anything would be better than this, even living next to the lion's very own den.

Amused by how quickly she had reacted, Nathan tried to keep his tone serious. "Of course, living in such a small room does have certain advantages. You could keep the area warm enough in the winter by heating bricks over the kitchen stove then bringing them in here just before bedtime. But then again you probably won't be here long enough for that to matter. And I'm afraid, in the summer months ahead, there will be no way to cool it properly, what with no window."

He waited until she'd had ample opportunity to scan the walls for a window before continuing. "But if this is what you truly want, I'll do what I can to help you fix it up and make it a little more livable. But it would be a lot easier on both of us if you'd reconsider taking the room upstairs. I wouldn't have to lug furniture down two flights of stairs, because the bedrooms upstairs are already furnished. And your bedroom has a large, double door which opens out onto the second-floor balcony."

"It does?"

"It also has several large windows along two walls, which should help keep it nice and cool in the warm summer months ahead. Plus, I think you'd enjoy having a lovely view of the lake."

Josie chewed on the inner lining of her lip while she gave her repulsive surroundings another quick, disdainful glance. The acrid smell of dust mixed with mildew was starting to make her feel nauseated.

Nathan sensed her discomfort and hurried to make his invitation even more enticing. "If you're worried about your privacy, you'll find both doors to the room have sturdy iron bolts, which should keep any unwanted intruders out. At the end of the day, if you decided you wanted some time alone, you could easily bolt your doors and be alone."

That was certainly reassuring. Josie looked at her surroundings again, knowing she could never tolerate three months in such a horrible little room.

"I guess it would be better for us both if I simply took one of the bedrooms upstairs," she finally admitted. Now was not a good time to let her stubbornness get in the way of common sense. "Show me the room upstairs."

Nathan grinned, pleased but not surprised to hear her decision. He wasted no time leading the way up the main stairs, down the hall, and into one of the larger bedrooms near the front of the house, where he had planned for her to stay right from the beginning.

Originally he had chosen the bedroom because he'd thought the ruffled curtains and cheerful colors would have special appeal to a little girl. In fact, the room looked as if it had been specially decorated with some pretty little girl in mind. But even after he'd discovered the little girl he'd expected to find in Cypress Mill was actually a beautiful woman, all grown up, Nathan had decided the room would still be the most suitable of the five vacant second-floor bedrooms. Especially after he'd heard when they played poker how partial she was to the color yellow.

"It's lovely," Josie said with true appreciation when she stepped inside and glanced around at the spacious, sun-filled room. She was in such awe of her surroundings, she forgot to feel threatened by the fact she'd entered a bedroom alone with Nathan Garrett.

"I thought you'd like it," he commented with a pleased smile.

Like it? Josie loved it, or at least what she could see of it. Though white sheets still draped the larger pieces of furniture nearest the windows, the sheets which had at one time covered the tall four-poster bed, the wide dresser chest, and the ornately designed clothes armoire had either slipped to the floor on their own or had been purposely removed to make the room appear more livable.

"Like the rest of the house, the room needs a good dusting," Nathan pointed out as he set her valise down again, several feet inside the hallway door.

He immediately headed for the nearest set of windows, which he quickly unlatched and pushed opened. "And I'm sure the bed will need fresh linens and the covers airing out. And after the floors have been cleaned, the carpets will need to be unrolled and tacked down at the corners. But by nightfall, you should have the room in suitable condition for sleeping. You will find the linens you need, and most of the cleaning supplies, downstairs in a small closet beneath the stairs."

He waited until he had all the windows open and a gentle breeze had begun to drift through the large bedroom, taking away any stuffy feeling, before he turned to leave. "You may go ahead and get started doing whatever you need to do to make the room what you'd like it. Meanwhile, I'll go back down and fetch your trunk for you before I start unloading my own things."

Josie waited until she was alone, then began by gently peeling back the remaining sheets, delighted to find a lovely rococo parlor suite complete with a writing desk hidden beneath. A fine layer of dust covered most of the furniture, having sifted right through the linens, but it was nothing like the thick coating of dust and dirt that had scattered across the floor. Studying the unusual amount of dust that had settled onto the moldings and windowsills, she realized Nathan had been away from home for quite some time. She wondered why.

After finally uncovering the last of the furniture, her next thought was to simply pitch the dusty linens out the window and be done with them. But knowing she would never get away with such an act, she instead bundled them up and carried them out into the hallway where she heaped them into a neat pile near the stairway.

"I'll carry them downstairs later," she promised herself, fighting the urge to sneeze again from all the dust that coated her clothing when she turned back toward her room. It startled her to find Nathan standing at the top of the stairs with her trunk resting precariously on his shoulder, a peculiar expression on his face. Her heart jumped when she realized he'd heard her talking to herself.

"That's fine," he answered, realizing how foolish she must feel. If he could have shrugged to show his indifference on the matter, he would have, but the trunk was too heavy. "Where do you want this?"

"In my room, next to the armoire," she told him, turning quickly to lead the way, brushing the dust from her skirts with short, self-conscious strokes as she went. She felt deeply embarrassed despite the fact he'd thought her comment had been directed to him.

Shortly after Nathan set her trunk exactly where she wanted and had gone outside to unload the rest of the things from the rented buggy, Josie went downstairs to see what cleaning supplies there might be. She dearly hoped she would find the instructions for their uses, knowing she might not be able to figure that sort of thing out on her own. Though she still did not relish the thought of living in that house alone with Nathan Garrett, or having to clean it all by herself, she was unaccountably eager to do something about her bedroom. If she was going to have to live there for the next three months, she might as well make the best of it.

It was almost one o'clock before Nathan had all the supplies put away. He'd considered leaving most of the items in the boxes until Josie had time to put everything just where she wanted, but when he'd found her so hard at work cleaning her bedroom, he decided he could at least save her that much trouble.

After all, he'd never really intended for Josie to clean anything, much less cook their meals. That had merely been a ruse to get her there. The very morning before he left for Cypress Mill, he had asked his father's attorney to locate the temporary help he would need to get the house in selling order. And as soon as he could notify Mr. Haught of their return, he was certain Oakhaven would be quickly supplied with at least two qualified housekeepers, a reliable cook, and a groundskeeper.

Luckily, his father had thought to set aside a certain amount of money to be used for the upkeep of Oakhaven in the interim months before his will was finally read. Nathan really had never planned for Josie to help with the cleaning at all.

So why hadn't he informed her of that fact? Why didn't he simply tell her the truth and be done with it?

Because it was too late for the truth, and he knew it.

92

If he was to admit anything to her now, she would become so angry over all he'd done, she'd leave. In the two short days he'd known her, he had come to know exactly how stubborn she could be, even about little things. And after having seen the deep resentment she felt toward her grandmother, he was afraid she might not react reasonably at all, and would refuse to stay on — even for the inheritance. He simply could not take that chance.

It was as much for her own good as it was his to let her believe their meeting had been fate and that the only reason he had brought her back with him was because he'd happened to win her services in that card game. After the three months had passed, and it was finally time for the will to be read, he would tell her everything. Then it would be too late for that stubborn streak of hers to interfere with their getting that inheritance for by then it would already be theirs.

Still, he felt a nagging twinge of guilt from having to keep such secrets from her — and from the fact she was upstairs at that very moment, down on her hands and knees, scrubbing away at all the dirt and dust that had accumulated since his father's death, sneezing at least once every two minutes.

Aware it was an injustice to allow her to work so hard when she should be allowed the same rights as he, he decided not to ask her to prepare their lunch after all. He set about cooking them each a plateful of scrambled eggs, fried potatoes, and sausages. It was a not a very conventional lunch, but it was about all he'd ever learned how to cook.

By the time Nathan called upstairs to announce lunch was ready, Josie had become so deeply frustrated that she wanted to scream. The longer she attempted to clean away all the filth in her room, the worse everything seemed to look. Rather than produce a brilliant shine as she had hoped, the beeswax and lemon oil she'd found — and had decided to use despite the lack of instructions—had proceeded to cloud and badly streak everything she'd attempted to clean with it.

The harder she tried, the worse it got, until she became so angry with herself, she could hardly stand it—and angrier still that she'd allowed Nathan Garrett to take such obvious advantage of her. He could have at least mentioned the fact his house was the size of a small castle, or that it had not been lived in for what was obviously weeks, possibly months.

Despite the soothing aroma of the food Nathan had prepared, Josie remained very out of sorts when she came downstairs to find out just what it was he'd said about lunch.

"What is it you wanted?" she asked moments later when she entered the dining room, determined to know why he'd felt it so necessary to interrupt her work.

Nathan tried not to laugh when she tramped so regally through the door, but he couldn't help it. Her dark hair had come undone and was all askew, her dress was badly rumpled, and she was streaked with dust from head to toe like some poor lost street urchin.

Glowering at him for having dared make fun of her appearance, she crossed her arms in a defiant gesture and stated angrily, "You have some nerve. You purposely neglected to tell me just how much work would be involved in cleaning your house, didn't you?"

"Who me?" he asked, his blue eyes wide with innocence as he placed the two steaming plates of food onto the small area he had just cleared along one end of the huge dining table.

"Yes, you!" she answered, narrowing her eyes as she noticed the portion of table where he had pulled back part of the linen and wiped away the dust.

It bothered her to see how beautifully the smooth surface shined, reflecting the different highlights of the wood. If it had been anyone else but him, she'd have demanded to know exactly how he'd gotten such a clear shine—when her own efforts upstairs had produced

94

nothing more than an ugly mass of gray streaks.

As she stepped closer to examine the gleaming portion of the table more carefully, her brow notched with disbelief. Still, she mentioned nothing about the curious fact that he seemed to know more about housecleaning than she did. "You took clear advantage of me by not warning me of the amount of work that would be involved, and you know it," she went on to complain. "You are a cold and heartless man, Mr. Garrett. This house is far too large for one person to clean, especially the way it is now."

One delicate eyebrow rose quizzically when she reached out to run a fingertip over the smooth surface of the table and found not a speck of dust; nor was it gummy with wax.

"You're right," he agreed readily, watching curiously at the keen interest she showed in the table.

"I am?"

"About everything but the accusation that I'm cold and heartless. This house really does need more than one housekeeper. I'll see what I can do about hiring someone else tomorrow when I go back into town to return that buggy."

Josie jerked her gaze up to meet his, unable to believe she'd heard him right. "You will? Just like that, you're willing to hire another housekeeper?"

"Just like that," he answered with a quick shrug of his shoulders, then motioned toward the two plates of food he'd just placed on the table. "Now that we've settled that, I think we'd better eat before our food gets cold. I know it's not much, but it'll have to do for now."

When Josie considered the alternative, which was oatmeal and boiled eggs, she offered no complaints at all.

"It smells wonderful. But why did yo—I mean, why didn't you—?" she started to ask, but then decided not to question this unexpected show of generosity after all. Instead, she chose to accept it graciously, and immediately sat down to take full advantage of the proffered meal.

After having spent several hours struggling to bring a faint semblance of a shine to her bedroom floor so she could then replace the carpets and go to work on the furniture, she had worked up a voracious appetite. Never had scrambled eggs tasted so good and never had well water felt so pure and clean sliding down her throat. For the moment she forgot her antagonism and simply enjoyed her meal.

"I'd say you were hungry," Nathan commented when he noticed how quickly the food on her plate disappeared.

Josie nodded agreeably and smiled, feeling much better now that she had something in her stomach. "I want to thank you for being nice enough to prepare our lunch when we both know it is really my duty to do so."

"You're welcome," Nathan responded simply, his eyes drawn to her contented expression. A strange floodtide of sensations passed over him when he'd looked at her then — gazing up at him with those huge green eyes of hers while smiling ever so shyly. The feeling was similar to the one he'd experienced before, back when he first noticed her in the saloon. It was an odd feeling of familiarity, as if he knew her from somewhere, as if she held a definite place in his past. Yet he knew he'd never met her. He would never have forgotten having met such an alluring young woman. Still, the feeling that he knew her from somewhere was there, gnawing deep inside of him.

Aware Nathan was staring at her again, and feeling extremely uncomfortable because of it, Josie pushed her chair back and stood. Without giving a thought to the dirty dishes, for they had never been her responsibility before, she quickly excused herself. Not only was she eager to get away from his probing gaze, which made her oddly nervous, but she was equally intent on returning upstairs and figuring out exactly how Nathan had managed to get such a gleaming shine from that dining-room table. There had to be a trick to it, and she was more determined than ever to figure out just what that trick might be.

By the time Nathan returned from town the following afternoon, not only had he already found the additional help he'd promised to look for, he had part of that help with him.

Two women, sat beside him. Next to the shabby trunks lay several other items near the back of the wagon he'd borrowed while in town. Having had a better chance to look around the place, he'd discovered a few things needing repairs and had purchased the lumber and tools he would need while he was in town.

Having heard the clattering approach of the lo-boy wagon through the open windows of her bedroom, Josie hurried to look out. She squealed with a combination of relief and delight when she noticed the two women at his side and hurried to wipe her face and hands with the back side of her apron before rushing out her bedroom and down the stairs, eager to greet them both.

Even if it turned out they were not the housekeepers he'd promised her, they were people, and would finally bring an end to the awkward situation that came from having to live alone with an unmarried man.

When Josie arrived at the bottom of the stairs only minutes later, she found Nathan standing beside two well-worn traveling trunks, but no sign of the women.

"I saw from the window. Where are they?" she asked excitedly, her eyes darting all around.

"I've already shown them to their quarters, but they decided they wanted to clean it up a little before moving their things in."

"B-but I didn't pass anyone on the stairs," she said,

perplexed as she glanced back the way she had just come.

Surely they couldn't have gotten up those stairs and into one of the other bedrooms before she'd had time to emerge from her own room. True, her muscles were sore and she was unable to move around as easily as she would like, but she was not yet *that* slow.

"They won't be staying upstairs," Nathan said, swallowing suddenly when he realized she was about to discover one of his many deceptions. He could feel his own lies closing in on him. Why hadn't he thought ahead to this moment? "They will be sharing a room downstairs."

"You mean that horrible little rat's nest you showed me?" she asked, angry he could even suggest such a thing. "I won't hear of it. Not when there are still several very comfortable bedrooms upstairs."

Quickly, she turned away from him, eager to find the two women. She wanted to let them both know there were other, far more suitable rooms upstairs.

"Josie, come back here," Nathan called, then took off after her, through the dining room, toward the kitchen. "There's something you should know."

"No, there's something *you* should know," she called back to him as she hurried on through the kitchen, toward the back portion of the house, with two determined fists swinging at her sides. "Those two women deserve the very same consideration you gave to me. There is no reason at all for either of them to have to live in that horrible little room."

"Josie, you don't understand," he shouted, hurrying to catch up with her. "I've had time to do a little rearranging down here." It amazed him how easily the lie had slid from his tongue, and at how quickly one deception led to another—until he now had a whole string of deceptions to worry about.

Josie didn't want to listen to any further explanations. All the rearranging in the world could not make that room presentable and she knew it. She never paused a step.

Stubborn woman! he muttered to himself as he hastened his footsteps, determined to catch her and make her listen. "Josie, wait!"

By the time he reached her side, she had pushed open the door to the tiny room he'd shown her just the day before and stood staring into the musty darkness, confused. "W-where are they?"

"That's what I've been trying to tell you. While you've been so busy getting your own room in order, I've had time to do some rearranging down here. I have prepared two servants' rooms in another part of the house, which should prove to be very comfortable. The two housekeepers I brought back with me will share the larger one."

"And the other is for me?" Josie asked, clearly disheartened. Though the large room upstairs was proving almost impossible to clean, she had already come to think of it as her own. After Nathan had served yet a second meal of scrambled eggs and sausage late the evening before, she had spent several hours sitting out on the balcony, resting her weary body in a reclining wicker chair, listening to the many different night sounds. She had loved every minute of it and hated the thought of having to give it up.

"No, of course not," he answered, shaking his head adamantly. "The other room is for the cook, who is supposed to arrive later this afternoon."

"A cook?" she asked, surprised. "But I thought I was going to have to take care of the cooking around here."

"Well, you can help if you want because you will be in full charge of both the new cook and the housekeepers." It was the least he could do.

"Sort of the head servant," she said, realizing the advantages that would mean. Nathan would never have to know how inept she really was when it came to any truly domestic chores. She fell silent while she thought

99

more about it.

Nathan watched her changing expressions, not sure if she was angry or pleased. "If the three women are not enough, just let me know. I don't want you to continue thinking of me as that cold and heartless man."

Josie smiled apologetically, but refused to actually recant the words she'd spoken so angrily the day before. Instead, she chose to change the subject entirely. "How did you ever manage to find them all so quickly? You weren't gone from here six hours. And how did they ever get their things packed so quickly?"

Nathan's eyebrows rose mischievously.

"For a person who does not like to answer personal questions, you sure do ask a lot of them." He then turned to proffer his arm. "Do you really want me to stand here and recant every little detail about how I arranged to hire all my help in one easy trip? If you must know, I even have a groundskeeper due to arrive at the end of the week. Or would you rather go meet the two already here?"

Remembering the body-jolting reaction she'd had the last time she'd taken his casually offered arm, she chose to avoid any further physical contact with the man. For some reason, touching him had proved somehow dangerous. Instead, she crossed her arms awkwardly in front of her as she walked back the way they'd come. "I'd rather go meet my new assistants. Where are they?"

To her dismay, though they never actually touched while he guided her across the kitchen then down a separate hallway, just the mere thought that she could be touching him if she'd only allowed it stirred her senses into a wild frenzy and caused her heart to take several amazing little leaps beneath her breast.

Chapter Six

With the capable help Nathan had provided, Josie started cleaning the house that very afternoon inside and out. Taking Nathan's suggestion to heart, she started with the rooms that would be used most often, then moved on to the areas which, for the most part, would be used only when there were guests or special occasions. To her own amazement, after having been given a few helpful hints from Shirley and Ruby, the two housekeepers Nathan had found on such short notice, Josie not only did her share of the work, but did it well.

As it turned out she had been trying to use far too much beeswax and lemon oil at a time, when only the tiniest bit was needed. She had also failed to first clean away the excess dirt with good old-fashioned soap and water. But once she'd been shown the proper way to bring a shine to wood surfaces and to clean away mildew, glass streaks, and tarnish, she had no problem keeping up with the two women. The hard work was like a soothing balm. It helped keep her mind off the other things she'd rather not have to think about, like a certain master of the house who seemed determined to always be in her thoughts, if not actually in the way.

To Josie, it was far easier to go to bed each night bone tired than to risk tossing and turning half the night, trying to push all thought of the tall, imposing man and his infuriating behavior from her mind.

During the day, it provoked her to know that about

the time she would finally get the man out of her thoughts, he would find his way right back in by either calling out to her from another room or by actually coming into the room where she worked to see how everything was progressing. Just knowing he might pop in at any moment made it hard for Josie to concentrate on her work, and it made it harder still to keep her emotions on an even course.

Within days, Nathan managed to make a nervous wreck out of her, but at the same time, she and the other women made amazing progress. The house had begun to shape up nicely. Being able to actually see the rooms, one by one, return to their original showcase beauty gave Josie a lofty sense of accomplishment. After a while, she even became accustomed to the dust and eventually stopped her incessant sneezing.

At times, especially when they finished a particularly difficult task, she wished her cousin Trey could see the amazing results of their work. He would have a hard time believing the difference a few days had made. The end result of their labors was truly something to behold and be proud of.

Nathan, on the other hand, was steeped in guilt. It bothered him to see Josie work so very hard, when in truth, she had no reason to work at all. In line to be a half owner of Oakhaven, he knew she should not have to bother with anything more than the simple overseeing of everyone else's work.

He shuddered at the thought of what would happen when she finally did find out the truth. She would be furious. As stubborn-headed and short-tempered as she was about certain matters, he had no doubt she would immediately pack up her things and leave. But only *after* she had tossed a few well-chosen words his way. She would care nothing about the stipulation of his father's will and even less that her actions could cost him his inheritance as well.

Nathan knew his only hope was to keep her from

finding anything out too soon. While Josie and the women he'd hired to help her continued to work at such a frantic pace, Nathan continued to convince himself that the present situation was really to her advantage. He tried to make himself believe that what she didn't know about her present situation could not hurt her. By not knowing the real reason she had been brought there, he was saving her from having to make a difficult decision — and what he truly feared might be the *wrong* decision. Besides, he knew a cleaner house would bring a higher price. In the end, she, too, would benefit from the many fruits of her labor.

But Nathan's attempts to convince himself he held only her best interests at heart did not always work and he attempted to lessen the underlying feelings of guilt by helping with some of the more difficult chores whenever he could, which was why he was now on his way upstairs. He'd gotten his boots soaking wet while helping Shirley and Ruby dump a huge tub of used wash water out onto the west lawn, where it would drain away from the lake.

Cringing at the squishy sounds his wet socks made inside the wet leather, he hurried to change into dry ones. But when he reached the top of the stairs, he noticed the strange, grinding noises coming from one of the smaller bedrooms down the hall from his own. He decided such a noise needed investigation.

"Don't do that," he called out to Josie the second he entered the bedroom and discovered her standing on top of a small wooden chair, trying to lift an extremely heavy picture and frame off the wall. "You could hurt yourself."

Nathan's sudden appearance gave Josie quite a start, causing her to almost topple off the chair when she spun to face him.

"But I have to move it so I can clean the wall behind it," she complained, having dedicated herself to doing the very best job possible, still finding the end results extremely rewarding. "All that's left to do in this bedroom is wash this one last wall, then I can polish the floor I've already mopped then roll out those two carpets. After that, it'll just be a matter of resituating the furniture and I'm through."

Placing her hands on her hips, she returned her attention to the huge wall hanging and stated with clear determination, "That picture has to come down."

Again, she bent forward and attempted to lift the heavy frame from its stout iron hooks. But when it still refused to do more than rub back and forth against the wall with a protesting growl, she paused again.

Clearly perturbed, she reached up to push away with the back of her wrist an annoying curl that kept straying out from beneath her red bandana. The action produced a dark smudge across her forehead as she continued to frown at the stubborn wall painting.

Studying the situation as best she could from her precarious position atop the small desk chair, she finally crossed her arms and admitted defeat with a heavy sigh. "I guess I'll have to call Shirley in here to help me with this. Goodness! I never saw a house with so many paintings."

Nathan wondered if she had yet made the connection between this painting and the others in the house, most of which had been painted by his father at different times in his life. They were the favored few he had refused to sell and, like James Haught had told him, each was worth a small fortune back East.

"Shirley and Ruby are both outside hanging out all those sheets they washed this morning. Don't bother them for something as minor as this," Nathan said as he stepped farther into the room. When his eyes caught sight of the bare toes peeking out from under the damp hem of her woolen skirt, he felt a sudden urge to tickle them with the tips of his fingers, a thought which was followed by an invigorating need to grin. "I'll help you get that painting down from there."

Josie considered protesting. After all, he was the boss and shouldn't have to come to her aid as often as he did and it puzzled her that he even wanted to help. But in all honesty, especially in this particular instance, she could use his assistance. That painting was a lot heavier than she had ever imagined.

"Well, if it is not too much trouble—"

"No trouble at all," he assured her, and came to stand behind her. Tilting his head to one side, with his hand cupped around the strong curve of his chin, he carefully considered just how he wanted to go about it. There was a devilish glimmer in his blue eyes that Josie could not see from her precarious position atop the chair when he finally spoke. "I think I should be able to lift the painting high enough to free it from the hooks."

Josie looked down over her shoulder at his solid build and had no doubt that indeed he could. Everything about the man exuded pure, male strength, from his taut, muscular thighs to his wide, stout shoulders. Though his personality certainly was flawed, she was hard-pressed to find fault with his build. Her toes tingled at the thought of how truly magnificent he was—at least in appearance.

Nathan's smile deepened at her sudden and obvious appraisal, but he directed his next comments to the matter at hand. "When I do have this thing high enough to clear both hooks, I want you to pull it away from the wall and keep it there while I gently lower it to the floor."

Josie turned back to face the picture, then gasped aloud when suddenly his arms came around on either side of her, grasping her just inches below her waist and pressing her forward as he grabbed hold of the frame with a sturdy grip. She felt the front of his body push intimately against the back of hers, and the resulting jolt to her system almost took her breath away.

"You ready?" he asked, his tone completely innocent of any wrongdoing.

"Mr. Garrett! I should say not!" she cried out in strangled outrage, trying to twist herself out of his grasp, but finding herself unable to.

"Why? What's the matter?" he asked, stretching his neck to one side so his words could be heard over her shoulder. The warm vibrations came up to tickle the underside of her ear. Suddenly, even her toes felt weak.

"What's the matter?" she repeated in shocked disbelief, her heart floundering inside her chest. The startling feel of his hard chest molded intimately against the gentle curve of her lower back caused a sudden streak of white-hot fire to shoot through her body, like a flaming bolt of summer lightning.

"Sir, will you please let go of my — of my —" Her dust-streaked face turned bright crimson when she realized just what part of her anatomy this man held so firmly pressed against his midsection.

"Oh! I beg your pardon. I guess I wasn't thinking," he said, as if he'd just realized what a truly prohibitive thing he'd done. Reluctantly, he released his hold and took a small step backward. "Maybe you should move your chair over to one side so I don't have to reach around you like that."

"Yes, maybe I should," she agreed wholeheartedly, wondering then if she'd been partially at fault for not having realized that herself. Angry and flustered, she jerked her skirts up away from her feet as she climbed safely down from the chair onto the floor.

Nathan caught a glimpse of her slender white ankles and pressed his lips together as he again fought the ridiculous urge to reach out and tickle the bottoms of those bare feet. How he'd love to hear her laugh.

When Josie finally had both feet securely on the floor and had spun about to face him, she noticed the devilish glimmer in his pale-blue eyes. Judging by his pleased and cocksure expression, she realized he'd behaved that way on purpose. Her face flushed bright crimson.

The rogue! How dearly she'd love to reach out and slap him soundly. He deserved at least that much. It was while she considered the different retributions that could follow such a brash action that she became all too aware of how close they stood to each other. She would not have to reach very far to carry out her desire to slap him. He stood barely inches from her, and just knowing he was that close made it decidedly difficult for her to pursue any real train of thought.

"Do I bother you?" he asked after she stared dazedly at him for several minutes, offering no further comment about the awful thing he'd done. His smile deepened when he realized his bold actions had left her uncommonly speechless.

In a desperate effort to calm herself, Josie drew in a deep, exasperated breath and held it for several seconds. She had to find a way to slow the boiling turmoil that raged wildly inside her.

"Do you bother me?" she repeated, unable to believe he'd asked such a question. "Since the very first moment we met, you have bothered me." Angrily, she turned away from him, yanked up the chair with both her hands, and moved it to one side. Not certain she had enough emotional strength left for any form of verbal battle, she decided not to make an issue of his brash behavior, this time. "Now, if you were at all sincere in your offer to help me—"

"Of course I was sincere," he protested, pouting indignantly at the insinuation he might have been anything less than sincere.

"Then move forward and carefully lift up on that painting while I pull it away from the wall, like you yourself earlier suggested," she stated through firmly clenched teeth as soon as she had climbed back onto the chair and gotten her balance, unsteady though it was.

"Anytime you say."

His voice was a shade too cheerful. She looked at him suspiciously.

Grinning from the remembered warmth of her body pressed firmly against his, Nathan stepped forward as told and grabbed a firm hold at the bottom of the large wooden frame. Unfortunately, this time there were no soft or curving obstacles to block his way. "Just say when."

"Now would do nicely," she muttered, then leaned forward to catch hold of the upper portion of the wooden frame, unaware that when she lifted her arms, the soft material of her pale-blue bodice pulled tightly against her most feminine curves, something Nathan was quick to notice and thoroughly enjoyed.

"Okay, now it is," he chirped, a devilish dimple twitching at the corner of his mouth while he continued to watch her every move.

When he then lifted the huge painting up off its main hooks, Josie pulled back on the upper part of the frame, separating it the few needed inches from the wall. But in her eagerness to get the job over and done with so she could send Nathan Garrett on his way, she yanked a little harder than she'd originally intended. Suddenly, the top of the painting lurched forward, jerking her off balance as it fell.

Somehow, Nathan managed to lower the painting safely to the floor in time to reach up and catch her as she came tumbling off the chair.

"Mr. Garrett!" she cried out when she suddenly found herself once again locked in his arms — again held firmly against his hard body. Only this time it was front to front. Her heart took a strong, frantic leap when she noticed just how different their bodies were.

"I thought I told you to call me Nathan," he stated, his voice low and taunting, his expression suddenly very serious.

Finding it an absurd time to squabble over what she chose to call him, Josie tried to wriggle herself out of his viselike grasp. When she realized he had no intention of letting her go, clearly pleased with the present situation, she decided to try reasoning with him. "Mr. Garrett, I do appreciate that you broke my fall. I might have been hurt. But my feet are securely on the ground now. No further harm can come to me. It is perfectly safe for you to let go of me now."

Nathan's gaze centered itself on the determined movement of her lips. "Not until you promise to start calling me Nathan instead of Mr. Garrett. I've already told you how I feel about that. It's time you respected my wishes on at least one matter."

Aware her lips seemed to hold some sort of fascination for him, Josie felt compelled to dampen them with the tip of her tongue. When she spoke again, her voice sounded far calmer than she actually felt. "All right. I understand. You prefer to be addressed by your first name, and I promise, from this moment on, I'll try my best to remember to call you Nathan. Whether I'm working or not. Just, please, let me go. Now."

"And, in return, I'll call you Josie," he added, but did nothing in the way of obeying her command. "Is that all right with you?"

"You already do call me Josie," she pointed out, her brows drawn low with warning.

Nathan's cheeks dimpled again.

The two of them stood like that for several moments, Josie helplessly locked within Nathan's strong embrace, before she realized what he was waiting for. He was waiting to hear her actually make use of his first name. He wanted proof of her promise.

"Nathan—" she began, stating his name slowly and carefully. But that was as far as she got, for at that moment she made the mistake of glancing back into the glimmering depths of his pale-blue eyes. Suddenly she forgot just what it was she'd intended to say. It was hard for her to think clearly about anything at that particular moment. It was hard for her to even breathe.

"Yes?" he responded huskily, leaning forward to catch the womanly scent that even a fine coating of beeswax, dust, and lemon oil had failed to hide.

"Nathan, don't." The command had come out nothing more than a tiny squeak. Even she had barely heard it. Panic crept slowly up the sensitive muscles in her throat, crested, then cascaded helplessly down her spine as an unfamiliar ache centered itself deep inside her—somewhere in the vicinity of her stomach, only lower.

"Don't what?" he asked, searching her impossibly green eyes in an effort to discover the answer to what it was about her that fascinated him so. Why did she already seem such a vital part of him when he hardly knew her? What was it about her that had immediately imposed itself into his heart? There had to be a reason he could not get her off his mind, even in sleep.

Josie stared at him helplessly, his face so close to hers she felt his sweet, warm breath against her cheek. Tiny shivers skittered across her delicate skin when she became aware of his intentions. He was about to kiss her. As sure as the sun, he intended to kiss her.

Motivated purely by instinct, she parted her lips and swallowed back the painful tightness that continued to grip her throat, only to have it finally break loose and settle deep in her chest.

"It's wrong," she muttered weakly like a frightened child. The words she'd spoken were fervently true—it *was* wrong. They should not allow anything like that to happen between them. It could only lead to more unnecessary complications in an already impossible situation.

But despite the validity of the words she'd spoken, her voice had held no conviction. It was then she realized with startling clarity, she wanted him to kiss her. Just once. Just to see what it was like.

Silently, she stood, waiting.

Every nerve in her body came alive with ever-growing anticipation while she drank deeply of the moment. Her heart beat fiercely, sending its message of uncertainty and panic through her while she quietly savored the features of his handsome face.

"How wrong can it be?" he asked with a deep groan, desperately fighting the urge to bring his lips down against hers. Though a kiss was what he, too, wanted, he was afraid of what her response might be. One kiss might be all it took to send her running. She'd made her feelings perfectly clear. She wanted theirs to remain strictly an employer-employee type relationship—one which had no room for familiarity. He had to keep in mind exactly what was at risk. Not only would he chance losing her, he'd chance losing Oakhaven as well. Finally, he broke away.

"You're right. I'm sorry. Forgive me for behaving so foolishly," he stated abruptly, then, after taking several deep, sustaining breaths, he turned away from her and headed immediately for the door.

"Nathan?" she called out, confused by the abrupt change in his behavior. Her heart still pounded a wild, erratic rhythm against the sensitive inner lining of her chest while her mind raced randomly in a frantic effort to figure out why he had reacted so strangely. It bothered her that in one moment, he could seem so very intent on kissing her and yet in the next, he'd turned his back on her and walked away.

Responding to the gentle sound of his name on her lips, Nathan stopped just short of the doorway and glanced back at her.

"How will I ever get this painting back on the wall?" she asked, though it was not the question she'd wanted to ask.

"Call me when you are ready to put it back. Until then, I'll be downstairs. I'm expecting a visitor." Then giving no further thought to his still-wet boots, he headed straight for the library downstairs, where he could find temporary solace in a good stiff drink. Maybe two.

Josie watched him go, still wondering what had

111

caused him to behave so strangely and just who the expected visitor might be. She also wondered why he hadn't mentioned anything about a visitor earlier. As the temporary house supervisor, a title she had proudly bestowed upon herself, she should be told of such things as expected guests. What if there were no iced cakes to offer him? Or what if there was no fresh pitcher of lemonade or chilled apple cider ready when he arrived? What sort of host would he think Nathan to be?

Wondering how long until the visitor was due to arrive, she hurried toward the door, planning to go downstairs and see if he'd at least thought to mention his intended guest to Jeanne, his new cook. If not, they needed to see what they could put together on such short notice. Nathan should want to offer him *something*.

Suddenly Josie's hand flew to the tiny pulsebeat at the base of her throat. It occurred to her that Nathan's guest might not be of the "him-he" variety. She stopped only a few feet outside the bedroom door to consider the very real possibility that Nathan's guest might turn out to be a definite "her." After all, a handsome, obviously wealthy, and unmarried man like Nathan Garrett probably had dozens of young women in eager pursuit. The thought of it made her stomach ache. For the first time, she wondered what the women in his life were like. She did not care for the strikingly beautiful images her mind immediately conjured forth, elegant pillars of society no doubt.

She decided that if Nathan had thought no more of the women who called on him than to forget to warn his help of their expected arrivals, they could just do without. She'd not put herself out to cover his neglect.

With a haughty toss of her head, Josie spun right back around and returned to work. If Nathaniel Garrett had wanted treats to offer his pretty little visitor, he should have thought to mention that visitor a little sooner.

In an effort not to dwell on such a trivial matter

when there was still so much work yet to be done, Josie dipped her yellow sponge into the tall bucket of wash water, wrung out the excess, and began cleaning the now-bare bedroom wall with a vengeance.

An hour and a half later, just as she placed the final pieces of furniture back into place and had begun wiping away any missed fingerprints with her buffing cloth, she heard the faint but definite jangling sound of a carriage as it hurried along the graveled drive toward the house. Nathan's visitor had arrived.

With a mixture of childlike curiosity and cold dread, Josie hurried to the window to catch a quick glimpse of the carriage below. A warm surge of relief washed over her when she discovered the lone occupant to be a man, an older man at that—thin with silvery white hair and thick, round spectacles.

She watched while he climbed down with agile ease, tethered his horse to a nearby post, then walked briskly toward the front of the house. After he'd rounded the tall bush at the front corner and she could no longer see him, she quickly returned her attention back to her work with renewed vigor. She wondered who the visitor was, but didn't really care. She was happy enough knowing it had *not* been some extremely beautiful young woman eager to get her hooks into Nathaniel Garrett.

The fact that she had even cared about such a thing startled Josie, but she swiftly pushed such thoughts away, not ready to analyze anything so silly. After all, she didn't even like Nathan. She decided the only reason she'd felt so relieved was because she had not liked the idea of having to take time away from her regular duties to help pamper some already spoiled young socialite. There was still too much work to be done.

Within a very few minutes, Josie was finished with the bedroom she'd started cleaning hours earlier—except for rehanging the heavy landscape that stood tilted against the wall. She remembered Nathan's offer to help her put it back, but decided to wait. She did not want to disturb him while he had company.

Instead, she picked up her large pail of water, her bucket of cleaning supplies, her wet stockings, and still-damp shoes, then headed for the next room. She set everything down again at the end of the hall, near the staircase, then tried to open the next door. Surprisingly, she discovered it locked.

"That figures," she muttered aloud, clearly annoyed.

Thinking there might be another entrance, since so many of the rooms in the house were interlinked in one way or another, she went on into the next bedroom. When she stepped inside, she hoped to discover an adjoining door between the two rooms.

There was indeed just such a door. But to her growing dismay, she discovered it, too, was locked.

Aware she would have to wait until Nathan had returned upstairs to get the key, she decided to take the rooms out of order, and turned her attention then to the room she had just entered. She started with the furniture, then moved on to the walls, ceiling, and floor.

With two other upstairs bedrooms yet to clean, Josie soon forgot all about the locked room. It was late in the afternoon, hours after Josie had heard Nathan's guest leave and just as she was getting ready to quit work for the day, before she again remembered the painting.

Nathan responded immediately to her request for help. Within minutes they had the beautiful landscape back on the wall and with far less incident than it had taken to get it down. It wasn't until they'd stepped back out into the hallway that Josie thought to ask about the locked doors she'd come across.

"Nathan, while you are still up here, do you think you could unlock that bedroom for me?" she asked, indicating the door in question with a forward nod of her head. "I don't plan to actually get started on it today, but I'd like the door to be already unlocked when I do."

Nathan jerked his gaze to the door, as if it offended him somehow. Carefully evading her question, he looked away again. His gaze was drawn to her work-reddened hands and to the wide water stains along the hem of her skirt when he decided to ask a question of his own. "Aren't you working a little too hard trying to get this place back in order? I never said you had to have it clean by any certain date. You're starting to make me feel like a slave-driver."

His obvious concern touched Josie's heart. "I know you didn't demand to have everything clean by any certain date. And I assure you, I'm working no harder than any of the others," she answered honestly, then explained it to him in the same way it had been explained to her. "But the sooner we finish giving each and every room that first good going-over, the better. After the house has been thoroughly cleaned once, it won't take nearly as much effort to keep it that way."

"Still, I think you are working at all this a little too hard. Why don't you just forget about cleaning that room at the end of the hall. No one goes in there anyway," he told her, knowing he couldn't let her in even if he wanted to. He had yet to locate the key that fit either door.

"Why? What's in there?" she asked curiously.

That was a good question and one Nathan dearly wished he could answer. Though he had no way to know for certain, he suspected the locked door led to his father's private art studio. If only he could be sure. "What's in there? Just a lot of odds and ends. Nothing with which you should concern yourself."

"But why not move all those odds and ends upstairs to the attic? Shirley and I have been up there. Though it's pretty cluttered near the door, there's still plenty of storage room against the north wall. And if you were to use some of that attic space instead of storing things away in the bedroom there, you could eventually make use of that room again."

Heading for the stairs, hoping to get the door and all the frustrations that it brought with it both out of sight and out of mind, he shrugged. "Why do I need another empty bedroom? I've already got several."

Josie found no argument to that as she picked up her cleaning supplies and followed him down the stairs. Feeling bone-weary from all she had accomplished that day, she decided to let the subject drop entirely and think of it as one less room they would have to worry about.

"Well, that about does it," Josie said with a tired smile as she turned to glance at Shirley. "It took us four days, but, except for airing out the books in the library and then dusting off the shelves, it looks like we are finally finished."

"Aye, and since we will 'ave to wait for a bright, sunny day before we bother with those books, I think we can finally call this one a day." Shirley said with a satisfied nod of her head, grinning back at Josie with round, rosy cheeks and sparkling blue eyes. Happily, she surveyed her surroundings. "Now, Mister Garrett can show 'is 'ouse off proud and proper. Even this old cellar, if 'e's a mind to." She sighed aloud her relief. "Sure am glad to finally 'ave the worst of it behind us. Maybe Mr. Garrett will slip a bit of a bonus in our pay dockets this week for 'aving worked so extra 'ard. I think we deserve a little something extra. Wot do you 'ave to say about it, Rube?"

"I say I'm pooped," Ruby answered with her usual tight-lipped grumble, sagging onto a nearby stool and wiping her deeply grooved forehead with the back side of her apron. "I also say, bonus or no bonus, we're cutting our own throats by getting everything clean so quick. What if the man decides not to wait no three months before trying to sell this place? What then?" She did not wait for an answer. "I'll tell you what. We'll all be out on our duffs, that's what."

Josie frowned, confused by Ruby's statements. "He's hoping to sell this place?"

"Sure. Didn't you know?" Ruby asked. Her slate-gray eyebrows arched high over her hazel-colored eyes. Being nearly as underweight as Shirley was overweight, the skin along the sides of Ruby's face revealed every curve and dent of her bony skull. "Our jobs are only temporary. He told us both that the day he hired us. Didn't he tell you?"

"No, he didn't," Josie admitted, her frown deepening. She could not imagine the man wanting to sell such a lovely home — unless he had some need to be closer to town. Because other than being stuck out in the very middle of nowhere, Oakhaven was a magnificent place to live — so peaceful, so quiet, so incredibly beautiful. But if he was no longer happy living here, it at least explained why he had stayed away for so long, long enough to have let all his previous help go.

"Oh, sure," Ruby went on to say. "The way I understand it, Mr. Garrett plans to stay on here only a few more months, just long enough to get this place in selling condition and to square away a few personal affairs. By the end of summer, we'll probably *all* be back looking for new jobs, even his handyman, Rafe. I suspect the new owners will bring in their own help. Yep, in no time at all, we'll all be out there looking for work again. Unless, of course, he plans to take *you* with him." Ruby then gave Josie a quick once-over. "Which just might be what he plans to do. After all, you do seem to get more privileges than most housekeepers I ever know'd — like having that upstairs bedroom all to yourself, and being allowed to call the boss by his given name. Even being asked to eat at his table."

"Oh, Rube, quit insinuating the worst!" Shirley admonished sharply. "The man 'ates to eat alone is all. And if you were 'im and 'ad to make your choice of a table companion from the three of us, which would you

117

choose?"

Josie felt grateful to Shirley for her comments, but she still felt compelled to defend herself. At the same time, though, she was reluctant to explain the strange situation that had brought her there. "You might also consider that I've also been here the longest. I deserve any seniority. But I truly doubt he plans to take me with him when he leaves here." Her insides fluttered at such an outrageous thought.

Ruby did not respond, merely shrugged her shoulders as if it didn't matter to her either way. "Long as I get my three months of work."

"That's right, 'e 'as promised us at least three months," Shirley put in quickly, as if to somehow reassure herself. "And with jobs so scarce to find these days, I'll be needing every one of those three months. I've got a wee one to take care of."

Josie glanced at Shirley, surprised. The girl didn't look old enough to be married, much less have children. "You have a child?"

Shirley beamed with the unmistakable pride of a mother, glancing from Josie's stunned expression to Ruby. Ruby appeared to have very little interest in what was being said as she closed her eyes and gently massaged the muscles at the back of her neck and shoulders with her long, bony fingers.

"Aye, I 'ave a bright little lad named Eric, just two years of age. But since 'is father died just over a year ago, 'e's had to stay mostly with me mum. Wot with times being so 'ard and all, I've 'ad to take to the road to find work to 'elp support 'im. On me days off, that's where I 'ope to go, to visit with me mum and me precious Eric over in the next county. So, you see, I truly do need this job—all three months of it."

"Oh, you'll get your three months," Ruby assured her. The older woman's expression turned hard, causing leathery wrinkles to form along the narrow corners of her eyes and at the outer edges of her thin lips. "He promised us both at least that long." Her tone was low and menacing. "I don't know about you two, but nobody ever breaks a promise to me. Not nobody. We'll get our three months."

Josie felt deeply apprehensive when she watched the older woman push herself up off the stool then abruptly disappear into the shadowy stairwell that led up toward the kitchen.

Aware he was finally alone, Nathan quietly approached the locked door with the small brass key he'd found hidden behind a painting in the library downstairs. Patiently, he'd waited for the right moment when he could be absolutely certain no one would disturb him. He wanted to browse through the room's contents at will, with no unwanted interruptions and no one peering over his shoulder. His heart sped with eager anticipation, certain he was about to discover the room's hidden secrets at last.

Although he was aware his father had turned to his artwork with far less frequency during the later years of his life, Nathan was also just as aware the man had indeed continued to paint. Over the years, he'd personally viewed his father's works in various different art galleries back East, making note of each new painting he came across and the subtle changes that had appeared in each.

Because he had always made it a point to see his father's work whenever possible, Nathan had kept up with at least that part of his father's life. Secretly, he'd even purchased several of his more intriguing art pieces for himself, many of which now hung in his own home back at Quail Run.

While Nathan tried to fit the key into the first lock, he continued to reflect back over the different art shows he'd attended through the years. Suddenly, he realized why Josie had seemed so oddly familiar to him that first day. She *was* familiar to him, very familiar.

"I'll be damned," he muttered aloud. He paused in his effort to make the key fit when the revelation struck him full force. Josie was the very image of the beautiful woman who had appeared in so many of his father's paintings.

His suspicions had been right all along. The beautiful, beguiling woman who'd constantly appeared in so many of his father's works was indeed his father's mistress—later made his wife. Josie's grandmother.

"Of course!" It also accounted for the mysterious fascination he'd felt for Josie from the very first moment his gaze had touched her. It was because of his father's paintings. Nathan had always felt emotionally drawn to those particular paintings—paintings of such deep, vibrant emotions, such true inner depth that they brought actual tears to the eyes. They were paintings depicting a beautiful, seductive woman. A woman deeply in love with her artist.

Because Nathan had always suspected the woman in the paintings to be his father's mistress, he'd never had the courage to actually buy one and hang it in his home, for he'd felt it would be an act of personal betrayal to his mother's memory. Yet he had stood and studied the different works of her for hours on end, until he had all but memorized every tender brush stroke.

Though disappointed the key failed to unlock either door to the mystery room, Nathan felt strangely satisfied to have discovered such sudden insight into his father's life, the life of the late Carl W. Garrett—a well-known artist, who had turned wanderer and sometime riverboat gambler during his younger years, and who had amassed a small fortune before his untimely death several weeks ago.

Because his father had chosen to be away more often than he was ever home during those impressionable years of Nathan's youth, what memories he did have of the man were extremely vague. He knew that he looked a lot like his father had at that age, only taller. But he was never sure if that knowledge came more from everything his mother had told him or from his actual memories. The images in his mind were too faded, too blurred, to be sure which was the case. Yet he knew it was true.

Another fact he had also known, even in his early childhood, was that his father had openly kept a mistress. She had been a woman of questionable reputation, several years older than his father — a woman his father had loved despite the bitter pain and humiliation it had caused his only son and his deeply devoted wife. Yet in all those years, Nathan had never actually met his father's mistress, not even after his mother's death ten years ago, when his father suddenly married the woman.

Now he had an actual face for her — more vivid than the inanimate one in his father's portraits. He had Josie's face, a face of many moods. A face with many emotions. For some reason, this made Nathan feel less resentful. It became easier to understand why his father had been so completely taken by the woman.

But Nathan then recalled how very quickly the two had married after his mother's death, as if they had been secretly waiting for it to happen. He also remembered how very quickly his father had then sold everything he owned just so he could build his new wife a truly grand estate out in the country. Oakhaven. A place where the two could live in peace. A place where neither would have to suffer any further scorn from those who did not understand their scandalous relationship.

It was shortly after Oakhaven reached completion that Nathan had received the letter that had been signed by both of them. The letter had been a personal invitation to visit their new home whenever it was convenient for him to do so. But he had never bothered to accept that invitation, and had purposely stayed away.

Now, as he stood silently staring at the locked door before him — sadly reliving tiny snatches of what few memories he still had of his father — he wished he had come to visit them. At least once.

Slipping the key back into his pocket, he turned away from the still-locked door. His heart weighed heavy with regrets.

Chapter Seven

Standing at the very top of the small, three-rung folding ladder, Josie bent down to give Shirley another handful of the dusty volumes she had just taken down off the top shelf.

"Some of these books haven't been touched in years," she said. Her nose crinkled from the unpleasant odor, the musty smell making her want to sneeze again.

"I 'ave to agree with you there." Shirley nodded. Quickly, she dusted the four cloth-covered books with a rag then placed them into her basket to be carried immediately outside and set in the bright morning sunshine. "I'll wager these books 'aven't seen the light of day in ages. It's a wonder this entire room doesn't smell of must and mold."

Scowling as usual, Ruby nodded in full agreement. "And the sooner we get them outside and opened up to some clean fresh air, the better," she muttered as she picked up the basket she also had just filled with books. She then turned and headed toward the hall door, still muttering as she went. "It'll take a full week of sunning to help these books any."

"Wait up," Shirley called out, aware she was about to be left behind. Hurriedly, she lifted her own basket and followed Ruby down the main hall to the nearest outside door.

Temporarily, Josie was alone again.

Stepping down off the ladder, she attempted to relieve the muscle ache in her arms by swinging them gently back and forth while at the same time bending her elbows and wiggling the tips of her fingers. Restlessly, she paced the narrow space between the bookshelves and the large mahogany desk. The room reminded her of Nathan, since he'd spent so much of his time there lately, and being reminded of Nathan was the last thing she needed. She was eager to get the job done and be out of there.

Aware it would be several minutes before Shirley and Ruby returned for another load of books, Josie decided to sit down and rest her feet. Though there were several small chairs, the oversized, richly upholstered desk chair suddenly looked far too inviting to resist. Sighing at the mere thought of resting in such luxurious comfort, Josie stepped over and sank gently down into the chair's depths. How good it felt to finally rest her aching feet.

Sitting at an angle to the desk and tilting her head back against the high, cushioned back, she closed her eyes and wondered if Shirley and Ruby had taken similar advantage of the chair during their own turns at being left behind. If God had given them any sense at all, they had, for it was truly a most comfortable chair.

Despite her exhausted state, Josie was too filled with nervous energy to remain perfectly still. Absently, she opened her eyes and reached for a few of the books that were strewn across the top of the desk. She wanted to see if they should be carried outside as well.

By separating the pages of the books and breathing cautiously between them, she was pleased to discover none of them needed to be aired out. They were obviously used often enough to keep them from collecting any musty odors. Curiously, she glanced around for more books and, without bothering to actually get out of the chair, she stretched an arm back and took a few of the worn volumes from the shelf directly behind the desk.

To her surprise, when she pulled that first handful of books off the most accessible shelf and brought them to rest in her lap, she heard a muffled clatter. Oddly, the noise had sounded as if it had come from inside one of the books.

Puzzled, she kept her hands wrapped securely around the books, then shook them purposefully. Again, she heard the curious rattling sound. Her green eyes widened.

Separating the books and placing them aside one at a time, she carefully gave each individual volume a hard shake until she discovered the last book to be the culprit. Immediately, she noticed the book felt much lighter than the rest. When she opened it, she found the book to have a false heart. To further the intrigue, she discovered that the clattering noise had been caused by a small brass ring that held several tarnished keys. Yet, there was nothing to indicate what the keys might fit.

Hoping for a clue, she glanced again at the spine of the dark-brown, cloth-covered book. The title of the false volume read *Hidden Treasures*, its author, Mark Founder. She smiled at how appropriate the title, and wondered just what sort of hidden treasures those keys unlocked.

Her next thought was of the mysterious room upstairs, the one that had caused Nathan to act so peculiar. Did one of those keys unlock either of those two doors? The idea that it just might, sent her thoughts racing ahead with a wondrous sense of adventure.

What if it did? What if she'd just found a means of getting inside the room without anyone knowing? Her insides tingled with undeniable excitement. Though logic told her that in all probability the room held nothing more than what Nathan had said it held, her heart did not want to believe it. Surely if it contained only various odds and ends he had no present use for, he'd see no need to lock it. After all, he didn't keep the attic locked. But, what if, instead, the room held some deep, dark secret from Nathan's past?

"Then, there would be every reason to keep it locked," she reasoned aloud.

Having been born with an extremely active imagination which had already begun to run rampant, Josie conjured all manner of speculation. Just what would she discover inside that room? She could hardly wait to find out.

Aware Shirley and Ruby might not share her keen sense of adventure, and might instead feel it was their duty to tell Nathan about her grand discovery, she decided to keep the keys her secret. At least for now.

Bursting with excitement over all the prospects the keys offered, she returned them to the book, then placed the well-worn volume exactly where she'd found it. She planned to convince the others not to touch that particular section of books. She would explain to them that those books were used often enough that they did not need airing. They need never touch the book with the hidden keys.

As she stepped away from the bookshelf, she started formulating her plans. She would need to wait and sneak the keys out of the room at a time when no one would be around to catch her. She would have to find something for Shirley and Ruby to do in another part of the house and while Nathan was still up in his room, or perhaps after he'd gone outside to take care of the stock. Then, as soon as she had removed the keys unnoticed, she could slip upstairs and try them on those two locked doors.

If for some reason, she was unable to get the keys safely out of the library that afternoon, she could always wait until after dark. After everyone else was in bed sound asleep, she could then sneak back downstairs and get them without being seen or heard. Either way, she intended to try the keys before another day passed.

She would simply have to be careful and not get caught.

Nathan grew more frustrated by the hour. After having carefully gone through the contents of his father's desk downstairs, and then through the personal effects he'd found in the bedroom, Nathan was starting to believe he'd never find the key to fit that room. He hated the thought of having to forcefully remove one of the doors from its hinges just to finally find out what was hidden behind it.

The whole situation bothered him. The more time he had to think about it, the more he wondered why his father would find it so necessary to hide the key at all, especially if the room was nothing more than his art studio. To lock intruders out of such a room was one thing, but to hide the key where no one could find it was quite another. Another thing that bothered him was the fact he had yet to find a key to the front or back door, or to the storage room in the carriage house. He could bolt the doors from the inside for now, and padlock the front door from the outside using the lock the lawyer had installed while the house had been vacant, but that wasn't good enough.

There had to be keys. He was certain of it. Some-where in that house was an entire set of missing keys— and he knew there was a good chance his aunt would know where those keys could be found. But the thought of seeing his father's only sister again spilled chills down his spine. There was something about the insincerity of her thin-lipped smile and the cold glint of her slate-colored eyes that sent sickly shivers through him— always had. For now, he'd just rather Aunt Cynthia not know he was living there at Oakhaven. He'd prefer to solve the mystery of the missing keys without her help. He'd go to his aunt *only* as a last resort.

Finally, after having exhausted his own search of the

most logical places, Nathan decided to ride into town and see if his father's lawyer had found anything helpful. He hoped to discover something in his father's legal papers that would finally help locate those confounded missing keys—before he lost his mind entirely.

"I'm headed into Silver Springs for a while," he announced to Josie when he entered the library only minutes later. He was already dressed for travel in a pair of dark-blue trousers that clung to all the right masculine contours and a loose-fitting, pale-blue cotton shirt, open at the neck, exposing a portion of his tanned throat.

"You're what?" she responded with a gasp. Not having heard his footsteps out in the hallway, he'd startled her. Swiftly, she jumped to her feet and made several self-conscious swipes at her dusty apron with the side of her hand. She felt awkward at having been caught lounging around in his personal chair when there was still so much work to be done.

But if Nathan was upset to discover she had taken such liberties, his expression showed nothing to reveal it. He was too deep in thought to care. "I'm headed into town for a while. I'll probably be gone most of the day."

Josie's green eyes widened, unable to believe her luck. With Nathan gone for the day, and the others made busy in another part of the house—or better yet, outside—she could easily make off with the keys that very afternoon without having to worry at all about getting caught.

Smiling a little too enthusiastically, she asked, "Will you be lunching in town then?"

"Yes, I suppose so," he answered, not having given the noonday meal much thought. "But I imagine I'll be back in plenty of time for supper. I have only two stops to make. Be sure to tell Jeanne that I'm going. I don't want her to go to the trouble of fixing lunch when I won't even be here to eat it."

"Of course I'll tell her." Josie's green eyes danced with eager anticipation.

Nathan studied her happy expression, disheartened to know she found such pleasure in his plans to be gone. "Though I don't plan to be in town very long, I will be making a stop at Nelson Brothers before heading back. If there is anything you want me to get while I'm there, I'll be happy to add it to my list."

"Nelson Brothers?" she asked. Clearly the name was unfamiliar.

"The mercantile."

"Oh, the mercantile." Eager to give him reason to stay away for as long as possible in case there were complications she had yet to foresee, she nodded agreeably. "Why, yes, there are several things we are almost out of—salt for one, turpentine for another. Do you have time for me to make a list?"

"As long as you hurry," he told her, following when she immediately left the room.

For the first time since breakfast, Nathan was able to think about something other than the elusive keys. At the moment, his attention was drawn to the gentle way Josie's hips swayed before him. He became so caught up in the sensual movement that he did not at first notice Shirley and Ruby, who were both in the hallway, headed back to the library with their empty baskets.

"Where ya be going, Josie?" Shirley asked, watching as the two hurried past her, wondering if she should return to the library or follow.

"First, to the closet underneath the stairs. I have to write out a supply list for Nath—Mr. Garrett," Josie was quick to correct herself. Though she did indeed call him by his first name whenever she addressed him personally, she had sensed Ruby's growing irritation over such a breach of propriety and tried to remember to call him Mr. Garrett whenever she was talking about him and not to him. "I'll be right back."

"Do you want us to continue emptying those book-shelves all by ourselves or wait for you to get back?" Ruby asked with a disgruntled twist of her thin lips. She was obviously irritated by the fact Josie had found something more pleasant to do. Being older and far more experienced, it was clear that Ruby resented Josie being in charge.

"The bookshelves?" *The bookshelves!* Josie's heart slammed hard against her chest at the thought. She didn't want to chance either of them coming across the keys and sharing in her secret. Worse yet, they might decide to alert Nathan to the fact his hiding place had been discovered. Josie was hoping he would not realize the keys were right where she could find them until it was too late.

"No. I'd prefer you wait for me. In fact, I'd rather you didn't touch a thing until I get back," she told the two women. Instantly aware her voice had sounded a little too harsh, she quickly softened her tone before they or Nathan himself decided her reaction peculiar. "After all, you two have worked very hard these past few hours. You both deserve to take a short rest."

For once, Ruby couldn't have agreed more. "When you get through making that list of yours, you'll find me in the kitchen. I need something cool to drink. Come on, Shirley."

Shirley offered no comment, either in agreement or protest, as she turned to follow Ruby in one direction while Nathan and Josie went off in another.

While Josie glanced through the different cleaning supplies on the tiny shelves in the closet, she kept a cautious eye turned toward the library door. She wanted to be sure the two did not return to work too soon—or they might accidentally discover her secret.

Barely twenty minutes later, Nathan was on his way

130

into town with Josie's supply list tucked away in his pocket. Since his main concern was to meet with his father's attorney, he planned to leave the list at the mercantile first so they could fill his order while he hurried on over to James Haught's office to see what he could learn about the missing keys. By the time he'd finished his business there, the order would probably be filled, his supplies already boxed and waiting for him. He could then be back in plenty of time to take advantage of whatever clues the lawyer might have discovered for him concerning the whereabouts of those keys.

By noontime, all the dirtiest books were dusted and already outside soaking in the fresh sunshine — and Josie's secret was still safe. She'd had no trouble convincing the others to leave the books directly behind the desk where they were.

"I've already checked them and they don't need to spend time out in fresh air," she had told them, and Shirley and Ruby had readily agreed. "And until it's time to bring all those books back inside, there's really not much for us to do in here but give these bookshelves a really good dusting," she added, approaching the subject carefully as they prepared to break for lunch. "I really don't see much sense in the three of us coming back in here after lunch when it'll take only one of us to finish the work. The other two can get started on all the laundry that's been piling up."

"Aye, that makes sense," Shirley said, nodding agreeably.

But before either of the other women had a chance to volunteer for the easier chore, Josie hurried to add, "I'll have Jeanne start heating the wash water right away. That way, you two can get started on the laundry just as soon as we've finished eating. The clothes should still have plenty of time to dry before dark. I'll be out to help right after I've finished in the library."

"I'll just bet you will," Ruby muttered under her breath, just loud enough to be heard, but without looking directly at Josie.

Rather than start another argument with the quarrelsome woman, Josie chose to ignore the comment. "Let's go see what Jeanne has prepared for lunch. I'm starved."

Later, after she returned to the library alone, she went immediately to work dusting the shelves, in case Shirley or Ruby should return with some initial problem that needed her attention. She waited until they were both outside, deep into their labors, before doing anything about the keys.

Aware Jeanne was still in the house, already preparing for their evening meal, Josie ever so cautiously eased the library door closed as an added precaution. Then, as soon as she heard the door click into place, she hurried across the room and quietly eased the book *Hidden Treasures* from the shelf.

Biting her lower lip, she struggled to control the excitement that swelled inside her as she carefully removed the keys and slipped them into the hidden pocket in the folds of her skirt before returning the false book to the shelf. As soon as she had the book back where it belonged, she hurried back across the room toward the closed door. Her heart thudded with such force against the inner walls of her chest, she felt the resulting rush of her blood throughout her entire body.

Filled with a pulsating sense of adventure, eager to see her daring escapade through without getting caught, she carefully eased the door back open and peered cautiously out into the vacant hallway.

Moments later, she was on her way up the stairs, stopping halfway just long enough to glance back and be certain no one had entered the entrance hall. Eagerly she continued up the stairs, anticipating all she was about to discover, delighted to know Nathan had not yet had time to reach Silver Springs. It would be hours yet before his return.

"Josie!"

Her heart jumped skyward.

Although the voice had not been close enough to worry she'd in any way been discovered, it was a clear indication she was wanted for some reason, and if she didn't answer, whoever it was would no doubt come in search of her.

"Yes?" she responded reluctantly as she turned and hurried back toward the library. Though she knew she could invent a plausible excuse for being on the stairway, she'd rather not have to. "What is it?"

"Could you come here for a minute?"

It was Jeanne, calling from the kitchen.

"I'll be right there," she responded, then breathed a heavy sigh of disappointment before heading toward the back of the house and into the kitchen to see what the woman wanted.

"What is it?" she asked as soon as she'd entered the kitchen, eager to get back to her daring escapade.

Jeanne, the large Negress Nathan had hired to do all the cooking and to take care of the kitchen, stood in the center of the room. Her right hand was wrapped in a large dishtowel and held protectively against her ample bosom with the left. Several cabinet doors stood open around her, as did many of the drawers. Josie knew by her pained expression that she had injured herself.

"What happened?" she asked as she rushed forward.

"I cut myself on that knife," she said, glowering indignantly at the dastardly implement of destruction where it lay beside a huge pile of freshly peeled potatoes. "And now I can't find nothing to put on it." She turned her sad brown eyes to Josie.

"Surely there's some carbolic acid somewhere," Josie said, less annoyed at the interruption now that she'd discovered the seriousness of the situation. "First, let me see how bad the cut is."

When she reached for the injured hand, Jeanne pulled back and brought her chin down protectively over it. "You're not gonna hurt me none, are you?"

"Not if I can help it. I just want to see how serious it is and be sure it has stopped bleeding. Then we'll have to see what we can find to put on it to help prevent any inflammation."

Reluctantly, Jeanne held out the injured hand and grimaced while Josie slowly and carefully unwrapped the bulky dishtowel from around it. Josie felt her annoyance return the moment she discovered that the big, bad, terrible cut was just a nick—barely half an inch long—and had long since stopped bleeding. But aware the woman expected her to give the wound a certain amount of attention, she searched the cabinets for something to treat the wound. Eventually—aware precious time was slipping away—she made up a worthless poultice from baking soda and lard then carefully applied it to the tiny cut.

"There, let that set for at least half an hour, then you should be able to go on about your work with nothing more to worry about," she said reassuringly as she secured a small strip of linen around the woman's index finger, effectively covering the tiny wound.

Satisfied that she had been sufficiently doctored, Jeanne looked at her new bandage and smiled happily. "Good thing you know'd what to do."

"Just be more careful in the future," Josie warned, not about to admit to the insignificance of the wound. "I'll check back on you later, but for now, I have a lot of work to get done."

When she left the kitchen only seconds later, her heart had already begun to beat frantically with renewed anticipation. Aware she had lost another precious hour of time, and that Nathan could well be on his way back by now, she did not bother with the library at all. Instead she hurried directly to the stairs.

Again, she paused halfway just long enough to listen for footsteps both above her and below, but that proved to be an unnecessary precaution, for there was no one around. Eagerly, she suppressed her fluttering heart as she lifted her skirts with her left hand, then continued on up the stairs. By the time she'd reached the top step, she'd slipped her right hand into her pocket and had come out with the keys.

The third key Josie tried did the trick and the door came easily open. A little surprised by her own daring, but not about to stop now, she glanced around once more to make sure no one had started up the stairs behind her, then quickly stepped inside. Her breath caught and held while she quietly closed the door behind her.

Suddenly she was surrounded by darkness.

Since it was still the middle of the afternoon and the room was one that should have at least one southern window, Josie had expected to find sufficient light inside and had not thought to bring a match. She turned to scan the darkness and discovered that what windows there were in the room had been covered with thick, heavy drapes, which blocked all but the tiniest rays of sunshine.

Stumbling in the unfamiliar darkness, she slowly made her way around the clutter that filled the room, trying not to knock anything over that would alert Jeanne to the fact someone was upstairs, almost directly over her head. Finally, Josie reached the windows and found the cord that would allow her to draw the first set of drapes back. Gently, she pulled down on it.

Her pulses quickened when bright sunlight poured forth, filling a portion of the room. Eagerly, she turned back around to catch her first glimpse of whatever was so important it had to be kept under lock and key. She

135

was surprised to discover the room filled with huge waist-high work tables, ceiling-to-floor cabinets, and paintings of all sizes. So *many* paintings. Some stood on easels, others hung directly on the walls, while yet others leaned helter-skelter against table legs and cabinet doors, or were precariously propped against chairs.

Was Nathan an artist? Was that his big secret?

Intrigued by the thought, she stepped forward to examine some of the work. First, a beautiful landscape very much like the one hanging in her bedroom caught her eye, then an unfinished painting of the sea. Next, a picture of a small child with a yellow kitten and a ball. Finally her gaze fell across a large portrait of a woman, hidden halfway in the shadows.

Her eyes widened with shocked disbelief when she stepped closer and discovered her own image staring back. But how could that be?

She hurried to pull back another drape.

Chapter Eight

"Have you told her yet?" Jason asked while leaning back in his chair and gazing up at the impatient young man who stood before him. "She has every right to know about her inheritance."

"No, I haven't told her. I haven't found the right moment," Nathan hedged, aware he had no intention of telling Josie anything until he had to. "Besides, that's not what I came to discuss. I came to find out if you've discovered anything more about those missing keys. Are you sure you've gone through everything? I can't believe Father left no clue at all to where his keys might be found."

"I've been through everything your father left here in my care. There is no mention of having hidden a set of keys. But then, I don't think your father expected to die so quickly after he'd made out his last will. You have to keep in mind that his death was an accident. He probably figured he still had plenty of time to finish getting all those more minor details in order. The only thing really bothering me about those missing keys is that I'd seen him with a full set of keys in his pocket more times than I can count."

"You did?"

"Yes. And I can't understand why he didn't have them with him when he fell. After all, except for his boots, he was still dressed. And another thing, what about a spare set of keys? Everybody keeps a spare set hidden away just in case the regular set gets mislaid. I can't imagine why you haven't found any keys by now. When I put the padlock outside the front door, I figured it was just temporary, until a more thorough search could be made of the house."

"No keys when he died, and no mention of a spare set in his letters," Nathan muttered softly as he thought more about it. "Tell me, did he still have his wallet?" Suddenly, he suspected foul play.

"Yes, and there was money still in it. I know what you are thinking, young man, but there's no indication his death was the result of a robbery. Not only was there still money in his wallet, there were plenty of valuable items lying around the house that could have been taken and easily sold. Why, his paintings alone are worth plenty. No, his death was an accident all right. I'm almost certain of it. Somehow he tripped or lost his balance and fell down those stairs, breaking his neck in the fall. It was most unfortunate, but clearly an accident."

"Still, it does not explain where those keys are. If he was so used to carrying them around with him, why would he go to the trouble of hiding them so well on the night of his death, especially when he lived alone—?" Nathan's eyes widened. "Unless he thought he'd heard someone prowling about either downstairs or outside and decided to hide the keys as a precaution before he went downstairs to investigate. Maybe his housekeeper remembers hearing something. Did you ever get a chance to talk with her?"

"Yes. Pearl Beene was questioned thoroughly. But she wasn't even at Oakhaven the night it happened. She'd left that very afternoon to visit her sick mother and had stayed with her through the entire weekend."

"What about anyone else. Was there a groundskeeper or a stockman around at the time?"

"No, your father took care of the stock himself, in much the same way you are doing now. All he had was a handyman named Travis Morris. But Travis always spent his weekends up in Clarksville, where he had family. Your father was there all alone the night of his accident. In fact, if your aunt hadn't come by needing to speak with your father when she did, his body might not have been discovered for days. But we are getting off the subject here. I wanted to talk with you about the way you're handling the situation with Josephine Leigh. I think she has a right to know what's going on. She also has a right to make her own decisions on the matter."

"I know. And I told you, I'm going to tell her. I just haven't found the right moment yet."

"Well, you need to do something about finding that right moment. You can't go on letting that poor girl believe she is there simply because of some silly wager made between the two of you. She deserves to know the truth. She deserves to know about your father's will and about everything she stands to inherit. Besides, the buyer I told you about earlier is eager to have some sort of reassurance. He wants to know that when the three months are up and you two have finally obtained true ownership of Oakhaven, you will *both* be wanting to sell. He'd hate to wait out the three months only to discover something had gone wrong at the last minute."

"The only thing that could go wrong at this point would be a sudden decision on her part to leave Oakhaven before those three months are up. And if we aren't careful, she might do just that. Especially if she somehow manages to find out the truth about all this before I'm really ready for her to."

Nathan ran his fingers through the thickest part of his hair in a disgruntled gesture. He was fully aware of the fix he'd gotten himself into, but saw no easy way out of the situation. He'd simply have to ride it out and hope for the best.

"Surely she wouldn't think of leaving after she's

learned exactly how much is at stake here," Jason argued, tilting his head to one side, finding the man's attitude a little irrational. "She has too much to gain by staying."

"That woman is a lot more stubborn than you realize. And if she gets angry enough, nothing will keep her here." Though there was plenty Nathan still did not know about Josie Leigh, of that one thing he was certain. Josie put her pride above all else.

"Not even for her grandmother's sake?" Jason asked, hoping to reason with him.

"Especially not for her grandmother's sake. Though she won't really talk about her reasons, she has made it perfectly clear that she does not think very kindly of her grandmother."

"Why not?"

"I'm not sure. The way I understand it, she never even knew the woman, which means there was never a real bond between the two. Therefore, you can pretty well rule out any attempt to get her to stay for sentimental reasons. What's worse—" Nathan closed his eyes for a moment, trying to push aside the sudden feeling of impending doom. "She has stated more than once how deeply she despises anyone who is not entirely honest with her."

Which was why he knew Josie would hate him beyond all reason the moment she discovered the sort of secrets he'd chosen to keep from her. It was bad enough she displayed such obvious annoyance whenever he was around, but the thought of having her actually hate him hurt far more than it should.

"Which you certainly haven't been," Jason stated bluntly, seeing the problem there.

Self-consciously, Nathan picked up a small wooden pencil from the lawyer's desk and began to fiddle with it. How was he ever going to get out of this terrible mess without losing everything—including Josie? "I agree I

140

haven't been very honest with her. But at the time I thought it was the best thing to do. You've got to admit, it got her here."

"But can you keep her here?"

"I don't know." Nathan shook his head dismally, wishing now he'd taken a more direct approach with her from the very beginning. But even that might not have worked with a woman like Josie. In fact, it probably wouldn't have since she had taken too much of an instant dislike to him.

Pressing the capped end of the pencil underneath his chin, he leaned forward against it and sighed heavily. "She is going to be one angry woman if and when she learns the truth about all this. Especially when she realizes how dishonorable my intentions were right from the very beginning. She's going to know I intentionally manipulated her into coming here, completely against her will, just to suit my own purposes."

"Still, I think you should tell her. It would be a far better approach than chancing the girl finding out on her own."

"I wish you'd quit calling her a girl," Nathan stated emphatically, tossing the pencil back onto the desk with a resounding clatter. "I think that's what threw me for such a loop that first day I met her. I was expecting to find some small, helpless child with guardians who could be easily handled. *Not* a fully grown, wildly attractive, and fiercely independent young woman. But then, maybe I'm worrying needlessly. After all, as long as I keep my father's personal things stashed away in my bedroom, and as long as Aunt Cynthia stays away, how is Josie going to find out?"

"And what happens when you father's dear sister discovers you two are now living there. Just how do you plan to keep her away?"

Nathan tilted his head back and stared at the ceiling, his shoulders weighing heavy with defeat. "You're right, of course. Aunt Cynthia will eventually learn that there is someone living at Oakhaven again. It's inevitable. Living as close as she does, I'm surprised she hasn't already found out. And, once she's heard the news, she will come immediately to investigate. There will be no stopping her."

He sighed with further resignation as he looked back at Jason. "Okay. I'll tell her. In my own way, and in my own time, but I will tell her."

"Just don't wait too long. It will be a lot better if she hears it from you than from someone else."

What's going on here? Josie wondered. After opening another set of drapes, she was able to examine the painting in a better light. Although the portrait of the woman could not possibly be of her, as she had first thought, the face did bear a striking resemblance to her own. From the thick, curling mahogany-brown hair and vivid green eyes, to the slight dimple at the side of her mouth, the similarities were astounding.

Beside this portrait was yet another one, again of the same woman, and again the resemblance was uncanny. The artist signature on both was clearly Garrett, though the preceding initials were so poorly scrawled one would have to already know what they were to read them. It looked to Josie as if they were possibly C.N. She wondered what the C stood for.

With mounting curiosity, she looked around to see if there might be yet more paintings of this woman and, to further her interest, her eye caught sight of several more similar portraits hanging on the wall near the door. Two were definitely of this same woman, one seeming more youthful than the other; and centered between the two was a portrait of Nathan himself.

Moving closer, she thought the painting of Nathan poorly done. The hair was the wrong shade of brown and the eyebrows were much too thick; but the likeness in that devil-may-care smile was accurate enough to set her heart into rapid motion. Suddenly, it felt as if the portrait had taken on life and now stared back at her, mocking her for having shown such an inappropriate interest. Frowning over the different emotions that stirred to life within her, she pulled her gaze away — as if that should show him she was not really so interested after all.

It was then she noticed that the signature at the bottom of this painting was different. Though hard to believe, the portrait of Nathan had been painted by someone whose penmanship was even worse than his own. The last name, barely a scrawl, was not at all discernible.

Still feeling awkward at the way Nathan's portrait appeared to be staring at her, Josie turned her attention back to the paintings of the woman who looked so very much like her, curious to know more about her. It was obvious, whomever she was, that she had at one time been, or perhaps still was, very important to Nathan. Otherwise, he wouldn't have chosen her to be the subject of so many of his paintings.

And it also was just as obvious by the adoring expression on the woman's face, that she, too, was deeply in love with her artist. Deeply in love with *Nathan*. For some reason, that realization did not set well with Josie Despite all the obvious things she had in common with the woman in the paintings — or perhaps because *of* them — she found herself wanting to hate her.

Suddenly it became clear to her why Nathan had stared at her in such a peculiar manner that first day back in Cypress Mill. She remembered his startled expression when he'd first noticed her. The expression had been one of surprised recognition, almost as if he had seen a ghost. And even now, she constantly caught him staring at her, his expression questioning, his gaze

143

deeply probing.

The reason was now obvious — she reminded Nathan of the woman in these paintings. Though such knowledge brought a sense of logic into the strange manner in which Nathan had behaved toward her from the very beginning, the thought of it annoyed her, and also frightened her. Did Nathan think he had found a replacement for his lady love? Is that why he was always finding so many reasons to touch her? Is that why he looked at her with such a strange expression? In his mind, had she already become his lady love?

While still lost in such a disturbing thought, the sound of hoofbeats penetrated her thoughts, startling her back to the present. Nathan had returned.

Filled with panic at the thought of getting caught inside his secret room, Josie hurried to close the drapes, then quickly stumbled her way through the darkness, across the room, to the door.

She barely had the time to yank her skirts clear before the door closed behind her. Quickly she jammed the key back into the lock. Her hands trembled with mounting frustration when the key refused to turn. Finally, she felt the lock give and heard the metal move inside.

After one quick test to make sure the door was again securely fastened, she took off back down the stairs and hurried into the library. She had barely enough time to slip the keys back into the book and place it on the shelf before she heard the back door slam shut. On legs that had suddenly grown weak, she moved across the room, then turned to face the hallway door. She felt certain Nathan would come there first.

"You still haven't finished in here?" he asked, stopping shortly after he'd burst into the room.

Snatching up her dustcloth purely in afterthought, she began vigorously wiping the shelves nearest to her. "No, not yet. But I'll finish this later if you feel you need your privacy."

Nathan frowned, gave the liquor cabinet one last quick glance, then decided that was not what he needed after all. What he really needed was to tell her the truth and be done with it. "No, don't leave. Actually, I'm glad I found you here alone. I think we need to talk."

"What about?" Josie asked. She felt as if the air had been sucked right out of the room. Had he somehow guessed what she'd done? Could he have heard the door close? Or had he possibly heard her hurried footsteps on the stairs? Surely such small sounds could not carry all the way outside. Swallowing hard, she spun about to face him again, her eyes wide. She realized now what had given her away. He must have seen the drapes close!

"About honesty," he began. He was not yet certain how he should handle the subject, but knew he had to start somewhere. "I know what fine stock you put on such things and how you despise people who are anything less than aboveboard with you." He paused while he tried to think of just the right words to continue.

Josie tried to swallow again, but her mouth was too dry. Nathan wanted honesty. He obviously planned to demand a full confession from her. Unable to meet his gaze, she stared down at her hands. Vaguely, she noticed how red and work-worn they had become in the few days she'd been there.

"Yes, sir," she commented after the silence had stretched to unbearable proportions. She never looked up. Though a part of her wanted to be angry with him for the secrets she'd discovered in that room, another part of her reminded her that she had no right to know those secrets. Shame flooded her. "I do remember saying something like that."

"Well, I feel it is time we—" He paused again, still hoping the right words would come to him when he looked at her. How vulnerable she suddenly seemed.

What a heel he was for having kept such important secrets from her. Was there any possible way to explain his actions to her without her hating him forever?

At that moment, while they both silently considered the true seriousness of their separate dilemmas, the clattering sound of a carriage caught their attention. They both let out a mutual sigh of relief and glanced toward the open window. Josie studied the noise with curious interest. Nathan listened with dreaded fear.

"I wonder who that is," she asked, glancing at Nathan, aware he had suddenly gone pale.

"I don't know. I'm not expecting anyone. I guess I'd better go out there and see." He looked at her a moment longer, then, as if someone had suddenly given the command to *move*, he turned and hurried from the room.

Josie closed her eyes and slowly released the breath burning in her lungs. The reprieve would be only temporary, but at least it gave her a moment to collect her thoughts. She knew that as soon as his visitor was gone, he would be back, demanding to hear her excuses. She had to figure out just what he did know, or what he thought he knew, so she could be ready with believable responses. Had he indeed noticed the drapes close while he was still out in the yard? Or had something else given her away—something far more easily explained? Her misery grew to overwhelming proportions while she wondered how she would ever get herself out of this dilemma. Suddenly, honesty did not have quite the same virtue it once did.

Hoping to put off the inevitable by surrounding herself with others, Josie went outside to help Shirley and Ruby finish the laundry. Wanting to avoid him at all costs, she used a different door than she normally would to get outside.

Knowing that after they finished the laundry, they still had all the books to bring back inside and put back on their proper shelves, she felt certain she would not be forced to face Nathan again until suppertime. She would use that time to try to figure a reasonable excuse for having been in his studio.

The problem was, suppertime came all too soon, and in that time she was unable to think of a believable excuse, nor could she think of an excuse not to dine at his table as had become their custom. Reluctantly, she changed into one of her prettier dresses and went downstairs to greet her doom.

When she entered the dining room precisely at seven, Nathan was already there. Seated in his usual place at the far end of the table, he stared idly at his interlaced hands, preoccupied with his thoughts.

Her initial urge was to turn around and flee the room, but she did not react swiftly enough. When he glanced up and noticed she stood just inside the doorway, he immediately rose to assist her. His failure to show that easy smile of his seemed proof enough that time had in no way diminished his anger. He definitely knew, or at least suspected, what she'd done. Her stomach knotted with gut-wrenching apprehension while her heart ached to know what he must think of her.

"You look lovely as usual tonight," he said as he helped her with her chair.

It was the sort of comment that usually set her insides aflutter, but tonight it only served to make her feel guiltier. She had no right to any compliments, not tonight. She'd rather he tell her what a terrible and untrustworthy person she was. A woman he could never believe again. A woman who knew secrets she had no right to know.

"Thank you," she muttered softly, taking her napkin from the table and gently shaking loose the folds. She then made a larger production out of spreading it across her lap—anything to prolong the inevitable.

With neither of them able to think of anything appropriate to say, a thick curtain of silence fell between them as he reached for the dinner bell and rang it soundly. It was not until Ruby had served their plates and left them alone again that Nathan finally broke the heavy silence. "Did you get everything accomplished today that you had hoped to?"

Josie's eyes widened. Aware of the implication, she froze with her fork poised in midair. A small bite of roast beef clung precariously to the tip. "I—I guess," she answered hesitantly, then hastened to change the subject. She was not ready to confess her crime just yet. "And did you get everything accomplished in town that you wanted?"

Nathan nodded, even though the one thing he'd hoped to accomplish remained a mystery yet unsolved. He still had no idea what had become of those keys. "The mercantile had everything on your list except the peppercorn. But he expects to get some in at the end of the month."

"That's fine. We have enough to last another couple of weeks yet."

Again silence fell between them, awkward and accusing. After several, long agonizing minutes, Josie decided she could stand it no longer. She had to bring an end to the burning torment before she lost her mind. Taking a deep breath, she prepared to look him squarely in the eye, get her confession over with, and face the consequences. But in the end, when she finally did find the courage to speak, it was merely to ask, "And who was your visitor this afternoon?"

Nathan's muscles tensed. He was still undecided about whether to be relieved or apprehensive about his unexpected visitor. Although it had not been his aunt, as he'd feared, it *had* been one of the woman's personal house servants. That meant, by now, his aunt knew he was there. And though the servant had claimed his aunt was far too ill to travel at the moment, that was not a chance he dared take. The time to tell Josie the truth was running short.

"It was only a concerned neighbor," he commented, deciding that was truth enough.

"Concerned? About what?"

Realizing he should have used a better choice of words, he quickly sought to rectify. "Concerned to have heard unusual noises coming from this direction. She thought I was still away and was worried the noises might mean prowlers were about."

Another lie. How easily they came to him now. Actually the servant was sent over at regular intervals to make sure no one tampered with the house.

"Then she must be the neighbor who lives in the rented house you mentioned," she surmised. "How nice that she was so concerned about you."

"Yes, wonderful," Nathan stated less than enthusiastically as he prodded his braised potatoes with the tip of his fork. His appetite was gone.

Noticing he lacked the usual zest for his food, Josie felt her apprehension grow stronger. *He knew.* Just as sure as the sun rose in the east, he knew she had taken those keys and had used them to enter his private room. Why didn't he simply demand a confession and be done with it? It occurred to her then, he may have left those keys in the library on purpose, as a test of some sort. A test she had failed miserably.

Guilt spilled like acid from her heart, filling her bloodstream, while her brain cried out for her to simply admit her evil deed and be done with it. After all, he already knew. He obviously wanted to give her a chance to admit everything on her own. So why couldn't she get the words out?

Meanwhile, Nathan suffered a similar dilemma, still trying to find the right words to tell her what he'd done. In that past few hours, he'd come to the startling conclusion that he was not just afraid of losing his inheritance, but of losing her. In the few days he had known her, she'd become an important part of his life — though he still wasn't sure why.

Disgusted with himself, he pushed his plate back, slumped back in his chair, and stared helplessly at her, still puzzled over what he should do.

Josie misread his expression as one of annoyance and was unable to bear her guilt any longer. Heaving a frustrated sigh, she gave up all pretense of being interested in her meal and tossed her fork onto her plate. Unable to meet his direct gaze, she stared intently at the beads of moisture collecting along the sides of her water glass and blurted aloud the confession he obviously waited to hear.

"Okay. You're right. I did it. I took your keys, just like you knew I would, and unlocked one of those doors upstairs. Though I knew it was wrong, I went inside and looked around. But I was only there a minute or two. And other than to open and close the drapes so I could see, I didn't touch anything. I swear I didn't!"

Nathan's blue eyes grew wide at the mere mention of the word "keys." "You what?"

Josie looked at him then, her eyes pleading for him to understand. "I have no idea what got into me. I really don't. It's just that when I discovered those keys, and realized one might fit the door to that room, I couldn't stop myself. I had to know what secrets were hidden away up there. Had you admitted to me that it was your private studio to begin with, I wouldn't have been so curious." She looked away again, this time to the gleaming silver salt shaker which rested near the edge of her plate. "I'm sorry. It was wrong."

"Give me those keys," Nathan demanded, so eager to have his hands on them that he didn't stop to think how frightening his tone of voice sounded.

"I don't have them. I put them back where I found them," she admitted, swallowing back the tightness that

150

gripped her throat. "I had hoped you would never find out I'd used them."

It occurred to him then, this was the perfect time to tell her the truth—while she was still feeling guilty about having taken the keys. But first he wanted those keys. He wanted to touch them, to see that they actually did exist. "Show me where you found them."

"Show you? Don't you know where they are?"

"Just show me where they are. I'll explain later."

Quietly, Josie rose from the table and led him across the dining room, through the hall, and into the library. After taking a moment to light the lamp nearest the door, she went directly to the book she'd found and removed it from the shelf. She studied the incomprehension on his face when she then held it out for him. "You really don't know, do you?"

"No, I don't. What has the book got to do with it?"

Slowly, she opened it to reveal the false heart—and the small set of keys.

Nathan's mouth gaped with wonderment as he reached out and took the keys into his hand. "I never would have thought to—" he said, clearly amazed at how cleverly his father had hidden them.

"Something is not at all right here," Josie stated her thoughts aloud. "If those are your keys, why is it you had no idea where they were?"

Nathan knew the time had come to tell her the truth.

About everything.

Gesturing toward a nearby chair, he spoke softly. "Josie, sit down. We have to talk."

151

Chapter Nine

"Talk? About what?" Josie asked. She looked at him, clearly confused by the serious tone in his voice, but did exactly what she'd been told and sat down.

"About a very serious matter." Nathan explained, then headed across the room to close the door.

"No, don't do that," Josie called out when she realized his intention. "Ruby already thinks the worst about us. All because I'm allowed to dine with you and have also been asked to call you by your first name. If you closed that door and she happened to come by and notice it closed, she just might decide something truly scandalous was occurring in here especially when you have never asked any of them to call you by your first name. Nor have you ever asked them to dine at the main table."

"There's a reason for that."

"I know. And I realize my circumstances for being here are a little different than theirs. But, still, I don't want any more talk behind my back."

"Your circumstances for being here are far different than even you realize," Nathan said, deciding to plunge right in with the truth. Leaving the door partially open, he turned to face her.

"What does that mean?" Josie asked. But her breath caught in her throat when she realized just what he had meant. He intended to tell her about the woman in the portraits. Was he also about to admit that Ruby had been at least partly right? Was his overall plan indeed to try to seduce her like he had that other woman? Had she, in his mind, already become that woman from his past? If so, what did he expect of her?

A strong sense of panic filled her.

Nathan took several short steps in her direction then stopped, still a safe distance away. "I think you should know, things around here are not exactly what they seem. And I'm not exactly who I seem."

"Your name is not Nathaniel Garrett?" she asked, clearly confused and afraid. "Then who is Nathaniel Garrett? Why are his paintings locked away upstairs? And why have you assumed his name?"

"Hold on. One thing at a time. First of all, I *am* Nathaniel Garrett, but any paintings you may have found upstairs are not mine. At least, not yet. What I mean to say is that although they might be mine someday, I'm not the one who painted them. My father did—Carl N. Garrett." He waited then for a reaction to his father's name. When none came, it was his turn to be puzzled. "You do know who Carl Garrett is, don't you?"

Josie's eyes widened as she considered how she should respond. She was afraid to deny the man an answer, yet at the same time afraid her answer might be the wrong one. Something was not at all right here, and she did not want the situation getting any worse. "Y-you said he was your father. I assume that's true."

"But other than that, the name means nothing to you?" He moved toward her again, his expression serious but thoughtful.

Swallowing hard, Josie had no idea what the man was talking about, but she was fully aware he thought he was making perfect sense. Rising slowly from her chair, she began backing away from him. "No, the name means nothing to me. Should it?"

"Yes, I should think it would," he answered, stunned that she honestly had not recognized it. "My father was married to your grandmother."

"What?" Josie came to a sudden stop while she tried to digest that little piece of information.

"My father was married to your grandmother," he repeated for clarity. "You did know that your grandmother remarried, didn't you?"

"Grandmother Seger? No. All I ever really knew about my grandmother Seger was that one night, back when my mother was barely seven years old, the woman slipped off into the night with some passing stranger and never returned. She left my mother and my grandfather behind—both of them angry and heartbroken. They never forgave her for that betrayal." Josie blinked back a sudden rush of tears. "But then she never asked to be forgiven."

Josie's expression revealed such hurt and such inner confusion that Nathan was overwhelmed by compassion. "So you had to live with a terrible scandal, too."

"What do you mean, *too?*"

"That stranger your grandmother ran off with was married at the time, and even had a son on the way—me."

Josie's eyes widened with horror.

"That's right. My father was already married, but he made your grandmother his mistress. I grew up fully aware of it. Though he never bothered to actually divorce my mother, who was several years younger than he was and deeply devoted to him; and he even found it in his heart to come and visit us from time to time, he never tried to keep the feelings he had for your grandmother a secret from either of us. And, despite the four-year age difference between them, he cared for your grandmother enough to eventually marry her." Nathan's voice turned suddenly bitter. "They were wed only a couple of weeks after my

154

mother's death."

This was too much for Josie to comprehend. Feeling shaky, she reached out to grip the back of a nearby chair, hoping to steady herself. Her expression grew pensive and her mind became lost in deep thought when she spoke again. "She *married* him?"

Why had no one ever told her? She understood the reason her mother would not care to speak about such things. It would have been very painful for her. But why hadn't her father ever told her? He had secretly revealed so many other things about her grandmother to her, why not that? Was it because of the scandal associated with such a marriage, or had he simply never known? Or did their marriage take place after her father's death?

"Yes, she married him," Nathan answered, distracting her from her thoughts. "And it was right after that, he built this place for her. He claimed Oakhaven was to be a refuge where they could live together in peace, and not have to be bothered by scornful neighbors, who he claimed judged them unfairly."

"This was my grandmother's home?" Josie glanced around at her elegant surroundings with a totally new perspective. This was where the grandmother she had so often wondered about had actually lived—and loved. What a thrilling yet sobering thought that was.

"The way I understand it, he built it especially for her," Nathan said, nodding as he, too, glanced at the furnishings in the room. He tried to visualize it as his father must have.

Finally, it occurred to Josie that the woman in the paintings upstairs was her grandmother—not some lost lover from Nathan's past. Josie had often been told how very much she looked like her—and, at times, how much she even behaved like her. How often had she been severely punished just for having done something that reminded her mother of her

155

grandmother's recklessness? Far too many times to ever count. Instantly, Josie was caught in a whirlwind of bitter, yet fascinating memories — too lost to yet wonder how Nathan had come to know all these things.

"Your grandmother died here," Nathan added solemnly. "In this very house. She is buried in a small cemetery not far from here. My father is buried alongside her."

"Your father is dead, too?" Though she'd never as much as heard the man's name before today, somehow his death saddened her.

Nathan took a long, deep breath, knowing the time had come to admit the rest. "Father's death is the real reason we are here."

"What real reason? What are you talking about?" she asked, thoroughly confused. The more Nathan tried to explain things to her, the less sense it all made.

"My father died just a few weeks ago, leaving behind a very strange stipulation attached to his will."

"I don't understand. What does any of that have to do with me?"

"If you will sit down again, I'll try to explain," he told her, then waited until she had complied before he, too, sat down.

He decided the best place to start would be at the beginning. "Shortly after my father's death, I received a letter from his lawyer, asking me to set a date to meet with him, which I did the following week. That's when he gave me a letter of instruction my father had written less than a month before his death. From that letter and from what the lawyer had to say, I learned of the unusual provision in my father's will."

He paused to give her a chance to comment. When she said nothing, he went on to explain. "For some reason, he has demanded that you and I live here at

Oakhaven together before his will can even be read."

"He *what?*" she asked, barely starting to comprehend all the different implications. "For how long?"

"His last request was for the two of us to live here at Oakhaven for three full, consecutive months. We can leave the estate to take care of personal matters during the daytime, but we must both be here, in residence, at night. The will itself is not to be read, nor can his estate be settled, until we have either lived out the required three months in this house or until one of us has decided not to stay the required amount of time and leaves—in which case *neither* of us will inherit anything."

"You mean, if I choose to leave here now, you would lose your claim to any of the inheritance as well?"

"Yes, that is exactly what I mean."

"And just what do we inherit if we both stay?"

"Everything. The lawyer explained that if we last out the entire three months, everything my father owned will be ours, to be equally divided between us. And if we do last out the three months, and we do become the legal owners of Oakhaven, we will be free to do whatever we want with the place—except for a few acres that my aunt lives on. Although we are to become the legal owners of that land, too, we cannot dispose of it until after her death. She's to be allowed to live out her life in the house she's living in now. Plus, I think she's to be given an allowance of some sort for the rest of her life. But, if having to hold on to that land for so long bothers you, I'll accept that land in my half of the settlement. I'll also pay her allowance out of my part, if you'll just agree to stay the entire three months. The lawyer has already been out here to assure himself that we are indeed living here together. And he plans to make periodic, unannounced visits to make sure we both remain in resi-

157

dence as stipulated."

"He was the visitor who came calling the day I discovered your father's studio," she realized aloud. She recalled how authoritative the man had appeared.

"Yes."

"And we have to stay here for three months?" Her expression hardened when the full implication finally hit her. "For *three* months? Exactly the time limit you specified for our bet. That was no coincidence, was it? You knew about this even then, didn't you?"

Her tone was accusing, and her words came too close together to allow him a chance to answer in his own defense. "You went to Cypress Mill looking for me, didn't you?" Her voice trilled with anger. "You went there intending to find some way to force me to come back with you, and that bet was your way of doing just that. But, why? Why didn't you just tell me everything directly? Why the ploy to force me into coming back with you?"

"I wasn't sure you'd be willing to come with me, even after I explained it to you. As you probably recall, you didn't take too kindly to me that afternoon we first met. You didn't even want me to sit in on your card game. You may not have actually come right out and said as much, but those feelings were clear to me nonetheless."

"So you tricked me into coming back with you. How very clever! Not only did you get me here as planned, you managed to make a personal slave out of me in the process!" Her features flushed with rage. "You played me for a complete and utter fool! Rather than chance my refusal, you made a game out of the whole thing."

"No, you've got it all wrong," he tried to explain, but she was beyond listening.

"And I was blind enough to be led right into your little farce. I never once caught on to what you were

158

doing, much less why." Josie had never felt so humiliated, or so angry. "I played directly into your plans, didn't I?"

Tears burned her emerald eyes, causing them to look larger and sadder than Nathan had ever seen them. At that moment, he hated himself for what he had done to her.

"Josie—" He tried again to interrupt, but there was no stopping her emotional tirade.

"I can't believe I was ever that blind. I *let* you get away with the whole thing, didn't I?" She closed her eyes against the sharp pain that pierced her heart when she realized what grand sport he must have had—all at her expense. "And even after you managed to get me here, you continued to have your fun, didn't you? Of course you did. How amusing it must have been to see me down on my hands and knees, working like a beaten animal. You let me go on thinking I had to, all because of that—" Josie's emotions became overwhelming, to such a painful degree, she was unable to say anything more.

Fear gripped her when he suddenly took a step in her direction. Her gaze darted about the room, looking for the quickest and best means of escape.

"Josie, you've got it all wrong," he tried one last time to explain, approaching her cautiously, aware that in such an intensely emotional state, she might react unexpectedly.

Determined Nathan not be permitted to see her cry, and aware her tears were about to burst forth, Josie turned away from him. Her heart filled with panic. At that same moment, she noticed the open door and bolted from the room, with Nathan only a few steps behind her.

Running as hard as she could, Josie reached her bedroom door just seconds before Nathan. She slid the heavy iron bolt into place just as his hand reached for the handle then ran straight for her bed.

"Josie, unbolt this door. Let me in. We need to talk," Nathan shouted, jiggling the brass handle while he spoke. "You have to at least give me a chance to explain."

"I don't want to hear any of your lame excuses. Go away. All I want is to be alone. I need time to think," she cried out, lifting her face from the pillow just high enough to make her response. Her voice was so choked with emotion, her words came out strangled. It only served to frustrate her more.

"Josie, please. Open this door. Let me in." Though he continued to shout, to be heard through the door, his gruff tone had softened until he sounded more concerned than angry.

"You might as well go away and leave me alone. I have no intention of unlocking that door."

"Please, Josie," he tried one last time. "I don't want you angry with me."

"Why? Are you afraid I might pack my things and leave?" she asked, suddenly thinking the idea a fine one. But, at the same moment, she knew running away would be the coward's way out. What she needed was time to think. Time to sort through all she had learned in so short a time.

"Yes, that's exactly what I am afraid of," he answered honestly. "I don't want you to go."

"That's rather obvious," she retorted. If the pain filling her heart had not grown quite so unbearable, she would have laughed at the absurdity of such a truly obvious statement. "Of course you don't want me to go. You'd lose your precious inheritance, wouldn't you?"

"I'd lose much more than that," he stated, surprised by his own openness. "I'd also lose you."

Josie pushed herself up on one elbow, eyeing the door skeptically. A small part of her wanted desperately to believe him, but, logic winning out, she knew better than to accept any more of his lies. He'd already proved how far he was willing to go in his efforts to get his hands on his part of the inheritance. "Oh yes, now you are going to pretend you actually care about me. Well, it is a little too late for that approach, don't you think?"

"Josie, I do care. All I ask is a chance to tell you how very sorry I am for all I've done."

"I don't doubt that you are feeling pretty sorry about the whole situation about now," she spouted angrily. "But you are feeling sorry for yourself, not me. You're sorry that I ever had to find out the truth."

Knowing then how deeply worried he must be over the very real prospect of losing his half of the inheritance, she smiled. Suddenly, it dawned on her. She held in her possession the power to make him suffer even more.

"We can talk about all this tomorrow — after I've had a chance to pack my things."

Chapter Ten

"Josie, no!"

"Go away, Nathan. I'm tired of having to shout through my bedroom door."

"Then open it!"

Knowing the silence would do more harm than an angry retort, Josie decided not to respond to that at all. She merely lay in the semidarkness, waiting for him to finally leave her door so she could think.

"Josie? Please? Open this door. I won't stay long. I won't even come inside if that's what you want."

She remained silent, listening when he rattled the door handle again. Finally he walked away. She waited until she'd heard his own door slam closed, then heard muffled noises coming from within his bedroom before daring to turn her attention to other important matters.

The image of the woman in the portraits she'd discovered came first to her mind. Josie had always been told that she greatly resembled her grandmother, but until now she'd never realized just how close the resemblance really was. No wonder her mother had been so cautious of her—always so strict. She must have worried that the similarities between the two had run deeper than mere appearances. And in a way they had.

Her father had often commented on other similarities the two shared. Many times, he'd compared Josie's wild sense of adventure with her grandmother's strong, independent nature. But he'd done so without showing any of the animosity her mother sometimes displayed. That which her mother had always called Josie's "stubborn willfulness," her father had merely termed her "budding free spirit." It was a topic the two had argued about again and again.

But they had always agreed on one thing. They had agreed that the spirited side of their daughter had indeed come from her Grandmother Seger. Which had led Josie to wonder what other traits she might have in common with the woman.

Because Josie had been warned about all the many things she had in common with her grandmother, she'd shied away from emotional commitments of any kind. She was afraid, one day, she would discover that she, like her grandmother, could not remain committed to her obligations. The thought of hurting someone else the same way her grandmother had hurt those she should have held dearest to her heart terrified Josie, as did the thought of being the one to be hurt.

Rolling over onto her back, she stared at the curling designs and the intricate details of the ceiling above her bed, remembering how angry and bitter her mother had been as a result of what her grandmother had done.

Her grandfather, too, had grown hard with his hatred and had constantly tried to instill those same strong feelings of resentment and hostility in his only granddaughter, Josie. But Josie had never found a reason to truly hate the woman—something neither her mother nor her grandfather had ever understood.

Even after her grandfather had eventually killed himself, and her mother had claimed it to be an indirect result of the evil thing her grandmother had done so many years earlier, Josie could not bring herself to actually hate the woman. She found it impossible to hate someone she never knew. Her father had been the only person to understand that.

As a result of his deeper understanding, he had been the only one in the family she could talk with about her grandmother. He became her only real link with the woman. Whenever Josie's youthful curiosity surfaced, she knew she could ask him questions about that woman who'd chosen to no longer be a part of their lives, and he would willingly tell her what little he knew about her. He had always felt his daughter had a right to know something about that part of her heritage.

Though there were certain details he admitted holding from her, claiming she was not yet old enough to understand everything, what he did tell her had filled her heart with youthful wonder. The stories he told were marvelous. They centered around a woman filled with so much life, so much determination — and the same wondrous sense of adventure she herself often felt — that Josie found it impossible to hate her. They were too much alike for that.

The only thing she personally held against her maternal grandmother was that she'd never cared enough about her family to ever return, even for a brief visit. She'd never wanted to see what her daughter and her only granddaughter might be like. It was unnatural to not be at least a little curious about what had become of her family. But Josie's father had urged her not to condemn the woman for things she was too young to understand. It was her father who'd kept Josie from becoming bitter like her mother. It was his deep love and understanding that had made her hope to someday meet the woman and discover for herself the sort of person she really was.

The day Josie's mother had calmly informed her that her grandmother was "finally" dead had been quite a blow for Josie. Having already lost her dear father earlier in the year, she was certain she'd just lost her last real opportunity to get to know the woman who had secretly fascinated her throughout her youth.

Or had she?

Josie's heart filled with wonder. Could Nathan possibly know anything about the woman? Had he actually met her? If so, would he know personal details about her — What had made her laugh? What sort of things had made her cry? Or perhaps he'd know what flaw in her character had made it impossible for her to ever truly commit herself to anyone — even to her own family? Were there items still around that may have personally belonged to her grandmother? If so, what were they?

So many questions. Would Nathan know any of the answers?

Curiosity aroused, Josie decided the sensible thing would be to put aside her anger — at least long enough to find out if Nathan did indeed know something about her grandmother. The opportunity to meet the woman had long since passed, but she might yet discover the sort of person she'd been. She might yet learn the real reason she'd left her family behind, though Josie already suspected it would prove to be more than a passing fancy. It just had to be.

Eager to find out what she could, Josie dabbed the moisture away from her cheeks with the corner of her pillowcase, then climbed swiftly out of bed. Her heart filled with tiny rays of hope while she hurried across the room to the mirror. Quickly she made the necessary repairs to her hair, then unlocked her door and crossed the hallway to knock at Nathan's.

When he failed to respond, she knocked again. Louder.

Thinking it might be his way of getting even with her for what she'd done to him earlier, she tapped her slippered foot impatiently on the hardwood floor. There had to be a way to get into that room. She tried the handle, startled to discover the room unlocked.

"Nathan?" she called out timorously. Bravely, she stepped into the room. Having never been in Nathan's bedroom, she was surprised and dismayed by all the clutter. There were trunks, crates, and boxes everywhere, their contents spilled out onto the floor. The area looked more like a neglected storeroom than a bedroom. She wondered why he had refused to let them come in when it obviously was in such dire need of cleaning.

She took another tentative step into the room. "Nathan?"

He was not there. She looked out onto the balcony to see if he'd stepped outside. The bolted door assured her that was not the case. He'd obviously gone back downstairs.

Afraid he might return at any moment and discover her there, and of course immediately jump to the wrong conclusion, Josie did not linger in his room. Quietly, she stepped back into the dimly lit hallway. Then, just as she turned to close the door behind her, she noticed a door just down the hall stood slightly ajar. It was the door to Nathan's father's studio. Nathan had gone back downstairs for the keys.

Still eager to question him about her grandmother she gathered her courage about her like a well-worn cloak and bravely approached the open door. But the closer she went, the more hesitant her steps became. She wondered if she should bother him just now, knowing he might prefer to be left alone, at least for a while. She considered using that as an excuse to turn back; but, finally, her courage won out and she knocked.

"Who is it?" he asked in a gruff tone. Only a second later his muffled footsteps were heard crossing the room.

"It's me, Josie. I've had a chance to think. I am now ready to talk," she said. Her voice sounded far calmer than she actually felt.

The door had been left open only a crack, but enough so she saw his shadow moving about inside. She chose to wait patiently in the hallway until he opened it further. When it did finally open wide enough to see him, her voice caught on a startled gasp. The man was barely dressed. Though he still wore a pair of dark-brown denim trousers and a pair of gray woolen stockings, he'd removed both his shirt and his boots, which made him a full inch shorter and put his lightly haired muscular chest right at Josie's eye level. She tried her best not to notice as she took a tiny step backward. "B-but I can see you did not expect to be disturbed. It can wait. We can talk in the morning."

She had already started to turn away, her face flushed by what she'd seen, when he suddenly reached out and pulled her into the room. Her next sound was very much like the yelp of an injured pup.

"Oh, no you don't," he told her, his voice stern, the hold on her arm like a vise. "I don't plan to wait until morning. I want to have this out now." Then, without giving her an opportunity to protest, he kicked the door shut, effectively closing off the rest of the world in one lithe movement.

Aware they were quite alone—with Nathan still half undressed—Josie felt her pulses jump into rapid motion. Nervous apprehension scattered to every part of her body. "I wish you would leave the door open."

"Not this time," he stated emphatically, keeping a firm hold on her arm as he stepped closer. He wanted to see her expression. "I well remember how quickly you made use of that last open door. I'm not about to let you get away from me again. You are not leaving

167

here until you have given me a chance to finally have my say."

When she then tried to pull herself free with the intention of reopening the door herself, he grabbed her other arm and jerked her sharply against him. The feel of his warm, bare skin beneath the palms of her hands when she reached up to push him away again was maddening. Her breaths came in tiny little gasps as panic pierced her heart, paralyzing her against further action.

"Nathan, don't."

Josie was frightened. She did not understand her own awakening responses. Her body ached with a strange, startling sensation. She tried harder to push him away, but he reacted by tightening his hold. There was no escaping him. Not this time.

"Josie, please. We have to talk."

Though his voice fell low and soothing at her ear, Josie's heart continued to pound at a frightening pace beneath her breast. He continued to hold her close. Too close. She had to make him stop. She had to get away. But how, when he was so much stronger than she?

"I want you to listen to what I have to say." He continued to coax, his attention equally divided between her wide green eyes and her soft, inviting lips. "You must give me a chance to explain. I had my reasons for what I did, foolish though they might seem."

With her chin tilted rebelliously, Josie's mouth opened. An angry response fell ready on her lips. But before she could speak the words that would make Nathan finally let go, his mouth came crashing down on hers to claim it with a bold, thought-shattering kiss.

Whatever comment she had proposed to make became quickly lost to the whirling sea of shocking sensations. While his lips drank freely of her very soul, all traces of coherent thought slowly slipped away. It was as if he'd cast some mysterious spell over her. How easily he bent her will to his. Never had she felt such an all-consuming response to a mere kiss. Never had she known such a need to return that kiss and explore it for all it could offer.

It took all Josie's restraint to keep her own hands still. Secretly, she wished she had the courage to explore the hard muscles along his back and neck, feel the tingling warmth of his skin.

Finally, after several mind-reeling moments, Nathan gently pulled his lips from hers. Too spellbound to move, Josie gazed once again into his glimmering eyes. When he spoke, his voice came forth but a whisper.

"Please stay."

Josie knew she should protest his bold actions while she had the chance. But she couldn't. All trace of logical thought had left her. At that moment, the only thing she wanted to do was stand there and look at how exquisitely handsome he was.

"Stay with me," he whispered again.

His eyes searched hers for any indication of withdrawal when he then bent forward, bringing his lips back to within a scant inch of hers. He fully intended to kiss her again, but he had to be certain it was what she wanted, too. He had *taken* that first kiss, but he wanted her to give freely of the next.

Mesmerized by the stark, animal hunger glimmering from beneath his heavily lowered lashes, Josie did nothing to stop him from claiming her mouth in yet another wondrous kiss. Held breathless by her own awakening passion, she was unable to ask that he stop. As she stared into his stormy blue eyes, a strange, penetrating warmth slowly invaded her senses yet again, spreading instantly through her body like a hot, rolling mist. The effects left her lightheaded and weak. No longer able to think rationally, she leaned against him for strength and he brought his hand to the small of her back to offer gentle support, pressing her closer still.

The shocking intimacy of his hard body against her soft curves caused the hot, roiling mist inside her to ignite and burst into sudden flame. Never before had she experienced such a feeling of pleasure and eagerness. It was impossible to do the right thing and pull away. Timidly, her thoughts edged slowly beyond the kiss itself until, boldly, she wondered where such intense passion might lead. But before she could possibly find out, he again pulled away. This time more abruptly. This time he released her entirely.

Once freed from his embrace, she immediately stepped back, hoping to still the strange dizziness that surrounded her by putting distance between them. Desperately, she filled her lungs with deep gulps of air. She was so shaken by the sheer force of the passion that had so quickly taken hold of her senses, and by her own helpless reaction, that all she could do was stare at him numbly. She was far too stunned to yet speak her mind.

Nathan's eyes were dark when he looked at her then. "I guess I've wanted to do that ever since that very first moment I saw you," he said gruffly while struggling to control his ragged breath.

Josie had no idea how she should respond to such a bold statement, still too shocked by what had occurred to think clearly. Taking another backward step, she tried to understand what had happened, but couldn't. The whole thing seemed preposterous. A man she could barely tolerate had kissed her without warning, and she had done absolutely nothing to stop him. Instead, she had accepted the kiss and had actually enjoyed the new feelings he'd aroused. Hers had been

170

the wrong reaction—the wrong reaction entirely. And she had yet to make sense of it.

Nathan was just as startled by his bold actions as she had been. He had not planned to kiss her. It had just happened.

Turning quickly away, he, too, wondered about the kiss and about the powerful response he'd felt. It had been different from anything he'd ever experienced before.

"I think we'd better have that talk now," he said. His tone of voice became far more subdued when he stood with his back to her, his hands locked behind his back.

Grasping at any chance to return some state of normalcy between them, Josie's response formed quickly. "I do, too. There are so many things I want to ask you. For one, I've decided I want to learn more about my grandmother. Did you know her?"

Nathan turned to face her again and saw evidence of true concern on her face. Aware of the sincerity of her request, he wished he could be of more help. "Not really. About all I ever knew about your grandmother was that she had somehow become an important part of my father's life—and that he loved her dearly."

"Then tell me about your father. I'd love to know what he was like. Maybe by knowing him, I could understand why she left her family behind."

Nathan's expression hardened when he turned to face the portrait he'd been studying when she first knocked at the door. "That's him there."

"That's your father? I thought that was supposed to be you. The resemblance between the two of you is astounding," she told him as she looked from the painting to Nathan, then back to the painting. "What was he like?"

"I'm afraid I don't know very much about him, either. I really don't understand why he decided to include me in his will when you consider that I was barely included in his life," he said sadly. "When I was very young, he took very good care of us and came to visit fairly often. Because my mother had had such a hard time giving birth to me, she was unable to have other children and the ones she'd borne before me had died at very early ages. So I was an only child and he felt it was his duty to see that I was taken care of—that *we* were taken care of. Even when I got older, he continued to provide for us, but only because he felt it was his duty. His visits became further and further apart. Then, after my mother's death, which was about twelve years ago, I saw my father only once more. That was right after mother's funeral."

"Can't you tell me anything about him?"

"Certainly. I can tell you that he was fifty-three years old, twenty-three years older than I, and three years older than my mother. I can also tell you some of the things I've read in magazines and newspapers. I can tell you that he was an excellent artist, earning his reputation early in life. In fact, he was touted to be one of the best contemporary artists known. Some of his works have sold for tens of thousands of dollars. His special genius made him famous worldwide. But, at the same time, he was also a wanderer and a gambler."

Nathan turned away from the painting. He let his gaze idly sweep the room—his father's room. "It was while my father wandered the countryside that he met your grandmother, fell in love, and took her to be his mistress. Mother knew about the arrangement, I guess practically from the very beginning. It hurt her deeply, but somehow she learned to accept the sad fact she was no longer to be the only woman in my father's life."

His voice took on a bitter tone as he continued. "And it wasn't long before she came to accept the fact she held a definite second place in his heart. But, still, she preferred second place to no place at all, and remained devoted to him until her death. She loved him that much."

"How awful it must have been for her," Josie said, wishing the memories did not have to be so painful for him. She longed to comfort him somehow, but didn't know how. "At least she had you."

"That she did. I did all I could to make up for his absence. But it was never enough. She lived for his visits. When she caught the fever that eventually killed her, it was his name that came from her lips. I sent word to him as soon as the doctor had explained to me just how serious her condition had become. I am grateful to my father for coming as quickly as he did. His being there made dying so much easier for her." Tears glimmered in his eyes.

Josie's heart ached to reach out to him. How suddenly lost he seemed. "Then he must have still loved her, at least to some degree, or else he would never have come so quickly."

"Oh, he did love her. It just wasn't the same sort of love he felt for his Annabelle."

Josie felt suddenly guilty for the heartache her grandmother had caused. "How old were you when your mother died?"

"I had just turned eighteen. Old enough to be on my own. But my aunt Michalann felt it would be better if I stayed with her in Jefferson for a while. Being Mother's oldest sister, she felt it was her duty to take me in and care for me. I lived with her nearly a year before I finally struck out on my own."

Josie wondered what had happened after that, but felt she had probed into his personal life enough. "And you never had the chance to meet my grandmother?"

"Oh, I had the chance. I just didn't think I could

ever fit into that other part of my father's life so I purposely stayed away. I'm sorry I can't be of more help to you, but I just didn't have the heart to come here and actually meet the woman who had taken my father away from us. Or maybe I should say I could never quite work up the courage."

"I understand how you must have felt. My mother was much the same way. Shortly after Grandfather's death, my grandmother wrote to my mother. But Mother had wanted no part of the woman and returned the letter unopened. You see, she blamed Grandmother Seger for Grandfather's death."

"Why was that?"

"Grandfather was a weak man. Shortly after she left him, he turned to heavy drink. My mother was only nine at the time, but had to quit school temporarily so she could take care of him. His drinking forced her to have to grow up in a hurry. Later, when he found it impossible to drink his sorrows away, he chose to kill himself—with his own rifle. He shot himself in my bedroom."

Nathan's features paled when he realized what a traumatic experience that must have been for her. "How horrible."

"Don't look so concerned. In all honesty, I can barely remember the incident. I was only seven at the time. But the shock of it lived with my mother till her death, nine years later." Josie paused a moment to think more about her mother. "I wonder if Mama ever knew Grandmother Seger got married again."

Josie felt the same momentary surge of anger she always felt when she considered all the suffering her mother and grandfather had been forced to live through, and the fear she'd always lived with because of their suffering—fear that she, too, could end up like that if she ever allowed herself to fall in love. But the anger proved short-lived. There were too many

174

conflicting emotions building inside Josie at that moment to allow room for anger.

Torn between jealousy and sheer admiration, Josie thought more about her grandmother. Having seen the portraits, she better understood the deep love the woman must have felt for Nathan's father. What the two had shared must have been very special.

At last, Josie realized the courage it had taken for her grandmother to go against all the social conventions of the time in order to follow her own heart. The woman's reason for leaving had been far different from anything Josie had been led to believe.

Gazing then at one of her grandmother's portraits, Josie's expression grew wistful. "I wish Mother had been more willing to talk about her. I'd love to know more about her."

"Maybe Father's lawyer can help you. I imagine Jason knew your grandmother well enough to answer at least a few of your questions. The way I understand it, he and my father were friends for well over twelve years."

"Do you really think he could answer some of my questions?" Josie asked eagerly. Her eyes sparkled with sudden hope.

"Can't hurt to ask. Why don't I set up an appointment for you two to meet? Then you can find out for yourself just what he does and doesn't know about your grandmother." Nathan thought it might be a way to keep her there, at least for a few more days.

"He might even give me the names of other people who knew her," Josie added, finding all manner of possibilities ahead.

Nathan thought then of his aunt Cynthia. She had certainly known Josie's grandmother, but whatever memories his father's only sister might have of his father's lady love would no doubt be tainted with bitter feelings. Like himself, his aunt Cynthia had never fully accepted his father's second wife and had done all she could to prevent the two from ever getting married.

Unaware Nathan's attention had wandered to something else entirely, Josie's thoughts raced ahead, excited by the prospect of finally knowing more about her grandmother. "Yes, do set up an appointment. I want to find out all I can about my grandmother. Not only do I want to know why she left home the way she did, but why she never bothered to make any real contact with her family again. Oh, yes, she sent letters from time to time, but she never came herself. I want to find out why she never tried to see me when she obviously knew I existed. How else would your father have known about me?"

Suddenly, the truth struck her full force. Her stomach hardened into a painful knot. The answer was suddenly so obvious. Her grandmother had never tried to see her because she'd never been interested enough to make the effort. Her grandmother had known about her, and had obviously convinced her new husband to see that certain provisions were made upon his death, but she had never cared enough to actually go to the trouble to see her—to meet her. The pain of knowing that was unbearable. She lashed out at that pain with anger.

"On second thought, forget the appointment. I don't want to speak with your father's lawyer after all—about anything. And I don't want any inheritance that is linked in any way to someone who showed so little regard for her family. I think I'd rather just leave here now and forget the whole thing."

"You can't," Nathan said, hoping to reason with her. "I'll see to it that Father's lawyer keeps away from you, if that's what you want. But you have to stay. You have to see this thing through, for both our sakes."

"I don't *have* to do anything," she retorted, feeling suddenly defiant.

"Yes, you do. I have your written word. You promised to stay. Remember? You signed a document promising me you'd stay here with me for three months." He hoped she would not realize the document was invalid.

"But you purposely led me into that."

"Whether or not I led you into such a bet doesn't change the fact that you agreed to it. Nor does it change the fact you have only been here a week. You still owe me well over two and a half months."

"*What?* You can't expect me to live up to that bargain, not after having learned how you tricked me into making the bet in the first place."

"I may have tricked you into making the bet, and it may be a bet you might not otherwise have made, but I won that poker hand fair and square. You know that's true because you dealt the cards yourself. That agreement between us is still as binding as it ever was." He chose his words carefully. "Even though I won't expect you to continue to clean the house or even help with the cooking as a part of that agreement, I do intend to hold you to the three-month stay."

"That's not fair!"

"What's not fair about it? You agreed to the bet and you lost. It is as simple as that. You gave me your word—in writing—that you would stay with me for exactly that amount of time. Do you now plan to go against your own word?"

When he put it that way, how could she refuse and still keep her pride? "I can't believe you really plan to make me stay here against my will."

Stepping closer, he reached out and took her gently by the shoulders. His gaze searched hers for some indication she understood. "I had hoped you would

177

want to stay."

Josie's body responded to Nathan's unexpected touch with such a vibrant jolt, it again frightened her. Suddenly she realized the danger she would constantly have to guard against if she did stay. He had stirred to life something inside her that might best be left alone, something she might not be able to keep under control, something she found hard to control even then.

"Is that why you grabbed me and kissed me earlier?" she lashed out, as much in fear as in anger. She jerked her shoulders out of his grasp and took several steps back. "Was that kiss merely another clever ploy on your part to make me want to stay? Did you really think your manly charms would prove that overwhelming? How arrogant can one man be?"

Angered by such an unexpected response, Nathan curled his hands into tight fists and held them stiffly at his sides. "Is that what you really think? That I had hoped to seduce you into staying?"

"Yes, that is exactly what I think. Is there no limit to what you are or aren't willing to do to try and keep me here?"

"Yes, there is a limit. A definite limit. To everything. And I think I have just about reached mine," he said. His jaw clenched with anger as he took several slow, menacing steps in her direction.

"Don't you dare touch me again," she warned, eyes wide with sudden fear. Taking another step backward, she was horrified to discover her retreat suddenly halted by a large, sturdy worktable. Her heart vaulted forward with a wild surge of panic as she searched for a means of escape. "Don't you even come near me."

"Why? What will you do to stop me?" he asked, clearly unimpressed by her angry demands.

Knowing there was little she could do, Josie decided the perfect time had come to strike another bargain.

"I'll stay."

Confused at having been given such an illogical answer, he twisted his face into a disbelieving frown. "You'll what?"

"I'll stay. The full three months. Providing you agree to certain terms."

"And what terms are those?"

"I'll stay, as long as this house can be divided equally between us."

"It will be. The lawyer plans to see to that."

"I mean now. As of this very minute." She hurried to explain further. "Before I'll agree to stay on for the remainder of the three months, you must promise to keep to your half of the house and I will of course keep to mine."

"But why?"

"How can you ask that after what just occurred between us? I would think the reason would be perfectly clear, even to you. The only rooms we should even consider sharing between us are the dining room, the bathing room, and the privy—since there are only one of each and they are each necessary to both of us. And of course we'll have to share the hallways and entrances, for obvious reasons. But the moment we have clear title to this house and everything else your father owned, we will waste no time selling what we can and dividing the money equally."

Nathan scowled at Josie's proposition. He didn't like the idea of not being able to see her whenever he wanted. But if it meant she would stay, he had to at least consider it.

"So, what do you think?" she asked when he did not immediately respond.

Nathan continued to stare at her, his expression grim. Several moments passed before he finally threw his hands into the air in a display of annoyance. "To tell you the truth, I don't know what to think any-

179

more. All I did was kiss you."

Josie had an unexplainable urge to grin, but kept a solemn face when she asked, "Will you agree to those terms or not?"

"I really don't think I should have to agree to anything. After all, I already have a signed agreement from you in which you have clearly promised to stay here for three full months. It is in my rights to hold you to that agreement as it is."

Josie knew he spoke the truth. Whether or not he'd planned the whole charade didn't really matter. She was honor bound to fulfill her promise. She was defeated. She had no choice but to face the personal dangers that lay ahead, dangers that could easily surface every time they found themselves alone together.

Or did she?

"You're right," she agreed. "I did promise to stay. But since I'll no longer be required to cook or clean for you, there's nothing in our so-called agreement that says I can't stay locked away in my own room for the remainder of those three months, is there?"

Nathan rolled his eyes heavenward, unable to believe she'd even consider such a thing. After all, it was just a kiss. Powerful, granted, but just a kiss all the same. He hadn't even *tried* to make it into anything more, which in itself was surprising considering how beautiful and tempting she was. "You can't mean that."

"Oh, but I do. Just because I have to stay here in this house does not mean I have to subject myself to any more of your unwanted advances."

Drawing in a long, exasperated breath, he saw no real point in arguing with her. Her mind was made up. He might as well give in and be done with it.

"Okay. If it will keep peace between us, I'll agree to divide the house equally between us. At least for now. But like you said, we will have to share certain areas like the hallways, the stairs, and the dining room." He hoped they could at least continue to meet in passing.

"Fine," she said, smiling with relief, unable to believe he'd conceded on the matter. "And since your room is on the east side of the house and mine is on the west, that's how we'll divide our space. For the remainder of our time together, and except for the areas already mentioned, I'll keep to the rooms along the west side of the house while you stay on the east side. Because of the hardship it would place on Jeanne to cook separate meals, I suppose we should continue to dine together, but that's all."

"What about this room?" he asked, looking around at the many paintings and artist notes he had yet to explore.

"What about it?"

"It's situated as much on the east side of the house as it is on the west. Who is to have the run of this room?"

"I guess we can share it, too. We'll just have to work out a reasonable schedule. That way we won't ever have to be in here at the same time."

"Anything else?" he asked, still clearly displeased over the whole concept.

"Only that the moment your father's will has been read, and we finally become the legal owners of Oakhaven, we will try to sell everything but the land your aunt is living on just as quickly as we possibly can. We can then split the money equally and go our separate ways."

"That was my intention all along," he muttered earnestly, though for some reason he now felt far less enthusiastic about the idea than before.

Chapter Eleven

Nathan was furious. There was only so much any man should have to tolerate. Something definitely needed to be done. And soon.

For the past week, Josie had indeed kept to her part of the house and fully expected him to keep to his. Whenever he dared cross over the imaginary boundary between them, especially during those first few days, she immediately took to her room and stayed hidden away for hours. They were in each other's company only during lunch and supper.

For breakfast, they were never up and about at the same hour. Constantly, though unintentionally, they switched back and forth between who rose early and who rose late. It became rare for the two of them to share a morning meal, and even when they did, they barely spoke to each other.

There had to be some way for Nathan to get around that blasted stubborn streak of hers. There had to. Steeped in the heated memories of their kiss, he could not bear to let their relationship continue in the direction it was now headed. The thought of being reduced to stealing quick glimpses of her as she passed through the hallway was degrading—and downright frustrating. Something *had* to be done. Even if it meant having to risk everything.

It was while Nathan suffered through the annoying silence of yet another supper, during which Josie gave him barely a thread of her attention, his frustrations finally reached their breaking point. The time had come to do something about the present situation. At last his mind began to formulate a plan that just might work. Though the risk was great, almost fool-hearted, the end result might very well prove worth it. Enough so, he had to try.

"Josie, before you leave, there is something I want to discuss with you," he called out only seconds after she'd pushed her chair back from the table. She was already halfway to the door, no doubt headed upstairs where she would then lock herself inside her bedroom for the rest of the night. He could not bear the thought of it. "I have a proposition for you."

Josie paused only a few feet from the doorway, so physically shaken at having heard her name on his lips that she felt suddenly weak. How she had longed to hear him call her back. For whatever the reason. She was tired of spending so much of her time alone, yet far too proud to openly admit what a terrible mistake she'd made by demanding they stay apart. But, a mistake it had been. And she was miserable because of it.

During the past few days, as the hours of each day grew unbearably longer, she had come to realize just how grand her mistake had been. Constantly, she berated herself for having behaved so irrationally, but she didn't know how to go about undoing what she'd done without humbling herself in front of him. Desperately, she hoped he would do something that might force her to bend to his will.

She hated spending most of her time alone. Ever since the other three women had discovered she was actually their mistress and not one of them, they had purposely shut her out, refusing to let her help with any of the work and appearing extremely uncomfortable whenever she was nearby.

Eventually, Josie found herself left completely out of

their conversations. Whenever she entered a room in which they chattered away, hard at work, the room fell silent. Josie had become an outsider and, because of that, she was forced to spend the unbearably long days alone with nothing to fill the endless hours. She couldn't even read because, unfortunately, the library was on Nathan's side of the house, and he spent much of his time there, still going through his father's things.

How she longed to forget their ridiculous agreement entirely. Not only did she want to venture into the library whenever she felt like finding something to read, she wanted to share at least a part of her day with Nathan. She missed him far more than she ever would have imagined possible.

Filled with hope, she drew in a deep breath, then turned to face the man who had occupied her thoughts constantly over the past few days. Her pulses froze when she noticed Nathan had risen from his chair and was already headed across the room toward her. A look of pure determination glittered in the pale-blue depths of his eyes.

Wondering if his expression meant that he intended to demand she bring an end to their foolishness, her heart fluttered back to life. If he did make such a demand, she wondered if she would have the good sense to hold her pride at bay and not allow her emotions to overrule her head. Curling her hands into tight fists, she willed herself to listen to her heart for a change and resist any further arguments with the man.

"What sort of proposition do you have in mind?" she asked, amazed at how clear and concise her words had sounded when her throat remained so painfully constricted.

How she hoped his proposition would be a compromise that would allow them both to come away from this situation with their individual prides intact. Though she did not truly enjoy the thought of being forced to bend to his will, she no longer felt the strange need to force him to bend to hers. All she wanted was for the two of them to somehow be friends again.

Aware she waited for him to speak, Nathan tried to keep his gaze properly placed on the bright glow of her emerald eyes, but when he came to a stop only a few feet in front of her, his attention was drawn to the rapid rise and fall of her well-rounded bosom beneath a starched white blouse. Though the blouse was buttoned to the collar, the manner in which she filled out the crisp white material made him more aware than ever of the woman who stood before him. It was a moment before he lifted his gaze to again meet with hers, and another brief moment before he answered her question.

"Actually, it's more an opportunity for you to win back your freedom."

Josie's heart sank to the aching depths of her soul. How she had hoped to hear that he'd missed her company almost as much as she had missed his. Although he'd continued to find plenty of ways to keep busy, either in his father's library or out in the barn, she'd hoped to discover he had missed being able to enter whatever room she was in and antagonize her into another of their ongoing arguments. But, no, the exact opposite was true and Josie did not think she could bear it. Nathan was ready for her to leave Oakhaven all together—even though he risked losing his inheritance by her leaving. "I—I don't understand. How can I possible win back my freedom?"

"It's simple really. I'm sick and woefully tired of having to stay in my half of the house. I'm way too used to having the run of things. I want to be able to go where I want, when I want. Therefore, I've decided to offer you a chance to win your freedom back."

Josie wondered why he didn't just send her away but realized he was much too proud to do something like that. "How?"

"In the same way you lost your freedom in the first place. We'll play another hand of poker. It shouldn't take but a few minutes and could do an awful lot toward changing things around here."

"How so?" she asked and wondered if such a change would be in her best interest. She wasn't at all sure she wanted to leave just yet. She had started to find the whole idea of his father's will and her grandmother's involvement with the man intriguing.

"If you win, I'll tear up that agreement you signed sixteen days ago. You will then be free to leave here with a clear conscience. Simple as that."

"But what if I lose?" she asked, wanting to be sure she understood all sides of his proposition.

"If you lose, you have to give up this silly nonsense about the two of us keeping to separate halves of the house while we live out the last of our three months. I will be allowed to come and go in this house — where I please, when I please. And in addition, I will be allowed to claim another kiss from you, payable on demand."

Intrigued at the thought of such a bet, Josie considered the situation further. Though the part about the kiss seemed a little extreme, she saw no real reason to refuse the bet all together. The truth of the matter was, whether she won or lost, the game would serve the same purpose. It would finally bring an end to her self-inflicted days of solitude. She felt something inside her come alive at the mere thought of being able to spend more time with Nathan — of joining him in the library to see if any of his father's papers possibly mentioned her grandmother.

"I guess it sounds fair enough," she finally answered. "Where do you propose we play this hand of poker?"

"Since this appears to be neutral territory for us, I suggest we play right here," he said, motioning toward a portion of the huge mahogany dining table that had remained clear of any dishes or decorations. "I just happen to have a deck of cards with me."

"Why does that not surprise me?" she asked with a meaningful lift of her brow as she turned toward the table.

"Shall we?" Though he ached to touch her, he stood aside, giving her enough room to pass unassisted.

"I see no reason to delay this."

A strong, apprehensive feeling crept over Josie while she clutched her dark-brown broadcloth skirt and maneuvered her way around him. Though her main means of livelihood had always come from her uncanny ability to win at cards, in this particular instance, she was not so sure she wanted to win. Did she really want the total freedom it would give her? Having her fate thrust upon her as it had been over recent weeks made things so much easier than having to worry about decisions she wasn't at all certain she was ready to make.

"Who's to deal the cards?" she asked, glancing briefly at him while she settled into the chair he had gallantly pulled back for her. She was unprepared for the funny little jolt through her heart when his hand accidentally brushed against her shoulder.

"You can deal," he stated. His demeanor remained outwardly calm, though his insides had become a boiling cauldron of apprehension just knowing that, in a matter of minutes, a part of his entire future would have been decided.

"What'll we play?" she asked, trying not to concentrate on the heavy, almost painful pounding of her heart — also keenly aware of how very much depended

187

on what happened over the next few minutes.

"Dealer's choice," he said agreeably.

Josie thought about it. She'd much rather know her chances as they accumulated. "Stud. Five card."

"Then stud it will be," he said, handing the cards to her, then watched, fascinated by the agile movements of her hands while she coaxed the cards together again and again.

"Don't I get to cut them?" he asked when he was sure she'd finished.

"Of course," she said, pushing the shuffled deck across the table toward him.

Rather than cut them on the table, as was his custom, he casually lifted them off the table, dropped them to his waist, just out of her sight, then made one single movement with his hands.

Josie considered protesting that he'd dropped the cards out of her view, but as she accepted the cards back, she glanced up at his stony expression and decided it would be best not to even mention it. Her heart hammered wildly while she carefully adjusted the cards in her hand, then lifted the first card off the top. Wondering if he'd cheated, and if so, in whose favor, she hesitated only a second before turning it over and placing it directly in front of him. She did not glance down to see its value until she'd drawn her hand away and was disappointed to find that his card was a three of clubs. Suddenly she felt betrayed. He hadn't even *attempted* to fix the deck.

Nathan's jawline hardened when he, too, looked down at his first card, but he said nothing while he waited for her to turn over the next card.

Unnerved by his continued silence, Josie slowly turned her first card up and laid it on the table in front of her. It was an ace of diamonds. Of all times to get an ace! Now she felt as if she'd betrayed herself, but there was no time to reason why on earth she should feel that way. Nathan waited for his next card.

Quickly she dealt out another card to each of them.

But the next cards made no real changes in either hand. A six of hearts became partnered with his three of clubs. And a ten of diamonds joined her ace. Those four were immediately followed by another three for him, this time spades, and second ten for her, also spades. Now they each had a pair.

Hers tens.

His threes.

The fourth cards proved to be of little consequence. Nathan received the eight of spades. Josie got the three of hearts — which she realized cut his chances of getting another three-card in half. Her pair of tens kept their advantage.

With the wager already clearly established, there was little reason to lay the fifth and final card face-down as was the custom in five-card stud. Still, Josie felt ill prepared to look at either of them just yet. Finding Nathan's gaze locked on her own stony expression, instead of on the cards still in her hand, she hesitated to reveal his final card. His lips were but a grim line, his jaw rigid. Clearly he understood the seriousness of his situation.

"Here goes," she said bravely as she flipped his card over and placed it beside the other four. With difficulty, she pulled her gaze away from his to glance at that final card. The way his luck had run the first time they had played, she fully expected to see that she'd handed him the other three.

But it wasn't a three after all. It was a six. Still, that gave him two pair. Unless she handed herself that final three, another ace, or one more ten, she'd still lose.

Drawing in a long, unsteady breath, she lifted her own final card off the top and slowly turned it over. Her heart froze in midbeat. There was her lucky queen of hearts! All Josie had was a pair of tens. She'd lost.

Slowly, she lifted her green eyes away from her cards and blinked as she realized the startling truth. She'd actually wanted to lose. More than anything else, she had wanted to lose that particular hand of poker. Instead of disappointment or dismay, she felt as giddy as a schoolgirl at a spring dance.

"Looks like you win," she stated with a gambler's calm, though her insides were a tumbling combination of overwhelming relief and childlike excitement. "I guess that means you now have the run of the house again. No more imaginary lines to stay behind."

But the moment of relief proved very short-lived. A foreboding chill raced down her spine, causing her to swallow hard when her next thought arose, unbidden. The resulting spark of apprehension grew steadily stronger with each thudding beat of her heart. "I guess you'll be wanting your kiss now."

"No, not just yet. Don't forget, I said the kiss was to be payable on demand," he told her. His eyes glimmered from having been clever enough to put such a stipulation on the kiss. "But don't worry, I'll let you know when I think it's time."

He smiled, knowing he would not wait too long before claiming his kiss—just long enough to make sure the kiss would be undisturbed by the help!

Josie released a slow, trembling breath while she wondered just when and where he might demand this kiss. Her heart pounded in wild rhythm as she considered the many dangerous possibilities. Suddenly, she felt a great need to be out of his sight. She needed to think.

"Well, ah, then, since you don't intend to claim your kiss right away—and since we really have no further business to take care of at this particular moment, I guess I will retire to my bedroom." Feeling as

190

awkward as a small child facing a scolding, she quickly stood in preparation to do exactly that, aware he carefully studied her every move.

"Just don't go locking your door," he called out to her, his tone forbidding, while he watched her hurry toward the main hall.

Nathan's words brought Josie's footsteps to an abrupt halt. Her eyes were wide with fear when she spun about to face him. Her hand flew protectively to the hollow of her throat.

"And why shouldn't I lock my door?"

Nathan shrugged as if the reason should be obvious. "I just won the complete run of the house. Remember?"

"But surely you didn't mean to include my bedroom." The pulsebeat beneath her fingertips quickened.

"Didn't I?" he asked with an ominous lift of his brow as he leaned casually back in his chair. His eyes never left hers.

"B-but you never said the bet was to include my own bedroom."

"I guess that's because you never bothered to ask just what it did include," he stated simply. A pleased smile stretched across his face, causing two distinct dimples to press into the rugged perfection of his cheeks while he studied her flushed expression. "You really should learn to ask more questions."

Josie stared at him a long moment, blinking with stunned disbelief while she thought more about it. Her face suddenly paled. Did he intend to have that kiss in her bedroom?

Nathan tilted his head while he continued to smile, clearly delighted with himself and his present situation. "Don't look so upset. I'll probably knock first."

His cocky attitude made her furious.

"How very considerate you are," she responded with

a determined lift of her chin, offering him a look of angry defiance that would have withered lesser men. "Knock all you please, but you'll find both the doors leading into my bedroom securely locked!"

Afraid he might do something drastic to make her change her mind, she spun immediately back around and ran from the room just as fast as her legs and her skirts would allow.

To Josie's surprise, Nathan did not attempt to disturb her when he came upstairs less than an hour later. Other than to continuously plague her every waking thought, he left her alone. And instead of knocking at her door, demanding to be let in as she had fully expected him to, he went directly into his own bedroom and carefully closed his door.

Even so, Josie did not dress for bed right away. She still halfway expected Nathan to come bounding out of his room at any moment, demanding she unlock the door. It was only after no further noises came from his room and she felt certain he'd gone to bed that she dared slip out of her regular clothing and into her soft white nightdress.

Eager to push Nathan's image aside and finally find peace of mind through a blissful night of sleep, Josie climbed immediately into bed and pulled the covers to her chin. Though she turned out her bedside lamp and pressed her eyes tightly closed, sleep refused to come. For some reason, the harder she tried, the more she tossed and turned — until her bed had become a twisted jumble of sheets and quilts.

Finally, she gave up such futile efforts and relit her bedside lamp. Untangling herself from her sheets, she quietly slipped out of bed in search of something to occupy her thoughts for a while. But there was nothing.

Restlessly, she paced about the room. She considered slipping downstairs to search for a book, but was too afraid she'd run into Nathan. She was not at all ready to face him again. It was almost like being held a prisoner in her own bedroom.

Annoyed by the fact she no longer appeared to have any real control over her own life, Josie sank down into a chair and tried to figure out exactly when everything had started to fall apart. There she was, in a place she had absolutely no desire to be, in a situation that was in no way of her own making, living totally by someone else's rules. How had it all happened? When did she first start losing control over her own destiny?

Josie closed her eyes and heaved a dismal sigh. The answer to that last question was obvious enough. It had all started the very moment Nathaniel Garrett stepped into her life and quietly took over.

Frustrated that she had allowed him to manipulate her yet again, and even more frustrated to realize she had wanted him to, Josie had to get out of the close confines of her bedroom. She had to find breathing room.

Knowing of only one safe option, she pulled on her dressing robe and stepped out into the cool darkness that shadowed the second-floor balcony. Instantly, she found solace in the soft breeze that whispered against her heated skin.

Taking special effort to be quiet, she slowly pulled the door to her bedroom closed. She did not want to alert Nathan to the fact she had stepped outside.

Aware that at any moment he might glance out his bedroom window and see her standing there, she moved immediately away from the dim light that fell from her bedroom windows. Heading in the opposite direction of his room, she carefully remained in the darkest shadows nearest the wall until she reached the portion of railing farthest away from his room. No longer worried over being seen from his window, she pushed her troubled thoughts aside and gazed out upon the tranquil lake beyond.

Smiling, she breathed deeply the cool night air as she leaned forward against the sturdy, waist-high banister and braced herself with both arms. The delicate scent of pine and honeysuckle drifted on the gentle breeze, capturing her attention only until she noticed the silvery ribbon of moonlight that glittered across the water's dark surface.

While staring out across such breathtaking beauty, Josie wondered when the lake would become warm enough to wade in comfortably. She suspected it would be weeks yet. Though the days had become much warmer as April finally played itself out and the first of May approached, the nights themselves remained very cool, far too cool for the water to reach a temperature comfortable enough for wading. But it wouldn't be long before she could kick off her shoes and enjoy the feel of the water against her ankles.

Josie's next thought was of her grandmother. She wondered if Annabelle had ever taken off her shoes and stockings and waded about in the cool shallows of the secluded, woodland pond. Or might she have ventured upon a midnight swim during some hot and sultry summer night, maybe with Nathan's father splashing playfully at her side? Josie smiled at the thought, almost certain the woman had felt the same sort of lure she herself felt now, a lure that made her want to become part of that beautiful body of water.

"Lovely, isn't it?" came an unexpected voice from behind.

Josie drew in a startled gasp. She spun about just in time to watch Nathan's silhouetted form step out of the dark shadows directly behind her and into the glimmering moonlight. She'd thought him to be sound asleep by now. But there he was, still dressed in the same clothing he'd worn at dinner, though he'd unbuttoned the top buttons of his shirt for his own comfort. How devastatingly handsome he looked, standing in the silken moonlight, gazing at her with such a peculiar yet heart-warming expression.

"What are you doing here?" she asked, her voice instantly accusing. She wondered how she could have possibly missed noticing him.

Feeling awkward at having been caught outside in nothing more than her dressing robe and gown, she quickly reached up to clutch the overlapping panels just below her throat. Every fiber of her being had become immediately alert to the startling situation at hand. The two of them were again alone, totally alone, on a moonlit balcony, with only a few yards stretching between them.

"I couldn't sleep," he answered simply, shrugging as if she really should have guessed that. His gaze never strayed from hers while he continued to move forward, shortening the distance between them only inches at a time. "I've been sitting out here for quite some time. And you? Why are you out here at such a late hour?"

"I—I—" Not wanting to admit her own inability to sleep for fear he might guess the reason, she struggled to find another plausible excuse for having come outside at such an unusual hour. "I often come out here late at night. I find it very relaxing, very peaceful. Don't you?"

Nathan took another slow but determined step in her direction. Silvery beams of moonlight reflected from his hair and caught the clear blue of his eyes. "Yes, I do find it peaceful out here. It's just that I figured you'd be asleep by now. After all, it has to be after eleven o'clock by now."

It was closer to midnight, but Josie decided not to

impart that bit of information.

"I guess I really should be asleep, but I simply could not resist coming out and enjoying at least a few moments out here before heading off to bed. Aren't the stars magnificent?" she asked, in an attempt to steer the conversation in a new direction. She wanted to discuss anything but her reason for having gone outside.

Nathan turned his face skyward. "Yes, they are. Very beautiful. So's the moon. It should be full in a few nights' passing. Possibly by Thursday," he told her. But his gaze stayed with the spectacular sight overhead for only a moment more before he returned his full attention to her. "Still, the beauty overhead pales in comparison to yours."

Josie's eyes were enormous when she looked at him then. She was too surprised by such complimentary words to make any immediate comment. So surprised she was not at all certain she'd heard him correctly. She studied his serious expression only a moment longer before forcing her attention back to the star-filled sky overhead—all the while wishing he would do the same.

But he didn't. The stars held no further interest for Nathan. His interests lay solely with the woman who now stood before him. He studied her profile, bathed now with silvery splashes of moonlight. With her attention still drawn to the sparkling treasures in the night sky, he allowed himself a long moment of pleasure by allowing his gaze to travel over every perfect detail of her upturned face. She was truly the most exquisite woman he'd ever seen.

Suddenly, looking at her was not enough. He wanted to reach out his hand and touch the velvety smoothness of her skin. He wanted to sample yet again the honeyed sweetness that lingered along the gentle curve of her lips. And at the same time, he longed to trail his fingers through the thick, soft tresses of her long brown hair, which fell in quiet disarray about her shoulders.

Never before had he felt such an overwhelming urge to seduce a woman. He ached with want of her.

"It's time," he said in a low, silky voice.

Josie again lowered her gaze to meet his. She felt an instinctive urge to swallow, but couldn't. Instantly aware of what he intended to do, her pulses raced forward through her body, driven by a sudden leap of apprehension. There was no mistaking the dark passion that caught the moonlight and reflected from his eyes.

"Time?" she asked, hoping to sound confused, though at the moment the only thing that really confused her was her own unexpected willingness to be kissed.

"Yes. Time. For our kiss," he answered, then wasted no more time with silly explanations. Instead, he took the final step that brought them together. His arms came around her as he gently lowered his lips to take hers in what proved to be a truly masterful kiss.

Held motionless by her own blossoming desire, Josie did nothing to stop him. Instead, she convinced herself that he had at least one kiss coming to him and tilted her face upward to better accommodate the gentle pressure of his mouth as he slowly pulled her closer, drawing her soft body firmly against his own sturdy frame.

A shockwave of sensations resulted, gently cascading over Josie like a warm waterfall and awakening a response that both amazed and alarmed her. It was as if the kiss had set fire to her very soul. Warmth invaded every hidden crevice of her body while her heart soared to a new and dizzying height. Frightened by the overwhelming power of it all, she tried then to pull away, if only to steady herself. But he would not allow it. He drew her closer still.

The feel of his arms around her and the hungry pressure of his lips as they refused to relinquish possession of hers sent wave after burning wave of unfamiliar need coursing through her body. The need became so strong and so basic and bore down on her with such force, it became almost frightening.

A distant alarm sounded somewhere in the back regions of her mind, warning her of the danger, warning her not to give in to the overwhelming intensity of her own womanly desires. But reason was slowly giving way to something she did not fully understand. Something so powerful, so all-consuming, she knew she would be powerless to stop it if she didn't do something right away. Again, she tried to pull away—only this time, he let her.

His hands rested gently along the outer curves of her arms while he stared at her a long, maddening moment. His chest rose and fell sharply with each needed breath he took. There was something in his eyes that looked to be akin to anger. But it was not quite that. Josie wasn't sure what the emotion might be and was afraid to find out. She swallowed apprehensively as she took a tiny step back.

The muscles along Nathan's jaw flexed in and out while he continued to stare at her for another moment. Then, without uttering more than a simple good night, he turned his back to her and walked away, headed straight for his bedroom.

Dazed and breathless, Josie stood motionless while she watched him go—more aware than ever of the very real danger that lay ahead.

Chapter Twelve

When Josie approached Nathan the following morning, it was with extreme caution. As had become his custom, he had retired to the library shortly after an early breakfast. He sat behind his father's desk, bent forward reading when she entered.

Not wanting to disturb his concentration, she waited for him to either set aside what he was reading or glance up. Meanwhile, she stole the opportunity to study his rugged masculinity. How truly handsome he was, even dressed in his everyday work clothes. Just being in the same room with him caused an odd stirring somewhere in the vicinity of her heart. She could no longer deny that she was starting to care deeply for this man. Maybe too deeply.

The memory of their moonlight kiss lingered, stirring fire into her blood. She reached up to touch her lips in a purely reflexive gesture. It was the simple movement of her hand that caught his attention. Afraid the sudden tightness in her throat might hamper her speech, she drew in a deep, stabilizing breath before daring to speak.

"Nathan, I hate to bother you when I know you are so busy," she began. Her movements were uncharacteristically awkward when she stepped closer to the desk. "But now that it's pretty clear I'll be staying, I need to ask you to do something for me."

Afraid her next words would be another request

that he stay away from her, he hesitated to respond in the affirmative. Though, privately, he had vowed not to allow last night to repeat itself—as much for his own sake as for hers—he refused to go back to partitioning himself off into a separate area of the house.

"That depends on what it is you want me to do," he replied cautiously while he set aside the heavy ledger book he'd been studying. For the moment, she had his full attention.

Finding his probing gaze distracting, she looked down at the many papers scattered across the desk, only vaguely aware of how hard they would be to decipher. The handwriting was atrocious. "A little over a week ago you said something about setting up an appointment with your father's lawyer so I could meet him. Can you still do that?"

Relief washed over him. She was not asking him to stay away, nor was she demanding he never touch her again. She was merely asking for his help—on another matter entirely.

"Of course I can still do that. But I thought you'd decided against meeting with him."

"I've changed my mind. The more time I spend in this house, the more aware I become of the fact this was once my grandmother's home. I find myself thinking about her more and more often. I want to know more about her. I know I run the risk finding out things I might not like, but I have to discover what sort of person she was. I have to know why she chose to live her life the way she did, why she did what she did to my grandfather. It has become very important to me to know what she was like."

Able to see the sincerity in her request, Nathan's heart went out to her. He could tell by her downcast expression that she was hurting inside. Slowly, he rose from his chair and stood only inches away. How he wished he had the courage to reach out and comfort her. But after last night, he was afraid to. He was afraid of what might happen. "I'll help in whatever way I can."

The tenderness in his voice came unexpected, causing Josie a moment's pause. Fighting an overwhelming rush of emotion, she continued to glance down at the odd assortment of items on his desk. "Then you'll talk to him for me."

"Of course I will," he answered, suddenly so full of compassion for this beautiful young woman that he ached. When she then brought her gaze up to finally meet his, he was momentarily lost in their huge green depths.

Josie was afraid to place too much hope on what the lawyer might be able to tell her. The man might know nothing at all about her grandmother. "Do you really think this lawyer will know something about my grandmother?"

"Yes, I do. I think he will at least be able to tell you that he's met her. After all, Jason was Father's personal friend in addition to being his attorney, and your grandmother was Father's wife. They had every reason to meet. I'll send Rafe into town right away with a message asking Jason to come out at his next earliest convenience. I figure he'll come right away. He's been wanting to meet you."

"He has?" Josie looked at Nathan, puzzled. "Then why didn't he simply have you call me downstairs that day he was out here?"

It was Nathan's turn to feel awkward. "Oh, he asked me to. But, as you probably recall, at that time I was still trying my level best to keep you in the dark as to the real reason you were brought here. I was afraid he would let something slip that might arouse your suspicions. So I firmly refused to let him talk with you. But I did let him slip upstairs and catch a glimpse of you from the hallway while you worked. The only reason I allowed that was because he claimed he had to see you for himself before he could officially mark the start of our three months."

Amazingly, Josie no longer felt angry about all that. She'd come to accept his deception as a poorly conceived plan to get her there and nothing more. And she had to admit the ploy had worked. It certainly got her there. Despite the very real risk he'd taken of losing all that money, he had managed to come away with exactly what he wanted. She had to admire him for that.

"How could he be sure I wasn't just another housekeeper without actually coming into the room and talking with me?" she asked, thinking the man had been too easily satisfied.

"That's what made him so nervous about the whole situation. He couldn't. He had only my word that you were who I said you were, which was the word of a man he'd never met. Sure, he knew my father was a man of fair integrity, but he has no way of knowing what sort of man I am." Nathan laughed. "I'm sure he had some pretty clear doubts about me, especially after I told him the story behind how I got you here. I imagine he's wondering if the story might have been a ruse I'd come up with in order to keep him away from you. And if it was merely a way of keeping the two of you apart, his next worry would be why I'd even want to. That's why I figure he'll waste no time getting out here to finally meet you. Hearing you officially state your name will clear his conscience at last. It's my guess he'll drop any plans he has made for this afternoon and come today."

Nathan couldn't have predicted the man's actions any better. Less than half an hour after the groundskeeper had returned with Jason Haught's written confirmation that he would be on his way within the hour, the man's oversized carriage was heard bumping and jingling along the narrow drive that circled the lake.

Josie was on tenterhooks as she waited for Nathan to formally greet the man at the front door then escort him into the library where she waited.

"There she is," Nathan commented as the two men came into view. A gleaming smile came immediately on the heels of his reassuring words while he followed the thin, silver-haired man into the room. "Just like I said she would be."

Coming to a dead stop in the center of the room, the older man's eyes grew wide with recognition. "The resemblance is amazing."

Josie's heart froze, aware of the indication but still afraid to hope.

"Then you did know my grandmother?"

"Of course I knew her," Jason answered, blinking hard and adjusting his wire-rims as if unable to believe his own eyes—even after he'd moved closer. "I knew her very well. And you, my dear, are the very image of her."

Tears of joy sprang to Josie's eyes. "Please, come and sit down. I want you to tell me about her."

Taking the chair offered him while Nathan rested a well-muscled thigh over the corner of his desk, Jason continued to stare at Josie with open fascination. "What is it you want to know?"

"Everything. I want to know what sort of person she was. What she liked to do. What it was like to be around her." But mostly Josie wanted to find out why her grandmother had chosen to run away and leave her family behind.

Jason smiled with remembrance. "Your grandmother was a fun sort to be around. Even when she was feeling down, she still found a way to make those around her laugh. She was a true and caring

203

lady, that one. Beautiful and high-spirited, too, yet at times fragile as a kitten. But, then again, there were other times when she was almost more woman than poor Carl could handle."

"Was she? In what way?" Josie was delighted by his words and eager to hear more.

Jason laughed. "Ah, she had a mind of her own, that one did. And she had no qualms about letting you know it."

Nathan grinned, unable to resist an insert. "It's a family trait, I'm afraid."

Josie narrowed her eyes and looked at Nathan with clear warning, though her next words were still directed to the lawyer. "Just ignore him. You'll find he's harmless enough. Please, do go on."

Nathan's eyebrows rose, amused, but he held back any further comment, giving Jason the opportunity to continue.

"I don't really know what to tell you. Your grandmother was a beautiful, kind-hearted woman. She brought such joy to Carl's life. I know most people did not fully understand their relationship, nor did they wish to. I have to admit I didn't really understand it at first, either."

"Why not?"

"Well, when he first told me that he actually planned to marry Annabelle, I didn't understand how Carl could be quite that taken with a woman three, almost four years, his senior. But that was all before I met her. To tell you the truth, after Carl finally introduced us, I was quite taken with her myself," he told her, smiling when he then reached inside his coat pocket. "By the way, I have some letters here for you."

"Letters?"

"Yes. Your grandmother wrote them years ago."

"And they are for me? I can have them?" she

asked eagerly.

"Of course you can have them. They are written *to* you. I had originally planned to wait and give them to you the day Carl's will is finally read, I guess because they are mentioned in his will. But after I read Nathan's letter explaining how concerned you'd become over the matter, I realized there was nothing in Carl's instructions to prevent me from giving them to you now."

When his hand came away from his coat, it held a stack of yellowed envelopes, several inches deep, bound together with a small black ribbon. "As you can see, I have not opened them. I have no idea what sort of information they contain, only that Annabelle wrote the letters herself. I hope they will provide you with a few answers."

Josie's hands trembled as she reached out to accept the precious bundle.

Realizing how very close to tears Josie had become, and how embarrassed she would feel if she did indeed break down and weep before them, Nathan attempted to draw everyone's attention to himself by slapping Jason soundly on the shoulder in what was purely a friendly gesture. "What do you say to a good stiff drink about now? I imagine you could use one after that long, dusty ride out here."

"Actually, I'd prefer you offer me a nice hot cup of coffee," Jason suggested instead. "I was up all night trying to solve a personal matter, and I very nearly fell asleep on the ride out."

"Coffee it is," he responded with a firm nod. "What about you, Josie? Would you care for a cup of coffee?"

"What?" Josie asked. Her expression was as lost as a child's when she looked up from the letters held tenderly in her hands. She had been so engrossed with seeing her name written in her grandmother's very own handwriting that she'd heard her name and nothing else.

"Jason and I are about to have a cup of coffee. Would you care for any?"

"No. None for me."

"Oh, that's right," Nathan said, frowning. "I forgot. You don't drink much coffee. How about a glass of lemonade instead."

Eager to concentrate on the letters, Josie nodded agreeably. "Lemonade will be fine."

"I'll see if I can't round up a few teacakes while I'm at it," Nathan promised just before he left the room, with that sad little look on Josie's face embedded in his heart forever.

Already having returned her attention to the letters that rested gingerly in her lap, Jason studied Josie for a long moment before attempting to say anything more. "I gather by the condition of some of those envelopes, especially those near the top, that the letters date back quite a few years. Of course, I realize they have to date back at least to 1867 to have been written in her own hand, but some look even older than that."

His words served as a grim reminder. Annabelle Garrett had been dead for nearly eight years. Odd, it didn't seem that long ago to Josie.

"How did my grandmother die?"

Jason looked toward the elaborately designed bay window, as if trying to see the past through its tiny leaded panes. "Annabelle was ill for several months. It started out just like another one of those weak spells she was always having, only this time she was unable to pull herself out of it. Instead, she grew steadily worse, until finally she died. I'm really not sure what the illness was that took her. I never felt it was my place to ask. But then she was always such a fragile woman healthwise."

Josie couldn't imagine it. Not the strong-willed, high-spirited woman her father had so often told her about. "Fragile? In what way?"

"I don't know how to describe it exactly. Though she was always strong in both heart and spirit, there were times when, physically, she was as weak as a child."

"I wonder why?"

"I don't know. She never talked much about her ailments, leastwise not with me." Jason's expression grew more distant. "I imagine Carl knew."

Josie felt an odd kinship with this man, who obviously had cared very much for her grandmother. She felt she could ask him anything. "In your talks with her, did she ever mention me? Or my mother?"

"On occasion," Jason said, smiling as he recalled a particular conversation. "I remember once, she'd just gotten a letter from your father telling her about some important spelling bee you'd won. She was so bursting with pride, she couldn't wait to tell someone. You should have seen her. She was waltzing about this very room waving the letter in front of our faces, but never holding it still long enough for us to actually read it for ourselves while she jabbered something about how incredibly smart you were. But, because she was just getting over one of her weak spells, Carl had to catch her in his arms and physically force her to sit back down."

"My father wrote her?"

"Yes, didn't you know?"

"No, I didn't," Josie admitted, her eyes wide at the thought of it. "I had no idea."

Jason's face grew pensive. "I gathered by the way Carl talked, your mother had refused to have anything to do with Annabelle, not even enough to answer her letters. So your father took it upon himself to keep your grandmother informed of what was

207

going on with the family. How I would have loved a chance to thank that man for all those wonderful letters did for Annabelle. I know it may be hard for you to believe, but she loved you and your mother dearly."

Josie felt years of suppressed emotions burst forth. How she had longed to hear such words. She looked again at the letters resting in her lap. Would they serve to reinforce what Jason Haught had just told her? Did her grandmother truly love her? But if that was so, why had she never tried to see her? Why had she never mailed these letters? What kept her away?

When Nathan entered the room moments later, he found Josie still very near tears, and for a moment he fought the urge to go to her and take her into his arms. How he wanted to reassure her that whatever her fears, even if they should prove to be true, she could overcome them. But he didn't dare take such a risk.

"Coffee was already on the stove. I told Ruby to bring it in just as soon as she can get it into a serving pot and then onto a tray."

"And the teacakes?" Jason asked, turning in his chair to speak to Nathan.

Seeing that the lawyer, too, was very near tears, Nathan felt another hard tug at his heart. If he didn't do something to change the mood in that room and soon, he also would find himself on the verge of tears. Yet he had no idea why.

"I'm afraid there won't be any teacakes this time. But Jeanne made some sugar cookies early this morning and has promised to put a plateful on the tray."

Josie turned her thoughts away from the conversation between the two men. Her interest lay with the letters Jason had given her and in the sort of messages they might contain. She was only vaguely aware when Ruby entered with the coffee, cookies, and lemonade, until she heard the woman's harsh tone of voice, but finally, she pulled her thoughts back to what was going on around her.

"Why can't he just reach over there and get 'em hisself," Ruby asked, her narrow face drawn into an annoyed scowl. "I put them on the table right there in front of him just so he could get to them. What's the matter with him? He got a broke arm?"

"Ruby! That's quite enough," Nathan reprimanded her, shocked by her rude display. "I want you to apologize to Mr. Haught immediately."

"Me? Apologize to the likes of him?" Ruby puckered her face with outraged disgust. "Why should I? Just because he's got lots of money and I don't?"

"No. Because if you don't apologize to the man, you will find yourself out of a job," Nathan stated in a low, grating voice. The muscles in his jaw tightened to show that he meant what he said.

Ruby stared at him defiantly for a moment, then turned her hardened gaze on Jason. Her lips pressed into a grim white line while she studied her situation further.

"Please, Ruby," Josie encouraged. "He's our guest."

Ruby glared at Josie angrily, as if she thought Josie had no right to intrude on this matter. The muscles in her withered jaw pumped in and out. "All right," she finally said. Her nostrils flared and her expression twisted until she looked as if she'd just bitten into something vile. "My apologies, *sir*."

Then before anything else could be asked of her, the little woman spun about on her well-worn boot and marched determinedly out of the room, giving Josie and Nathan one last hate-filled glance before disappearing from sight.

"I'm sorry about all that," Nathan said, staring after the woman with stunned disbelief. "I can't imagine what got in to her. She's always been the cantankerous sort, but I've never seen her behave with such belligerence. I'll see to it she is properly reprimanded."

Jason sighed and gave a tired shake of his head. "It's perfectly all right. I can't very well blame you for her rude outburst. Actually, I have only myself to blame. After all, I'm the one who found her for you. I should have researched the woman's character a little better before agreeing to recommend her to you. I don't know why I didn't. I had plenty of references I could have checked out. She just seemed so sincerely in need of work, and you know how hard jobs are to find around these parts. Still, I should've taken the time to check her background. If anything, I'm the one who should apologize to you."

"That's true. You did recommend her," Nathan agreed with an easy laugh. "I take back my apology."

"Just as long as you don't take back your coffee," Jason responded with a laugh of his own as he raised his cup to his lips again. "This is really very good. At least I managed to do one thing right. I did find you a competent cook."

With the tension gone, the two men turned their discussion to some of the things they had in common. Josie barely listened, idly fingering the black ribbon that held the letters bound tightly together while she continued to wonder about them. Finally, she couldn't wait any longer to find out what was in them.

"If you two will excuse me, I think I'd like to go up to my room now. I'm anxious to read a few of these letters."

"Of course, we understand," Nathan said. And, though he wished it was something she could share with him, he did understand. He had felt the same need to be alone when he first entered his father's studio.

Josie tried not to let her frustration get the better of her while she searched her bedroom for a pair of scissors. Having discovered the ribbon to be so securely knotted she could not possibly untie it, she realized she would have to cut it before she could get at the letters. But there were no scissors to be found.

Finally, she came across her silver manicure file and decided to saw her way through the surprisingly thick ribbon. The process was maddeningly slow.

By the time she'd lifted the first envelope off the top of the stack and slipped the folded yellow paper from inside, her hands trembled. She was eager to read what her grandmother had to say, yet at the same moment she was afraid. Confused, tears burned her eyes, blurring her vision. She had to take the time to dash them away before she could read the neatly penned words on the pages before her.

The date at the top of the first letter surprised her: April 3, 1861. The letter had been written on Josie's ninth birthday. She wondered if that was merely a coincidence, or if her grandmother had somehow known the exact date of her birth. She felt a sharp ache of anticipation while she carefully pressed the folded paper flat across her small writing desk before she leaned forward to read.

My Dearest Josephine,

I'm afraid your mother has yet to find it in her heart to forgive me. My letters continue to be mailed back to me unopened. Your father, Lowell, writes from time to time. He encourages me not to give up hope. He believes Stella has started to change some in her feelings toward me, but I find myself afraid to put too

211

much faith in that. I fear my daughter is lost to me forever. I only hope you do not feel the same.

I understand from Lowell that today is your ninth birthday. He also tells me you are growing like a weed and can climb through the trees like a little squirrel. Your father claims you are going to be tall and willowy like me. He says you even look a lot like me. I wish I could see that for myself. I have asked him to bring you for a visit, and he says he is truly considering it, but I fear he will in the end refuse. He doesn't want to hurt Stella. He loves her dearly and believes she has suffered enough.

And I must agree. Stella has truly suffered enough. It breaks my heart to know that I am the cause of so much of her grief. But I simply could not stay in a loveless marriage. I had to get out and find happiness while I had the chance.

I wish she would give me the opportunity to explain that to her. My leaving was in no way meant to reflect against any of my feelings for her. I loved her. I still do. Just as I love you. It broke my heart to have to leave my precious little girl behind, just as it breaks my heart that she has yet to find it in her soul to forgive me. But what sort of life could I have offered her?

She was better off there, surrounded by family. I wish I could make her understand. It was because I loved her as much as I did that I was able to leave her behind. The only one I no longer loved was your grandfather. Someday, when you are older, I will try to explain why that was. For now, it is enough that I tell you how very much I love you. And I do hope you are having a wonderful birthday, just as I pray you are having a wonderful life.

Oh, but wouldn't it be grand if I could tell you these things in person? Yet I doubt I can even find the courage to mail this letter. What point would there be? Stella would simply return it to me unopened, just like she has all the other letters I've written. I don't know why I even continue to write them. But I do. I guess it's that I do so cling to the hope that someday your father will see fit to carry my letters to you. He's such a good man. I think maybe he will agree to take some of them to you after you get a little older. I do so look forward to that day. Then, maybe you can write to me.

With Love Always,

Your Grandmother
Annabelle Seger

While Josie refolded the letter and slipped it back into the faded envelope, she thought about what she'd read. She thought about all the heartache her grandmother had suffered, then she thought about all the heartache and bitterness her mother had borne. Then she thought of her own heartache.

It hurt to know everything might have been resolved and compromises met if only her mother had opened one of her grandmother's letters. If only her mother had been willing to learn her grandmother's reasons for leaving, whatever they'd been. At least her mother would have died knowing Annabelle Seger had not left her behind because she didn't love her. Instead, it had been because she had loved her so dearly.

All these years, Josie had believed the woman had been incapable of really loving anyone. It was startling to discover she might have been wrong. The woman might not have loved her husband, but she had truly loved her daughter.

The pain that resulted from such a startling discovery started small, but grew until it became far too much for Josie to bear. Silently, she covered her face with both hands and wept.

Chapter Thirteen

"Nathan, you'll be glad to know that because Saturday was the first of the month, I released the money to cover the expenses you've incurred thus far," Jason commented as he bent forward to set his empty coffee cup on the tray in preparation to pour himself more. "I went ahead and paid that mercantile bill myself to save you the trouble. But because the rest of your expenses came directly from your own pocket, and because at the time I didn't know I would be coming out this way anytime soon, I simply transferred the remainder of the money to a special account at the town bank—in your name, of course."

"Thank you, I appreciate that," Nathan responded with an understanding nod. "But I'm not exactly hurting for the money just yet."

"I didn't think you were. Not after winning as much as you say you did while you were in Cypress Mill. But it's my duty as the temporary guardian of your father's estate to see to all the expenses on the first of each month. So I went ahead and took care of everything you'd turned in so far. If I'd thought about it in time, I guess I could have stopped by the bank and withdrawn the money for you before coming out here. But I'm afraid it completely slipped my mind."

"That's perfectly all right. I don't really need it

yet, but it is nice to know the money's there whenever I do need it."

There was a short pause while Jason arranged his cup just so. He then reached for the tall handle on the silver serving pot and asked, "Is it safe to assume, by the simple fact I haven't heard from you in over a week, that you've finally found those keys?"

"Yes, in a way. Actually, it was Josie who found them," Nathan admitted with a shake of his head. "Strange as it may seem, while I was in town trying my darndest to find out if you had any idea where those keys might be, Josie was in this very room cleaning, and happened across them quite by accident."

Jason looked at him, puzzled. "Oh? I thought you said you'd gone through everything in here."

"I thought I had. Seems they were hidden away inside a fake book of all things." Nathan set his own empty cup amid the clutter on his desk, then circled around to the shelves directly behind him. Picking out the volume titled *Hidden Treasures,* he carefully removed it from the rest and held it out to Jason. "They were hidden away inside here all that time."

Jason pursed his lips while he thought about it. "That seems awfully strange to me. Why would he keep his keys in here? Why not in his room where he could get to them at a moment's notice?"

"Maybe he wasn't in his room."

"Had to be. His boots were up there, right beside his bed, when your aunt discovered him. It appears to me he was up there already getting ready for bed when something lured him downstairs. I just don't see why those keys would be hidden away in here when he was obviously upstairs in his bedroom."

"Maybe he put them in here just before he went

216

upstairs," Nathan said, trying to find logic in the situation.

"But then he'd have to come back down here in order to get them if and when he needed them."

"Could be that was what he was doing when he fell. Maybe he hadn't intended to leave them down here. Maybe the whole reason he was coming down those stairs was to get his keys."

"Possibly, but it just doesn't seem like the sort of thing your father would do. He was too used to having those keys with him when he needed them. I just don't understand why they were down here of all places."

Nathan thought about that while he shut the false book and returned it to the shelf. "Come to think of it, there's something else not quite right. Those keys." He reached into his pocket and brought them out.

Jason rose from his chair and crossed the room to have a closer look.

"Look at how tarnished they are," Nathan said, speaking more to himself than to Jason. "If Father had used them as often as you say he did, why hasn't the tarnish worn off from constantly using them?"

Jason took the keys to examine them. Nathan was right. They were almost black with tarnish. "These are not the same keys he carried around with him. I'm certain of it. Look at the scratches that were made from your recent use. The brass shows right through. You are right. Until lately, these keys were not used at all."

"Then this must be a spare set," Nathan said.

"Which means his personal set is still missing."

Nathan and Jason stared at each other a long moment before Jason made the comment, "It might mean that someone else stopped by here before your aunt did, found your father on the floor, looked him over, and took the keys. But why?"

"Maybe whoever it was hoped to return after everything had settled down. Maybe to empty the place."

"Could be," Jason agreed. "Could very well be. But then again, it's still possible our original notion is correct. You may find those keys yet, hidden away in some very clever spot. Just the same, I'd be careful to use not only the regular door locks at night, but any inside door bolts as well. If someone does have your father's keys . . ." He let the thought trail off, then shook away the ill feeling. "I'm probably just letting my imagination run away with me. Still, it's something to think about."

By the time Josie opened the fourth letter, she'd noticed that her grandmother's letters had been kept in perfect chronological order.

The second letter, dated the second of June, 1862, had turned out to be a very touching one, covering such light-hearted topics as the litter of puppies her neighbor's collie had just had and the capricious honey bees that had flown down the dress front of the bosomy preacher's wife.

Josie had to laugh right along with her grandmother when she thought of what the woman must have looked like, hopping about and flailing her arms. She thought her grandmother's final comments were so very appropriate, she read them twice. "And her being so set against dancing in public the way she is! I thought I'd never stop laughing. Ah, Josie, so many things in life are just. If only everything in life could be."

In the third letter, her grandmother mentioned Carl Garrett. The letter was dated October 16, 1863, and this first mention of the man revealed that the two were deeply in love and were soon to be married. Josie wondered if her grandmother's unwillingness to tell her more about him was because she would have been only eleven at the time, and an eleven-year-old was not yet of an age to truly understand such things. Or had her grandmother felt her granddaughter might not want to hear about the man who had so easily stolen her away from her family.

Whatever the reason, by the fourth letter Annabelle was over her initial reluctance and Carl Garrett was the main topic of concern.

According to that fourth letter, which was dated February of 1864, she and Carl were indeed married and in the process of building a very special house out in the country — a haven where they could be alone with each other. She talked of the spring-like weather, of the bright yellow jonquils blooming early by the lake, and of the overwhelming love she felt toward her new husband. If Carl was even half the man her grandmother had made him out to be, it was no wonder he had stolen her heart away. He was far more sensitive about some things than most men, yet he was the very bulwark of her grandmother's existence. And it was with obvious pride that her grandmother had signed that fourth letter, Annabelle *Garrett*.

Josie had already started opening the fifth letter in the stack when she suddenly detected footsteps near her bedroom door. Aware someone was about to knock, she quickly pulled her thoughts away from her grandmother's mysterious past, back to the present.

"Josie?" she heard Nathan call out. At the same moment he knocked. "May I come in?"

Aware the door was unbolted, and also knowing he could still claim his rights to enter her room whenever he liked, she considered the small courtesy to be a true gesture of kindness. She couldn't help but smile with appreciation.

"Yes, Nathan, come in."

There was a moment's hesitation before the door actually opened. When Nathan finally did appear, his face was filled with such honest concern, Josie felt a definite urge to leave her chair and run to him. She longed to feel his strong arms around her. She wanted to be reassured that the deep, hollow ache she felt after having read the first of her grandmother's letters was only a temporary affliction—that the pain would soon pass.

But she didn't dare go to him. She remained seated at her writing desk, the fifth letter still in her hand.

Awkwardly, Nathan stepped farther into the room and immediately noticed Josie had been crying. Though the tears themselves were now absent, the telltale traces lingered. Her eyelids were red and still swollen near the edges, and her eyelashes remained clumped together with tiny droplets of moisture. Sadly, he wondered if the tears had come from the sheer joy of finally knowing something about her grandmother or because of some terrible truth revealed in the letters. Knowing how vulnerable she was at the moment, he prayed the tears were the result of her joy. At least she was smiling now. That was a good sign.

When Nathan did not bother to speak right away, Josie set the letter aside and turned her attention to him. Lifting her hand to tuck an errant curl back into her upswept hairdo, she wondered what she must look like after all she'd just gone through. She hoped he did not find her appearance too appalling. "Yes, Nathan? What is it?"

"Nothing really. It's just that—well, it's after seven now and you haven't been down to eat supper yet. I was worried."

"Seven?" Josie asked, unable to believe so much time had passed. Her gaze flew to the Jeffrey clock on the mantel. He was right. It was twelve minutes after seven. Her gaze then went to the nearest window for visual confirmation. It was nearly dark.

"I'm sorry," she said, returning her wide green eyes to his concerned blue ones. "I hadn't realized the time. I hope you didn't wait supper for me."

Nathan pulled his gaze away from hers and admitted truthfully, "Actually I have."

"But why?"

He shrugged. "I didn't feel much like eating alone." He'd kept his answer simple, though he knew it was only partly true. He also didn't like the thought of her eating alone, or, worse yet, not eating at all. "That's why I came up here. I wanted to find out what was keeping you."

"I've been reading my grandmother's letters."

Nathan nodded to show he understood. "And have you finished them?"

Josie frowned, for in three hours' time she really should have finished. "No. I haven't read them all. I guess I'm a little too enthralled by each new detail I discover about the woman. I stop to give each new tidbit of information my full consideration before going on."

"That's understandable. But do you think you might spare enough of your time to come downstairs and have supper with me?"

221

He sounded so hopeful, Josie hated to tell him no. But she was too eager to finish reading her letters. Solemnly, she glanced down at her hands folded delicately in her lap, then back into his concerned blue eyes. "I'd really rather not eat right now. I'm not that hungry. I hope you can understand that."

"Certainly I do. You want to finish those letters. I'll have Jeanne or Shirley bring a tray. Hungry or not, you really should eat something." Because of the earlier incident in the library, he had purposely neglected to mention Ruby's name. He had yet to have a talk with her about her behavior and could not be sure what the woman might do if asked to take Josie a supper tray.

"That would be nice," Josie answered gratefully and reached again for the fifth letter, thinking he would now leave.

Though Nathan had no further business there, he lingered just inside the door. His hand closed over the brass knob, but he did not bother to turn it. He desperately wanted to ask her about the letters, though he knew their content was none of his business.

"What is it?" Josie asked, aware something still bothered him.

"I was just wondering about those letters. Does your grandmother mention my father at all?"

Suddenly she understood. He was just as curious about his father as she was about her grandmother. Josie smiled, then answered. "Of course she does. Would you like to read the letters?"

"No, they were written especially to you. They're private. I couldn't possibly intrude like that," he stated firmly, though his gaze lingered on the opened letters.

"Go ahead," she said, taking the four she had read and handing them to him. "Take these with you. I can trust you to return them to me when you've finished."

Nathan hesitated again, but in the end accepted the letters she offered, leaving her to finish her reading alone. Though Josie had felt a strong urge to go after him, she didn't. Instead, she wasted little time unfolding that fifth letter, pleased to discover her grandmother had begun using her nickname instead of her full name. She suspected her father might have had something to do with that.

June 6, 1864

My Dearest Josie,

For weeks now Carl and I have had to sleep in one of the servants' quarters downstairs while he and his two helpers worked practically day and night to finish the upstairs. But I'm proud to say that today we were finally able to move into our new bedroom. I had such fun arranging everything just so. I wish you could see it, for it is a truly glorious room which overlooks a beautiful little wooded lake. You would love it. And because I still hope that one day soon you will be allowed to come visit me, I am having the bedroom across the hall prepared especially for you.

Your father, Lowell, has told me how very fond you are of the color yellow. He mentioned that if I was to ever ask you to wear a ribbon in your hair, it had better be a yellow ribbon. Therefore you'll probably be glad to know that the room is being decorated in the brightest yellows I can find. It, too, overlooks the small lake that lies just outside our house, and it even shares the same balcony with our room. I do so hope you like it.

Josie stopped her reading, her face suddenly pale as she looked about the bedroom Nathan had chosen for her. Everything was so cheerful and yellow, even the bedcovers. And the room shared the main balcony with Nathan's room. Obviously, Nathan had taken over her grandmother's bedroom, and she now slept in the very room that had been decorated for her.

Tears burned to her very soul when she thought about everything her grandmother had done in hopes that one day her only granddaughter would come visit.

Well, she thought miserably as she dabbed away yet another tear. *She has finally come to visit.* Only it was too late for Annabelle to ever know. Taking several deep breaths, hoping to alleviate some of the intense pain that compressed her heart, Josie continued with the rest of the letter.

Your father also mentioned how very much you love to swing. Carl said to tell you that he plans to hang a very sturdy wooden swing from one of the oak trees nearest the lake. It is a beautiful spot for a swing. The perfect place for a twelve-year-old girl like you to spend hour after hour in play. You will enjoy it.

Carl has also just this week brought home an adorable little kitten. He named him Scoundrel. When the animal gets older, he is to take residence in the barn and keep mice out of the feed room. But for now, he has the run of the house. You'll love him. He's yellow, and frisky as they come. I do so look forward to the day when you can come to Oakhaven and see him for yourself. Maybe it will be soon.

Love Always,
Your Grandmother
Annabelle Garrett

Already feeling very morose in her thoughts, Josie wondered if the little cat had outlived her grandmother. The letter had been written in the summer of '64. At that time, her grandmother had barely three years yet to live. Josie hoped to discover through the remaining letters that those last three years had been very happy ones.

With a heavy heart, Josie opened the sixth letter, pleased to discover that the only true sadness in her grandmother's life during that time was the fact she had yet to be reunited with her daughter, nor had she finally been allowed to meet her granddaughter. The seventh letter proved no different. Other than the one main disappointment, Annabelle Garrett's life at Oakhaven remained joyous.

But by the seventh letter, written in the fall of 1866, Annabelle's writings took on a far more serious tone and became progressively longer. It was as if her grandmother understood how little time she had left—and there remained so much she still wanted to tell her.

The remaining five letters were all composed within scant months of each other. In them, Annabelle tried to convince her granddaughter to look for the joys in life, to follow her heart in all things—in essence, to do whatever it took to find happiness in her life. It wasn't until the final letter, written just months before her death, that Annabelle finally explained to Josie why she had run away so many years earlier.

Josie's hands trembled when she began reading the very last and longest of her grandmother's letters:

May 12, 1867

My Dearest Josie,

I've received another letter from your father and it couldn't have come at a better time. I was feeling a bit low when the letter arrived. I guess because I've been so very ill recently.

Josie swallowed back the burning ache that had swelled instantly in her throat. The letter her grandmother mentioned must have been written about a month before her father's carriage accident. It was probably the last letter her grandmother ever received from him. Just knowing that made it very difficult for Josie to read on, for she had loved her father dearly.

But I don't want to bore you with the petty details of my illness. I only mention your father's letter, because in it he's made me a promise. He wrote that when you finally come of age, and if we have not yet been brought together by some other means, he will tell you exactly where you can find me, or at least how to get in touch with me by mail. At that time, he will also explain to you how dearly I have always wanted to meet you, how I have dreamed of the day when we can sit together and have long talks about whatever crosses our minds.

Yet, until that day does come, I must be content with writing these letters. And, although I'm aware you are now barely fourteen years old, by the time you are ever allowed to read any of my letters, you will probably be a grown woman. That is why I have decided to say now what I have so longed to tell you. I do so want you to understand why I ran away from your grandfather nearly twenty-three years ago.

Though you may not be aware of it, your grandfather was sometimes a truly cruel and heartless man. I know he did not always show that ugly side of himself, and at times he could be really quite tolerable. But whenever he'd go out and drink too much, or whenever his personal problems reached the point where he could no longer handle them, he would become cruel and abusive. There was very little room for compassion inside Grant Seger, especially when it came to his feelings toward me. He didn't care that I had needs of my own. I was his wife, and he had certain expectations of what a wife should be. He expected me to bend to his every whim, but never saw fit to bend to any of mine.

Whenever he drank too much, which was often, he'd usually come home violent. He then took whatever hostilities he felt out on me. I can't remember that he ever took his anger out on Stella, or even on any of his animals. Only on me. I never understood what I'd done to make him hate me the way he did.

Finally, his violence reached the point where, because he had battered me so badly, I was too ashamed to show my face in town. I was afraid someone would notice the bruises and think I'd done something to deserve such brutal beatings. Because of that, I became a prisoner in my own home. At times, I was so distraught over the way he treated me, the only thing that kept me from taking my own life and ending my pain forever was my precious little Stella. I saw nothing else worth living for.

Until I met Carl.

Carl changed everything for me. He made me see that I was not at fault for the way Grant treated me. He made me feel beautiful again, and needed. He even made me laugh again. And when he then asked me to run away with him, he'd offered me my one real chance to ever find happiness.

When I left with him, I had no way to be sure that what he felt for me would last. But I did see it as a way out of the horrible life I had been forced to live. I did not take Stella with me because I didn't know how long Carl would be willing to help me along. I did not yet understand the true depth of his love for me.

Leaving Stella behind was a decision I've regretted all my life. Just as soon as I was settled and earning my own way as a notions seamstress, I wrote to Stella. I wanted her to come visit me. Secretly, I hoped she'd want to stay. When I received the letter back, unopened, my first thought was that Grant had intervened. But on the envelope, Stella herself had scrawled a message telling me not to bother writing to her again. I was no longer to be a part of her life. I considered going to see her then, but I was too afraid of what Grant might do if I did. I knew he would be very angry with me for what I'd done. I just didn't realize how angry.

Going by the address I'd placed on Stella's letter—in hopes my daughter might write me—Grant attempted to find me. Luckily, I was not home the weekend he visited my house. I was traveling with Carl at the time. But when I came home to find the inside of my home in shambles, all my clothing torn, and my furniture destroyed, I knew it had been Grant's doing. Out of fear, I was forced to move. After that, I used the addresses of post offices in towns other than where I lived and made regular trips to them to see if, by chance, Stella had finally decided to write me. But, as you already know, each time I was gravely disappointed.

Yet, by using the post offices in neighboring towns, I was able to keep Grant from catching up with me until 1859.

Josie's brow drew into an immediate frown. The color drained from her face. Eighteen fifty-nine was the year her grandfather killed himself. She wondered if the two incidents were in any way related.

I was living in Marshall Crossing when suddenly he appeared at my door demanding I pack my belongings and go home with him. He became furious when I told him I had no intention of going anywhere with him. For the first time ever, I chose to fight back, truly fight back. Before the neighbors were able to come to my rescue, he'd broken both my arms and several of my ribs. One of those ribs cut into my lung. I almost died. Much later, I learned that just two days after he'd attacked me, Grant killed himself. You might think I would've at least felt sorry for the man, but, God help me, all I felt was relief.

Understand, I am not telling you any of this to make you hate a man you may very well have had every reason to love. I just want you to understand why I felt I had to run away. And why I stayed away.

After having learned of Grant's death, I tried again to contact Stella. I thought with him out of the way, the two of us might have a real chance to become a family again. Because I was still too weak after what Grant had done to me to make a lengthy trip, I tried to convince her to come and visit me. But, like before, my letter was returned unopened—only this time there was a brief note attached. In it, Stella told me she blamed me for Grant's death and never wanted to hear from me or see me again. If it hadn't been for Carl, I think I'd have lost all will to live after that. But I didn't. I eventually recovered from my injuries enough to go on with my life.

It was shortly thereafter I received my first letter from your father. He had seen the address on the letter I'd sent Stella and had decided to write me, though he said Stella must never find out. It was the first I ever knew about you. How delighted I was to learn I had a granddaughter, even if it was a granddaughter I would probably never be allowed to meet. You were already seven years old by then and, I must say, the very apple of your father's eye.

Once, when Lowell had business in this area, he stopped by for a short visit and brought me a picture of you. You were almost eleven at the time and already pretty as they come. He has promised me other pictures, but it seems you've never been one to sit still long enough for such nonsense. So, for now, all I have is the one photograph but an imagination lively enough to guess what you must look like by now. Just don't ever let your beauty go to your head. It's what a person is inside that counts.

Always live by your heart. Follow it wherever it may lead you. Worry about the consequences only after they occur.

Love eternally,
Your Grandmother,
Annabelle Garrett

As Josie gently refolded her grandmother's final letter, she wondered about that last bit of advice and about the general tone of the letter. Did her grandmother somehow know it was to be her last letter? Josie read the last few lines again. It was almost as if the woman was trying to encourage her to fall in love with Nathan.

It was a ridiculous notion, for Nathan had never once been mentioned in any of the letters. Still, her eyes widened at the thought.

Chapter Fourteen

In the days following, Ruby continued to be angry with Josie for having interfered with the incident in the library. Though she never actually came right out and stated as much, she stubbornly refused to look at Josie, even when addressed directly. Instead, Ruby stood with her back rigid and her chin thrust high, staring stubbornly into space whenever Josie spoke to her. Her responses to Josie's comments amounted to little more than a simple "Yes, ma'am," or "No, ma'am," or "So sorry, ma'am."

Though Josie found Ruby's childish behavior irritating, she decided not to tell Nathan, thinking Ruby's anger would pass with time. She realized the woman's pride had taken a severe blow and needed a few more days to heal. Besides, Nathan had already given Ruby a stern lecture for having behaved so rudely toward his guest. In that lecture, he'd clearly warned that any repetition of such behavior would ensure her immediate dismissal, and Josie didn't want to have any part in causing the woman to lose her job—whether she was obstinate or not. Rather than report her then, Josie chose merely to avoid her. Whenever she needed help with anything, she sought either Shirley or Jeanne, but left Ruby alone.

Meanwhile, Nathan's attention was centered elsewhere. As he became more and more involved with the search through his father's belongings, Josie saw

232

far less of him. He had explained that the main reason he kept so busy sorting through everything was because Jason had requested that he compile a detailed list of everything his father had owned. Jason claimed the list would help move things along far more efficiently once it came time to sell everything.

But, to Josie, Nathan seemed personally driven in his never-ending quest to examine and list every single item to be found. As a result, he spent increasingly more time either in his father's studio or in the library, the two rooms he'd requested everything be kept that had yet been put on his list.

It was as if he'd developed some strong, obsessive need to familiarize himself with as many of his father's personal belongings as possible before selling them. And the more he learned about his father through the things they found, the darker his mood.

Worried for his emotional well-being, Josie tried to lure him out of his sullen mood several times, but each attempt had failed miserably. It was as if Nathan was being haunted by the unknown elements in his father's past. And, though Josie certainly understood his desire to know more about his father, she did not think it was good for him or anyone to dwell on such matters quite as much as Nathan did.

Finally, on the Monday following, Josie decided she could not tolerate Nathan's brooding another day. Determined to pry him away from his desk, at least for a few hours, without bothering to knock she marched into the library where he sat pouring over his father's many ledgers and the different lists he'd been making. She refused to give him the opportunity to ask that she leave him alone.

"Nathaniel Garrett! I've had just about enough of this! I demand that you stop whatever it is you are doing in here long enough to take me on a picnic.

You've been working way too hard lately and I've been in this house with nothing to do for far too long. We both need to get outside and simply enjoy ourselves for a while."

Nathan looked up, surprised by this sudden outburst. With blue eyes stretched wide, he opened his mouth to respond, but was not given the opportunity, for Josie had more to say.

"And, let me warn you right now, Mr. Work-all-the-time Garrett," she continued, wagging her finger only inches from his nose, "I have no intention of accepting a no for an answer. Nor do I intend to listen to any feeble excuses." In truth, she had already spoken with Jeanne and a basket was at that very moment being filled with everything they might need in the way of food and tableware. He was going with her if she had to drag him at the end of a rope.

Still stunned by her sudden burst of assertiveness, especially since the two of them had barely had time to even speak to each other over the past several days, Nathan leaned back in his chair and stared at her. He pressed his mouth shut for a moment and blinked as if he could not believe her brash behavior; but when he finally responded to her simple demands, it was with an agreeable nod.

"You're right. I think a picnic out by the lake is exactly what we both need," he said, tossing his pencil aside and rising instantly from his chair. "Here we both are, heading into our fourth week at Oakhaven, and we have yet to put aside any time to actually enjoy these beautiful surroundings. You'd think one of us would have thought of some sort of outing weeks ago."

Josie smiled. Slowly, her body relaxed. As moody as Nathan had been over the past few days, it was a relief to discover that he intended to accept her demands with no argument. Her green eyes sparkled with delight when she tilted her head shyly and admitted, "Actually, I've been wanting to go on a picnic for several days now, but you've been so terribly busy ever since Jason suggested you catalogue everything before the sale that I was afraid to bother you."

"What made today different?" he asked, quickly marking his place by folding the corner of the page that he had been working on. He came around the desk and when he stopped only inches from where she stood, he looked down at her questioningly.

"I—I'm not sure," she stammered, unnerved by how close he now stood. Suddenly, she felt the urge to put a few more inches between them. Self-consciously, she gestured toward the window with a slight wave of her hand while she took a tiny backward step away from him. "I guess it was all that beautiful sunshine out there that gave me the courage to finally come in here."

"Yes, it would be a real shame to let all that sunshine go to waste," Nathan agreed, already rolling his sleeves in anticipation of the warm, soothing sunrays on his skin. He was far too used to being outdoors to remain cooped up inside that house even one more minute. "Tell you what. You go on out to the kitchen this very minute and tell Jeanne to prepare us a real feast while I run upstairs to find a couple of thick quilts to take along with us." The thought of sharing a quilt out by the lake made his blood race in eager anticipation.

"I've already ordered Jeanne to have our basket made ready," she admitted sheepishly, feeling an unaccountable urge to stare at the floor.

"Oh, you have? Pretty certain of yourself, aren't you?"

"No, not really," she answered, glancing at him now through lowered lashes. If anything, she had expected him to flatly refuse her invitation. "Even had you decided against it, I still intended to take my noonday meal outdoors. I'm tired of being inside with nothing more to do than read yet another book or help sort through your father's things as they are brought down from the attic."

"Well, I have *not* refused. And now that you've suggested it, I find myself suddenly very eager to be outside, too. I'm also suddenly *very* hungry. Go hurry Jeanne along with our food while I get those quilts. I'll meet you out in the kitchen in just a few minutes," he said, already headed for the door.

Josie watched the strong, smooth movements of his legs and arms as he strode out of the room, again reminded of his undeniable virility. She then hurried to the kitchen to do as she'd been told.

When Nathan arrived moments later, with two thick quilts already tucked under his arm, Jeanne stood at her favorite work counter, slicing bread to top off the sandwiches she was making. No sooner did she complete a sandwich than Josie snatched it up and put it directly into the basket, wasting no time to wrap them in individual napkins. Now that Josie knew there was indeed to be a picnic, she was eager to be off.

By the time she and Nathan stepped outside with their basket and quilts in hand, the bright-yellow, early-summer sun had risen high into a brilliant, azure-blue sky. Huge, billowing clouds drifted leisurely on a slow west wind, offering occasional respite from the sun's gentle rays. As they followed the path that led away from the house, a warm breeze swept gently down to tug playfully at Josie's dark-blue skirts and tug lightly at the tiny tendrils of hair that had come loose from her looped braid and curled attractively about her face.

Overhead, while they passed beneath the huge, spreading oaks and towering elms that surrounded the lake on three sides, birds of all shapes, sizes, and colors flitted about from limb to limb. Mockingbirds, blue jays, cardinals, robins, and meadowlarks all chirped and chattered excitedly, determined to keep a cautious watch over the intruders.

When Josie and Nathan neared a small, sunny knoll along the northeast side of the lake, where the huge, shade-giving trees parted and the grass grew green and thick, Nathan moved ahead of her. He placed the basket on the ground and quickly spread out the two quilts he'd brought, one atop the other. It was a lovely spot dotted with bright-yellow wildflowers and dark-green patches of clover. Josie felt it odd she had never noticed the sunny glade during her long vigils on the balcony outside her bedroom.

Glancing back toward the house, now several hundred yards away, she saw why she had never noticed the parklike haven: a tall row of hollyhock blocked her view of all but a small portion of the house. Her pulses reacted vigorously when she realized that, not only were they quite alone out amongst all this beauty—where whatever they chose to say to each other would be very private—but if she allowed Nathan to place the quilts in his intended location, they would be pretty much out of everyone's sight as well.

Lifting her eyebrow, she wondered if Nathan had carefully planned ahead to pick that particular location. But, in the same second, she remembered he'd had no time to really plan anything. The picnic had been her idea, not his. She was making more of the situation than really existed and she tried to push such provoking thoughts aside.

Unaware of Josie's sudden discomfort, Nathan knelt beside the quilts and smoothed as many of the dents and wrinkles from them as possible. His movements drew her attention long before he decided to say anything.

"I don't know how my father ever found this place, being out in the middle of nowhere the way it is, but, I must admit, it is truly beautiful out here," he commented, standing again to regard their surroundings. His expression grew wistful while he glanced around at the beauty of it all. "Sometimes, I actually hate the thought of having to give it up."

Josie felt a sharp tug at her heart. She, too, hated the idea of selling her grandmother's special haven. But what other choice did they have? Neither she nor Nathan really wanted to live there. He had already told her that much. And even if she did eventually find herself wanting to stay on and make Oakhaven her home, she didn't have the kind of money it would take to buy his half from him. Glancing at him curiously, she wondered if *he* had the sort of money it would take to buy her out if he should decide to stay. Because he rarely talked about himself, she had no way of knowing what his financial situation was. She actually knew very little about him and it was time to change that.

"Nathan? I realize it's really none of my business, but I'm curious to know a little more about you," she began hesitantly, testing to see how he would react to a lot of probing questions.

"Like what?" he asked, showing none of the animosity she had feared.

"Oh, like where you live for one thing. Yes, I know for the time being, you live here, but where did you originally come from? Where do you call home?" she asked, watching while he lifted the basket in one easy movement then placed it on the far corner of the quilts. With his shirt-sleeves rolled high, she noticed the way the muscles in his forearms rippled with each movement. How strong he looked. The delicate skin along her neck and shoulders tingled with renewed awareness. "Do you live anywhere near here?"

"No, actually I live a good day's ride from here. I have a small cattle ranch off to the southeast, near a small East Texas town called Kellyville, which is on the road between Jefferson and Daingerfield, though it's a lot closer to Jefferson. The railroad has not yet come into that area, so the only way to get there from here is by horse or buggy, and on roads that leave a lot to be desired."

Knowing that Jefferson lay upriver from Alexandria, Louisiana, just inside the Texas boundary, Josie had a fairly accurate notion where Nathan's ranch was located.

"What's your ranch like?"

"It's pretty nice. The land around Kellyville is similar to around here. There are lots of hills and trees in the area, but I've pretty well got my land cleared. And by selling off the timber as I cleared and fenced my pastures, I earned enough money to build a nice house and get a good start on my herd. When compared to other ranches and plantations in the area, mine's still considered a small operation, but it's gotten big enough here lately to afford six full-time hired hands."

"I imagine you miss the place," she commented, trying to visualize his ranch.

"To tell you the truth, I haven't had much time to think about Quail Run lately. But then, I've left it in a pair of pretty reliable hands. Though the men are probably having a hard time of it, being one helper short while I'm away, I'm really not too worried."

Judging by that last remark, Josie decided Nathan worked with the other men on his own ranch, which accounted for the sun-darkened tone of his skin and the thick calluses on the palms of his hands. Looking at him then, she noticed that his skin had started to lose a little of its tanned color, but he was still clearly a man of the outdoors. How he must hate having to do all that inside work.

"Still, I imagine you miss being there," she commented, her tone distant as she realized that soon he'd be returning there and she'd never see him again.

Nathan noticed her reflective mood and decided she was homesick. She obviously missed her many friends in Cypress Mill. He wished there was something he could do to make the three-month stay easier for her.

"Yes, I guess I do miss it some," he admitted, "but not nearly as much as I had thought I would." Hoping to cheer her sullen mood, he smiled and quickly added, "Besides, it won't be long now before we can both go back home. In another nine days, we will have the first of those three months out of the way. Before you know it, the other two will have gone by and we will be free to start selling everything. And that certainly shouldn't take very long, since Jason has already found a buyer interested in the property and knows of several people interested in Father's paintings."

Instead of cheering her, as was intended, the thought of having to sell Oakhaven to a total stranger made her feel worse. Now that she understood why her grandmother had done all she had done, and how very attached she'd been to Oakhaven, Josie felt almost as if she would be betraying the woman

240

by selling her share of the house. But, on the other hand, what choice did she have?

"Who is this buyer?" she asked as she settled onto the quilts and absently tucked her skirts about her.

"Don't really know who it is. I suppose someone around here. Probably a neighbor whose land already borders with Oakhaven," Nathan suggested, his face twisted in thought. "To the best of my recollection, Jason has never really mentioned any names, but chances are I wouldn't know the person even if he did."

So they would indeed be selling to a total stranger. The thought of it made Josie even sadder.

Misreading her long face, thinking it resulted from her homesickness, Nathan knelt beside her and chucked her lightly under her chin. "Cheer up, rosebud. I'm certain whoever it is, he's very serious in his offer to buy. We won't have any trouble selling the place."

"That's good," she answered and tried to smile, though her heart was not in it.

Deciding the time had come to change the subject to something that would bring her out of her sulky mood, Nathan settled down beside her and began poking around in the basket to see what all Jeanne had packed. "Speaking of good, have you looked to see all the good food we have in here?"

"Like what?" she asked, just as eager to get onto another topic.

"Like ham sandwiches, macaroni salad, pickles, and two large bowls of blackberry cobbler."

"Blackberries? Already?" she asked, leaning forward to look for herself.

"Looks like blackberries to me." Nathan tilted the basket so she could see. He smiled and breathed deeply the gentle scent of lilacs when she bent closer.

He tried not to be too affected by it as he hurried to keep her thoughts off her homesickness. "I haven't had a chance to tell you, but I came across a picture postal card that my father sent to your grandmother back before they were married."

"You did?" Josie asked, glancing up, her curiosity immediately aroused. "What did it say?"

"Evidently it was written while my father was back East showing some of his paintings," Nathan told her while he continued to peruse the contents of the basket, lifting the more interesting items high enough so she could see them, too. "The message on the back was dated late 1859, probably while your grandmother still recovered from the severe beating your grandfather gave her."

"What did he write?"

"Because he was beside himself with concern, he mostly apologized for having to leave her behind with only a nurse and a housemaid to look after her. He seemed very anxious to get back, as if just by being gone, he could cause her more harm. I set the card aside so you could see it. It's still on my desk somewhere. But I imagine I'll have to read it to you. For someone so very meticulous with a paintbrush, my father's handwriting certainly left a lot to be desired. It's not nearly as legible as your grandmother's."

"Speaking of my grandmother's handwriting, do you realize that you haven't yet told me what you thought of her letters?" Josie said, ready to know his opinion of the unusual relationship his father and her grandmother had shared.

Nathan set the basket aside and turned to face her, his expression questioning. "I wasn't at all sure you were ready to talk about them yet."

"Well, I am. I would like to know what you

thought after having read them."

"I felt your grandmother's letters were very touching. I'm glad she thought to write them. They make it easier to understand why she did some of the things she did."

Josie didn't like the way he worded that. "What exactly do you mean, why *she* did some of the things *she* did? Are you blaming *her* for what happened between them?"

"No, not really. But I admit I used to. When I was younger, I didn't want to believe that my father had turned his back on us the way he did because he wanted to. I wanted to believe that Annabelle had done something so evil, so terrible, it forced him to stay away from us against his will, maybe something in the way of blackmail. But when I got older, I realized that was just not true. My father spent most of his time away from us because he chose to."

"Then what did you mean about understanding why she did some of what she did?"

"I was referring to why she left *her* family. After having read those letters, I realized it had not been an easy decision to make. Running away, leaving her daughter behind the way she did, had been very painful. But after reading what your grandfather put her through, it was easy to understand why she did it. It was also easier for me to understand what had brought her and my father together in the first place."

"How's that?"

"I put myself in my father's place and realized my own reactions would have been very much the same. Annbelle's terrible situation had clearly touched his heart. My father had wanted desperately to save her from further cruelty. And somewhere in the process of saving her, he fell in love with her."

"Is that what you think? You don't feel it was a case of love at first sight?"

Nathan pressed his lips together and thought about that a moment before answering. "I'm not sure I believe in love at first sight. It's more to my way of thinking to believe in 'attraction' at first sight." He studied her thoughtful expression while he explained further. "I believe love is something that develops slowly, over a period of time."

"But you do believe in love?" she wanted to know.

"Yes. Of course I do. Don't you?"

Josie glanced down and plucked a piece of broken grass from her dark-blue skirts. She was not sure what she believed about love anymore. Until recently, she'd felt incapable of ever truly loving anyone. Knowing she was supposed to be so very much like her grandmother, who had been known for her careless heart and reckless ways, Josie had always considered herself incapable of ever sharing a true man-woman relationship.

As a result, Josie had always been too afraid to commit herself to anyone or anything — afraid to discover the truth about herself. Afraid she would hurt someone else in much the same manner her mother and her grandfather had been hurt — or worse — afraid she'd be the one to end up bitter and broken-hearted.

But now that she had read through her grandmother's letters, all that was changed. She now understood that there had never been a real commitment between her grandfather and her grandmother, not the sort usually shared between husband and wife.

Whatever feelings her grandmother may have at one time felt toward the man she'd originally married had been quickly destroyed by his terrible outbursts of violence. Love had become a bitter experience, yet her grandmother had somehow come through it with her ability to love still intact. And Josie did not doubt that Annabelle Seger had truly loved Carl Garrett, and, because of that love, had committed herself to him with no reservation. That loving commitment continued to flower and grow ever stronger until her very death.

Her grandmother did not have a wild and careless heart at all, just a lonely heart in search of a little happiness. How very tragic her situation had been.

Noticing Josie had become lost to her own dismal thoughts, Nathan waited before questioning, "What do you believe about love?"

"I believe my grandmother loved your father with all her heart." Josie said, her eyes brimming with unshed tears as she lifted her gaze and scanned the sun-dappled lake before them.

"A love my father obviously returned in full," Nathan said, wondering why he felt such a sudden need to take Josie in his arms and kiss her again. He had promised himself not to become more involved with her than he already was because, in a very few months, which was no time at all, they would both leave Oakhaven and go their separate ways. It was inevitable. Allowing a personal relationship to develop between them would only make their parting that much more painful. He'd suffered enough pain in his life. And so had Josie. So why was he finding it so difficult not to touch her?

Josie glanced at Nathan again. When she did, she became instantly mesmerized by the tenderness in his expression. "It frightens me to think what my grandmother's life would have been like if your father had not come along when he did."

"Frightening," Nathan agreed, though he'd barely

heard what she'd said. His thoughts were on the kiss he longed to take. On the sweetness he knew lingered on her lips.

Aware Nathan's attention had become centered on the movement of her mouth, Josie ran her tongue across her lower lip apprehensively. Her own attention was divided between the uncanny blue of his eyes and the enticing way his mouth parted as he slowly leaned toward her. She felt the walls of her chest tighten around a fiercely thundering heart. "Nathan?" she squeaked.

"Yes?"

She cut her gaze toward the house, only to be reminded of their total privacy. She swallowed hard and returned her gaze to his and looked at him beseechingly. "I don't think we should allow this. It can only complicate matters between us."

"I know," he answered in a deep, vibrant voice as he reached forward to slip an arm around her waist, gently drawing her nearer. "And I fully agree." His head bent forward, his lips coming ever closer. His actions in no way matched the words he whispered against her cheek. "We shouldn't allow anything like this to happen between us."

The kiss that followed was maddeningly sweet. A tender sampling of something now familiar to both of them. A gentle touching, not just of lips, but of hearts as well, followed immediately by a stronger, far more demanding kiss.

Josie was instantly overwhelmed. His sudden possession of her mouth was just as warm and just as masterful as she remembered, causing her heart to soar instantly to the lofts of her soul. She still believed it was wrong. Allowing herself to care for Nathan the way she did could only complicate their lives in ways she hadn't even considered, yet she refused to pull away. She couldn't. Her hands moved first to touch the strong, corded muscles of his back, then slid timidly upward until she felt the solid curve of his neck. Finally her fingertips ducked into the soft thickness of his hair and pressed against the back of his head. She moaned aloud her pleasure when he responded to her exploring touches by drawing her closer.

The kiss continued to grow ever stronger until it was like nothing she'd ever experienced before. Warm, tingling shafts of pleasure poured through her, creating such a fiery turmoil of emotions, she grew weak from the onslaught — consumed by passion never before explored. An unfamiliar ache settled low within her, growing stronger, more powerful with every throbbing beat of her heart. Never had she felt such a true and basic need coursing through her depths. It became hard to catch a breath, and harder still to hold on to a thought. She was lost in a new world so startling, so wonderful, she no longer sought a way out.

Starved for more than Josie had given thus far, Nathan pressed the tip of his tongue past her lips, urging her to part them further. When she did, he dipped his tongue into her mouth, sampling the honeyed sweetness within. To his delight, she responded in kind. He could not remember ever having known such sweetness, nor ever having craved a woman so fiercely. His desire for her pounded through him like a driven thing, making him ache with the need to take his passion another step.

While continuing to support the small of her back with one hand, he slowly brought the other hand forward with slow, circular motions, thrilling at the feel of her taut body beneath the material of her blouse, until his hand rested just below her rib cage.

When he met with no resistance, he moved the hand slowly upward, until he was at last able to cup the underside of her breast with the curve of his thumb and forefinger.

Despite the clothing between them, Nathan's touch burned right through to Josie's delicate skin. She gasped in surprise when his hand moved intimately beneath her breast, and though her brain cried out for her to pull back before it was too late, her body refused to listen. She wanted to know more of the magic Nathan alone possessed. She wanted to find out if what happened next could possibly be as wondrous as all that had gone before.

Though her brain continued to cry out its warning of doom, her heart hammered out a louder message. A message she did not quite understand but could in no way ignore. She was as helpless to pull away as Nathan.

Constantly afraid Josie would at some point again turn away from him, Nathan was careful to go slow. Keeping the one hand where it was, just beneath her breast, he began edging the hand at her back slowly upward. He waited until she was used to the feel of the gentle pressure near her neck before he began to unfasten the many buttons and stays along the back of her dress.

He became so very involved with what he was accomplishing that he did not at first notice the distant sound of an approaching carriage. When he finally realized the noise indicated a visitor was on the way to Oakhaven, he was not sure whether he should curse his luck or be grateful for the timely intrusion. Though he had sought to find a place that would ensure their privacy, hoping for a chance to get to know her better, he had never intended for anything quite that powerful to happen.

His senses still whirled and his heart pounded a wild and furious rhythm when he drew back and turned his head to listen to the sound more carefully.

"Someone's coming," he warned her.

Josie gasped with horror. She heard it, too. Suddenly aware of what she had almost allowed to happen, she drew away, furious with him for having dared been so bold, and with herself for having allowed it. Color stained her cheeks when she wondered what her hair must look like. At the same time she realized the top buttons of her dress were undone and her embarrassment turned to mortification, causing her stomach to knot when she realized that whomever was coming would be in sight at any moment. They would notice her dress undone and know what had almost happened there by the lake. Shame flooded her.

"Who do you think it is?" she asked fearfully while she frantically reached behind her to refasten the tiny buttons near the top of her dress.

"I'm not sure," Nathan answered, his tone grim when he leaned forward to help her with her dress. He knew of only two people who had any reason to visit them.

He hoped it was Jason Haught, simply stopping by to visit again as promised. But the strong, sinking sensation in the pit of his stomach warned him that his aunt Cynthia was on her way, come to check on him at last. Though he'd tried not to think about it, he'd been expecting a visit from his *dear* aunt since the day her house servant had come by and discovered he was living there.

No sooner did he have Josie's dress refastened and the stray tufts of hair tucked back into the twisting braid at the back of her head than the carriage came bounding into sight and his worst fears were realized. Though he did not recognize the driver, the woman in the back was indeed his aunt. Dread settled over him like a leaded weight.

"It's my aunt Cynthia," he told her quietly, never once taking his gaze away from the carriage as it came to a clattering stop along a stretch of drive nearest the lake. "And I think I can safely say she has already spotted us. Prepare to make her acquaintance."

"Is she the aunt you lived with after your mother's death?" Josie asked, squinting her eyes in an effort to get a better look at the woman, who now waved a white, lacy handkerchief high in the air as if she had yet to catch their attention. The woman then climbed immediately down from the carriage, headed in their direction.

Though still some distance away, Josie could already tell by the grayness of her hair and by the manner in which she walked, Nathan's aunt was probably in her early to mid-fifties. And she appeared barely over five feet tall.

"No," Nathan answered her question, his expression somber. "The aunt I lived with right after my mother died was my mother's oldest sister, Michalann. Aunt Cynthia is my father's sister. His only sister. She's the one who lives on father's land, and will for the rest of her life."

"Oh." The word formed on Josie's lips, but no sound came forth. She could tell by the bitter tone in Nathan's voice, he did not hold his aunt Cynthia in high regard. She wondered why.

"I suppose I should go meet her halfway," he muttered, slowly pushing himself up from the quilt.

"Should I come with you?"

"No, stay here. You'll be meeting her soon enough."

Having said that, he brushed some of the grass from his trousers, heaved a heavy sigh, then strode reluctantly toward his aunt, who stepped ever so carefully while making her way through the tall grass toward them.

Feeling awkward at still being seated, though it would be several minutes yet before she was actually presented to his aunt, Josie stood. Self-consciously, she brushed some of the loose grass and wrinkles from her skirt, hoping the woman would not suspect what she had interrupted.

Then, realizing her actions themselves might draw unwanted attention to the rumpled skirt, Josie stopped what she was doing and waited with her hands held politely behind her back. While she watched the two from across the way, she wondered if she would be called forward to meet the aunt, or if the woman would be brought to meet her.

"Nathaniel!" Cynthia called out after she'd glanced up only briefly and saw that he was on his way to greet her. Clearly, she feared she might stumble and fall if she didn't carefully pick and choose every step she made. "It is you. What on earth are you doing back here?"

"Right now I'm enjoying a nice picnic with a friend," Nathan answered simply while he continued to close the gap between them. His carefully guarded expression revealed none of his inner emotions when he gestured back toward Josie with a backward toss of his head. "Would you care to join us?"

"I'd love to" came the immediate response as she stepped forward, holding her skirts with one hand while extending the other toward her nephew. Obviously she expected a proper escort the remaining distance to where Josie now stood nervously waiting.

Because of the manner in which the high grass

251

continued to snatch at the hem of Cynthia's heavy woolen skirts, she kept her gaze to the ground while they carefully made their way to the picnic site.

"First, I suppose I should introduce the two of you," Nathan said when he felt he was near enough to the quilts to be heard by both women.

"Of course, I'd love to meet your . . ." His aunt's voice trailed off into startled silence when she glanced up and noticed Josie for the first time. The woman's face turned a deathly shade of pale as her blue-gray eyes grew to enormous proportions. "You!"

Josie felt the sharpness of the woman's angry response and looked to Nathan for a possible explanation. He seemed just as confused by his aunt's outburst as she was, and just as horrified.

"But, then, it can't be you!" Aunt Cynthia cried out as if trying to convince herself. Her hand fluttered to the starched collar at her throat while she slowly began to back away. Her chest rose and fell rapidly while she spoke. "You can't be here. You are dead! You have to be dead. I stood there and watched them lower your coffin into that black hole myself! I watched them cover you with dirt then pack the earth down over you."

Then before either Nathan or Josie could say anything in response, or even move to catch her, the woman buckled at the knees and sank slowly to the ground in a billowing cloud of gray skirts and old lace.

Chapter Fifteen

"She must have thought you were Annabelle," Nathan stated needlessly as he and Josie both knelt beside Cynthia and began to rub her pale hands vigorously in an effort to revive her. "Or maybe she thought you were her ghost."

"Poor woman," Josie said, aware of the traumatic shock his aunt must have suffered. Worried when Cynthia did not immediately regain consciousness, she glanced up at Nathan, deeply concerned. "I hope we haven't caused her to have a heart seizure of some sort."

Nathan raised an eyebrow at the thought while he continued to rub her hand between his. He'd never considered Aunt Cynthia having a heart.

Slowly the color returned to Cynthia's frail cheeks and her eyes fluttered open, again widening with horror the moment she glimpsed Josie's face hovering directly above her.

"Annabelle!" The word pushed passed Cynthia's pale lips in a terrified whisper. Her whole body trembled.

"Aunt Cynthia, no, you've got it all wrong," Nathan said, hoping to capture her attention before she panicked again, or worse, became violent. "This is not Annabelle. This is her granddaughter."

Cynthia's gaze finally pulled away from Josie's worried expression to blink hopefully at Nathan.

"She's not Annabelle?"

"No," Josie quickly responded, patting Cynthia's hand reassuringly. "I'm not Annabelle. My name is Josie. Josie Leigh. And I'm very pleased to meet you."

Cynthia returned her attention to Josie while Nathan helped her to a sitting position. Her pale eyes narrowed while she studied the young woman more closely. "Of course you aren't Annabelle. What could I have been thinking? I apologize for behaving like such an old fool."

"There's nothing to apologize for," Josie assured her, smiling for the first time, glad to see some of the natural color return to the woman's cheeks. "I understand how you might have made such a mistake. I know how very much I resemble my grandmother."

"That you do," Cynthia remarked brusquely as she allowed Nathan to help her to her feet. Standing again, she clung weakly to his arm while she continued to stare at Josie, her expression disapproving. "I'm afraid you do look remarkably like your grandmother."

Aware the woman's words had come across with the sharp edge of an intended insult, and also aware Cynthia had yet to return her smile, Josie felt suddenly awkward and a little angry. Part of her wanted to tell the woman just what she thought of the cutting remark while another part of her desperately wanted to keep peace between them. She reminded herself that this was Nathan's aunt and the woman had a right to her own opinion, however foolish.

"I know," Josie said, striving to be as polite as possible. "Jason Haught told me that the resemblance between the two of us is truly amazing. I have to agree. I've since seen several of the portraits your brother painted of my grandmother. We do have an awfully lot in common."

"Jason Haught? Has Jason been here?" Cynthia asked, suddenly unconcerned with Josie. Glancing at Nathan, who still held her steady, her brow drew into an immediate frown. "Why would he come by here?"

"Mostly to see how we are getting along," he explained, wondering why Jason's visit should upset her so. As his father's lawyer it was Jason's duty to oversee the estate in the interim period before the will was read. His periodic visits should be expected.

"*We?*" Cynthia's gaze cut back to Josie. "Is she *staying* here with you? I thought she was just here for an afternoon picnic."

Rather than go into all that just yet, Nathan gestured toward the thick padding of quilts with a sharp nod of his head. "Aunt Cynthia, you are still a little shaky. I think it would be best if we all sat down for a while. Have you eaten?"

"I had a late breakfast," she said, clearly unconcerned with food at the moment. "I must say, I was quite surprised to find out you'd returned to Oakhaven so soon. I thought you told me that you had no plans to come back until we were called together for the reading of the will. How long have you been here?"

"Since April 12," he admitted after he had helped her settle comfortably onto the quilts.

"Since April 12? Over three weeks ago? Why didn't you send word you were here?" she demanded to know, her tone suddenly accusing. "Why did I have to find out from my *servant.*"

"I didn't want to bother you," he told her, hoping to avoid the truth. He knew it would make her angrier to learn that he'd hoped not to have to see her at all during his three- to four-month stay. Having seen her that day of the funeral had been more than enough.

"What bother?" Cynthia wanted to know, looking insulted. "You are my only nephew. You should have told me you were here. How long do you plan to stay?"

Her brow rose with keen interest while she waited for his answer, making Nathan wonder if she had somehow found out about the three-month stipulation in his father's will. According to Jason, she had yet to be told about Carl's strange bequest, and in fact had grown rather impatient with him for not calling the family together for a reading of the will right away. Until her illness—which Jason had viewed a godsend—Cynthia had come into his office regularly to find out what progress was being made toward getting all the legal details worked out.

"Plans are to stay for a few months," Nathan answered, sitting down on the opposite side of the quilt closer to Josie, whose presence felt reassuring somehow. "Just long enough to get Father's estate settled."

Josie glanced at him questioningly, but said nothing. She sensed something was not quite right in what they said to each other and in the cautious manner in which they said it.

"Well, it's about time someone did something," Cynthia retorted with a defiant toss of her gray head. Scowling, she explained, "I've asked Jason several times to get on with the reading of that will, but he has refused to listen to me. He claims he has good reasons for putting everything off. I gather there are legal complications of some sort. But he wouldn't ever explain to me what those complications might be. It's as if he doesn't think I'm smart enough to understand all the legal concerns in the matter."

Nathan knew why Jason had kept stalling her, and

it had nothing to do with whether or not she would understand. Jason had delayed telling her anything because he'd wanted Nathan to be the one to tell his aunt about the strange request attached to the will — a request that did not include Cynthia. Jason had avoided telling her anything, knowing how upset she would be when she discovered that except for the fact she'd be allowed to stay in her present home with a regular monthly allowance, her brother had obviously left her out of the inheritance entirely. Besides, Carl's letter had indicated it should be up to Nathan to explain why he'd decided to handle his will the way he had.

"Aunt Cynthia, Jason wasn't behaving so secretively because he thought you would not understand all the legal aspects. He simply wanted to get in touch with me first," Nathan told her, choosing his words carefully.

"Oh, of course, I should have realized," she said, glancing then at Josie. "But I don't understand what *she* is doing here. How, pray tell, did the two of you ever happen to meet?"

"We didn't happen to meet. Because there is a very real possibility Josie could end up inheriting half of everything, I was asked to find her."

"Her? Half of everything?" Cynthia asked, clearly upset by the news.

"Yes, if she stays here at Oakhaven with me for three months, she will get half of everything Father owned," Nathan explained, ready to get it over with, aware his aunt would eventually learn all the details anyway.

"If she stays here with you?" Cynthia asked, clearly appalled by the thought. "All alone? Just the two of you?"

"We're not exactly alone. We have two housekeepers, a cook, and a handyman living here with us," he explained.

"Not what I would call proper chaperones," Cynthia muttered with a disapproving shake of her head. "Maybe I'd better move in with the two of you so there won't be any talk."

"That's not necessary," Nathan responded quickly. The last thing he wanted was to have to see his aunt on a daily basis. "We've already lived here together for over three weeks. If there's going to be talk, I'm afraid it is too late. Besides, I really don't care. I don't know these people. After we've lived out our three months and the will has finally been read and the estate settled, I won't be around to hear what they have to say about me anyway."

"But I will! I live here. And I do care what my neighbors think. After all, I'll have to face these people each and every day for the rest of my life!" Cynthia tried to reason with him.

"Well, it can't be any worse than the talk that went around about my father and his older mistress, can it? At least, in our case, we are sleeping in separate bedrooms. The help can attest to that. Besides, what can happen in just three months? Josie and I barely know each other," he said, hoping to make it sound all so innocent. He fought the urge to glance at Josie and see what she thought of his righteous little speech.

Cynthia studied him a long moment, then looked at Josie. This time there was open contempt in her expression when she asked, "Why do you keep mentioning three months? Why so long to settle Carl's affairs?"

Nathan wasn't sure at which of them his aunt had directed her questions, but decided he should be the one to answer. "Because that's the time limit Father

258

chose. In a letter attached to his will, he requested that Josie and I live together at Oakhaven for three months before the document can even be read."

Cynthia was quiet for a moment. "How very like Carl to do something like that—to make the reading of his will into a contest of some sort," she finally said, her expression hard and her tone bitter. Then suddenly her whole demeanor changed. She bent her head forward, slumped her shoulders, and became instantly teary-eyed. "Poor Carl. I do miss him so. He was such a dear, dear man. We loved each other so much. I'm the one who found him, you know."

"Yes, I know," Nathan said, closing his eyes for a moment. "You told me all about it after the funeral."

Aware Nathan's was not a sympathetic ear, Cynthia turned to Josie while dabbing at the corner of her eye with the dainty handkerchief she still carried. "I had a feeling something was wrong when I first came by to check on him. That's how close we were. I always knew when something was wrong with Carl. I could feel it in my bones. And when he did not answer the door after I knocked, I *knew* something was wrong, terribly wrong."

"What did you do?" Josie asked, not really wanting to know.

"Finding the door unlocked, I hurried inside and discovered my beloved brother lying on the floor. At the foot of the stairs. So pale. So very, very pale. If only I had come by earlier—" she broke into a series of short, rasping sobs, glancing up to see Josie's reaction.

"There's nothing you could've done for him," Josie tried to assure her. She remembered Nathan telling her how the man had fallen down the stairs and died instantly.

"Don't be too sure about that," Cynthia replied,

cutting her teary gaze to Nathan. "I think Carl would still be alive today if only I'd come by sooner."

"You think by being there you might have prevented the accident?" Josie asked, not fully understanding.

"Accident? I'm not so sure it was an accident," she responded, never taking her gaze off Nathan.

"But of course it was an accident," Josie said, unable to believe Nathan would lie to her about something like that. Why should he? "And there was nothing anyone could have done for him. As I understand it, your brother died instantly."

"But if someone had been here, I'm not so sure he would have had that accident," Cynthia stated, almost accusingly.

"You think he would have been less careless if someone had been with him?" Josie asked, also looking at Nathan curiously.

Nathan reached up to readjust his collar.

"I don't know," Cynthia responded. "It just seems odd to me that such a thing happened while there was no one around to witness it. Think about that. Why was no one else here? Pearl, his housekeeper, who rarely ever left Oakhaven, told us later that she had been given Carl's permission to go visit her mother for a few days. That's why she wasn't around to see or hear anything. But if that was true, why didn't he mention her intention to spend the weekend away when I was by earlier that same afternoon?"

"You suspect the housekeeper of having something to do with Father's death?" Nathan wanted to know. A strange, prickling feeling crept along the skin at the back of his neck as he waited for her answer.

"Well, it does seem a bit strange to me that she disappeared from sight shortly thereafter."

260

"Disappeared?" Nathan and Josie asked in unison.

"What else would you call it? Pearl left here only hours after the funeral and no one has seen her since. In fact, she left very shortly after you did, Nathan. Some people think she ran away in an effort to protect herself from something—or someone. Perhaps the sheriff. A good guess might be that she was afraid some clue would be found that would link her to a murder."

"Murder?" Josie's hand flew to her throat.

"Others believe she was innocent of the crime itself but had somehow discovered something she'd been better off not knowing and was killed because of it. Or, knowing that contrary little woman, she tried to use whatever information she'd discovered to blackmail the real murderer. Most folks think her body may yet be discovered somewhere around here."

"That's ridiculous," Josie said, trying not to believe such tales. "With your brother dead, and no one else living here at that time, there was nothing to hold her here any longer. I imagine she went off to find work elsewhere. And the way I understand it, that sort of work is extremely hard to find around here these days. She may have left the area in order to find work."

"Maybe," Cynthia said, though still unconvinced. She then glanced at Nathan with a speculative lift of her brow. "But I still believe if I'd only come by earlier, my dear, sweet brother might still be alive today."

"I think you are grasping at straws. Why would anyone want to kill your brother?" Josie asked, more in an attempt to show Cynthia how preposterous her theories were than to have an answer.

"Who knows what motivates some people?" Cynthia said, keeping her speculative gaze on Nathan.

"Some people just have a lust to kill."

Wanting to change the subject before it became any more morbid, Josie turned her attention to the picnic basket. Quickly she pulled it closer. "I wonder what time it is getting to be. My stomach tells me it must be well past noon by now."

"Your stomach is probably right," Nathan chimed in hurriedly, just as eager to get off the topic of his father's death as she. "Why don't you start getting everything ready while I run back up to the house and bring back another plate, another fork, and an extra drinking glass for Aunt Cynthia. I'll be right back."

Then, before either woman could find a logical reason to keep him there, Nathan hopped to his feet and headed for the house in long, determined strides. He wanted to be away from them for a few minutes so he could think over some of the things Cynthia had said.

"That boy looks very much like his father did at that age," Cynthia commented, watching Nathan for a moment. Then suddenly she cut her gaze back to Josie. "Just be careful whenever you are alone around him."

Josie's eyes widened, wondering if Cynthia suspected what had gone on between them just moments before her arrival. "Careful?" she asked, her voice weak, trying to smile but finding it too difficult.

"Yes, very careful. There's always been something not quite right with that boy." Cynthia paused as if lost in dreary thoughts of the past, then continued. "Mind you, I'm not saying he had anything to do with his own father's death, but the way I understand it, Nathaniel had been in dire need of money for quite some time. Because of that, there's been

262

some speculation that he may have scraped up just enough money to pay the housekeeper to be conveniently gone that weekend. Then it's possible she made the mistake of trying to get even more money out of him by threatening to tell someone what little she knew."

"That's ridiculous," Josie said, coming immediately to Nathan's defense.

"It very well may be ridiculous, but I've known Nathaniel since he was born. I've seen that boy's selfish nature firsthand. I also know what he is capable of doing when he doesn't get his way. Now, mind you, I'm not saying that the rumors are true. I'm just warning you to be extra careful while you are living here with him. Because, if it is true, if he did indeed have something to do with Carl's death, and if he then got rid of the housekeeper so she could not tell what she knew, you could be in grave danger."

"What sort of danger?" Josie asked, finding it hard to believe the woman had practically accused Nathan of such a horrendous crime.

"I seriously doubt Nathaniel plans to let you leave here owning half of everything the way my brother obviously wanted. He'll do something to stop you from claiming half of what he no doubt feels should be his. That's probably why he was so adamant I not move in here. I think he senses that I'm on to him."

"And I think you have been listening to too many idle rumors. As a result, you are letting your imagination get way out of hand," Josie said, still not ready to believe Nathan could be so sinister. "Nathan's not like that."

"Oh, but he is. You might not have seen that side of him just yet, but let me assure you, it's there. I have seen it. I know from experience how easily that boy can lose his temper, and how violent he becomes

263

when he does. Let me ask you something. Who will inherit your half of Oakhaven if you should die before the entire three-month period has passed? If you happen to die *afterward,* your part of the money would probably go to your own next of kin, but what if you died *before* the three months? Who would get your part of the inheritance then? Think about that."

"I don't want to think about such nonsense," Josie stated firmly. "And I don't think you should, either."

"It's always wise to look at all sides, my dear. Especially when your very life may be at stake. And since Nathaniel obviously is not going to let me move in here to help protect you from whatever plans he has for you, I really think it would be a wise thing for me to stop by here regularly. Just to make sure you are safe."

"You are welcome to come visit any time you wish, but I assure you I'm in no danger here," Josie said, although not too convincingly. Because of what had happened only moments before Cynthia's unexpected arrival, Josie had to wonder if she spoke the complete truth. But, even if she was in danger, she didn't believe her danger was in any way the sort Cynthia implied, but instead lay more in the fact that she was slowly starting to fall in love with Nathan. Her only real danger was ending up with a broken heart. After the three months were over and they finally had his father's estate settled, the two of them would then go their separate ways, never to see each other again. Suddenly, it felt as if her heart was already breaking.

"Please don't take my warning too lightly," Cynthia said, unaware Josie's thoughts had taken off in a different direction. She cut her gaze toward the house, then added in a cautionary voice, "You must keep your eye on him at all times, but especially at night. His type usually works under the cloak of darkness."

"Nonsense," Josie stated, this time sounding more adamant. "You are letting a lot of stray gossip go to your head. I personally don't want to hear any more about it."

Cynthia pursed her lips with an expression that clearly meant to emphasize her message of impending doom. It was as if she wanted it understood that she had tried her best to warn her. Whatever happened to Josie now would be of the girl's own doing for not having heeded her warning.

The sharp, clattering sound of a door as it closed across the yard caused both women to look up with a start. Feeling guilty without reason, Josie watched while Nathan headed back toward them with a plate, a glass, and a fork in his hands. Noticing his grim expression when he came nearer, she wondered if somehow he had sensed his aunt's accusations. Josie hoped not. Nathan had enough worries on his mind already.

Though Cynthia did not again mention the ugly rumors she'd heard, and in fact tried her best to be quite pleasant for the remainder of the afternoon, Josie was unable to enjoy herself after that. She could not cast the terrible accusations aside as if she'd never heard them. Nor could she cast her anger aside.

It infuriated her to think someone actually believed Nathan was capable of harming his father — of *killing* him. Gossips. All of them. True, Nathan had never felt very close to his father, but that was Carl's fault, not Nathan's. In the weeks that had passed, she had come to believe Nathan regretted the fact he and his father had grown so far apart. She believed Nathan had always secretly longed for a closer relationship with his father, and she could tell he still hurt because they had never found a way to be close. No, she truly believed Nathan could never physically harm his father, no matter what the reason.

Even after Cynthia had left Oakhaven and Nathan had returned to his work in the library, Josie could not push the woman's carefully worded accusations from her mind. Though Cynthia had never come right out and said that she believed her nephew was guilty, she had certainly left that impression.

By bedtime, Josie was so outraged by all the woman had told her during Nathan's short absence, she couldn't sleep. Each time she closed her eyes, she visualized people huddled together discussing in hushed whispers the possibility that Nathan had killed his own father for the inheritance. She kept hearing Cynthia's high-toned voice in the distance, warning her repeatedly to be careful until she thought she would lose her mind.

Eager to find something less upsetting to occupy her thoughts for a while, Josie finally gave up her efforts to fall asleep and elected to go downstairs and search for something to read. Perhaps a book of poetry would soothe her.

Quietly, so not to wake Nathan, she slipped out of her room into the darkened hallway. Aware the hallway lamp had burned out, she considered stepping back into her room for a candle to carry with her but decided she could find her way easily enough without it. Slowly she headed toward the darker shadows at the top of the stairs. As she reached out to touch the narrow banister, she thought she heard a noise downstairs.

Thinking it might be Nathan, and not wanting to be caught in her dressing robe again, she called out softly to him. When no one answered, she called out again, louder, but not so loud she would disturb those sleeping at the back of the house.

"Nathan, is that you?"

There was a soft, ruffling noise, but still no reply.

"Who's down there?"

She turned an ear toward the dark stairwell to listen for a response, but heard only the sound of muffled footsteps, as if someone was walking around barefoot or in a pair of very soft slippers.

"Shirley? Is that you? Ruby? Jeanne?"

She thought she heard a door close, but could not be sure. Suddenly afraid an intruder had entered the house, she turned back and hurried to Nathan's bedroom door. Rapping lightly at first, then much harder when there was no response, she tried to wake him—pausing just long enough to listen again for noises downstairs. If the intruder decided to come up the stairs and confront her, she wanted to be forewarned.

Finally, fearing the intruder might do just that, she tried the handle and discovered the door unlocked. Stepping inside, she hurried toward Nathan's bed only to discover he was not there.

Confused, she returned to her bedroom and bolted the door, wondering if it was Nathan she'd heard rummaging around downstairs and, if it was, why he had refused to answer her. It angered her that he could be so secretive.

Again, she heard Cynthia's voice warning her to be careful.

"Can you believe that I slept more than half the night outside on the balcony?" Nathan asked upon entering the dining room early the following morning. He groaned when he then arched his shoulders

267

back, as if to stretch the stiffness out of them.

"On the balcony? What were you doing out there?" Josie asked, wondering if he was making excuses for having been gone from his room or if he'd actually been right outside sleeping when she had entered his room looking for him.

"I couldn't sleep, so I stepped outside to get a little fresh air," he said, rolling his head from side to side, still working the stiffness from his muscles. "I sat down in one of those lounge chairs out in front of your bedroom, sort of hoping you would have a little trouble sleeping, too, so I would have someone to talk to. But you never came out, and the next thing I knew, I was waking up from a very sound sleep and it was almost three o'clock."

Josie wanted to believe him. "Why couldn't you sleep?"

"I don't know. I guess seeing my *dear* Aunt Cynthia again got to me. I never have been able to get along with the woman. But you probably already guessed that much," Nathan said, shrugging as he sat down at the table beside her, facing her at an angle. "What are we having for breakfast?"

"I don't know about you, but I'm having biscuits and strawberry jam," she said, opening one of the three biscuits on her plate and filling it with a spoonful of the ruby-red confection.

"Sounds good, if you add a few heaping mounds of scrambled eggs and hash-browned potatoes," he said, reaching for the tiny bell that would call Jeanne or Ruby into the room. "I'm hungry as a bear this morning."

Josie felt torn. She wanted to believe that Nathan had indeed been outside on the balcony sound asleep when she had gone looking for him. But at the same time, she found herself questioning such a story. If he'd gone outside because he couldn't sleep, then how had he managed to fall so very soundly asleep once he'd gone out there?

Though she hated to admit it, Cynthia Garrett had placed some very strong doubts in her mind, doubts so grave and so very real, she decided not to ask him about strange noises she'd heard downstairs—not just yet. She wanted to see if anyone else would admit having been up and moving about during the wee hours of the night before she pointed any accusing fingers at Nathan.

Chapter Sixteen

"What are you doing out here?" Nathan wanted to know, surprised to find Josie entering the barn.

Pleased to see her, he set aside the bucket of oats he intended for the horse trough and wiped his hands on the back of his close-fitting denim trousers. The top four buttons of his pale-blue cotton shirt had been left open for comfort; although it was still morning, the temperature was already entering the eighties.

When he headed toward her, Josie found it hard not to center her attention on the dark hair curling softly across his muscular chest. Her heart jumped at the brazen memory of what that chest felt like beneath the gentle pressure of her palms.

"There are only so many games of solitaire a person can play before losing interest," she answered, feeling a little awkward at having finally decided to actually do something about the way they had begun avoiding each other lately. Lifting her pink gingham skirts just high enough to keep the hem from touching the thick layer of sawdust and hay that covered the earthen floor, she stepped closer. "And since I have nothing else to do at the moment, I thought I'd come out here and see what you were up to."

"Just tending the stock," he said, shrugging as he glanced back at the wooden bucket he'd just abandoned. "After that I promised to help Rafe fix a broken gate out back. Now that I've gotten most of my father's things written down on that list for Jason, I can afford to spend a little of my time helping with some of the chores around here."

"Doesn't Jason want the things in the outbuildings listed?" she asked, studying the way his dark hair had fallen forward during his morning labors giving him a rather roguish appearance. He had not had a haircut since their arrival over a month ago and Josie decided she definitely liked his hair long. The thick, dark brown was an attractive contrast to the pale blue of his eyes and the handsome ruggedness of his facial features.

"Yes, he does, but it shouldn't take long to finish that," he explained. "I still have nearly two months to get everything that's left listed and priced. Meanwhile, there are lots of other things that really do need my attention. After all, I really should do my share around here."

But, mainly, he wanted to find something to lift his plunging spirits. Having to be around his father's personal things all day, casually listing them for eventual sale, had started to put him into a very dark, melancholy mood.

The more he searched through his father's things, the more he wished he could somehow have gotten to know the man—and the gloomier his mood became. In truth, he still had a lot more of his father's things to sort through and list, but he had reached a point where he simply could not go on with it. It hurt too much. He had to get away from it for a few days and get a stronger grasp over his emotions.

"Besides," he went on to explain, not yet ready to admit to his innermost feelings, "I'm not used to being indoors so much of the time. I had to find something to do that would allow me more time

271

outdoors. And believe me, once I started looking around, I found plenty of work needed to be done."

"Is there something I can do to help?" Josie asked, eager to be included.

Having had over a week to think through all the terrible things Cynthia had said about Nathan during the day of their picnic, Josie had finally reached what to her appeared the most logical conclusion. The woman simply did not know her nephew as well as she thought she did.

Though Josie never did figure out just who she had heard rummaging about downstairs later that same night, or why that person had failed to respond to her calls, she had long since decided Nathan had nothing to do with it. If Nathan said he'd fallen asleep on the balcony outside, then that was what he'd done. She refused to believe anything else.

If forced to select the person most likely to have been moving about so late that night, Josie would probably pick Ruby. When she had casually questioned everyone the following morning, Ruby was the only one who refused to answer anything concerning that previous evening. She had been quick to remind her that the night hours were hers to do with what she wanted, and whether or not she had gotten a good night's sleep was her own business and no one else's.

Rather than try to force a response out of the old woman, which might bruise Ruby's already battered pride even more, Josie decided to simply let the matter drop. Nothing had become of the incident anyway. Nothing was discovered missing or broken that next day, or even left out of place. Whoever had been making that noise had done nothing wrong.

But when Cynthia came by two days later, in pretense of bringing two loaves of freshly baked raisin bread, Josie had purposely neglected to mention the strange incident to her. Because of the secretive manner in which Cynthia had taken her aside to question her about any suspicious happenings, Josie decided not to say anything to throw any more fuel into the woman's highly active imagination. Instead, she'd done what she could to assure Cynthia everything was fine at Oakhaven. Still, Josie was not sure the woman had left convinced.

Unaware Josie's thoughts had drifted, Nathan asked, "Do you happen to know anything about repairing broken gates?"

Having effectively brought her thoughts back to the discussion at hand, he smiled at her teasingly. His dimples sank deep into his lean cheeks while he waited for her answer.

"No, but there has to be something I can do to help around here. We've been here for over a month now and I'm becoming very restless. There's nothing for me to do. I'm tired of reading and I'm tired of playing solitaire. I need to find something more constructive to occupy my time."

"What would you like to do?"

Josie frowned. There really wasn't that much she even knew how to do. Her father had pampered her shamelessly in the fifteen years before his death. And then, barely ten months later, she began living with her aunt and uncle, who also chose to cater to her every whim. What little she did know how to do had been forced on her by a mother who had worried her only daughter might grow up to be a completely useless human being, which was exactly how she felt now.

"I don't know what I want to do," she answered, shaking her head. "I just know I want to help in some way. I want to do something to make me feel

273

worthwhile—like when I helped out with the house cleaning."

"And now there's not that much housecleaning to do," Nathan said with an understanding nod.

"Barely enough to keep Shirley and Ruby busy," she agreed. And Josie certainly didn't want to cause either woman to lose her job by taking any of their work away from them—especially knowing how very important those jobs were to both of them.

"Why don't you take another walk?"

"I'm tired of taking walks by myself." Mainly because those walks usually seemed to end at the tiny cemetery nestled beneath a tall stand of walnut trees on a neighboring hill.

Nathan lifted his hand to stroke the strong lines of his chin while he thought about it further. Finally, he asked, "Can you paint?"

"Like your father did? I don't know. I've never tried," she said. Having always liked to draw, she wondered if she might indeed have such artistic talents hidden inside her somewhere. Her eyes widened at the thought.

Nathan's teeth tugged at the inner edge of his lower lip while he considered her response. Then he smiled sheepishly. "Actually, I was thinking more along the lines of painting the barn, but I don't see why you shouldn't try your hand at painting on canvas."

Feeling embarrassed for having jumped to the wrong conclusion, Josie became suddenly interested in the angular shapes of the hayloft overhead.

"Oh" was her only comment.

"Why *not* try your hand at painting pictures?" he went on to ask as he reached into his pocket for the keys. "Why don't you go on upstairs right now and see if there are any clean canvases lying around

Father's studio? I'm sure you'll find all kinds of paints and brushes, and plenty of turpentine. Who knows? You might have what it takes to become a world-famous artist just like my father," he said, hoping to make her feel more at ease over having misunderstood him.

"Maybe I'll do just that—after we've finished painting this barn," Josie said, smiling when she looked at him again. "What color do you think we should paint it?"

Nathan was pleased she wanted to participate. "Rafe and I were discussing the color just this morning. We couldn't quite decide whether to stay with white because it matches all the fences and the two bridges that cross the stream down near the lake or go with a light gray to match the color of the house. What do you think?"

"Gray is a nice color for stone, but I'd prefer to see the barn stay white," Josie said with a firm nod. She did not like the idea of making too many unnecessary changes. She'd rather see Oakhaven stay the way her grandmother had known it.

"That's what I thought, but Rafe kept telling me how we could get by with less paint and a lot less work if we went with the gray. He also claimed it might not need to be repainted quite so soon."

"Still, I think it would be worth the extra paint, and the extra time, to keep it white," she said. Then, as if that should make the decision final, she asked, "When do you want to start?"

"You really don't have to help. I was only trying to think of something you could do that might not be too strenuous. I feel like you've done more than enough of the hard work around here."

He felt a twinge of guilt as he remembered her down on her hands and knees rubbing the hard wooden floors first with soap, then with lemon oil until they gleamed.

"But I want to help," she insisted.

Nathan studied her determined expression. "Have you ever painted anything before?"

"No, but I'm sure I can handle it."

Knowing it was not a job that allowed one to keep both feet on the ground, he asked, "Aren't afraid of heights, are you?"

"Who, me? Not at all. When I was a little girl, I climbed to the very top of the tallest trees in our yard without giving it a second thought."

"Good," he responded with a huge grin. Though he would never admit it, he already looked forward to the chance to spend more time with her. Ever since that unfortunate incident out by the lake, she had carefully avoided being alone with him. He certainly didn't blame her for that, but, even so, he had longed to find a reason for the two of them to spend more time together. "Then I guess we should plan to get started on it later this week. Maybe even as early as tomorrow. I'll fix the broken gate myself. That way, I can send Rafe on into town to get the paint this afternoon. Would you like for him to stop by the mercantile to buy a drape of some sort for your clothing?"

Remembering what a hindrance skirts were when climbing and how much easier it had been to get around when she'd worn her cousin Trey's trousers, Josie decided a drape was not at all what she wanted. "No, thank you. But you might ask him to stop by and purchase a pair of men's trousers for me, and possibly an inexpensive workshirt. I have no idea what size I'd wear, but maybe he can guess."

Nathan's grin widened, certain Rafe would not need to look among the men's clothing at all. Judg-

276

ing by her tiny waist and slender hips, the clothing found in the *boy's* department would come far closer to fitting her.

Thoroughly intrigued over the thought of seeing Josie in trousers, he asked, "Will you be needing men's underclothing to go with that?"

Reddening at the thought, she answered, "No, of course not. I'll wear my own underclothes."

Nathan wondered if that underclothing might be frilled with the ruffles or lace that so often appeared on women's underthings. The thought of lacy underdrawers under a sturdy pair of denim trousers made quite an odd combination, and Nathan found it hard to keep a straight face.

"I'll see what I can do about getting you a pair of trousers," he told her, knowing that was one promise he definitely planned to keep.

Later that same afternoon, Rafe returned with fourteen gallons of white paint piled into the back of the wagon, along with many of the other items Nathan had requested.

"Why so much paint?" Josie asked, when she came outside to watch them unload the supplies, which included everything from a brand-new, six-foot folding ladder to four different-sized paintbrushes. She picked up one of the smaller brushes to examine it.

"Since it's almost a two-hour ride into town, I didn't want to chance running out and having to go back for more," Nathan explained. "Besides, I can always use whatever paint is left over to touch up some of the fences around here. Any improvements we can make between now and the time we finally sell this place will help bring that much more money in the end."

Not wanting to think about having to sell Oakhaven, or about Nathan's determination to try

277

and get all he could for the place, Josie set the brush back down. "When do we start?"

"I'm afraid Rafe discovered several washed-out places along the carriage lane this afternoon and wants to repair them before he gets started on the barn," Nathan said, handing the paint to Rafe four gallons at a time.

Though Rafe was shorter than Nathan, he was just as solid in build and had no trouble handling the bulky load as he stacked it on the ground near the barn.

While Nathan continued to grab the things in the wagon, pulling everything closer so it could be easily lifted out, he added, "But I don't see why the two of us shouldn't get started first thing in the morning."

The thought of working alone with Nathan both pleased and frightened Josie. Her heart thumped at the thought.

"Did he get my trousers?"

Nathan glanced at Rafe questioningly, wanting to laugh at the clear discomfort the man felt over discussing a pair of trousers bought to be worn by a woman.

"Yes, ma'am, I got the trousers and the shirt you asked for," Rafe said, glancing in her direction but never actually looking at her. The skin along the back of his neck and at the crest of his cheeks became as red as the bandana that protruded from his shirt pocket. "They're in that box there with the other supplies I was asked to get for the house. I'll carry it inside directly. Just as soon as we get the rest of these other things unloaded."

"Don't bother," Josie said, hurrying to see what else was in the box. "I'll take it in."

Finding the box heavier than expected, Josie wished she had not volunteered so readily. But unwilling to admit she had misjudged the situation, she heaved the wooden box up into her arms and headed quickly for the house.

By the time she reached the back door, her fingers had grown numb and the box was starting to slip out of her grip. She barely managed to get inside the door before the entire thing collapsed to the floor, scattering the contents in all directions. She glanced back outside to see if Rafe and Nathan had heard the noise, relieved to find they had not.

Rather than put everything back into the box and carry it on into the kitchen, where most of the items belonged, she gathered the items in armloads and spent the next half hour putting it all away, finishing just moments before suppertime.

It was nearly bedtime before she finally had a chance to try on her new trousers. To her delight, they fit very well. They were a little loose around the waist, but the leather belt Nathan had thought to purchase easily solved the problem.

Admiring her new outfit in the mirror, she could hardly wait to see everyone else's reaction when she went traipsing into the dining room the following morning. She remembered how horrified her aunt had been that first day she'd been caught wearing a pair of Cousin Trey's trousers, cut off just below the knees to make it easier to climb trees, and one of his old shirts with the sleeves rolled all the way to her shoulders. Her aunt had eventually decided she could wear the clothing, as long as no one outside the family saw her dressed that way. Even so, her aunt Nadine had never quite adjusted to seeing her niece run about in her son's trousers. But then, there was a lot Josie did that her aunt Nadine had a difficult time adjusting to.

"Like my new outfit?" Josie asked upon entering

the dining room the following morning dressed in her new black trousers with the dark gray workshirt tucked neatly inside the waistband.

Nathan almost choked on a piece of ham when he looked up to see her march casually toward him. The trousers fitted her far better than he had dared hope. The material clung to her hips and molded against her shapely legs when she walked. Curves he'd been forced to only imagine had become clearly evident.

Reaching for his water glass as he stood, he gulped half its contents before attempting to speak. "Yes, I do like your new outfit. Very much." His eyes widened.

"Very practical, don't you think?" she asked, delighted by his startled reaction, and spun around so he could get the full effect.

"You shouldn't have any problem getting up and down the ladder in those," he agreed, almost forgetting to pull her chair back for her. His attention was centered on how very tiny her waist was and how well rounded her hips, fully aware those same trousers would not look quite so fetching on anyone else.

"You're right. I don't think I'll have any problem in these," she said, nodding agreeably as she settled into her chair.

Nathan decided that was an honest enough statement. She should have no problem moving about from ladder rung to ladder rung in those trousers. The only problem he foresaw would be entirely his—because he was going to have one hell of a time keeping his mind off her outfit long enough to see to the matters at hand.

"I guess I'd better have a larger breakfast than usual if I'm to be climbing up and down ladders carrying a bucket of paint," Josie said, reaching for the dinner bell and jingling it slightly.

Within minutes, Ruby appeared, her usual tight-lipped scowl on her thin, wrinkled face, until she rounded the table and caught sight of Josie's apparel. Suddenly, her mouth dropped open and her eyes popped wide. For the first time in Josie's memory, the woman was speechless.

"Ruby, could you bring me an egg and two slices of ham with my usual biscuits and jam?" she asked casually, as if there was nothing out of the ordinary in the present situation.

"Y-yes'm," Ruby said, taking a tiny step back as if Josie posed some unknown danger to them all. "Right away." She stared at Josie only a moment longer, clearly shocked and disapproving, then spun about on her skinny heel and hurried from the room.

"I'd sure like to be a fly on the ceiling of that kitchen when she goes in there and tells the others what she just saw," Nathan said, chuckling. "For someone who claims she doesn't want the help talking about her, you sure do have a way of keeping the chatter alive."

Josie grinned, but refused to comment as she placed her napkin in her lap and waited for her breakfast.

Nathan and Josie went outside to start painting shortly after Josie finished her breakfast. Because Nathan had already scraped and sanded the areas where the old paint had cracked or come loose from the walls the afternoon before, there was nothing to delay their work.

Josie was shown how to load her brush with enough paint to last several brush strokes, but not so much that it dribbled off the brush in globs. Nathan offered her the use of the new folding ladder while he climbed onto the taller, straight ladder propped against the side of the barn and began painting the highest areas. The idea was for them to meet somewhere in the middle.

Rafe joined them shortly after lunch, but had a hard time coping with the fact Josie was dressed in men's trousers. It made him nervous to paint beside a woman so scandalously dressed, so nervous, he eventually had to take his own ladder and brush to the opposite side of the barn and work alone. This suited Nathan just fine, for he liked the thought of being alone with her, though he recognized that in reality Rafe remained always within earshot.

"I need more paint," Josie called out after she dabbed the last of the white from her bucket and spread it as far as it would go. "Looks like someone will have to climb down and open another pail."

"I'll do it," Nathan responded quickly, eager for a reason to climb down. He'd quickly discovered that the view, whenever she stretched to reach the most difficult areas, was far more enjoyable from below than from above.

"Bring me some more, too," they heard Rafe call out from his side of the barn. "I'm just about out."

"Will do," Nathan said agreeably as he sauntered across the small corral to where the paint had been stacked near the front gate. While he busily worked to pry another lid off, he kept his eye constantly on Josie, who had taken advantage of having run out of paint and was stretching her muscles in a most provocative manner.

Though splattered from head to booted toe with tiny droplets of white paint, and though part of her shirttail had pulled out of her waistband, hiding much of that curvaceous waist, Nathan couldn't remember ever having seen a woman more alluring than Josie. He ached to take her in his arms again, to kiss her until she was compelled to respond. It

282

took valiant effort on his part not to rush to her side and snatch her right off that ladder.

"What's keeping you?" Josie asked, turning on the ladder to face him. She glanced first at the crooked smile on his dimpled face, then beyond to a rising trail of dust in the distance. "Uh-oh. Looks like we've got company coming," she said, and nodded in the direction of the dust.

Shading his eyes from the harsh glare of a late-afternoon sun with his hand, Nathan tried to see whose carriage approached. Squinting, he noticed the dark shapes of two people. One was a driver seated in front and the other a woman seated in back, dressed almost completely in gray.

"Aunt Cynthia," he muttered, stepping away from the not-yet-opened can of paint. "I wonder what excuse she has for coming over here this time. More bread perhaps?"

Josie felt a prickling sensation in the pit of her stomach when she climbed down from the ladder. Though she, personally, had no reason to dislike the woman, she found Cynthia not only annoying but extremely tiring. "Should I go inside and ask Jeanne to prepare a pot of tea?"

"No," Nathan stated adamantly. "If she wanted tea, she should have let us know she was coming. This is the third time she's come by to visit us without warning. To tell you the truth, I'm getting very tired of it."

"Should I at least go inside and change into something—ah—more appropriate?" she asked. Aware how very opinionated Cynthia could be, Josie suddenly felt extremely awkward over her unusual choice of attire.

"Why? I like what you have on. Besides, we still have two full hours of daylight left. I see no reason

283

for us to stop work just because my aunt thinks she needs to stop by and check on us again."

Josie wondered if he suspected the real motive behind his aunt's visits. "What do you plan to do?" she wanted to know when he began wiping his hands on an oily rag. His expression was grim and his movements forced while he dipped his hands into a bucket of water to rinse them.

"I intend to find out what she wants," he said, then tossed the rag to her. "Here, use this to get some of the paint off. Just be careful when you try to get that big splotch off your nose. The turpentine on that rag will burn your eyes."

Josie frowned, crossing her eyes in an attempt to see the paint splattered across the tip of her nose.

Nathan chuckled, feeling some of the tension ease out of him as he studied Josie's comical expression. "Quite a fetching pose. I wish I had my father's talent for painting, because I'd sure love to capture you just as you are now."

Josie's eyebrow shot up as she uncrossed her eyes to glower at him. She opened her mouth for a quick retort, but didn't have enough time. His aunt's carriage had already pulled to a stop only a dozen yards away.

"Good afternoon, Aunt," Nathan said, turning to greet her with a cordial nod. "What brings you out this way so late in the afternoon?"

Cynthia did not answer. She'd already caught sight of Josie and sat staring at her with eyes wide and mouth agape.

Feeling awkward at the dumbstruck expression on Cynthia's face, Josie wiped as much paint away from her face and hands as possible, rinsed the turpentine off with water, then stepped bravely forward to greet the woman.

"What in the name of our dear Lord are you wearing?" Cynthia asked when she finally found her voice.

Josie looked down as if she had no idea what Cynthia had found wrong with her.

"Paint mostly," Nathan commented with a deadpan expression. "She appears to have a real problem in getting the paint out of her bucket and on to the wall. But she's improving."

In no mood for flippant remarks, Cynthia tossed her shoulders back. "I was referring to the trousers."

"Oh, those," Nathan said with a slow nod of his head, as if just starting to comprehend. "Josie wanted to help us paint the barn and thought she might be of more help to us if she was able to get up and down a ladder. And she has been helpful. Very helpful."

"You allow her to climb up on ladders?" Cynthia demanded, clearly disapproving. "Isn't that a little dangerous?"

She looked pointedly at Josie, though she continued to speak to Nathan. "Isn't she risking serious injury by climbing to such heights? Or doesn't that matter to you?"

The muscles in Nathan's shoulders tensed.

Chapter Seventeen

"I'm not in any danger, I assure you," Josie said, coming quickly to Nathan's defense. "Besides, the decision to help paint the barn was mine. There isn't anything else for me to do around here and I was starting to feel bored."

"And whose idea was it for you to dress like that?" Cynthia asked, cutting her accusing gaze back at Nathan. Her thin nostrils flared when she huffed out a disapproving snort.

"Mine," she admitted. "I didn't think I could be of much help to anyone unless I was able to climb up a ladder, and climbing a ladder in skirts is far too cumbersome."

"And dangerous," Nathan quickly pointed out. "In skirts she might trip on the hem causing her to fall off the ladder and breaking no telling how many bones in the process."

"Then you admit that a fall from that ladder could indeed hurt her," Cynthia stated, thrusting her chin proudly forward and her shoulders back. "Yet you allow her to climb it anyway."

"It's very unlikely I'd fall," Josie told her, hoping to make the woman understand. "When I was a little girl, I was always climbing up trees and ladders, and anywhere else I found a sturdy foothold. I have very good balance."

"I'm glad to hear it," Cynthia muttered. Aware she

was not getting her point across to those two, she made one last driven comment. "Just be very, *very* careful when climbing that thing. Accidents can happen no matter *how* good your balance." She continued to stare at Nathan pointedly, as if sending some silent message. "Just look at what happened to Carl."

"Oh, I'm always careful," Josie said quickly, not wanting to stray to that subject again. Reaching for her skirts, only to be reminded she wore none, Josie moved forward, eager to turn the conversation in a different direction. "Would you care to come inside for a while?" she asked politely. "Perhaps you'd like a cup of cinnamon tea? It shouldn't take Jeanne very long to brew a small pot."

"On a hot day like today? No, I think not. But I would enjoy a tall glass of cool water. Moses, help me down." Cynthia moved to the edge of the carriage where she waited for the driver to assist her. The elderly black man, who had tried to appear disinterested in the events around him, quickly came to attention as he tossed a wooden block onto the ground for her to use as a step.

"I hope you won't be terribly offended if I don't join you two ladies," Nathan said, frowning because Josie had actually asked his aunt inside when he'd hoped to have her on her way by now. "But I really do have a lot of work to get done around here and only a couple of hours of daylight left."

"Of course, we understand," Cynthia assured him with a smile that lifted the corners of her mouth but never quite penetrated the depths of her blue-gray eyes. "You go right ahead with your work. Josie can see to my needs. I don't plan to stay very long anyway. The only reason I came by at all is because I was on my way back from town. Since I was so close, I decided to stop in and see how you two were getting along. After all, you are my only nephew. I feel it's my duty to see to your welfare."

Lifting her heavy gray skirts gracefully, Cynthia then turned her back to him and walked with Josie into the house.

"My but the place looks nice," Cynthia commented when she entered the main parlor only moments later. Because Nathan had managed to keep her out of the house during her previous visits, she took full advantage of being inside at last. While plucking her white traveling gloves from her hands one finger at a time, her gaze darted from tabletop to tabletop. "To tell you the truth, Carl's housekeeper, Pearl, never bothered to keep the place quite this clean. You should feel proud of the way it looks now."

"Thank you," Josie responded with a pleased smile. "But in all fairness to Carl's housekeeper, we do have three women, all working very hard to take care of Oakhaven. And, as I understand it, Pearl Beene had no one helping her at all. She was responsible for both the cooking and all the housecleaning."

"But did neither very efficiently. Why Carl continued to put up with her is beyond me. The woman was obstinate and unruly. She had a very sharp tongue and, in all honesty, was getting too old and was just too contrary to take care of my brother properly."

"I gather you did not get along with her," Josie commented, secretly wishing she could have seen the two at odds with each other. It would have been interesting to find out who had the sharper claws.

"No one could get along with that woman," Cynthia replied with angry remembrance. "Except Carl, of course. But then Carl had a way of getting along with everyone." She paused as she thought about her brother. "Sometimes I think he was too soft-hearted for his own good. He let that woman get away with whatever pleased her, and she certainly took advantage of that. There were times when she flatly refused to do any work at all. She complained of her back all the time, though she had no trouble plopping down on the couch for a rest. I tried to get him to send her packing, but he just couldn't bring himself to fire her. He was a very weak man in some respects."

"I'm not so sure that having a kind heart is a sign of weakness," Josie said, noting the similarities between Carl and Nathan.

Like his father, Nathan had been unable to make himself fire Ruby though the woman continued to be cantankerous. At least Ruby got her work done, Josie reasoned, suddenly remembering that one of Ruby's responsibilities was to help Jeanne in the kitchen whenever needed. Ruby would probably be the one to answer the service bell should she ring it, but knowing what Cynthia would think of Ruby — who behaved very similarly to the hated Pearl — and knowing what Ruby would think of Cynthia's inbred haughtiness, Josie decided it would be better to go to the kitchen and get the water herself.

"Why don't you sit down and make yourself comfortable?" Josie asked as she headed toward the narrow door that joined the parlor with the formal dining room. "I'll be right back with a small pitcher of cool water and a glass."

Knowing it was considered rude to leave a guest alone for very long at a time, Josie rushed through to the kitchen. She returned within a very few minutes with the water, but upon entering the parlor from the dining room, she discovered Nathan's aunt nowhere in sight.

"Miss Garrett?" she called out, setting the tray

aside before hurrying toward the only other door to the room, which was a wide, double door leading out into the entrance hall. "Where are you?"

"I'm in here," Cynthia responded as she came out of the library, her brow drawn into a deep, studious frown.

"What were you doing in there?"

"Looking around," she answered simply, as if she had every right to snoop through the house if she wanted.

"For what?"

"Nothing in particular. I just wanted to find out what Nathaniel has been up to these past few weeks," she admitted. "I see he has been making a grand list of everything in the house, even going as far as to write out suggested sale prices. I guess he wants to be sure nothing gets past him. That boy always has been driven by his obsessive greed."

"It's not like that," Josie explained, angry that Cynthia persisted in believing the worst. "Nathan is making that property list at Jason Haught's request. Jason wants him to compile a detailed list of everything so he can settle the estate as quickly as possible after the three months have finally passed."

"Nathaniel told you that?" Cynthia asked carefully, as if hoping to prove something. "You didn't hear Jason say anything about such a list yourself?"

"No. I didn't stay in the room during the entire conversation. I had other things to do," Josie admitted. "But I have no reason to doubt Nathan's word."

Cynthia shook her head grimly. "What has he done to make you so completely blind to his faults?"

"Nothing. I see his faults," Josie quickly replied.

"Which are?" Cynthia asked, curious to find out if she'd told her the truth.

Josie frowned while she thought for a moment.

What were Nathan's faults? At one time she thought he had nothing but faults—major, unforgivable faults. But for the life of her, she could not remember even one of them. Still, she knew he had to have faults. Everyone did. Finally, she thought of something.

"He doesn't cut his meat into small enough pieces," she said, pleased with herself for having come up with something so quickly.

"And you consider that to be one of his worst faults?" Cynthia wanted to know, clearly unable to believe the simplicity of Josie's answer. "The young man is driven by his own greed, willing to do whatever it takes to get what he can, and all you can find fault with is the way he cuts his meat?"

"He also scatters bread crumbs all over the table," she added, knowing it wasn't much in itself but thinking maybe the two together would account for something.

"My dear child, what can I do to make you see what sort of man my nephew really is? He's dangerous enough when you know to watch out for him. It truly worries me that you continue to be so blind when your very life could be at stake."

Josie had had enough. "And how can you continue to judge Nathan the way you do when you really don't even know him?"

"I know him far better than you think."

"How can you say that? Without including the day of Carl's funeral, when was the last time you spoke with Nathan?"

"At his mother's funeral twelve years ago," Cynthia admitted reluctantly. "But before that I saw him regularly. I went with Carl for a visit at least once a year."

"But, until his father's funeral two months ago,

291

you hadn't even seen Nathan for twelve entire years," Josie pointed out. "Nathan was barely eighteen when his mother died. He's thirty years old now. You can't possibly know what sort of man he's become."

"I know him well enough. He was a rebellious young man, full of selfishness and spite. The only person he ever cared about is himself. And, believe me, he hasn't changed. He could very well be the one responsible for his own father's death, and he might even be responsible for Pearl Beene's death, too. I'm warning you again. Be careful whenever you're around him. Be very, very careful," Cynthia stated, her expression harsh. Then, without arguing the point further, she spun about and marched briskly out of the house, not returning to the parlor for either her gloves or her water.

Josie's nostrils flared as she watched Nathan's aunt leave. She'd become so incredibly angry with Cynthia for having based her suspicions on what amounted to little more than malicious gossip and a personal dislike she refused to follow her and convince her to stay. Knowing that Cynthia was just as angry at her for having come to Nathan's defense yet again, Josie wondered if they possibly had seen the last of her. But in the same moment, she knew they hadn't. Even though Cynthia had left furious with her for her unrelenting belief in Nathan, she would be back. There was no doubt in Josie's mind. Cynthia Garrett would be back.

Sighing heavily, Josie spun about and headed immediately for the library, where she intended to wait until she heard Cynthia leave. When she noticed a movement and glanced toward the stairway, she found Shirley and Ruby standing near the top, both staring down at her, dumbfounded.

Angry to think they might have heard everything,

she came to a sudden stop and glared up at the two of them. "And just what right do you two have to spy on me?"

"We wasn't spying on you, ma'am," Shirley said quickly, her eyes wide and her cheeks pale. "We got finished cleaning the upstairs and was already on our way downstairs to put away these cleaning supplies when that lady suddenly came stalking out of the library. We stood 'ere, thinking she would surely follow you back into the parlor. We didn't mean no 'arm, ma'am. 'Onest we didn't."

Knowing Shirley probably spoke the truth, but still very frustrated to also know they'd probably overheard everything she and Cynthia had said about Nathan, she continued to glare up at the two.

"Well, don't just stand there gawking at me like a couple of mindless ninnies," she snapped. "Don't you two have more work to do?"

"Aye, ma'am, we certainly do," Shirley assured her, swallowing hard as she hurried on down the stairs, then ducked into the dining room, carrying her bucket of supplies with her.

Ruby remained where she was, watching with a hardened expression while Josie stalked angrily into the library and slammed the door closed.

That evening, after a long, hot, soaking bath, most of the tension that had been building inside Josie slowly slipped away. By the time she donned a comfortable dress of pale yellow gingham with white cuffs trimmed in white lace and then joined Nathan in the dining room for a late supper, she felt very relaxed, almost lethargic.

Because Nathan had decided to work until it was too dark to see, then still had all the brushes and

293

buckets to wash up afterward, their usual mealtime had been pushed back by almost two hours. By the time they both sat down at their usual places and were ready for Ruby to serve their food, it was well past Josie's usual bedtime.

Yawning repeatedly throughout the meal, she did her best to stay awake. Though she was bone-weary from the full day of work and had become thoroughly relaxed from her long bath, she made every effort to stay awake. She wanted to have a talk with Nathan after supper.

The time had come to tell him about his aunt's malicious tongue. He had a right to know the sort of things that were being said about him. But she wanted to make sure their talk would go uninterrupted and she knew Ruby would continue to be in and out of the dining room until they were finished with their meal. Aware the nosy little housekeeper already knew far more than she should, Josie decided to wait until Ruby was safely tucked away in her room before telling him anything. She continued to fight an overwhelming desire to drift off to sleep.

"Why don't you go on up to bed?" Nathan commented when he looked up from his plate and found her leaning forward over the table, her chin propped on her hand, her beautiful green eyes barely open. "You look exhausted."

"I am," she admitted, lifting her heavy eyelids just high enough to be able to see his face a little better. "But I want to have a talk with you first."

"About what?"

"I'd rather wait and tell you later, when we are alone."

Nathan glanced curiously about the room, then back to her droopy expression. "We are alone."

"I mean *really* alone. It concerns a very personal

matter that I don't want overheard."

"I see," Nathan commented, setting his fork aside, eager to hear of this very personal matter. "Well then, why don't we go out onto the balcony to have this talk? It's a nice night and no one can possibly overhear us there."

"That'll be fine," she said. Her head bobbed agreeably as she fell back heavily against her chair.

"Why don't you go on upstairs? I'll join you there in a few minutes, just as soon as I check to be sure the doors are securely locked and all the front windows latched," he told her, pushing his chair back. Despite the fact the evening temperatures had gradually grown warmer, Nathan refused to leave any unprotected window open while they slept. He always checked the windows that had no wire mesh covering to be sure they were not only closed but securely latched as well.

"Just don't take too long," Josie said, nodding agreeably as she, too, pushed her chair away from the table. "I'll be waiting for you in one of the lounge chairs upstairs."

"I'll be right up," he assured her, eager to find out what she wanted to talk with him about, but even more eager to be alone with her again on the balcony. Well remembering what had happened the last time they had found themselves alone out under the stars, he hurried from the room.

Quickly but carefully, Nathan checked the proper windows, assuring himself that they were closed and latched, and that the doors were not only locked, but also bolted shut. With his father's personal set of keys still missing, Nathan continued to take all the added precautions he thought necessary for their safety. But as soon as he had the final lock locked and the last bolt shoved into place, he wasted no time turning out the lights then hurrying upstairs to join Josie.

"Sorry it took me so long," he said as he stepped out onto the darkened balcony and headed immediately toward the small group of lounge chairs at the far end. He had only a sliver of a moon to guide him but it provided just enough light to see which chair she'd chosen. Eager to enjoy such a romantic setting with her, he hurried toward her and asked, "Now, what was it you wanted to talk with me about?"

When there came no immediate response, he moved closer, studying her lifeless form in the dark. Although he had just enough light to make out her shape, there was not enough to see her expression at any distance.

"Josie?"

Still she did not respond. When Nathan knelt beside her chair, he discovered why. She was sound asleep.

"Josie?"

He tried again, hoping to revive her enough to at least have their talk, still curious to find out what she'd been so secretive about. "Are you awake?"

He reached forward to run his fingertip lightly down the gentle curve of her nose, thinking it might gently wake her. He smiled when her only response was a slight twitch near the corner of her mouth. He felt a strong rush of tenderness toward her.

"Poor thing, I guess you worked a little too hard today," he whispered softly, while studying her ethereal beauty in the faint moonlight. How truly beautiful she was, even in sleep.

Unable to resist, he trailed the tip of his finger first across the soft curve of her cheek, then down along the slender column of her neck, stopping just short of the deepening curve between her breasts. He watched with fascination when tiny goose bumps formed beneath her ivory skin.

"Josie?" He tried again to wake her, disappointed when she still did not respond. He pressed his cool hands against her cheeks. "Josie, wake up. You can't sleep out here."

"Nathan? Is that you?" she asked, finally opening her eyes and blinking groggily. She smiled when she found he was so close. "What time is it?"

"Obviously past your bedtime," he said with a begrudging smile of his own. Though he ached to take her in his arms and kiss her, he had to consider what was best for her. She was exhausted. "You need to get on to bed."

"But we have to talk," she reminded him, making a valiant effort to keep her eyes open, but finding it close to impossible.

"We can talk tomorrow. Right now, you need your rest." Standing, he reached out a hand to help her up out of the chair. "Come on, rosebud, off to bed with you."

Josie accepted the hand and allowed him to pull her to her feet, then stumbled sleepily against him. At the feel of his warmth against her cheek, she closed her eyes, a lethargic smile on her face.

Still struggling against the very real urge to take advantage of the situation, Nathan pulled her into the crook of one arm and gently led her toward her bedroom door. Tilting his head, he leaned his cheek against her hair and breathed deeply the sweet scent of lemons and soap that lingered there.

"Can you manage it from here?" he asked, standing back after they'd entered the dimly lit room, watching cautiously while she stumbled off toward her bed.

"Yes, thank you," she called back to him, but didn't have the energy to turn around. "I'll be fine."

Then, without bothering to as much as take off her clothes, she pulled back her covers and crawled right into bed.

Nathan stood in the doorway, watching for several minutes. A smile lingered on his lips as he considered how tired she must be. She had worked just as hard as he and Rafe and had not complained once. She was truly amazing.

Thinking she would be more comfortable without her shoes, he considered walking over and removing them for her. He took several steps toward her, trying to convince himself he would be doing her a favor; but in the end he left without touching her for the temptation to remove far more than her shoes would be too great. It might do him good to sleep in his own shoes that night — anything that might take his mind off the growing desire he felt for the beautiful woman asleep in that bed.

When Josie awoke the following morning, she was surprised and a little embarrassed to discover she was still fully dressed in the clothing she'd worn the evening before. What surprised her even more was the late hour. The clock on the mantel revealed that it was nearly nine o'clock. She should have been up and about hours ago. Why hadn't someone wakened her?

Hurriedly, she changed back into her work clothes, only to discover that both her trousers and her shirt had become uncomfortably stiff with dried splotches of paint. But, stiff or not, she knew they would still provide more freedom than skirts. Then, remembering what a problem she'd had getting a comb through the dried pieces of splattered paint that had clung to her hair the evening before, she quickly swept her thick mane into a tight knot then wrapped it with a colorful scarf.

Only minutes later, when she first stepped out of her bedroom, she noticed that many of the muscles along the back of her legs and across her abdomen were sore from yesterday's strain—not enough to prevent her from going right back to work, but enough to make her walk with a funny little stiff gait.

"I'm sorry I'm late. I overslept." Josie began making her excuses the moment she entered the dining room and saw that Nathan had already finished eating and had just risen from the table. "Why didn't you wake me?"

"Didn't see any reason to. You obviously needed your rest and I still have a few chores to see to before I start back painting."

"What chores?"

"First, I need to feed and water the horses, then I have to take a quick ride out to the east section to check on the new calves. It'll be at least an hour before I get back. I noticed Rafe was already out by the barn getting ready to paint, but there's no sense you going out there until I get back so, you should have plenty of time to enjoy a good, hearty breakfast. And since we never did get to have that talk last night, I'll try to get back as quick as I can so we can talk before we start to work."

"It can wait until this evening," she assured him, glancing down at her boots as she thought about the way she'd fallen asleep the evening before.

"Whatever," Nathan said with a light shrug, aware of her discomfort. "I'll see you in a little while."

Disappointed to have missed breakfast with Nathan, Josie considered skipping her morning meal, but then realized she would need the added energy. As soon as she heard the back door close behind him, she stepped reluctantly to the table and rang the service bell.

Seconds later, Ruby entered the room with more than her usual tight-lipped scowl. Her face was rigid and her jaw set. Josie wondered if Ruby's sour expression had anything to do with what she'd overheard the afternoon before. Was she angry with Cynthia for having said such awful things about Nathan, or angry with her for having defended him as quickly as she did? Or did Ruby actually believe what she'd overheard and fear she was working for some sort of monster?

Josie considered discussing it with her, but realized it would do little good. Whatever conclusion Ruby had jumped to was already solidly a part of her. That opinion would not be easily changed by anything she had to say, and her attempt to try might be misconstrued into a feeble effort on her part to hide the facts. She felt Ruby would eventually realize the truth, if given time. And time was something Josie had plenty to give.

Later, as soon as Josie finished her breakfast of biscuits, jam, and sausage, she joined Rafe outside. Feeling invigorated from having had a good night's sleep and from the bright, morning sunshine, Josie decided not to wait for Nathan. Pouring an ample amount of white paint into a wide bucket, she tucked the handle of her paintbrush into her waistband and went directly to her ladder.

"Think we'll be finished by tomorrow?" she called out to Rafe, who was already hard at work just around the corner from where she'd stopped painting the day before.

"At the rate we've been going, I'm sure we will," he called back to her, never pausing in his brush strokes.

"Think we'll have enough paint left over for any of the fences?" she asked as she set her bucket on the small shelf attached at the back of her ladder. When she then placed her foot on the first rung and pulled herself up, she grimaced. Not only were her muscles stiff, but the ladder wobbled noticeably beneath her weight causing her to put more strain on the sorest areas of her body.

"Hard to tell how much paint we'll have left. Looks to me like we are going to be cutting it awfully close," Rafe told her. "Why? Are you planning to help paint the fences, too?"

Thinking her ladder had been carelessly placed on an uneven area, she cautiously lifted herself onto the second rung. She didn't want to cause any more pain or jostle her paint bucket from its precarious position atop the tiny ladder shelf. "Actually I had thought about painting the fences all by myself."

"There's no need in that. I can paint those fences in no time at all," Rafe assured her. "There's no reason for you to even bother."

"But you've got other work to do," she reminded him as she reached down to slip the paintbrush out of her waistband. Dipping it carefully into the bucket, she started to paint with long, even strokes. Again, she was reminded of the true extent of her aching muscles, but was determined not to let the soreness affect her work.

Finding she was not quite high enough to overlap the area Nathan had painted the evening before, she cautiously lifted her foot onto the next step. No sooner did she place her full weight on the ladder rung than she heard a loud, splintering crack. She screamed as the board suddenly broke and gave way. Her foot bent into an awkward angle when she crashed helplessly to the ground. Grabbing at the ladder while she fell, she pulled it over on top of her as she landed first on the twisted ankle, then fell over on her hip. Her elbow struck something hard. Pain shot up simultaneously through her leg and across her shoulder as her head fell back and struck the earth.

"What happened?" Rafe shouted, dropping his paintbrush to the ground as he rounded the corner. His face paled with concern when he saw her on the ground with the broken ladder piled on top of her. The paint bucket had missed striking her head by bare inches. White paint was everywhere.

Too stunned to speak, Josie sat up and stared at him, slowly shaking her head with confusion.

"Are you hurt?" Rafe asked as he slid to the ground beside her, immediately tossing the ladder aside.

"I'm not sure. I hurt my elbow and I think I may have sprained my ankle," she told him, remembering the initial pain she'd felt. "But I don't think I hurt either one very badly. I don't feel any pain now."

"Are you sure? You may have broken something," Rafe said, bending over her, frantic with his desire to do something to help her but not knowing what. "Can you wiggle your foot?"

Josie gently moved her foot from side to side, yelping aloud at the pain that resulted. "Yes, but it hurts."

"We'd better get you inside," Rafe stated matter-of-factly, his thick eyebrows raised as high as they could go. "We need to put cool rags on that ankle before it starts to swell. Do you think you can walk?"

"Help me up and we'll find out."

While Rafe worked to help Josie to her feet, Nathan rode into the yard, instantly aware there had been an accident.

"What happened?" he asked, swinging his leg over and dropping to the side of his horse even before the animal had come to a complete stop.

"The ladder broke," Rafe explained while Josie held his arm for balance. "She hurt her ankle when she fell. May have hurt her elbow, too. I was going to try and help her get to the house so we can wrap cool rags around the injuries."

Wasting no time, Nathan scooped Josie into his arms and headed immediately toward the house. Rafe hurried past them to open the back door.

"Are you bleeding anywhere?" Nathan wanted to know as he crossed the yard with long, determined strides. His eyes darted over her in search of more possible injuries.

"No, I don't think so."

"That's good," he said, relieved, then shouted out so Rafe could hear, "Rafe, I want you to ride into town and get the doctor. Tell him to hurry."

Josie shook her head, startled by the magnitude of his concern. "I don't think that's really necessary. I'm not that badly hurt."

"Necessary or not, I want a doctor to examine you. I want to be absolutely sure that you have no broken bones. I won't rest easy until I hear *him* tell me that you are not badly hurt."

Aware his mind was made up, Josie did not argue with him. Instead she laid her head against his chest and allowed him to carry her into the house and up the stairs, where he gently placed her on her bed then immediately ordered her out of her boots — and her breeches.

Chapter Eighteen

Rafe returned with the doctor shortly after one. After having sent Nathan from her room, Josie had already changed out of her breeches and workshirt into a loose-fitting dress so the doctor would be able to examine her more easily. She'd barely had time to bathe away some of the dirt before Nathan had demanded he be let back into the room so he could start applying cool cloths to the injured ankle and elbow. Despite her staunchest protests, he'd been doing that ever since.

"You must be Dr. Harrison," Nathan said, rising from the chair he'd set at Josie's bedside as he turned to greet the older man. Immediately he shoved the small ladder-back chair out of the way with his boot, wanting to give the doctor plenty of room to work with the patient. He offered his hand as he stepped forward. "I'm Nathan Garrett, Rafe's employer. And I am very pleased you managed to get out here so quickly."

"Me, too," Josie muttered, sighing heavily as she crossed her arms in a disgruntled fashion. "I can't seem to get anything through this man's thick head. I've tried my best to explain to him that I am not seriously injured. Asking you to come all the way out here was really unnecessary. But, then, the way he's been acting, you'd think I was on my deathbed."

"I just want to be sure she didn't hurt herself

seriously," Nathan said in his own defense. "Josie's had quite a fall, Doctor. I think she may have broken her ankle."

"It's not broken," she tried to reason with them. "I'd know if it was. I've just twisted it is all."

Dr. Harrison smiled encouragingly as he set his medical bag on the small table beside Josie's bed then carefully removed his coat. "Sometimes you can't tell about these things. A broken ankle can play tricks on you. At least Nathan did the right thing by applying cool compresses to the injured areas," he said as he rolled his white shirt-sleeves up past his elbows. "Now, if you don't mind— Josie, isn't it?"

Josie nodded that it was.

"Well, then, if you don't mind, Josie, I'd like to examine that ankle," he said as he moved closer to the injured ankle.

"Her elbow, too," Nathan insisted, also moving to the foot of the bed so he could watch.

Nodding briefly, Dr. Harrison leaned forward and raised the hem of her skirt from midcalf to knee before he slowly lifted her foot and began peeling away the cool, wet cloths that had been applied to the ankle. "Tell me, Josie, have you two been married long?"

"Married?" she responded with a startled gasp, wondering how the doctor could even think such a thing. "Us?"

"Aren't you?" He paused long enough to glance at the two of them questioningly.

"Not at all. We're just friends," she stated emphatically.

"And at times barely that," Nathan quickly added.

"I'm sorry if I offended anyone, but the way you two have been talking to each other, I just assumed you were married. It was an honest mistake, I assure

305

you," the doctor said as he reached up to pull the skirt back down to midcalf. He then immediately returned his attention to the injured ankle while he gently finished unwrapping it.

"Hmmm, you have definitely bruised the area. And it does appear to be a little swollen in places," he said as he took the large towel that had been tucked beneath the injured ankle and began to gently blot the excess moisture away from the skin.

"But is it broken?" Nathan wanted to know, leaning forward until his head nearly touched the doctor's, wanting to examine the ankle, too.

"I keep telling you. It's not broken!" Josie complained, clearly exasperated that he had yet to believe anything she had to say about her own ankle. "What will it take to convince you of that?"

The doctor chuckled, shaking his head. "You two might not be married, but you should be. The way you go at each other, it sounds to me like you are already husband and wife."

Josie opened her mouth to comment, but really didn't know what to say about such a remark. She snapped her mouth shut again, puckering it into a bewildered pout.

If the doctor noticed her sudden loss of words, he didn't let on. Bending closer to the injured ankle, he first adjusted his spectacles to where he could see better, then began to probe the swollen area gently with his fingertips. "Tell me the moment I hit any tender spots."

Josie had no problem with that. She yelped the instant his forefinger came into contact with a damaged strip of muscle. She tried to jerk her foot away, but he had too firm a grasp. "There, Doctor. It definitely hurts there."

"How does it hurt?" he asked, narrowing his eyes

as he studied the sore area carefully.

"What do you mean *how?*" she asked, thinking it a stupid question. "It *hurts.*"

Nathan turned away, hiding a sudden grin, while the doctor's eyes met hers with an amused expression. "What I need to know, my dear, is the pain centralized in that area or does it shoot up into the leg?"

"It hurts mostly right there, around the ankle itself," she told him, biting down on her lip when he pressed down on the sore spot from a different direction. "But it didn't start hurting again until you began poking at it with your fingers."

When Nathan looked at her again, his expression was back in control, but his blue eyes sparkled with such mischief, Josie suspected his reason for having turned away. She stared at him accusingly. How dare he find her pain amusing.

"Hmmm," Dr. Harrison droned as he turned the ankle to a different position, causing her to forget Nathan for the moment.

"What is it?"

He pursed his lips and lowered his bushy gray eyebrows while he then pressed the flat of his outstretched fingers against the affected area and wriggled the injured muscle back and forth beneath them. "Exactly what sort of fall was it?"

"Didn't Rafe tell you?" Nathan asked, puzzled.

"He told me she fell from a ladder. But I'd like to hear her describe the fall. I will also want to examine her for other possible injuries. Sometimes after a fall like that, there are some pretty serious injuries that go unnoticed."

Nathan nodded. "I agree wholeheartedly. I want you to be thorough." He then leaned over the edge of the bed again to have a better view of the examination.

When Josie and Dr. Harrison both looked at him then, their eyebrows pulled low, their expressions perplexed, he stared back at them questioningly. "What have I done?"

"You've done nothing," the doctor said, cocking his head at an angle as if trying to decide if the man was truly that naive. A hint of a grin twitched at his lips. "Which is really the root of the problem. Because you are admittedly unrelated to this young lady, I think it would be a good idea for you to step out into the hall until I am finished with my examination. Do you have a housekeeper?"

"Yes," Nathan answered, finding it an odd thing to ask at a time like this. "I have two housekeepers and a cook."

"Good. I'd appreciate it if you'd ask one of them to come up here. I prefer having another woman in the room whenever I examine my female patients. It tends to make the patient feel more at ease and at the same time provides me someone to hold things for me."

"Oh, I get it, sort of like a temporary nurse," Nathan said, nodding vigorously as he hurried out of the room to find either Jeanne or Shirley.

"He seems very concerned about you," Dr. Harrison commented with a grin so wide it formed tiny crinkles at the corners of his eyes as he sat down to wait for the housekeeper. "I gather he is related to Carl Garrett. His son, perhaps?"

Josie's green eyes widened. "You knew his father?"

"Oh, yes. I had several occasions to treat him. And I've treated his sister, Cynthia. I was certainly sorry to hear about his accident. He was such a fine man."

"Everyone seemed to think so. Did you happen to

know Carl's wife? Was she ever a patient of yours?" Josie asked hopefully, thinking she might at long last learn what her grandmother had died from and if her death had anything to do with the injuries she'd received years earlier at the hands of her grandfather.

"No. I never had that pleasure. I've only been in this area for a couple of years. Originally, I practiced in Shreveport. I didn't move to Silver Springs until I heard that Dr. Edison planned to retire. I've always yearned to live in a small town. I was never happy in the city," he explained, unaware of Josie's disappointment. Propping his elbows on the arms of the chair, he linked his hands together and rested them in his lap. "But that's enough about me. You still haven't told me how your accident happened."

"It was just like Rafe has probably already told you. I was trying to climb a ladder when one of the top rungs suddenly broke in half and I fell."

"Ladders can be very dangerous," he admitted, gazing at her curiously. "How far did you fall?"

"About five feet, I suppose," Josie told him, feeling a twinge of discomfort as she remembered a similar statement having been made about ladders the day before. She wondered what Cynthia would say when she learned that her staunch warning about climbing that ladder had proven justified. If only they could keep her from finding out.

"And after the ladder broke, you landed on your ankle?" he asked, glancing again at the injured ankle.

"Yes. I then fell over on my left side and struck my elbow on something."

"Did your head hit anything?"

"Just dirt. But not hard enough to raise a bump or anything."

"You are very lucky. Head injuries can be very

309

serious."

Josie remembered how close the bucket filled with paint had come to striking her head and suddenly she felt very lucky indeed. She could have been far more seriously hurt.

"May I ask you how you plan to get all that paint out of your hair? Because if you plan to use turpentine or kerosene, I want to caution you to do it quickly and then wash and rinse the area thoroughly. Either chemical can blister the skin if not washed away immediately."

"Paint?" Josie lifted her hand, raking her fingers through her hair and discovering a large sticky splotch of paint near the back of her head. She then felt of her pillow and found she had ruined the pillowslip with paint, too. Disgusted over the mess she'd made, she wondered why Nathan hadn't mentioned the paint in her hair. Surely he had noticed. Or had he? Was he that concerned over her injuries? So concerned he had failed to notice the paint in her hair? A slow warmth spread through her. Suddenly the paint in her hair no longer mattered. She pressed her head back onto the pillow and smiled.

The doctor studied her expression with raised eyebrows.

Footsteps in the hallway broke the short moment of silence that followed. When Shirley entered the room seconds later, her eyes were wide with concern.

"Mr. Garrett told me you needed my 'elp up 'ere," she said, glancing from the doctor to Josie, then back over her shoulder to where Nathan stood, his broad shoulders filling the doorway.

"Yes, that's true," the doctor said, pushing himself out of the chair. "And the first thing I want you to do is close that door. Then come over here and stand next to me while I examine your Miss Josie for

310

further injuries. It shouldn't take long."

Which was true. Within minutes, the doctor was finished with the examination, having felt every major bone for injury and having probed each bruised area for signs of swelling.

"Everything looks good," he commented with a cheerful smile as he dipped his hand into his medical bag. "All I need to do now is cleanse that scrape on the side of your leg then bandage it and that injured ankle. As soon as I'm done with that, I'll be finished here."

Josie stretched her neck forward in an effort to watch the doctor's movements. She grimaced, but didn't complain when he tugged the slack out of the bandage a little too hard.

"You can leave now. I'm through," he told Shirley as he tied the bandage in place, then tucked the loose ends neatly out of sight. "And on your way out, you can tell Mr. Garrett he is welcome to come back in now."

Nathan did not need to be told anything. The moment the door began to open, he pushed it wide and stepped inside. "How is she?"

"No bones broken," Dr. Harrison reassured him, already putting his things away.

Shirley slipped quietly from the room and carefully closed the door behind her.

"See, I told you," Josie said, smiling triumphantly when Nathan moved closer. "No broken bones."

"But you do have a nasty sprain," Dr. Harrison reminded her. "Therefore I must insist that you stay off of that foot for at least three days, preferably four."

"What? You mean I have to stay in this bed for three whole days?" she asked, clearly upset. "I can't even go downstairs if I want?"

"Only if you can find someone to carry you," the doctor told her. "I do not want you to put any weight on that ankle."

Josie frowned. "And what if no one agrees to carry me downstairs?"

"Then you have a problem," the doctor acknowledged.

Nathan grinned, amused by her predicament. "If she'll promise to be a good girl through all this, I might see it in my heart to carry her downstairs from time to time." In all honesty, he looked forward to the opportunity. Not only did he enjoy carrying her in his arms, he liked the thought of her finally being dependent on him for something.

"See there?" the doctor said, turning to glance at Josie over the tops of his spectacles. "Problem solved."

"I don't know. I'm not sure I like the way he said that. Just how good do I have to be?"

"A damn sight better than you have been," Nathan retorted, then turned his attention back to the doctor. "How long do you plan to keep that bandage on?"

"Just until the swelling goes down. She can probably come out of it sometime tomorrow. If not, by the next day."

"And what about the elbow?"

"It's bruised, but should be fine. I saw no need to bandage it."

"Is there some medicine she should be taking?"

"Only if she complains of any real pain. Then you can give her a headache powder."

"The problem is in my ankle, not my head," Josie snapped in an attempt to get their attention. She was tired of listening to them talk about her as if she wasn't even there.

312

"Don't be too sure about that," Nathan retorted, raising an eyebrow meaningfully. "I think there may be a very *definite* problem with that head of yours."

Josie crossed her arms and sighed aloud, exasperated, but before she could make any real comment, the door swung open and Ruby entered, carrying a tray with a single glass and a folded napkin upon it.

"Here's the lemonade you told me to make," she said to Nathan, setting both the napkin and the glass on the table beside Josie's bed. "Nice and cold just like you wanted."

Quickly unfolding her arms, Josie reached for the tall, frosty glass. Smiling at Nathan's thoughtfulness, she was ready to forgive him everything. "Thank you."

"Will there be anything else?" Ruby wanted to know, already turning toward the door.

"Yes, you can show me to the door," Dr. Harrison said, grabbing his medical bag and hurrying to follow.

"No, I'll escort you out. After all, I haven't paid you yet," Nathan protested, also moving toward the door. "How much do I owe you?"

"Oh, I think two dollars should cover it nicely," the doctor told him.

Ruby's eyebrows shot up at what obviously seemed to her a ridiculously high fee, but for once, she held her tongue. Tucking the tray beneath her arm, she stepped back and waited until Nathan and Dr. Harrison had passed by on their way to the hall. When they were finally gone from sight, and their footsteps heard well down the hallway, she turned to Josie and stared at her a long moment, as if debating whether or not to speak her mind.

"She was right, you know," she finally said, stepping closer so she would not be overheard.

313

"Who was right?" Josie asked, taking a sip of the tart drink she still held in her hands.

"Nathan's aunt."

Josie nearly strangled when she tried to swallow. "Right about what?"

"Right about everything," Ruby said, her expression like stone when she glanced toward the open door then back at Josie. "Your fall was no accident."

"Don't be silly. Of course it was an accident. The ladder rung broke and I fell. It's as simple as that."

"The ladder rung did not simply break. It was tampered with."

"Tampered with? How?"

"Someone took a saw and cut a deep groove about halfway through the bottom of that rung. It broke only because someone wanted it to break."

"That's ridiculous," Josie said, shaking her head at such a foolish notion. "Where did you ever get an idea like that?"

Ruby cut her gaze toward the door again. "Don't you dare tell no one, but I overheard Rafe telling Mr. Garrett all about it. I heard him tell how when he went back outside to clean up the mess, he noticed something was not quite right about the way that board broke apart. The break was smooth and straight on the bottom but ragged along the top. He said that meant only one thing. Someone had taken a saw to it. He also told Mr. Garrett that two of the screws that helped hold the ladder together near the top were missing. He said that if the ladder rung hadn't broke when it did, the whole thing would eventually have fallen apart. Someone was out to hurt somebody. One way or another."

Josie wanted to reprimand Ruby for having eavesdropped again, but by the time she had heard all the woman had to say, she'd forgotten about scolding

314

her. Instead, she set her lemonade aside, wanting to know more. "And what did Nathan have to say about all that?"

"He told Rafe not to mention it to anyone. He said it was to be their little secret." Ruby nodded her head, her eyes narrowed accusingly. "My guess is Mr. Garrett don't want you to know nothing about it. He wants you to go on thinking it was just an accident."

"But why?"

"I think you know why," Ruby said. "And if I was you, I'd pay a lot more attention to what that aunt of his has to say about things from now on. She obviously knows Mr. Garrett a lot better than you do. He's a bad one."

"I don't believe it," Josie stated adamantly. "Nathan would never deliberately try to hurt me."

Ruby shrugged as if it didn't matter to her one way or the other as she turned toward the door. "Have it your way. I just thought you should know."

When Nathan did not return after having escorted the doctor to the front door, Josie had to wonder why. She also had to wonder why he had felt it necessary to see the doctor out, since he could have paid him his two dollars while they were still in the room.

Unable to do anything but lie in her bed and think unwanted thoughts, she carefully studied the situation from all sides. She wondered how much, if any, of what Ruby had told her was true. It was hard for her to believe someone had actually tampered with the ladder. Still, it was something to consider. Because if it was indeed true, it meant there was someone, somewhere, who meant to harm her. Or

315

Nathan. What if the harm had been intended for him? Did he have enemies she knew nothing about? Did *she?*

So many possibilities to consider.

She wished Nathan would hurry and finish whatever he was doing and come to her room. She wanted to discuss the matter with him. She also wanted him to carry her downstairs to the bathroom, where she could do something about the paint still matted in her hair.

Half an hour passed and still no Nathan. Tired of waiting, Josie began to call out, hoping to be heard downstairs. Several minutes later, Shirley appeared at her door.

"Can I do something for you?"

"Yes. You can find Nathan for me. I want him to carry me downstairs to the bathroom so I can wash some of this paint off."

"Mr. Garrett's gone into town," she said, frowning at the predicament his absence had clearly created, for there was no one else quite strong enough to carry her.

"Into town?" Josie asked, surprised. "What did he go into town for?" *And why hadn't he bothered to tell her?*

"I don't really know. I didn't think it was my place to be asking such things."

Josie sighed wearily with resignation. "Did he say how long he would be gone?"

"No. Just that 'e was 'eaded into town and 'ow 'e wanted us to take good care of you while 'e was gone."

Josie studied Shirley's expression, wondering if Ruby had yet mentioned anything to her about the ladder. "Did Rafe go with him?"

"No. Mr. Garrett set Rafe back to painting. 'E went into town alone."

"What did they do about the broken ladder?"

"Don't know wot they did with it," she answered with a disinterested shrug, clearly uninformed on the matter. "They probably put it inside the barn so they can repair it later."

Josie leaned her head back into her pillows, wondering why Shirley had· yet to hear Ruby's latest bit of gossip.

"As long as it is out of the way," she commented, not wanting to throw further suspicion onto the incident. "But that doesn't solve my problem, does it? Would it be possible to have a tub brought up here? And lots of warm water, a cake of soap, and a small jar with turpentine?"

"Aye, I think that could be arranged. Would you then like for me to stay and 'elp you work some of that paint out of your 'air?"

"I'd be forever grateful," she said, smiling when Shirley spun immediately about and left the room to do exactly what she'd been asked.

Later that afternoon, after Josie and Shirley had finally removed most of the white paint from Josie's hair and Josie lay in bed again on fresh linen, with her foot propped on pillows and her hair drying, Nathan returned.

"I'm glad to see you're resting," he commented as he came through the door. Though he smiled, the expression did not run deep. Something about his eyes let her know he was troubled. "I wasn't sure you would obey the doctor's orders. I was afraid you might decide to get on out of that bed just to spite me."

"Oh, but I did get out of bed," she admitted, gesturing to the tall metal tub that had been emptied and wiped dry but left in her room until she could manage the stairs alone. "But I promise, I didn't put any weight on my ankle. In fact, my foot barely touched the ground."

"How did you manage that?" he asked, eyeing her suspiciously.

"Shirley helped me."

"And what about the bandage? How did you keep from getting it wet?"

"I dangled my foot over the side."

"But you were told to stay in bed and keep your foot up."

"I wasn't in the tub for long."

"I hope not." Nathan then nodded toward a tray that sat on the table beside her bed. "I see someone thought to bring you something to eat."

"Yes. But I'll admit I wasn't very pleased to discover I had to eat my meal alone." She crossed her arms, hoping he would tell her about his unexpected trip into town.

"As long as you ate something," he said, deliberately avoiding any mention of his absence.

Deciding a more direct approach was called for, she narrowed her eyes and asked. "Where were you?"

"I went into town. I needed to speak with Jason about something," he answered vaguely, then quickly redirected the conversation. "By the way, he told me to send you his regards. He was upset to hear about your accident and is glad you weren't hurt any worse than you were. You know, that fall could have been far more serious than it was."

Josie noticed how readily Nathan still termed her fall from the ladder an accident. She pursed her lips as she thought more about the situation. Could Ruby have misunderstood? Or was Nathan purposely hiding the truth from her?

There seemed only one way to find out.

"Yes, I could've been hurt a lot worse," she agreed.

Then she asked, watching closely for a reaction, "What do you suppose caused the ladder to break like that?"

"Hard to say," he said, turning his attention to her bandaged ankle. He avoided her probing gaze. "I guess the wood was weak."

An eerie feeling crept through Josie when she studied his somber expression. Something was not quite right. "But it was a brand-new ladder."

"That's true," he nodded agreeably. The muscles at the back of his jaw flexed while he continued to gaze at her bandaged ankle. "I don't know what to tell you except that I feel terrible that it happened."

The muscles around Josie's heart constricted as her doubts continued to grow. She wanted to believe him, but the eerie feeling persisted. He was definitely keeping something from her. Something important. "I guess you and Rafe will have to finish painting that barn without me."

"Sure looks that way." He nodded, finally glancing at her face. "Speaking of which, there's still a full hour of daylight left. I guess I'd better get on down there and give Rafe a hand. I'll be back to get you when supper's ready."

"Just be careful climbing up any ladders," she called out to him when he headed for the door. "We don't want any more accidents."

"I'll be careful," he said, his expression grim. He paused to glance back at her, then left the room with no further comment.

Josie folded her arms protectively about her while she listened to the hollow click of his footsteps as they faded into the distance.

Chapter Nineteen

"I came as soon as I could," Cynthia said, her drawn face showing concern as she hurried into the bedroom.

Josie glanced up from her book. Having failed to hear a carriage, she was startled to see Nathan's aunt. "Miss Garrett? What are you doing here?"

"Well, since Dr. Harrison was out this way anyway, he stopped by to check on me earlier this afternoon. He wanted to see if I was over my illness," Cynthia explained, plucking her white gloves from her hands one finger at a time as she came to stand beside the bed where Josie sat staring up at her, supported by a mountain of feather pillows.

"And while he was there, he told you about my accident," Josie surmised, lifting her hand to twirl a lock of her long hair absently around her finger. A heavy feeling weighted her chest while she continued to watch Cynthia's every movement.

"Oh, but can you be sure it was an accident?" Cynthia wanted to know, indicating there should be some doubt.

Josie didn't know what to answer. She had no intention of telling Cynthia that the ladder she'd fallen from might very well have been tampered with. But at the same time, she didn't want to lie about the incident, either, so she kept her answer as vague as possible.

"What else would it be but an accident?" she asked, glancing up at her with wide, innocent eyes. "One of the ladder rungs broke under my weight and I fell. Landed on the side of my ankle. I'm lucky I just sprained it. But I guess it proves you were right about climbing that ladder. It really was a very dangerous thing to do."

Cynthia's face drew into a tight-lipped frown while she studied Josie carefully. Tiny worry lines dipped between her eyebrows. "But are you certain it was an accident?"

Josie released a long, weary sigh. She really was in no mood to listen to Cynthia cast any more doubt upon Nathan. "I suppose you think your nephew had something to do with it."

"Did he?"

"No, of course not," she answered a little too quickly as she glanced down to brush an imaginary piece of lint off her periwinkle-blue skirt.

"You didn't say that very convincingly," Cynthia pointed out, quickly folding her gloves together and putting them into her skirt pocket. Her blue-gray eyes remained alert to Josie's every movement as she stepped back and sank into a nearby chair. "Not very convincingly at all."

"I'm tired. I can't say anything very convincingly at the moment," Josie said, closing her eyes for a moment to prove just how tired she was—tired of Cynthia's constant accusations against Nathan, tired of trying not to listen.

Cynthia sat quietly until Josie reopened her eyes. "I imagine you are tired. You've had a terrible experience. I'm just grateful I was allowed to come up here to see you at all. I thought for a minute there Nathan was going to send me away. I guess he's afraid I'll try to warn you that there could be more

321

trouble ahead."

"If that's his worry, I hope he is proved wrong," Josie said, her tone deadly serious. She did not want to hear any more of Cynthia's frightening predictions. It was enough that she'd been right about the ladder. "I hope the real reason you came was to see if I was all right."

Cynthia's mouth twitched uncontrollably. "Yes, of course. I am deeply concerned for your welfare. But I am also concerned for your safety. I've come to beg that you reconsider your views about everything I've told you thus far."

"Which things?" Josie asked, knowing she was going to have to hear it all again anyway.

"What is most important for you to try to understand and accept is that Nathan Garrett is not at all what he seems. I have warned you to be careful when you're around him, but I don't think you are really aware of how deadly serious your situation is. I can feel the danger in my bones. That broken ladder may indeed have been an accident. There's no way we can be sure it wasn't. But if any more such accidents happen around here, my advice is for you to pack your things and get out of here as quickly as possible. Before you have to be carried out. Believe me, no inheritance is worth risking your life."

"I appreciate your concern" was all Josie was willing to say in response. And she did appreciate her concern. What she didn't appreciate, though, were the constant innuendoes about Nathan.

"If you had any sense, you'd leave now."

"That may be true, but I plan to stay anyway." Josie pressed her head back into the comfort of her pillows, wishing Cynthia would go away and leave her alone. Though she clearly suspected Nathan of hiding something, she refused to believe he'd had anything to do with causing her accident.

"I wish you would reconsider," Cynthia said, shaking her head with dismay.

"There's nothing to reconsider."

"I don't think you understand how concerned you should be with all that has happened around here since your arrival. Very concerned. Still, I want you to know that if things do start to get worse, all you have to do is find some way to get word to me and I'll come and get you. I'll bring the sheriff if I have to, but I'll come and get you out of this place. I promise."

"I doubt that will be necessary," Josie assured her. "But I thank you for the offer just the same."

Cynthia sank back in her chair, staring at Josie with a bewildered expression. "Can I at least do something for you while I'm here?"

Josie was puzzled by Cynthia's sudden determination to be so helpful. "No, I've got everything I need," she said, gesturing to the book in her lap, the pillows resting beneath her foot, and the water glass at her bedside.

"What about supper? Shouldn't someone be bringing you something to eat about now?"

"Not yet. Besides, Nathan plans to carry me downstairs in a little while. That way, I can dine at the table with him."

"Do you think that's wise?"

"What? Dining with Nathan?"

"No, letting him carry you down those stairs? What if he should take a notion to drop you? A fall like that could kill you. It certainly killed his father."

Rather than continue with their endless differences of opinion concerning Nathan, Josie agreed to hang on to him extra carefully when they were on the stairs. She then immediately changed the subject to something they could both agree on—how hot the weather had become that afternoon. And how handsome Dr. Harrison was for a man in his mid-fifties.

Barely twenty minutes after Cynthia left, Nathan appeared at Josie's door. His hair was still damp from having taken a hasty bath, and his shirt was only half buttoned.

"I know I'm a little late, but we decided to work until dark. We wanted to get as much done as possible. Are you ready to go eat?" he asked, still fumbling with his remaining buttons when he stepped farther into the room.

"I'm ready for anything that will get me out of this bed," she nodded agreeably, setting her book aside. When she looked at him then, she felt immediately drawn to his pleasant smile. Any doubts she might have unwillingly harbored about him melted away. She awaited eagerly to be taken into his arms. Her insides tingled with anticipation.

"How do you want to go about this?" he asked when he came to a stop beside her bed. Placing his hands on his lean hips, he glanced first at the injured ankle, then at the dark-blue skirts arranged neatly across her outstretched legs. "I don't want to do anything that might hurt your ankle even more."

Josie smiled, pleased he could be so thoughtful. "Just be careful."

A flurry of excitement clamored against her chest when he bent forward to gather her into his strong arms. Cautiously, he slipped one hand just below her knees and the other near the small of her back. Gently, he lifted her from the bed before adjusting her weight evenly in his arms.

"How's that?" he asked, his muscles bulging from

the strain as his gaze met hers. Tiny laugh lines formed at the outside corners of his pale-blue eyes.

"That's fine," she said, and boldly slid her arms around his neck. Tilting her head so she could see directly into the glimmering depths of his eyes, her heart danced to a lively rhythm. "After having put in such a hard day, do you think you will still be able to carry me all the way downstairs?"

"I'll certainly try my best," he said, making his voice sound strained as he slumped forward, pretending to find her a much heavier burden than she really was. "Just please have a little mercy on me. Don't eat too much while we are down there. I'd hate to have to leave you sitting at the table all night."

Grinning, Josie nodded agreeably, then pressed her cheek against his warm shoulder and breathed deeply the tantalizing scent of bath soap and bay rum. "I'll try to keep that in mind."

Nathan laughed, turning toward the door. "See that you do."

Josie chuckled in response to his laughter. Wanting to fully enjoy the feel of his sturdy arms around her, she closed her eyes while he carried her along the hallway toward the stairs. She did not bother to open them again until she felt the downward movement that came from his having made that first step.

"Tired?" he asked as he took a second step.

"Only of having to spend all day alone in that bed," she told him, studying the long, narrow dimples that had formed in his cheeks. The thought of how truly handsome he looked set her pulses into rapid motion. She wished she could stay this close to him forever. Suddenly, she realized their time together was almost half over.

"You don't like being in bed alone?" he asked, his

expression the epitome of innocence. "Would you prefer company?"

She felt a perplexing little leap of her senses. "And just what do you have in mind?"

Nathan focused his attention on the sensual movement of her lips. "Oh, I don't know. If you truly want someone to keep you company while in bed, I thought I might volunteer. I'm certain that, together, we could find something to do in that bed to help pass the time."

Josie's eyebrow shot up. "No doubt."

Nathan's eyes met hers, glittering with sheer deviltry while he continued to carry her down the stairs. Suddenly, his foot slipped and sent them both crashing forward.

"Nathan!" Josie screamed. Her mind filled instantly with Cynthia's harsh warnings as she felt herself break loose from his grasp.

After quickly capturing his balance on the next step, Nathan made a desperate dive to catch Josie in midair. Though he knew he couldn't prevent her striking the stairs completely, he wanted somehow to slow her fall. He hit the stairs below her on his right side as his arms came around her waist, bringing her down on top of him. Together they tumbled the remaining distance to the floor below.

"Josie? Are you all right?" Nathan wanted to know as soon as he had pushed himself into a sitting position. His face was pale and he could barely catch a breath.

Glaring at him accusingly, Josie sat up, jerking angrily at her tangled skirts. "I'm still alive, and I don't think I have any broken bones, if that's what you mean. Maybe you'll have better luck next time."

"Better luck?" Nathan asked, bewildered by her angry response. "You can't think I did that on purpose."

"I don't know what I think anymore." Tears stung her eyes, but the only pain she felt at the moment was to her heart.

Having heard the crash in nearby rooms, Shirley, Ruby, and Jeanne bounded into the entrance hall from three different directions.

"What happened?" Jeanne cried out as the three of them all came to sudden stops. "Are you two all right?"

"Yes, we're fine," Nathan snapped, still angry at Josie for having insinuated the fall may have been intentional. "I was bringing her downstairs for supper when my boot slipped on something."

"Slipped?" Ruby asked, glancing at Josie with a raised brow. "Another *accident?*"

"Yes, it was an accident. I slipped," Nathan shouted furiously as he pushed himself up off the floor. "Do you think that I enjoy falling down a flight of stairs?"

"Are you sure you're all right?" Jeanne asked, glancing nervously at Nathan while she knelt beside Josie, helping to straighten her dress. "Did you hurt your ankle again?"

"No, I don't think so. I'm just a little shaken is all," Josie assured her, and attempted a smile to prove it.

"Here, let me help you up off that floor," Jeanne offered, standing again.

"I'll do that," Nathan insisted. moving forward to intervene. "You three get back to whatever it is you were doing. I can handle everything from here."

Not about to disobey a direct order, the three women slowly backed away, returning in the directions they'd come.

Josie stared at him, horrified. She wondered if his anger was because he'd been falsely accused or because the fall down the stairs had not worked out the way he planned. She watched helplessly while the three women slowly disappeared from sight.

"I can get up by myself," she assured him, quickly leaning forward to do just that. She refused to give him another chance to hurt her.

Nathan knelt beside her and placed his hand on her shoulder to prevent her from doing anything foolish. His face was filled with concern. "Josie, you can't really believe I did that on purpose."

"Can you honestly tell me it was an accident?"

"Yes, of course I can."

"Just like that broken ladder was an accident?"

Nathan studied her paled expression. "Who told you about the ladder? Rafe?"

Then it was true! Josie felt a sharp pain pull her stomach tight. "Let's just say I found out."

Standing, Nathan raked his hand through his hair. "I was hoping you wouldn't find out about that. At least not yet."

"Why?"

"Because I wanted to find out more about it first. I wanted to make sure all the danger was passed before you found out about it."

"Why? If there is even a possibility of more danger, I would think I'd have a right to know. Why would you want to keep something like that from me?"

"I was afraid it would frighten you and you would leave," he answered honestly.

"So what you are really saying is that getting your hands on your half of the inheritance is more important than my safety." Or did he want to keep her there so he could have another chance to hurt her. But what did he have to gain by hurting her? If she left, he would lose his share of the inheritance, too, wouldn't he?

A cold, prickling feeling crawled over her as she remembered something Cynthia had asked days earlier. What would become of the estate if she happened to die before the three months had passed? Would Nathan then inherit *everything?* For the first time, she wondered why Cynthia was not to inherit anything. If she was so close to her brother, why had he left her out of his will? Something was not quite right about the whole situation.

"No, I'm not implying anything like that," Nathan said, shaking his head with exasperation. "Your safety is very important to me. I should think you would know that by now. It's just that I was afraid you'd decide to leave and I'd never get a chance to see you again. Here, let me help you up, then I'll try to explain."

Josie stared reluctantly at his proffered hand.

"Please, Josie, trust me."

Gazing up into the pure blue of his eyes, something told her she could indeed trust him. Slowly she lifted her hand to his. Warmth spread through her as she allowed him to pull her to a standing position. Balancing on her good foot, she then let him help her hobble over to the stairs, where they both sat down to talk.

"Explain then," she said. Knowing she could concentrate better if she didn't touch him, she immediately withdrew her arm from his and placed it in her lap.

"I've been concerned with your safety right from the beginning. The fact is, I've been taking certain precautions ever since I first started to suspect that something was wrong. At night, I've always made certain the house was locked. And during the day, I've constantly kept my eye out for anything unusual.

So has Rafe."

"Why?"

"Because I feel my father died under questionable circumstances. There is a very real possibility he was murdered, and an even better possibility that whoever murdered him has a set of keys to this house with definite plans to use them. The padlock the lawyer put on the front door just days after Father's death and then our coming here so quickly probably foiled those plans to some degree. It just stands to reason, if we manage to sell everything off before whoever stole those keys can find an opportunity to make use of them, there will be far less to steal. And chances are that whoever buys this place will immediately have his own locks installed, which will render those keys useless anyway. It just makes sense that whoever has those keys would want to scare us off before that can happen."

Josie looked at him questioningly. To come up with a story like that, he either had to be extremely creative or he was telling the truth. "Therefore, you've been expecting something like this to happen."

"After searching this house over, yet never finding that original set of keys, I felt it was a possibility. I didn't know whether to look for some attempt to run us off, or an attempt to make use of those keys while we slept. That's why I've been so careful about bolting the doors after I lock them and making sure all the windows that don't have wire screens were securely latched. And now that something has indeed happened, I'm becoming even more cautious. I've even supplied Rafe with a pistol so he can help protect the house. I've asked him to keep an eye out for *anything* that appears to be in any way out of the ordinary."

"Does anyone else know?"

"Jason does. That's why I rode into town right after Rafe told me about the ladder. I wanted to discuss some of the possibilities with him. And I wanted to tell the sheriff."

"And what are the possibilities?"

"There are several really, but nothing we can be sure about."

"Such as," she prompted, wanting to hear more of the details.

"I personally think it is someone who knew Father."

"Why would you think that?"

"Because there were no signs of forced entry the night my father died. No signs that he made any attempt to protect himself."

"But you no longer believe his death was an accident?"

"I really don't know. It could be that he did fall, then someone happened by afterward and discovered the keys on him. Or he might have been deliberately pushed and the keys stolen. The thing that really doesn't make sense, at least not to me, is why whoever has those keys waited this long before causing any trouble."

Josie thought it odd, too. "Another thing. Why didn't the thief use those keys in the days immediately following your father's death, back when no one was living here at all and before Jason had a chance to padlock the door?"

Nathan nodded that it was something he had wondered about, too. "Best I can figure, it was too soon after the murder. The person was probably afraid of getting caught in the house, afraid of being linked to my father's death."

"You think it took him all this time just to get his courage up?"

Nathan's jaw hardened. "Or *her* courage."

331

"*Her* courage? You think the killer might be a woman?"

"One of Jason's theories is that it might have been Pearl Beene, my father's housekeeper. Although she claims to have left for her mother's late that afternoon, hours before he fell, she was never really able to substantiate that claim. Father's handyman had already left to visit with his own family, which always was his custom, so he couldn't say when she left out of here. And Jason never found anyone, other than her own mother, who could back up Pearl's claim. No one recalled passing her on the road or seeing her when she passed through town."

"What about this handyman? Isn't he a likely suspect?"

"Not really. Travis and his brother were seen in town that evening by at least half a dozen people. But no one remembered having seen the housekeeper."

Josie's eyes grew wide. "And your aunt Cynthia mentioned how strange she thought it was that Pearl left so shortly after the funeral."

"It starts to add up," Nathan agreed, nodding. "My guess is she was tired of having to work for a living and saw an easy way to get rich quick. But, because she wanted the death to look like an accident and not a robbery, she had to leave everything in place so she took only the keys. That way, she could come back for his valuables later, after everything had quieted down. Only Jason took it upon himself to padlock the house and then we showed up only a few weeks later, upsetting her plans."

Josie's eyebrows notched with anger. "And she hopes to scare us off so she can carry through with her plans."

"Looks that way."

As Josie thought more about it, her mouth curled at the edges and she slowly started to laugh. "To think Cynthia suspects *you* of having had something to do with your father's death."

"What?" Nathan asked angrily, not seeing any humor in that at all.

"She does. She even went as far as to predict you would try to drop me down these stairs." Suddenly, Josie quit laughing and turned to glance back at the stairway. Was that fall truly a coincidence? Her stomach knotted as she considered it further. Was he telling her the truth?

"I didn't drop you," Nathan reiterated. "I slipped and fell with you in my arms." He then stood and retraced his steps, kneeling to examine each step as he did. When his hand ran across a slick spot about halfway up, his eyebrows shot skyward. "Ah ha! Here it is. This is the reason I slipped."

Josie craned her neck to see. She watched curiously while Nathan put his open hand to his nose and sniffed. His eyes widened instantly.

"Butter!" he proclaimed, then hurried back down to let her sniff the oily substance on his hand. "Whoever brought you your tray earlier must have accidentally dropped some butter on the way upstairs. Did you have anything with butter on it?"

"There was butter for my roll," Josie said, relieved to know it had indeed been an accident. "I didn't eat any, but there was a small dish of it on my tray."

Nathan sank down on the step beside her and smiled triumphantly. "There, you see, I really did slip. That fall really was an accident."

Josie reached out to press her hand against the solid curve of his cheek, smiling apologetically. "I'm sorry I ever doubted you. It's just that two accidents in one day seemed a little excessive, especially after

I'd already learned how the first one really wasn't an accident."

"And I'm sorry I decided to keep that a secret from you. That was wrong. From now on, I promise, no more secrets," he said, capturing her hand between his and pressing his lips gently against her palm.

The intimate touch sent a shockwave of sensations through Josie, making her feel a little light-headed. "And I promise never to doubt you again."

"Ever?" he asked, leaning toward her until their lips were but inches apart.

"Ever," she responded. Her heart pounded rampantly, aware he'd come close enough to kiss her if he so desired. She looked deep into his eyes, hoping to find just such a desire.

"And, from now on, you'll believe whatever I tell you?" he asked, testing her.

"Whatever you tell me," she nodded obediently.

"I'll be able to confide in you completely?"

"Completely."

"And you'll trust me no matter what?"

"Hardly." Smiling mischievously, she asked, "Just what kind of fool do you take me for?"

Nathan's eyes sparkled with amusement and something more as his mouth slowly came forward to claim hers in a passionately sweet kiss.

"Will you at least believe me if I tell you that I think I'm starting to fall in love with you?" he asked, drawing his mouth but a breath away.

Josie's heart soared. Though she hadn't fully realized it, those were the very words she'd longed to hear. "Only if you'll believe me when I tell you the same thing." She smiled, joyously blinking back a sudden rush of tears.

"Josie?" He spoke her name barely above a whis-

per. "I'm serious. I was terrified when I learned you'd —
had that accident. It made me realize just how important you are to me."

"And I am just as serious," she said, leaning forward to sample a second kiss. "I've never been more serious about anything in my life."

"How's your ankle?" he asked, his gaze searching hers.

"What ankle?" She was feeling too many other things to notice any pain. Her chest rose and fell in short, rapid movements as the air surrounding her became grossly inadequate for her needs.

"The ankle the doctor ordered you to take care of. You've had quite a second fall. I don't think we should take any more chances. I think I should get you right back into that bed," he said, also finding it suddenly hard to breathe.

"I think that's a very good idea," she told him, her eyes meeting his, sending a special message of love and acceptance.

Slipping his hands behind her, Nathan lifted her into his arms, then stood. Desire raged through him as he moved carefully back up the stairs, careful to avoid the area that still had traces of spilled butter.

Once he'd topped the stairs and was well away from the danger of falling again, he moved with long, urgent strides toward her bedroom. Upon entering, he paused just long enough to kick the door closed behind them. He looked at her questioningly then, and when she offered no protest, he carried her across the room and gently laid her on the bed.

Josie's eyes met his eagerly when he bent to kiss her again. His lips were warm, tender, and extremely persuasive. She moaned softly with pleasure as the warmth of his mouth pressed against hers. The gentle heat radiated through her body, making her yearn to draw him closer. She lifted her arms to circle his neck.

When Nathan pulled away a few seconds later, no words were spoken, yet his eyes promised a prompt return. Rising, he left her bedside barely long enough to extinguish all but one lamp. When he turned to look at her then, she lay in a single island of golden light, her long hair spilling across her pillows, her eyes dark with unfulfilled passion. Never was there a woman more beautiful or more desirable.

"Josie?" he asked as he knelt on the bed beside her. "Are you sure?"

Always live by your heart, her grandmother had told her in that final letter. *Follow it wherever it may lead you. Worry about the consequences only after they occur.* Josie smiled. Those had been words of wisdom from a woman who knew about love.

"Yes, Nathan, I'm sure," she said as she raised her arms to him. "I am very sure. I've never been more sure of anything in my life."

Worry about the consequences only after *they occur.*

Chapter Twenty

Nathan responded to Josie's declaration with a deep, guttural moan. Their gazes locked as he slowly unbuttoned his shirt, exposing the tanned skin across his wide chest. When he bent to take yet another devouring kiss, the only clothing still clinging to his muscular body was his trousers and the single garment beneath.

No longer able to resist the powers that be, Josie gave of herself fully, pressing her head back deep into her pillows when his lips left hers to trail tantalizing kisses first across the sensitive curve of her cheek, then down the gentle slope of her neck. A delicious, burning sensation rippled through her when his mouth lighted upon the delicate hollow at the base of her throat.

While she yielded eagerly to his feathery kisses, Nathan's hands slipped beneath the thick curtain of mahogany hair, first to stroke the sensitive skin along the back of her neck, then to find the opening of her dress. He prayed she would find no reason to stop him. He wanted her desperately.

Overwhelmed by the power of her own passion, Josie's hands moved upward to caress his neck and shoulders—both gloriously bare to her touch. She marveled at the feel of his taut, lightly haired skin as she moved her fingers over his powerful back. Muscles that had grown sleek and strong from years of hard work rippled beneath her fingertips.

Intrigued by her own explorations and by the feel of his hungry mouth when it returned to claim hers once again, she was only vaguely aware he'd begun to release the many buttons and stays along the back of her dress. One by one they yielded, until Josie felt the material slacken, followed by the shocking warmth of his fingers against the delicate skin along her back. Finally, after the last stay had yielded to his command, the bothersome garment was quickly removed. Her shoes, stockings, camisole, and bloomers swiftly followed, until she lay naked beside him, trembling with anticipation, filled with wonder. The thought of what was to happen next was a little frightening, but at the same time thrilling because she loved him.

Eager to feel the length of her body against his, Nathan wasted no time in removing the last of his own clothing. Soon he lay beside her just as gloriously naked as she. Drawing her close, he pressed himself intimately against her as his mouth returned for yet another passion-filled flurry of kisses. Hungrily, his tongue dipped past her lips to sample the sweetness. Timidly, she followed with her own, lightly touching the smooth edge of his teeth and the velvety surface of his inner mouth, delighted by his shuddering response.

Languorously, his palm moved to stroke the smooth skin along her thigh and hip. Tiny bumps of anticipation formed beneath her skin as the hand moved slowly upward toward her breasts, until, at last, it reached its destination. Shafts of sheer, white-hot pleasure shot through her when his thumb finally brushed against the straining peak.

Throbbing with his own growing need, Nathan fought the urge to conquer quickly. Gently, and ever

338

so slowly, he explored the trembling softness of her breast — caressing the fullness with the curve of his hand while his thumb stroked the tip until it was rigid with desire.

Josie's smoldering passions ignited, bursting into raging, uncontrollable wildfire. She ached to draw him closer, though their bodies were already molded to each other. Still, he was not close enough. She wanted to pull him closer — right into her very being, right into the very core of her soul. She wanted somehow to make him a part of her.

With bodies entwined, their passions soared. Tentative explorations became more and more frantic, their needs far more pressing. Willingly, Josie gave in to the whirling sea of sensations that had so quickly engulfed her. A floodtide of fevered emotions spilled from her heart, filling her with uncontrollable desire.

There would be no turning back. Lost now to her own passion, Josie became more and more aroused with each new place he touched, with each new place he kissed, until she ached with a boundless need to be fulfilled. His sweet taste and familiar scent only served to excite her further. Her blood raced through at an alarming rate, making her feel more vibrant, more alive than she had ever felt before.

Josie felt her pulses deep within her as they pounded with an unbelievable force, throbbing in every part of her. Her senses whirled in a wondrous state of delirium, intoxicating her, heightening her passion, causing her to yield eagerly, instinctively, to his masterful touch.

Consumed with the madness of desire and the sheer power of her love, Josie felt as if she was on fire, wild with a burning need. Her hands pressed into his back with all the strength she possessed. She wanted to bring him closer. She wanted to make him a part of her, so much a part of her that he would never want to leave her.

Though it seemed impossible, their soaring passions climbed even higher. Their hearts filled with wonder.

Nathan continued to work his magic on first one breast, then the other, until Josie wondered how much more of this bittersweet torment she could bear. Eager to bring an end to the exquisite torture, she tugged on his shoulders. Aching with needs she did not yet understand, she pressed herself against him with all her might. Her breasts flattened against his chest. Her mouth became more insistent at his lips. Desperately, she sought to pull him into the flames that burned inside her.

But Nathan was not yet ready to end the slow, sweet climb. He wanted to show her just how splendid lovemaking could be. Holding back his desire to take her, he bent down and mapped a burning trail of kisses first across her delicate collarbone, then downward between her breasts. Josie quivered with anticipation and arched her shoulders back as his mouth moved ever closer to the swelling mounds.

Slowly, he nipped and teased the sensitive skin only inches from one of the straining peaks, causing her to thrust her breasts out further still, eager to hurry him toward his destination. When his mouth finally closed over the rigid tip, she gasped aloud. The pleasure was unbearable, yet she wanted more. She took his head between her hands and pressed him closer, urging him on. But Nathan needed no urging.

Aching with desire, she clutched at him harder, praying he would find a way to bring an end to the bittersweet agony. With every skillful stroke of his hand and with every hungry caress of his tongue, she urgently wanted to bring an end to her torment, yet at the same time she felt eager to give him more.

"Nathan, please, I'm on fire," she cried out in a throaty whisper, thrashing her head from side to side.

Having heard her desperate plea, Nathan rose and looked down upon her naked beauty once more. He watched her breasts strain with the desire that burned inside her and knew the time was right. Eager to feel her warmth surrounding him, he took only a moment longer to gaze at her glorious beauty, then lowered himself to her once more.

Sparks of searing heat shot along Josie's every nerve when he finally moved to claim her. After a brief moment of discomfort, Nathan became a part of her. It was an exquisite feeling. A rapture beyond any she had believed possible, and yet it continued to build, causing her breaths to come in shallow, halting gasps. Her need grew stronger and stronger with each movement of their bodies, until finally, in a splendid burst of glory, she cried aloud his name.

Nathan responded with a deep, shuddering groan that wracked his entire body again and again, leaving him weak. Sated at last, he fell back to lie beside her, making no effort to leave. Instead, he gathered her into his arms and held her close.

Still in awe over what her love had brought her, Josie closed her eyes and pressed her cheek against the solid warmth of his chest as she lay beside him, unmoving, listening contentedly to the steady pounding of his heart as it matched the gentle throbbing in her ankle.

Oddly, she felt no shame as she lay naked beside him, her body still pressed against his. Having taken her grandmother's advice by following the dictates of her heart, she'd discovered what it was to be a woman in love, really in love. It was wonderful. She sighed contentedly.

Several minutes passed before either of them wanted to speak. Nathan took a long breath, then broke the silence with a low, soft voice. "If what my father felt for your grandmother was even half as strong as what I feel for you at this moment, I finally understand why he was so willing to give up everything he ever held dear—even at the risk of scandal—just to share a few stolen moments with her."

Josie blinked back a sudden rush of tears, for she also understood what the two must have felt. "I'm glad they found each other."

"I'm glad *we* found each other," he said, gently stroking her hair as he pressed his cheek against the top of her head. "And I'm glad you found what we just shared as satisfying as I did, because that was only the beginning for us. I intend to make love to you again and again."

Josie tingled at the thought of having pleased him, but at the same time felt troubled. Nathan had yet to say anything that truly committed himself to her. He had admitted to falling in love with her and being pleased with her. But did he want her to be a permanent part of his life or was she just something to occupy his time while having to stay at Oakhaven? She longed to know what was truly in his heart.

"Only the beginning?" she asked timidly, glancing up to see his reaction. "Does that mean you have plans for me?"

"Oh, I definitely have plans for you," he growled, pulling her over on top of him so that her breasts fell against the hard plane of his chest. Gazing at the bulging mounds of womanly flesh, he pulled her higher still until he reached one of the rosy peaks with his mouth. Suckling hungrily, he muttered his next words around the sensitive bud, "Starting right now."

His warm breath against her breast sent a tingling array of sensations through her, leaving her weak and wanting. Arching her head back, she allowed him to draw the nipple deep into his mouth, gasping at the pleasurable sensation it created within her. Though she had no way of knowing if his plans for her went beyond their three months at Oakhaven, she was powerless to stop him from taking all that he wanted from her. Because, if the truth be known, it was what she wanted, too.

It was after midnight when Nathan finally realized he hadn't yet locked the house. Nor had he latched the windows. Nor had they eaten. For the past several hours, he'd been too preoccupied with Josie to consider anything but pleasing her.

"I think I'd better go downstairs and find something to eat. Are you hungry?" he asked as he disentangled himself from the twisted mass of sheets atop her bed.

"Supper!" she gasped, feeling a sickening rush of horror laced with deep mortification when she realized Jeanne had probably waited for them to come back downstairs for hours before giving up and going on to bed. Her hand flew to her cheek as her eyes grew wide at the thought. "Oh no! We forgot all about supper. Do you think anyone suspects the reason we never came back downstairs to eat?"

"Probably," he said, sounding unconcerned as he bent over to retrieve his trousers. "But I doubt they really care one way or the other what we do. All that matters to them is that they get paid every other

Saturday and that Shirley is allowed to use the wagon to visit her family once a month."

"But what if they decide to spread the gossip to others?" she asked, grasping her rumpled sheet and pulling it up to her chin. Suddenly, she felt the need to cover her nakedness.

Nathan studied her while he fastened his trousers. "Are you ashamed of what we did?"

Though Josie knew she should be ashamed, very ashamed, she wasn't. She was too much in love with Nathan to feel any shame — not for having shared something so wonderful certainly. Still, she didn't like the thought of people turning what they felt for each other into petty gossip.

"No, I'm not ashamed," she admitted, though she didn't release her firm hold on the sheet.

"Neither am I. In fact, I intend to be quite open about what I feel for you. After I go downstairs and lock up, I plan to find something for us to eat, then come right back up here and spend the rest of the night in that bed, holding you in my arms."

Josie's heart swelled at the thought. Smiling timidly, though they were beyond any reason to be timid with each other, her hands loosened on the sheet. "Just don't take too long."

Watching as the sheet fell gently across the tops of her breasts, outlining the shapely treasures beneath in a thin white drape, Nathan grinned. "Don't worry. I'll be right back."

Then, without bothering to put on a shirt or his boots, he slipped quietly out of her room into the darkened hall. Discovering that someone had turned out all the lamps before going off to bed, he paused in the hallway long enough to relight the hall lamp nearest Josie's door. Placing the globe back on the lamp, he turned the flame higher until he had sufficient light to see the way to the stairs, then hurried toward them. He was eager to lock up, find something to eat, and return to Josie's arms.

Reaching deep into his side pocket, he pulled out his keys while he proceeded down the stairs. They jingled in his hands as he felt their shapes, but because it was too dark to see, he was unable to single out the keys he would need. He realized he would have to light another lamp as soon as he got downstairs so he could identify each key.

As his feet met with the bottom steps, he noticed a clattering noise off to his right, as if something had fallen to the floor. He paused to listen. Again he heard noises—muffled noises. It sounded as if someone was shuffling papers. Glancing in the direction of the library, he was surprised to discover the room closed. A faint crease of light peeked out from beneath the door. Someone was in there.

A cold, clammy feeling tugged at his stomach as his foot came off the stairs and he moved quietly toward the closed door. Unable to see much in the darkened hallway, he stepped slowly but deliberately, his toes curled to avoid stubbing them on any hard objects that might be in his path.

Planning to surprise whoever was inside, he carefully reached for the knob. But at that moment, as his hand closed over the metal knob, he realized the danger he might face if he entered the room unarmed. He needed to find something to defend himself.

In addition to the small handgun he'd given Rafe, he had two other pistols and a shotgun. He kept one of the pistols in the bottom drawer of his father's desk *in the library*. It was obviously of no use to him, but certainly could be to whoever was in there, should it be discovered.

The other pistol lay hidden beneath his shirts in a dresser drawer upstairs in his bedroom. Having no other choice, Nathan stepped away from the door and headed back up the stairs, trying to move as quickly but as quietly as possible. Every little creak and groan from the wood beneath his weight, which otherwise would have gone unnoticed, sounded like splintering gunblasts to his ears. Knowing the noises might have alerted the intruder to his whereabouts, he hurried. Though he fully understood the danger involved, he was eager to confront the intruder, angered by such an invasion.

Again hampered by darkness when he entered his bedroom, Nathan slowed his steps as he maneuvered his way across the cluttered floor to the dresser. Carefully, he slipped his keys back into his pocket, then eased the top drawer open. He cringed at the scraping sound of wood rubbing against wood. When the opening gaped wide enough to slip his hand inside, he quickly removed the pistol and returned to the hallway. He paused near the hall light to make sure the pistol was still loaded before daring to surprise the intruder.

As he examined the open cylinder, there was a sudden crash downstairs. It sounded like breaking glass.

Knowing whoever it was would try to escape after having made such an obvious noise, Nathan had no more time for precaution. Snapping the barrel in place, he hurried back down the stairs, taking the steps two at a time despite the darkness. His disappointment was overwhelming when he noticed the library door now open and no one in sight.

Stepping carefully toward the open door, aware whoever had been in there might still be hiding, he peered from the darkened hallway into the lighted room, his pistol raised in readiness. Desk drawers and cabinet doors had been left open and papers were strewn everywhere. On the floor was a broken vase. Beside the vase, he noticed splotches of fresh blood.

Taking a cautious step forward, out of the cloak of darkness into the lighted room, he listened carefully for any sound that might alert him to where the prowler had hidden.

Once inside, he noticed that the two smaller windows on either side of the larger bay window were open. It was possible the intruder might have squeezed through one and escaped, but not likely. Having found the door open again when before it had been closed, he felt the odds were more in favor of finding the person in another part of the house. He turned back toward the darkened hallway and took a deep breath, wondering which direction to search.

The first thing he noticed as he stepped back into the hallway was a faint, almost undetectable light against the far wall in the dining room. Aware the light came from the kitchen, he took another deep, steadying breath, then moved back across the hall, toward the dining-room door. The light suddenly went out. He listened carefully for any noise that would alert him to the prowler's location. Just as he reached the dining-room door and was about to step inside, he heard Josie's voice overhead. The unexpected sound startled him.

"What happened down there?" she called out to him. "What did you break?"

Not wanting to alert the intruder to his exact whereabouts, Nathan did not reply. He prayed she would sense the danger and turn back.

"Nathan? Answer me. What did you break?"

Glancing up, he saw her standing at the top of the stairs, clutching a blue silk dressing robe. He had no way of knowing if she could see him or not.

"Nathan?" she called out again, taking the first steps into the darkness. She leaned heavily against the banister to keep as much weight off her injured ankle as possible. "Nathan, where are you?"

At that moment, there was a rustling noise in the kitchen, followed by a sharp thud, then another splintering crash.

"Go back," he called to Josie, his voice coming out in a low growl. "Go back upstairs and lock yourself in your room."

"But why?"

"Don't ask questions, just do as you're told."

Josie hesitated, wanting to help, but at the same time not wishing to cause any unnecessary complications if there was indeed some sort of trouble. Finally she turned away to do exactly what she'd been told. But before she'd gone ten feet, she heard Nathan's startled gasp and her hand flew to her throat.

"Damnation, Rafe!" Nathan bellowed angrily. "You scared the bloody hell out of me! What are you doing in the house?"

"I thought I heard a crash. I came to investigate," Rafe explained. The pistol in his hand was pressed flat against his chest. Obviously he'd been just as startled as Nathan by their unexpected encounter. "When I discovered the back door unlocked, I got worried. I came on in to investigate. What did you break?"

"I didn't break anything. Someone was prowling around in the library and broke a vase. I think whoever it was is still in the house. Did you see anything suspicious when you came in?"

"Not really. When I first came in, I thought I saw

348

a shadow moving about in the kitchen, but when I struck a couple of matches to get a better look around, I found I was alone. After the matches burned out, I decided to light a lamp so I could see to get around in there. Having spotted a table lamp before the matches burned out, I thought I knew about how far it was from me. But I misjudged the distance. I bumped into the table while groping about in the dark. That knocked over the lamp and broke the globe. I'll pay for the damage."

Nathan was unconcerned with the broken globe.

"You thought you saw a shadow moving around in the kitchen?" he asked, and glanced toward the dimly lit doorway at the far side of the dining room. He wondered if the intruder had heard Rafe enter the house and decided to hide. "Maybe we'd better go have a second look, just to be sure. You head back through here and I'll circle around outside. If there is someone hiding in that kitchen, we'll find him — or her."

Josie stood frozen at the top of the stairs, staring down into the darkness, barely able to make out the shapes of the two men as she listened to their muffled voices. She caught only a few of their words, but enough to alert her to further danger. "Nathan, be careful."

Startled by her voice, Nathan's heart jumped and his eyes narrowed with anger. "I thought I told you to lock yourself in your room. Damnit, woman, do what I tell you. I've got enough problems without having to worry about your safety, too."

Feeling the sharp blow of his wrath, Josie bit into the tender flesh behind her lip, then turned and limped hurriedly back to her bedroom. Swiftly, she bolted both the hallway door and the door that led to the balcony. With her heart beating wildly beneath her breast, she then turned out the lights in her room and waited.

Meanwhile, Rafe and Nathan approached the kitchen from opposite directions. Though they knew the intruder might have slipped out a window and be long gone by now, they both held their pistols raised and ready. The danger could be anywhere.

Nathan entered from the outside, taking time to close and bolt the door behind him so the intruder could not use it to escape. After scanning the room and finding it apparently empty, he began searching the different hiding places he thought large enough for a body to fit, taking no chances. When the search turned up nothing, he motioned for Rafe to head down one of the two hallways that led toward the back of the house while he carefully made his way along the other, checking each room as he came to it.

Suddenly it struck him as curious that none of the women had heard either crash, especially when Rafe had heard the first noise all the way out to the bunkroom, at the very back of the barn—and Josie had heard it upstairs. Nor had they heard the second crash, and it had happened just down the hall from their bedrooms.

Cautiously, he moved toward the two servants' quarters near the end of the hall and pressed his ear against one of the doors. He heard nothing. Knowing Shirley and Ruby should be inside, he knocked lightly. He aimed his pistol toward the ceiling, but held it ready to lower and fire.

Ruby answered the door several seconds later, clutching her robe with one hand and rubbing her eyes with the other. "Yeah? What do you want?"

"Are you all right?" he asked, glancing past her into the semidarkness of the room. Ruby had taken the time to light a small candle at her bedside before coming to the door. Though the light it cast was dim, he could see objects within. To his amazement he saw Shirley lying in another bed, her cheek pressed against her pillow, covers pulled to her chin, still soundly asleep. Neither his knock nor Ruby's voice had wakened her. It was when he noticed the small metal flask on the table beside Shirley's bed that he realized the reason she slept so soundly. She had obviously taken a little nip before bedtime.

"Of course I'm all right," Ruby muttered as she stepped on out into the hallway, partially closing the door behind her. "Why shouldn't I be?"

"You didn't hear any strange noises?"

"Nothing out of the ordinary," she claimed, reaching up to scratch her head through her white nightcap. There was enough light from the kitchen for him to see her confused expression clearly.

"You didn't think the sound of a vase or a glass globe breaking in the middle of the night was a bit unusual?"

"Is that what those noises were? I wondered what you broke."

"Then you did hear them. But you didn't come out to investigate," he pointed out, wondering why.

Ruby shrugged. "I saw no reasons to get out of bed. Besides, I figured I'd find out what it was in the morning."

Nathan frowned as he studied her disinterested expression. "After you heard the vase and then the globe break, you didn't hear anything else unusual?"

"I went right on back to sleep both times. Why? What was I supposed to hear?" Her brows arched when she glanced down and noticed that Nathan held a pistol in his hands.

Just then, a door down the hall creaked open.

Nathan whirled to face the noise and was relieved to see Jeanne's wide-eyed face pop cautiously out of the doorway.

"Mr. Garrett, I heard something," she said in a low, guttural voice as she stepped hesitantly out into the hallway, clutching her robe with one hand and holding a huge brass candlestick in the other. The glow from the candle cast eerie shadows across her dark face as she stepped closer to them. "I'm always hearing strange noises in this house late at night."

"What sort of noises?" Nathan asked, relieved to be getting somewhere at last.

"Spooky noises, like someone is moving around looking for something." The whites of her eyes grew to enormous proportions while she glanced first one direction then the other, as if expecting to find someone watching her.

"Why haven't you mentioned these noises to me before?"

"Because I didn't think you'd believe me."

"Why wouldn't I?"

"Because most folks don't believe in ghosts."

"Ghosts?" he and Ruby asked in unison.

Nathan sighed with exasperation, wondering now how much credibility to place on whatever else she had to say. "Surely you don't think Oakhaven is haunted."

Jeanne tossed her heavy shoulders back, deadly serious. "Yessir, I do. I think it's your daddy's own spirit that walks this house at night. I've looked out of my room and seen his shadow on the wall and I've heard him moving things around in the darkest hours of the night."

Ruby's eyebrows drew together, forming a deep notch in her weathered forehead. "Now that you mention it, I've heard some strange noises, too, in

352

the middle of the night. But I figured it was just one of you up and around, looking for something to eat or drink. It never occurred to me that it might be a ghost!"

At that moment, Shirley snorted loudly, then rolled over in her bed, causing Ruby and Jeanne both to cry out in startled alarm. Jeanne jumped sideways and pressed her ample frame against the wall, her terrified gaze cutting first one direction then the other, so frightened that she trembled.

"Calm down, you two. That was Shirley — snoring in her sleep. Get a hold of yourselves. There are no such things as ghosts," Nathan tried to reason with them.

But there was such a thing as a prowler, and he'd wasted enough time listening to their nonsense. He had to get on with his search. Time was important. "I'm sorry I bothered you. Go on back to bed and get some sleep. We can talk more abut this in the morning."

"Might as well put that pistol away," Jeanne said, as she stepped slowly backward toward her room, her candle held high. "Don't do no good to shoot a ghost. They's already dead."

"I'll try to remember that," he muttered, watching while she gave the hallway one last quick glance.

"All a person can do about havin' a ghost in the house is stay clean out of its way. You sure don't want to go riling it none."

"I agree," Ruby put in quickly — too quickly. "I think the best thing we can do is keep behind closed doors whenever we hear him roaming about. Maybe if we don't interfere with his doings, he won't want to harm any of us."

Nathan studied her eerie gaze. "Ghost or no ghost, I have no intention of ignoring any noises in this

353

house. And now that you both have told me you've heard them before, I'll be paying a lot more attention to them. I fully intend to discover the source."

"That might not be very wise," Ruby warned.

"Like I said, we can discuss this further in the morning. Good night," he said firmly, letting her know he was finished talking with her.

"Good night, sir."

A cold, prickling sensation crawled along the back of his neck while he watched her step back into the shadows of her bedroom and slowly close the door. Turning away, he wondered why she and Jeanne seemed so anxious to have him believe Oakhaven was haunted. Did they have something to do with that prowler being in the library?

Lost to such thoughts, he headed back toward the kitchen, eager to find out what Rafe had discovered.

Just as he entered into the glow of the table lamp Rafe had lit earlier, he heard a sharp clunk of wood and the immediate clatter of metal. He turned just in time to see Rafe stumble sideways, then fall to the floor.

Chapter Twenty-one

"Rafe, what happened?" Nathan asked, dropping to the floor and rolling up against the protection of a worktable in one easy motion. He kept his pistol pointed in the direction of the narrow hallway Rafe had just tumbled out of. His heart pounded hard against the walls of his chest while he waited for something to happen, something that would let him know exactly what he was up against.

"I was attacked," Rafe muttered as he sat up, gingerly rubbing his jaw.

"By who?"

"By a damned door."

Nathan blinked twice as he replayed Rafe's response in his mind, then slowly lowered his pistol. "You were what?"

"Attacked by a door," he repeated, staring accusingly down the hall at the large wooden door in question.

"Rafe, be serious. Tell me what happened." Aware that the person who had really attacked Rafe was still somewhere down that small hallway, since it had no other outlet than through the kitchen, he edged his way toward Rafe. He wanted to get a look at his injury before confronting any more danger.

"I *am* serious," Rafe said with a dark scowl. "I was attacked by a door."

"How can a door attack you?" Nathan asked. While

glancing at the red welt along the side of Rafe's jaw, he kept a cautious watch over the hallway.

"Damned if I know. When I first went down that hall, the only doors open were the ones that open into the rooms and away from the hall. But when I finished checking those last two rooms near the end and turned to start back toward the kitchen, suddenly there was that door—standing wide open in the middle of the hall. I didn't see it in time and hit it square against my jaw."

Despite the seriousness of the situation, Nathan couldn't help but grin. "Sounds more to me like you attacked the door than it attacked you."

"What I want to know is how that door suddenly opened all on its own like that. It's almost as if a ghost had a hand in the incident."

"Oh, no. Not you, too," Nathan moaned, shaking his head as he stood. He'd heard all he wanted about ghosts and haunted houses. "Please don't tell me that you believe in ghosts, too. I've had enough of that nonsense."

"It may be nonsense to you, but something had to cause that door to open," Rafe declared as he pushed himself up off the floor and began searching for his pistol.

"Or *someone*," Nathan corrected. His gaze returned to the hallway where the dark wood door still stood open. He scowled as he watched for possible movement in the bleak darkness that rose out of the cellar. "And I think that someone is still here in this house, hiding somewhere down that hall."

"Why's that?"

"Because there is no way out of that hall except through this kitchen. There's only a pantry, a storage room, and the cellar down that way. None of which have windows or outside doors—except for the cellar."

"I was about to mention that there was a door down there when I looked just a minute ago. Don't you reckon whoever it was could have gotten out that way?" His shoulders slackened with disappointment.

"I doubt it. The outside door in the cellar is never used. It's kept locked at all times. In fact, I don't even have a key that opens that door. It's got a sturdy padlock and a chain on the outside keeping it shut. It can't even be opened from the inside. Not even with a key."

"You mean we've got him?" Rafe asked, his brow rising with renewed interest. Having spotted his pistol lying under one of the worktables, he bent to retrieve it. "There's no way he could have gotten out?"

"Sure looks that way," Nathan said, nodding agreeably and feeling a cold surge of excitement tempered with caution. "It appears we've got her trapped all right, somewhere down that hall. My guess is we'll find her hiding down in that cellar. All we really have to do now is flush her out."

"How can you be sure he's still there?" Rafe asked, not yet willing to acknowledge the culprit as a woman.

"Because I'd already returned to the kitchen when she hit you with the door."

"Hit me with it?"

"Or when she opened it so you'd run smack into it. The point is, I would have seen her if she'd tried to come this way. No, I figure she ran down into the cellar, hoping to hide from us."

"Well, what are we waiting for?" Rafe asked, dusting off the handle of his weapon, then heading back toward the hall.

"Wait a second," Nathan said, and grabbed Rafe by the shoulder. "I don't want to take any chances of letting her slip by us unnoticed."

"You still sure it's that runaway housekeeper, aren't

you?" Rafe asked. He finally noticed that Nathan kept referring to the intruder in terms of *her* and *she*.

"Who else could it be?" Nathan answered, moving with Rafe to the opening of the narrow corridor. "And I don't intend to let her get away from me. I want her in jail where she belongs. Even if she didn't intentionally kill my father, I feel certain she took his keys with the intention of using them to steal something from this house."

"Like what?"

"Paintings probably. And possibly his silver serving pieces, and his silverware. That sort of thing. What I want you to do is stand here and guard the hall for me so she can't possibly get by. If it is Pearl Beene, she knows all the little nooks and crannies of this house and will know the best places to hide. If I happen to overlook her hiding spot, I don't want her making a run for it after I've passed by."

"I understand. I'll wait right here with my eyes wide open and my pistol loaded and ready," Rafe promised, planting his feet to the ground in a show of force. "She won't get by me."

"Just don't take any unnecessary chances because she's a woman. Be ready to shoot if she's armed in any way. If she did kill my father, she won't hesitate hurting us in an attempt to get away," Nathan warned, then turned to face the dark corridor. With the light at his back, his shadow fell across a wide area, taking away part of what little light he'd had.

Nathan tilted his head for a moment, studied the situation further, then turned back to the kitchen. "I guess I'd better take a candle or a hand-lamp with me. It will be pitch black in that cellar."

Rafe agreed that would be best and watched while Nathan pulled a small, molded-glass hand-lamp off a high shelf. Minutes later, when Nathan approached the open door, he had his pistol in one hand and the hand-lamp in the other. Holding the small lamp high over his head, he moved cautiously down the steep staircase until he reached the planked floor at the bottom.

"Pearl?" he called out, holding perfectly still while he scanned the various shadows in the room. "Might as well come on out. You can't get away. I've got a man covering the hall. He's armed and ready to shoot."

Nathan's words were met with chilling silence.

Slowly, he moved about the room. He was careful about where he turned his back, aware Pearl could be armed with a knife or a club—or even a gun. Using the toe of his boot, he pushed crates over and scooted barrels aside, hoping to reveal her hiding place. When he didn't find her in any of the more obvious places, he started searching inside things. Carefully, he popped the lids off the larger barrels with a crowbar and lifted the tops off any wooden bin that looked large enough to hide a small woman. Still, he found nothing, not even in the open area underneath the main staircase.

He stood in the middle of the small, damp room, perplexed. He'd been so sure he'd find her in the cellar. It had seemed the most obvious place for her to have gone after opening that door.

Frustrated, he headed back up the stairs toward the hall, when he glanced back and noticed the wooden steps that led to the outside door. Though the space beneath was tiny, it was large enough for a small person to crawl through. He went back to check, but all he found was a small, mildewed satchel and a case of empty fruit jars. He rattled the door latch to make sure the outside door was still locked.

Disappointed, he returned to the hallway. When he

glanced back to where Rafe's broad shoulders filled the entrance, he saw the man's dark form silhouetted by the yellow light flickering from the broken lamp directly at his back.

"No luck yet," he told him. "But just in case I missed something down there, keep your eye on this doorway while I head farther back to check those other two rooms."

"She's not getting by here," he assured him, leaning casually against the wall and crossing his arms, the pistol still held tightly in his grip.

Smiling at Rafe's show of confidence, Nathan stepped farther down the hall to where the final two doors stood directly across from each other. Choosing the one on the right, he entered the pantry and searched it thoroughly. When he did not find anyone there, he again returned to the hall and faced the opposite door.

"She has to be in there," he said, glancing only briefly at Rafe before looking back into the blackness of the room before him. Filling his lungs with a deep, sustaining breath, he proceeded with the last leg of his search. As he entered the downstairs room he'd earlier let Josie think she would have to use, he held the lamp high and began to prod the scattered contents with his boot.

It was a tiny room, filled with boxes of chipped jars and useless pieces of broken furniture. There were very few places large enough for a person to hide. Soon he'd searched the room thoroughly and was even more frustrated when he failed to find anyone hiding there. He'd run out of places to look. Where was she?

When he stepped back out into the hallway, his expression was a mixture of anger and puzzlement. "I can't find her anywhere."

"But she's got to be here. There's no way she could

360

have gotten away," Rafe replied, stepping forward. "You said so yourself. Hand me that lamp and let me have a look around while you guard the hall."

Nathan willingly handed the lamp to Rafe and stood at the entrance of the hallway, watching while Rafe approached the three rooms, starting with the small storage room, then moving across to the pantry, and searching the cellar last.

When he came out of the cellar, Rafe's expression was just as puzzled as Nathan's had been.

"It's like she vanished into thin air. Maybe we are dealing with some sort of ghost," Rafe said, grabbing the knob of the cellar door and pushing it closed behind him. "Or maybe there's a hidden door we don't know about."

Nathan thought about that, but there was really no place for such a door. No space for a hidden room, which would give reason for a hidden door.

Rafe headed toward him, his bushy eyebrows drawn low as he thought more about it. "I sure thought we had her."

"So did I," Nathan muttered, shaking his head with regret. "I just don't see how she got by us."

"Nor do I."

While looking at the disappointment etched with deep lines onto Rafe's burly face, Nathan noticed a movement over the man's left shoulder. His blue eyes widened while he watched the cellar door slowly swing open all by itself.

"Rafe, look," he said, motioning toward the moving door with a brief, forward motion of his hand.

Rafe turned in time to see the door sway for a moment, then come to a stop out in the hall. Swallowing hard, he glanced back at Nathan. "Maybe you *do* have a ghost."

"Or maybe that door is off kilter," Nathan stated,

stepping forward to investigate. While carefully studying the doorframe, he slowly pushed the door closed again with the flat of his right hand. He noticed he had to push on it extra hard to make it to click into place. Lifting his brow curiously, he reached down for the knob to open it again. When he did, he felt something sticky.

"Blood," he said when he glanced down at his hand, more confused than ever. There was blood in the library and now there was blood on the cellar doorknob. Whoever had broken the vase must have come this way.

"Blood? Let me see," Rafe said, reaching out to touch the knob. When he did, they both noticed spotty patches of blood on his right hand. Upon further examination, they discovered he'd been cut.

"How did that happen?" Nathan asked, as he reached for his shirt pocket to retrieve his handkerchief only to be reminded he wore no shirt; it was still upstairs in Josie's bedroom.

"I don't know." Frowning as he took his bandana out of his hip pocket, Rafe shrugged. "I guess I cut myself when I broke away the rest of the glass off that lamp so I could light it."

"Then the blood on the knob could be yours."

"I guess so. I really hadn't noticed I was bleeding," Rafe admitted as he carefully wrapped his hand with the bandana, then tucked away the loose end. "And I did open that door earlier so I could glance in and see what was down there. I touched it again just a minute ago when I closed it."

"So the blood on the doorknob means nothing," Nathan uttered as he finished opening the door, then shut it, this time without letting it click. He watched it carefully when he stepped back. Seconds later, the door swung open to precisely the same angle as before.

"Damn!" he cursed under his breath, slamming the side of his fist hard against the wall. "Exactly what I was afraid would happen. No one opened that door. After you looked in, you must not have closed it back all the way. It opened again all by itself."

"I'm sorry," Rafe said, looking down at the rounded toes of his scuffed boots. "I thought I closed it."

"And while we were so busy searching around here for the prowler, I imagine she was just as busy making good her escape in another part of the house."

"Think so?"

"Bound to be. Would *you* stick around if you knew two men, both armed with guns, were out to get you?"

"I guess not," Rafe admitted, though reluctant to give up hope. "Still, I think we should give this entire house a good once-over. Just in case."

"I agree. We'll take the rooms one at a time, latching the windows and locking doors as we go." Nathan turned to start with the kitchen door.

"Want me to bunk in the house tonight?" Rafe asked as he fell in step beside him.

"Only if you feel you'd be unsafe sleeping in the bunkroom," Nathan told him. "After I've locked all the doors and secured any windows that are large enough for someone to climb through and that have no mesh coverings, I don't think she'll be able to get back inside. At least not without making enough noise to wake somebody. The only reason she managed to slip in unnoticed tonight is because I hadn't yet bothered to lock up for the night."

Rafe looked at him as if curious to know why not, but decided not to ask. "If you're sure you will be safe, then I'd really rather go back outside and sleep in my own bunk. All I have to do out there is put that wooden bar across my only door and no one can bother me."

"That'll be fine. I feel sure the house will be safe as soon as we get all the doors and windows closed and securely locked," Nathan said, his face twisted deep with thought. "But I think it does prove one thing."

"What's that?"

"That she's been out there watching, just waiting for a chance to get into this house. Jeanne and Ruby claim they've heard noises during the night, but they both decided it was my father's ghost roaming the house."

Rafe shuddered at the thought.

"Even so, they've both heard unexplainable noises during the night," Nathan continued. "Therefore, I think Pearl has been trying the windows and doors regularly, probably each night soon after she sees the lights go out." His lips flattened into a grim line when he realized how easily she had taken advantage of his carelessness. "I'll just have to take more precautions in the future."

Moving on to the front of the house, then slowly working their way toward the back, Rafe and Nathan closed and either latched or locked all the windows and doors while they discussed where Pearl might be hiding outside and how she had gotten out after she'd been discovered on the inside.

One by one, they checked every room, every closet, every hiding place they could think of, wanting to be certain Pearl was no longer in the house.

Upon entering the library, Nathan felt his anger flare again when he viewed the clutter a second time. Several of the cabinet doors had been left carelessly open. The papers and books inside had been shuffled around, but for the most part were still on the shelves. Most of the desk drawers had also been left open, the various contents scrambled, papers spilling out onto the floor.

Nathan felt his anger turn into cold rage as he moved toward the littered desk. His father's desk. "She was sure in a hurry. I wonder what she expected to find in here."

"Probably money. Did your father keep cash hidden away in his desk or maybe in one of these cabinets?" Rafe asked as he closed the cabinet doors.

"If he did, I never came across it," Nathan stated, straightening some of the scrambled papers before closing the first two drawers. "In fact, the only cash he had was what little was found on his body the night he died."

As soon as he'd closed that second drawer, Nathan bent lower to push the bottom drawer shut. Suddenly he felt his stomach tighten into a sickening knot. His blood turned ice-cold as the hardening sensations settled in the pit of his chest. "The pistol is gone."

"What pistol?"

"The small derringer I kept in this drawer in case something suspicious ever happened while I was downstairs. It's gone."

"Are you sure?" Rafe hurried to his side.

Nathan stared down at the empty space where the gun had lain and nodded. Only a small nest of rumpled papers remained. "I'm sure."

"That means she's definitely armed."

"With a gun. And that makes our situation far more dangerous."

Rafe's eyes widened. "And might give her a reason not to run. With a gun to protect herself, there's a good chance she is still in this house, hiding somewhere, waiting to surprise us. She could even be just outside that door." His face paled when he looked out into the hall. "Waiting for us. Both of us."

Nathan's next thought was of Josie upstairs alone and unarmed. "Or she may have gone upstairs—"

Not ready to voice his worst fear, Nathan burst from the room. With no thought for his own safety, he took the stairs two at a time. Rafe followed at a far more cautious pace, his back to the wall where he could glance back at where he'd been as well as at what lay ahead.

"Josie?" Nathan called out as soon as he had her closed bedroom door in sight. "Josie? Are you all right?"

He tried the door, but found it locked. Panic gripped his heart. "Josie! Answer me!"

Rafe soon stood beside him, his gaze cutting from Nathan's frantic expression to the locked door, then back toward the stairs. "She doesn't answer?"

A noise was heard inside.

"Josie!" Nathan cried. "Damnit, if you are in there answer me!"

"I'm fine," she responded barely seconds before he heard the metal bolt slide out of place. An instant later, the door opened.

"Then why didn't you answer me sooner?" he shouted angrily as he pushed his way into the dark room, looking around in every direction, wanting to be absolutely certain she'd told him the truth. The only light in the room came from the hallway, but it was enough to assure him Josie was alone.

"I was on my way to the door to open it," she explained, thinking that should account for something.

"Still, you could have answered me!"

"I'm sorry, " she apologized. Her forehead notched when she stepped away from him, studying the hard glint in his eyes. She wondered why he was so angry over something so trivial. "I didn't want to shout

366

through the door. Besides, I was only a few feet away when you called out. How was I to know you were too impatient to wait for a response, too impatient to wait what few seconds it would take to open the door?"

Seeing how his harsh actions had frightened her, Nathan quickly moved forward and took her into his arms. "I'm sorry I shouted like that. It's just that when you didn't answer right away, I was afraid you'd been hurt."

"Why?" she asked.

But before Nathan could answer, Rafe stepped into the room. As soon as he noticed Josie was not properly dressed, he spun around to face the doorway. His neck turned instantly red.

"Sorry, ma'am. I didn't realize," he stammered, reaching up to run a hand through his thick, curly hair. "I just wanted to say something to Nathan."

"What is it?" Nathan asked, grinning at Rafe's startled reaction, relieved it had been him and not Pearl.

"I was just thinking, if you're through with me I'd really like to get on back out to my bunk now."

"That's fine. I'll take care of shutting the windows upstairs," Nathan assured him, still holding Josie close. He was so relieved to know she was unharmed that the muscles in his legs felt weak. "Because most of these rooms are bedrooms that need a cross breeze during the night, there are only a few windows up here that aren't protected with wire mesh. It'll only take a few minutes."

Rafe took several steps toward the hallway, then hesitated, his back still to them. "I, uh, I need someone to unlock the back door and let me out."

Reluctant to let Josie go, but aware he was the only one who could let Rafe out, Nathan sighed. "Go on ahead. I'll be right there."

Satisfied his problem was solved, Rafe disappeared

through the door.

"I can latch the windows for you while you're letting Rafe out," Josie suggested, pulling away from his warm embrace to do just that.

"Oh, no, you won't. As soon as I leave this room, you are to bolt this door back and wait for me to return. *I'll* get the windows," Nathan told her in a stern voice, letting her know she'd better not argue with him. Though he felt the danger was past, he didn't want to take any unnecessary chances.

"But why?" A twisting combination of fear and utter panic gripped her when she looked down and noticed the pistol dangling from his hand. Until then, he'd held it at his side or behind her back, out of her sight. "Nathan, what's this all about? What happened down there?"

"I'll tell you all about it when I get back," he said, tucking the pistol into his waistband as if to assure her the trouble had passed. "Until then, I want you to keep this door bolted. Don't open it for anyone except me."

"I promise," she said, gazing up at him quizzically. "But do hurry."

"I will," Nathan promised. He bent forward to place a gentle kiss at her temple before turning toward the door. After he stepped out into the hallway, he waited until she'd closed her door. Then, after hearing the bolt slide into place, he tested it. Only after he was certain no one could get into her room without breaking the door did he remove the pistol from his waistband and go downstairs to open the back door for Rafe. Upon returning upstairs, he decided to go ahead and shut any unprotected windows that might have been left open.

He started with the room nearest to the stairs, an unused bedroom. Leaving the door open so he'd have enough light to see his way across the room, he curled his bare toes to prevent any painful accidents and crossed the floor to check the windows. They were both closed and latched, and both were protected by screens.

When he came back out, he headed immediately for the bedroom on the opposite side of the hall. As he passed his father's studio, he reached out and rattled the knob merely as a precaution. Because of all the valuable paintings inside, that particular room was kept locked, even during the day except when he or Josie had a reason to go in.

To his surprise, the door came easily open.

Stopping suddenly, he stared at the open door with disbelief.

His first thought was that Pearl had come upstairs and used her key to get in. But the logical side of his brain felt it just as reasonable to think Josie may have accidentally left it unlocked. It was possible she had gone inside to look over his father's paintings and for some reason neglected to lock the door back when she was through.

He tried to remember when she'd borrowed the studio key last. It had been days. Had the door gone unlocked for that long? Or had it recently been undone? The muscles along his throat constricted, making it hard to swallow while he stared into the dark shadows of the room beyond. Again he considered the possibility that Pearl had used his father's key to let herself in the studio. And if that was the case, she might still be in there. Hiding. Waiting.

Cautiously, he stood to one side of the doorway and stuck only his right hand inside, feeling for the wall lamp he remembered to be only a few inches from the door. After locating it, he carefully turned the knob to raise the wick, then removed the glass globe and set it on the edge of the nearby countertop. Next he felt around near the base of the lamp with the tips of his fingers until he found the tiny compartment that held the matches. After singling one out, he struck it across the metal base. Then, while he held the burning match between his thumb and forefinger, he used his other three fingers to feel the shape of the lamp until he located the proper place to touch the match. Soon the wick caught and the room filled with light.

He listened carefully for any sound inside the room, then, hearing only silence, he brought his hand back. Quietly, he transferred his pistol from his left hand back to his right and slowly cocked the hammer back. Bending low to make a smaller target, he then spun himself into the room, knocking over an easel in the process. The resulting clatter of wood caused his heart to slam hard against the walls of his chest as he dropped immediately to the floor. But after he scanned his surroundings, he discovered nothing else moved.

He was alone.

Letting out a slow, shaky breath, he stood and moved farther into the room. He was surprised to discover one of the windows open. Though he or Josie often pulled the drapes back to emit more light whenever they were in the room, they rarely took the trouble to open the windows. They were never in the room long enough to bother. So why was the window open now?

After turning down the light to a bare flicker to make himself less visible from the outside, he crossed the room and glanced outside through the open window. The drop to the ground was at least fifteen feet, with nothing below to help break a fall. There was little chance anyone had entered or left the house through the window. Still, he felt the open window was a bad omen. Taking time to close it and twist the latch into place, he left the room to see if Josie knew anything about the unlocked door or the open window.

He barely took the time to step inside her bedroom before asking her about what he'd found.

"I have no idea why that window was open," Josie answered, gazing up at him questioningly. "I've never bothered to open any of the windows in there. And I'm certain I locked that door back the last time I was in there; I always do."

"That's what I was afraid of," he said, then pressed his lips together as he thought more about it.

"Nathan, I don't understand what's happening around here. Who else could have unlocked that door?" she asked. Then remembering what he'd told her earlier that night, her eyes widened. "You don't think it was Pearl Beene? You don't think she's actually been in this house, do you?"

"Yes, I do. And more than once," Nathan commented, raking his hand through his hair and pacing restlessly about the room.

"More than once? How do you know that?"

Having promised no more secrets, Nathan told her the whole story, leaving nothing out, not even the part about the stolen pistol. When he finished, Josie was so stunned and so frightened, she had to sit down before hearing any more.

After taking advantage of the nearest chair, she stared idly into space while Nathan summed up his own thoughts on the matter. "So, not only did she manage to get in the house tonight, she's obviously been in here before. She's even been in Father's studio without us knowing it."

"Did she take any of the paintings?" she asked fearfully.

Nathan's gaze met hers. "I don't know. She may have. But how? How could she have gotten anything that large out of the house without someone seeing her? Slipping in and out unnoticed is one thing, but making off with a painting would be another matter entirely. Surely we'd have seen or heard her."

It sounded convincing, even to himself. Yet they saw the doubt in each other's eyes. Without speaking their reasons, they went together to the studio to see if anything was missing.

Because he was not absolutely certain all danger was gone, Nathan entered first, his pistol drawn. Seconds later Josie followed.

"The painting of the little girl with the yellow kitten is gone," Josie noticed right away. Having realized the feline subject was Scoundrel, the little kitten her grandmother had mentioned in her letters, Josie had become especially fond of that particular painting. Tears stung her eyes when she discovered it missing.

Nathan looked around to be certain the painting had not been accidentally set aside somewhere. But when he did not find it, he had to agree. The painting was gone. "I can't believe she managed to get that painting out of here without anyone seeing her. She must have taken it in broad daylight, or else in the early evening while we were all downstairs."

"How can you know that?"

"Because, even with a set of keys, she couldn't have opened the outside doors during the night because I've always taken the added precaution of bolting them from the inside. A key isn't going to open a bolted door. And unless she has a way of removing wire screens and renailing them afterward, she couldn't possibly have entered through the windows. The only time she could have gotten in this house is during the time we're awake and those doors are

372

unlocked. She must have slipped in while our backs were turned."

"That's scary."

"And it makes me wonder if she doesn't have someone inside this house helping her. Someone who conveniently turns her back when the time is right, and maybe even goes as far as to help make sure the others are safely out of the way."

"Who would do something like that?"

"There are only three possibilities."

"Four, if you count Rafe."

Nathan closed his eyes a moment while he considered Rafe as a possible accomplice. Was Rafe linked to Pearl? Had he purposely tried to distract him with the mysterious opening door so Pearl would have a better chance of getting away? If Pearl had known about the door, she could have told him ahead of time to use it if the need for a distraction ever arose.

Or had she indeed been hiding in one of those rooms, relying on Rafe to let her slip by while he himself was down in the cellar searching for her? One thing was for certain: if this incident was in any way linked with the ladder incident, Rafe would be a prime suspect. He'd had plenty of opportunity to tamper with that ladder without having to worry about getting caught.

"You're right," Nathan finally admitted. "At this point there are four possibilities."

"How do we know who we can trust anymore?" she asked, looking at him, bewildered by the thought.

"We don't," he said softly, then knelt beside her so he could see her better. "From now on, we can only trust each other."

"And Jason Haught," Josie reminded him. "When do you plan to tell him about all this?"

"I don't know. I really don't want to leave Oakhaven

373

unprotected, not even long enough to make the trip into town. No telling what could happen while we were gone. And I'm not about to leave you here alone again for any reason."

"I can take care of myself," she assured him. "Just leave the pistol with me and I'll be just fine."

"Look, rosebud, I'm not taking that sort of chance. Besides, the doctor told you to stay off that foot. You're supposed to be getting complete bed rest during the next few days."

"If putting any weight on my foot was going to cause any further harm to my ankle, the damage would already be done," she pointed out. "I've been down the hall twice tonight and have suffered very little pain as a result. The ankle is not as bad as the doctor seems to think."

"I don't care. I'm still not leaving you here alone. Too many things could happen." His gaze met with hers. "Besides, Jason intends to drop by and check on you within the next day or two. We can tell him then."

"But what will we do in the meantime?"

"Be careful," he said, taking her hand in his and pressing it gently to his cheek. "Be very, very careful."

Chapter Twenty-two

"Are you ready to go down for breakfast?" Nathan asked, returning to Josie's room to change into clean clothes barely ten minutes after he'd left.

"Yes, I'm starved," she admitted as she set her comb aside. She glanced at him through the mirror, finding he looked extremely attractive in his pale-blue shirt and dark-blue denim trousers. "We never did get to have supper last night."

After all that had happened, neither had had any real desire to eat. Instead, they had stayed awake the whole night discussing the possibilities of all that had happened and what might yet happen. Was it Pearl who'd stolen the painting? And if so, did she have an accomplice? But who could that accomplice be? Everyone had remained a suspect.

"Just give me a minute to pin my hair up and put on my slippers, then you can carry me downstairs, though I'm certain I can make it down there on my own two feet. My ankle barely hurts at all."

"Are you trying to deprive me the pleasure of carrying you?" he asked, moving across the room with long, determined strides. He frowned when he saw her gather her hair into one hand and, with nimble fingers, start to arrange it into a simple twist. "Why do you have to put your hair up? I like it better down."

Josie studied his little-boy pout for a moment, then

willingly released her hair, letting it spill past her graceful shoulders and down her back. "Then I'll wear it down. Do you mind if I at least slip a couple of combs into the sides to keep it out of my face?"

"If you must, you must," he said, shrugging and tilting his head. He smiled as he thought more about it. "Yes, it would be a shame to hide that pretty face of yours—even with your beautiful hair."

"My, my but the silver is dripping from your tongue this morning," she commented, matching his smile with one of her own. For the moment, all the worries of the night before were gone. "By any chance, are you trying to turn my head?"

"Only if it will make it more convenient to steal a kiss from those tempting lips," he murmured, bending low so that they both were visible in the mirror. His cheek was within inches of hers.

"And what makes you think you have to *steal* such things from me?" she asked, turning to face him. Her heart jumped when she realized just how close he really was. She felt his warm breath against her cheek. "What makes you think I wouldn't give of such things willingly?"

Nathan's blue eyes glimmered devilishly, darkening as he slowly bent forward, his lips parted, eager for that kiss. Josie jerked her head back playfully just as his mouth was about to touch hers, but he lifted his hands to capture the sides of her head and quickly pulled her back. When his mouth finally found and placed their claim on hers, the sensations that spilled forth were no less than astounding.

In awe of the undeniable power in his kiss, Josie tilted her head back and parted her lips, allowing his tongue to enter and tease. Slowly she rose from her stool, eager for him to take her into his arms and hold her close.

For the moment, all that mattered was their kiss. Though her legs felt immediately weak, her body stirred with an amazing abundance of energy. Leaning against him, she wondered how a man so incredibly powerful in build could have lips so tender and so very tempting—yet at the same time offer a kiss that was both firm and demanding. So many contrasts. So much to learn about him. So much to love.

Just as overcome by the effects of their kiss, Nathan's fingers moved gently through the soft tresses of Josie's long hair. He enjoyed the way it felt when it curled wantonly around his wrists and arms as he slowly trailed his hands downward to the gentle curve of her back. Pressing her forward, he molded her soft body against his. His passions flared instantly and his fingers moved immediately to the many buttons and ties along the back of her dress.

Just as eager as he, Josie's hands moved from the rounded muscles along his back to the flatter muscles across his chest and abdomen, finally touching the buttons on his shirt. Quickly, she set about freeing him from the garment.

Having had more experience with her garments, Nathan had the dress undone long before she'd finished with his shirt. Hooking his thumbs beneath the fabric, he slid the dress from her shoulders and continued to work with it until it was finally nothing more than a puddle of yellow cloth on the carpeted floor at her feet. He immediately turned his attention to the silken ties of her underskirts, and soon they, too, drifted easily to the floor. Only her thin cotton camisole and her bloomers trimmed with white lace and shiny yellow ribbons remained.

Taking the end of one of the ribbons attached to the top of her camisole between his thumb and forefinger, he gently untied the tiny bow. Her camisole parted

377

obligingly and the strap slipped willingly off her shoulder. The delicate fabric rested lightly across her breast.

Nathan's blood raged wildly. Aware she had finally finished with his own buttons, he swiftly tugged out of his shirt and tossed it aside. His gaze locked with hers while he then pulled the bottom of her camisole free from the waistband of her bloomers. Josie raised her arms to oblige when he drew the wispy garment up and over her head. When he then paused to look at her in the morning light, she made no effort to cover herself. Instead, she stood before him proudly.

"You are beautiful," he said as he lifted his hand to pull a thick portion of her dark hair forward to cover one ivory shoulder in a most beguiling manner.

Finding the slender column of her throat far too tempting, he bent forward to place a series of tiny kisses there. He heard her catch her breath before she rolled her head back to give him easier access. His hands circled her waist while his thumbs dipped beneath the waistband of her bloomers, teasing her delicate skin. Gently, he untied the string and worked the final garment down over her hips until it fell lightly to the floor at her ankles atop the rest of her clothing.

He drew her into his arms again and kissed her hungrily. Her lips were like warm satin, but the sweet kisses did little to douse the fire that raged within him. Eagerly, he bent down and lifted her into his arms. He carried her the short distance to her bed and gently laid her onto the soft mattress. Her dark hair spread over her pillows like a shimmering cape. His eyes drank in her beauty while he hurriedly removed the rest of his own clothing, tossing the garments haphazardly in every direction.

When he climbed onto the bed beside her, he wasted no time taking her into his arms again, crushing her warm body against his. Hungrily their mouths met while his hand moved to stroke the soft curve of her hip, then moved to the small of her back and around to the flat of her stomach. He edged the hand ever higher until his thumb finally met with the outer curve of her breast.

Remembering the incredible sensation his touch had unleashed before, and unwilling to be tormented any longer, Josie shifted, giving him easier access to her breast. When his hand moved to claim its prize and his thumb brushed lightly against the tip, she was rewarded with a startling burst of pleasure. Her hands moved over the taut muscles of his body in eager exploration.

Nathan lowered his head, first to kiss the pulsating hollow at her throat, then downward to claim the other breast. Josie's breath held, then broke from her lungs in a wild rush when his tongue curled around the straining bud and drew it deep into his mouth. Consumed by her own passion, she knotted her fingers into his hair and pressed him closer.

Slowly and deliberately, he brought her desire to maddening heights until she could bear no more. Tugging desperately at his shoulders and arms, she let him know the time had come. He had set her soul on fire. The time had come to put out the flames.

Nathan's body rose above her, then down. He became a part of her and she a part of him. She held him tightly. Together, they continued the long, sweet climb to love's most glorious summit. Each movement carried them higher. Each touch of their bodies made them that much more aware of each other until, finally, their love catapulted them to the ultimate height. Release came first for Josie as wave after thundering wave washed over her, causing her to cry out softly. Barely seconds later, Nathan, too, crossed that glorious plateau, then tumbled effortlessly into sweet oblivion.

As they lay beside each other, the world, which had melted around them, gradually began to reshape itself piece by piece, bit by bit, until Josie was finally aware of her surroundings once more.

Crooking her arm beneath her head, she turned to look at Nathan and found him carefully watching her. Silently, he reached out to touch her hair with a gentleness that was almost reverent.

"You are exquisite," he said, his voice a ragged whisper.

Josie smiled. "And you are going to starve to death if you don't eat something soon."

"At least I'll die a happy man," he commented, still gazing at her as if hoping to memorize every little detail of her face.

"You're incorrigible. I demand that you get out of bed this instant and get dressed," she said, laughing as she tried her best to push him out. "I have no intention of sharing my bed with a dead man."

"Is that so? Then you have just given me a very good reason to live," he commented and rolled effortlessly out of her bed. Swiftly he moved about the room picking up his strewn clothing.

Josie watched, fascinated, while he hurriedly put his clothes back on. For a moment, she forgot that she should be doing the same. Spellbound by his agile movements, she watched the muscles in his hips and thighs flex rhythmically as he slipped first into his underdrawers, then into his trousers, lifting one long leg at a time.

"Aren't you planning to get dressed, too?" he asked as he fastened his trousers, then reached for his shirt.

Embarrassed to have been caught in such a daze, she hurried out of bed to the pile of clothing that lay on the floor beside her vanity stool. Quickly, she separated the different garments and began to dress.

No sooner had she fastened the last and the most difficult button than she found herself being scooped into Nathan's arms and whisked toward the bedroom door.

"Wait a minute, I have to brush my hair," she protested, trying to wriggle free.

"Your hair looks fine."

"What about my slippers?" she wanted to know, kicking her foot out from beneath her hem so he could see that it was totally bare.

"You don't need slippers. You aren't supposed to be walking on that foot anyway, remember?"

When he reached the closed door, he shifted her weight, trying to keep her balanced in his arms yet at the same time have free use of his hand.

"I'll get the door," Josie finally volunteered, having given up on the idea of brushing her hair or the possibility of wearing shoes. She waited until she had turned the knob and pulled the door wide enough for the two of them to pass through before asking, "Why are you suddenly in such a hurry to go downstairs?"

"I just realized that I haven't eaten anything since lunch yesterday. That's an awfully long time for a man to go without food."

"A woman, too," she reminded him. Slipping her arms around his neck, she leaned her cheek against the warmth of his shoulder. She breathed deeply the masculine scent of bay rum. "As hungry as I am right now, I do believe I could eat an entire horse."

"Would sausage or bacon do? I'd hate to lose a good steed just to appease your appetite."

Josie's eyebrow rose, but she decided to let that remark slide. She was too engrossed in the wonderful way it felt to be carried in his arms. She closed her eyes to better enjoy the sensations his closeness aroused in her until they reached the stairs. Remembering their previous "trip" down the very same stairs, she opened her eyes to watch for any indication of trouble. If there was something there, she wanted to warn him. With each step he took, she waited for something terrible to happen.

"We made it," he said the moment he had both feet planted on the ground floor. He felt the tension ease out of her.

"Safely," she agreed, smiling at him. As she relaxed again, she laid her head back on his shoulder.

Nathan felt a warm stirring inside as he headed across the entrance hall and into the dining room. Josie had the sort of smile that made him think of angels.

"About time you two decided to come downstairs and eat," Ruby muttered when she entered the dining room from the kitchen moments later. She cut her gaze from Nathan to Josie, then crossed her bony arms in front of her. "Jeanne had to toss out last night's supper and was worried she'd have to do the same with today's breakfast."

"I'm sorry about last night," Nathan apologized as he tugged Josie's chair away from the table with his boot, then gently deposited her in the seat. "But after that frightening fall down the stairs last night, I'm afraid we lost our appetites. But I can assure you that those appetites have now returned. Tell Jeanne I want double helpings of everything."

"Me, too," Josie piped in as she placed her napkin across her lap.

Ruby glanced at her questioningly, but said nothing when she left the room. Upon her return, she held two plates, both filled with skillet-browned potatoes, scrambled eggs, and sausage.

"This will have to do to start," she told them as she bent to set Josie's plate before her. "But Jeanne said to tell you she's already cooking more. It should be ready by the time you finish this."

When Ruby brought her hand away from Josie's plate, Nathan noticed a small white bandage wrapped tightly around her right thumb and remembered the blood in the library. He lifted his gaze to study Ruby's face.

"What happened to your hand?" he asked when she bent to set his plate down.

Ruby looked at him, surprised, then glanced back at the plate she carried. "Someone broke one of the lamps in the kitchen last night and didn't bother to get up all the glass. I cut my hand while I was helping Jeanne pick up some of the pieces that had been left on the floor. She cut her hand, too."

"How badly?" Josie asked, knowing how even the tiniest injury frightened the poor woman into a near panic.

"Not bad. She just nicked the side of her finger. But you should see the bandage she made Shirley put on it," Ruby answered, shaking her head with disbelief. "You'd think she'd nearly lost that entire finger."

"Did you see her cut her hand?" Nathan asked. He tried to sound only casually interested.

Ruby looked at him, obviously finding it a queer question to ask. "No. She'd already cut herself and was having Shirley bandage it when I came out of my room. Why?"

"No reason, really. Just curious if you'd actually seen the injury," he answered, reaching immediately for his fork. He wanted to ask if the other two had seen her cut her own hand, but decided against it. Ruby was too suspicious of his questions as it was.

Still, both injuries coming the very morning after

383

he'd discovered blood in the library seemed a little too coincidental. He now wondered if it might have been either Ruby or Jeanne he had heard in the library. Either of them would have had plenty of time to make it back to her room during the time he'd gone back upstairs to get the pistol. Was one of today's injuries actually a way of covering up a previous injury, an injury from the night before? Suddenly he was not so sure Pearl was who he had heard in the library, though he still felt certain his father's housekeeper was involved in *some* manner.

"Ruby, there's blood in the library, on the carpet near the desk. Someone needs to go in there today and try to get it up." He watched closely for her reaction over his having mentioned the blood.

Ruby's face hardened, but whether it was out of fear, guilt, or just plain irritation, he couldn't tell.

"One of us will see to it," she said quietly, then took an audible breath. "Will there be anything else?"

"Just see that the rest of the food is brought out as soon as it's done."

"Yes, sir." She paused just inside the door to the kitchen, her small body held rigid, her shoulders pulled in. "I'll get it right out here. Then I'll see to that problem in the library." Having said that, she spun sharply on her work-worn heel and immediately left the room. Nathan noticed how stiff her movements had suddenly become as he watched her go.

Barely an hour later, Nathan entered the library while Shirley and Ruby worked on their hands and knees with turpentine, lye soap, and two stiff brushes trying to work the bloodstains out of the carpet.

"How's it coming?" he asked as he casually crossed the room to stand beside them.

"Slow," Shirley admitted as she continued to put all her weight, which was considerable, into her efforts. "But we're getting there."

Nathan sat down in the chair beside his desk and watched the women progress with their work.

"Strange thing about those bloodstains," he commented, studying both women. "I just can't figure out where they came from."

Shirley stopped working to look up at him. "You didn't cut yourself on that broken vase we just picked up?" She glanced briefly at his hands.

"Not me."

"Then this blood isn't yours?"

He shook his head. "Nor is it Josie's."

Shirley sat back on her heels and glanced at Ruby, who had yet to look up from the bloodstain she'd been working to remove.

"It is a complete mystery," Nathan continued. Having seen such believable confusion in Shirley's round-eyed expression, he centered his attention on Ruby. "The best I can figure is that whoever broke that vase somehow managed to cut himself. My guess is either the vase broke in his hand while he held it, or he was foolish enough to bend over and try to pick up the pieces. But then again, I guess he could have stepped on a jagged piece of vase and cut his foot. But he would have had to be either barefoot or wearing very thin-soled shoes for that to happen."

"He?" Ruby asked, glancing up only briefly while she continued to rub the pungent solution they'd mixed into the fading patch of blood.

"Or she," he conceded. "I guess it could have been either. But I honestly don't think this has anything to do with a ghost of any sort."

"A ghost?" Shirley asked, turning her head sharply to look at Nathan again. Her blue eyes widened at the

385

thought of such.

"Oh," he said, "you haven't heard Jeanne's theory that Oakhaven is haunted, I suppose. Although I don't really know very much about ghosts, I've always been under the impression that they don't have any blood. So I really do think we are dealing with a real live human being here."

Ruby stopped her work but did not look up. Instead she tenderly massaged the bandage on her right hand. "You think someone might have broken in last night? Was anything stolen?"

Rather than make any accusations just yet, Nathan was careful with his response. "I've discovered a few items missing, though I can't say for sure that they disappeared last night. All I can really say for certain at this point is that whoever was in here last night shouldn't have been."

Ruby resumed her work, but Shirley sat staring at him with wide-eyed horror. "I wonder who it was."

"I have my suspicions, but I'm not ready to state any of them just yet," he answered, continuing to watch Ruby closely. He wished she would look up again so he could find out if his staring at her made her feel uncomfortable. "What do you think, Ruby?"

"I don't know what to think," she muttered, pressing harder on her brush as she continued to scrub, putting all her energy into the process. "But I agree with you on one thing, ghosts don't have no blood, and this here is definitely blood."

"But whose blood? That's what I need to find out. Can I ask a favor of you two?" Nathan wanted to know, bending forward and talking in a hushed voice, as if he was about to say something that should be kept in the strictest of confidence.

"Wot's that?" Shirley asked, leaning toward him in turn.

"Whoever was in here last night may plan to return. And I sure want to catch him if he does. Can I depend on the two of you to keep your eyes open for anything that appears even a little suspicious? Will you both promise to come to me the minute you notice anything that seems even a little odd? Anything at all?"

"Aye," Shirley agreed, setting down her brush so she could place her hand over her heart in solemn oath.

"What about you, Ruby?" he asked, dipping his head over to one side to get a better look at the expression on her face.

Ruby looked up and met his gaze. "Do you really think he'll be back?"

"I'm certain of it."

Ruby studied him in silence.

"Can I count on your help?" he asked again.

Her hazel eyes seemed to stare right through him for a moment while she considered her answer. Finally, she replied, "I'll help if I can."

"I'd appreciate it," Nathan said, rising from the chair. "And if either of you does find something that eventually leads to the capture of whoever was in here last night, there will be a big bonus in it for you."

Shirley's face lit with excitement, but Ruby's expression remained extremely cautious when Nathan left the room. Pausing momentarily out in the hallway, he wondered what was going through her mind at that moment. Clearly something had her full attention. Was it because she was worried over being found out? Or was she merely trying to figure out a way to get her hands on that bonus? If only there was some way to find out.

When he entered the kitchen moments later, his thoughts were still with Ruby, but he noticed how startled Jeanne was to glance up and find him there.

"Can I help you, sir?" she asked, promptly putting aside the vegetables she'd just washed. She lifted the corner of her apron to wipe her hands while waiting for his response.

"Yes, you can," he said as he strode across the room to where she'd been working, then leaned casually against one of the work tables. "I'd like to know a little more about those noises you've been hearing during the night."

Jeanne's eyes widened. "What you want to know?"

"Things like when you usually hear them, and from which direction."

Jeanne glanced down as she straightened her apron over her voluminous skirts. "It's usually late at night when the noises start—long after everybody's gone off to bed. But because I don't sleep as good as most folks, the noises usually wake me."

"And from which direction do these noises seem to come?" he asked.

"Mostly from off toward the kitchen, but sometimes I hear them overhead. And sometimes it even sounds like he's gone outside to have a look around."

"He?" Nathan prompted.

"The ghost. Though most ghosts usually like to stay indoors, I think this particular one likes to go outside from time to time. I've heard his footsteps out in the backyard, sometimes right outside my window."

"And do ghosts usually make foot sounds?"

Jeanne twisted her face into a peculiar expression while she considered his question. "Some do and some don't."

"How do you know so much about ghosts?" he asked, watching the animation on her dark face. She was either deadly serious about believing in ghosts or was one hell of a liar.

"There was several ghosts living in Mr. Trent's

388

house." She pursed her lips, then corrected herself. "I guess 'living' isn't a good word for what ghosts do." Her forehead wrinkled as she thought more about that.

"And who is Mr. Trent?" Nathan asked, encouraging her to continue.

"He's a man I worked for several years back."

"A man who had ghosts in his house?"

Jeanne nodded. "Several."

"Weren't you afraid?"

Jeanne nodded harder, her eyes widening again. " 'Course I was. But I found out that if you just leave them alone, they'll leave you alone. After all, there's nothing you can do about a ghost once it decides to move in."

"How do you know?"

"Mr. Trent told me so. He explained it to me so I wouldn't be so scared."

Nathan wondered if her previous employer had told her such things to keep her from quitting or if the man had actually believed that nonsense. "Is that why you haven't left here? This Mr. Trent taught you not to be afraid of ghosts?"

"Oh, I'm afraid of them all right. But there's nothing you can do about them," she repeated with a firm shake of her head. "Best thing is to stay in bed with the covers pulled up over your head whenever there's a ghost about. As long as you do that, you're safe from them."

"Mr. Trent told you this?"

"Yes."

"But you told me you've seen the ghost's shadow. How can that be if you always duck under the covers whenever you hear the noises."

Jeanne glanced about her worriedly as if she was afraid of being overheard. "One night I just couldn't stand not knowing what this ghost of yours looked like so I opened my door just a mite and peeked out."

Nathan's eyebrows rose with interest. "And what did you see?"

"There was an eerie light in the kitchen which let me see a faded shadow as it moved slowly across the wall."

"And did this shadow appear to be in the form of a man or a woman?"

Jeanne looked at him curiously and lifted her bandaged hand to rest on her chin. "I don't rightly remember."

Nathan gazed at the bulky bandage and pretended not to know anything about it. "Goodness. What happened to your hand?"

"I cut it on a piece of glass. That ghost must have come right back out and knocked over one of the kitchen lamps last night, probably after you went on back to bed."

"Did anyone else cut themselves?"

Jeanne shrugged. "Not that I know anything about."

"Did anyone else help you pick up the broken glass?"

Turning to study the area where the glass had been, she puckered her face into a thoughtful frown. "Somebody must have. It's gone."

Nathan wondered why Ruby had not complained of her cut to Jeanne. And he wondered why Jeanne had not noticed when Ruby picked up the glass—if that really was what had happened!

"That must have been a pretty nasty cut to need such a large bandage," he said, stepping closer to have a better look at it.

"Sure was," she agreed, but no longer looked at him. "It bled and bled." She held the hand out in front of her and studied it.

Nathan didn't like the way she suddenly refused to meet his gaze. "It's a good thing you wiped away the blood before it dried. It would have been a lot harder to clean up if you'd waited."

Jeanne looked again at the area where the lamp had lain broken. "I didn't clean up that blood. I had to go to my room and lie down for a while. Ruby was afraid I might faint and hurt myself worse if I didn't."

"Then who cleaned up the blood?"

Jeanne drew her bandaged hand to stroke her chin again while she studied the area further. "I don't know. Ruby and Shirley, I guess."

Nathan's stomach knotted with apprehension. There were too many unanswered questions—too many people unwilling to look him in the eye. What he wanted to find out next was why.

Chapter Twenty-three

When Nathan returned to her bedroom later, Josie was eager to be told everything he'd found out. Although she felt that neither Shirley nor Jeanne had had anything to do with the previous night's incident, she found it just as difficult to believe that Ruby or Rafe could have had any part of it. Though Ruby was an obstinate old woman who sometimes spoke out when she shouldn't, Josie just couldn't believe she'd been involved with either the incident last night or the earlier one with the ladder. Nor did she believe Rafe capable of such things.

"What did you discover?" she asked as soon as he'd closed the door to her bedroom and had started across the room to where she lay propped up by half a dozen pillows. A closed book rested in her lap.

"Not much, I'm afraid," he admitted. "Shirley seems innocent enough, but Jeanne and Ruby are another matter."

"Why? What did they do?" Josie asked, noticing Nathan's troubled expression as she set the book aside. Clearly he was not pleased with whatever he'd uncovered.

"It's more what they didn't do. Neither was willing to look directly at me when I started asking them questions. And even when they did manage to glance my way, they were definitely uncomfortable for having done so. And neither of them gave me any real answers. Jeanne is sticking by her story about a ghost in the house, while Ruby was awfully quick to question the whole thing being a break-in of some sort."

"And what about Rafe? What was his reaction?"

"I haven't had a chance to ask him anything yet. He finished painting the barn this morning and even though it's Sunday and he should have the afternoon free, he's started in on some of the fences out front. I'll walk out there later and see if he has anything more to say about what happened last night."

"Just be careful. Whichever of those four is helping Pearl get in and out of this house might not like the thought of being asked too many questions."

"That is, *if* one of them is helping her."

"Have you changed your mind about that? Do you think she's done it all on her on?"

"I'm so confused now, I'm not sure what I think anymore," he said, bending his head forward and rubbing the back of his neck in an effort to relieve some of the tension. "I wish Jason would come on out here so I could talk it over with him. He just might know something I don't. Maybe, together, we could figure out exactly who was roaming around this house last night and who might have taken that painting. I'd also like to know if that same person had anything to do with sabotaging the ladder yesterday."

Josie studied the dark shadows underneath Nathan's eyes and the worn look on his face. "Nathan, you haven't slept since night before last. That's not good. You need to put aside enough time to get some rest. Not only would a little sleep make you feel better, but you'd be able to think a lot clearer."

Nathan's eyebrows arched when he lifted his gaze to meet hers. "Oh? Is that your coy way of asking me to join you in your bed? How brazen you've become."

Tilting her head to one side, Josie crossed her arms

and flattened her lips into a straight line. "Keep that up and you can add me to the list of people you need to watch out for."

Disappointment pulled his lips into a playful pout. "You mean you don't want me anymore? You're casting me aside like so much garbage already?"

The corners of her mouth tugged into a smile. He was so appealing when he looked like that. "No, I'm not casting you aside—at least not yet."

"Then I am welcome to share your bed?" he asked eagerly, and took a tentative step in her direction.

Rather than answer, she wriggled over to one side and patted the empty portion of bed beside her. She laughed when he responded by diving bellyfirst onto the mattress, skidding across the covers, and coming to an abrupt stop against her pillows. When he rested his elbow on top of the pillows beside him, his face had come within inches from hers.

Shaking her head, she reached out to push back a lock of hair that had fallen forward across his forehead and asked, "What am I going to do with you?"

"Are you asking for my suggestions?" he wanted to know, offering her a crooked smile as he reached an arm around her to bring her lips gently to his.

The kiss was brief, but enough to send Josie's blood coursing hot and tingling through her body. How she marveled the uncanny power of his kiss and the feel of his arm around her. But she was too concerned about his welfare to allow the moment to progress any further.

"There will be no more of that, Mr. Garrett—at least not until you've had some sleep," she told him, wagging her finger just inches from his nose.

"How much sleep?" he asked, rolling over and gazing up at her, his head pressing back against her pillow. A dimple dipped playfully in his cheek.

"Enough to get rid of those horrible dark circles under your eyes," she answered, again aware of how tired he looked.

Nathan's eyes narrowed as he studied her determined expression. "How come you don't have any dark circles under *your* eyes? You've been awake as long as I have."

"No, I haven't. I had the good sense to take a short nap while you were gone," she told him, though in truth, good sense had had nothing to do with it. She'd fallen asleep despite all efforts to stay awake. "Which is exactly what you are going to do right now — take a quick nap."

"But what about our prowler? What if she decides to pay us a return visit while I'm sleeping?"

"We've put most of the valuables into the studio and relocked it. If someone tries to open that door, I'm sure I'd hear it in here. After all, the studio is just down the hall and I'll be awake to hear any noises. So, quit your arguing and get some sleep."

"Yes, ma'am," he said obediently, then immediately folded his hands over his chest and pressed his eyes closed.

Josie watched while he pretended to be asleep, and was aware when, moments later, his facial muscles slowly relaxed. Soon his breathing slowed and his head tilted to one side. He was truly asleep.

Though she'd fully intended to stay awake and watch over him, feeling especially protective of him while he slept in her bed, it wasn't long before she, too, was asleep, cuddled next to his warmth.

It was midafternoon before the distant sound of a carriage startled them awake. Neither having planned to actually fall asleep, they awoke to a moment of sleep-muddled confusion.

"I wonder who that could be," Nathan said as he

swung his legs over the side of the bed and sat up. He blinked groggily, trying to clear the sleepy thoughts, while he listened to the jangling sound of the carriage through the open window.

"Maybe it's Jason," Josie suggested hopefully. She, too, swung her legs over the side of the bed, but when she caught sight of the bandage on her leg, she hesitated. Though the ankle barely hurt anymore, Nathan had remained adamant she stay off it.

"Jason?" Nathan responded, already on his way to the window to look. "I hope so. Maybe we can get some of the mysterious things that have been happening around here cleared up at last. I'll feel better just knowing someone else has been made aware of our troubles."

Pulling back the lace curtain, he stood off to one side and glanced down at the small portion of drive that curved below her window. When he glanced back at Josie a few seconds later, his dour expression told her their visitor was not Jason Haught after all.

"Cynthia?" she easily guessed once she'd seen the sudden look of annoyance on his face.

"In all her glory," he muttered angrily, tucking his shirt back into his waistband as he turned toward the door. "I'd better go see what she wants this time."

Several minutes later, when Nathan returned to Josie's bedroom, Cynthia was at his side. While his aunt rushed forward to bend and place a cursory kiss at Josie's temple, Nathan took only a few steps into the room. Clearly bothered by the woman's presence, the muscles in his jaw turned rock hard while he watched is aunt flutter about at Josie's bedside.

Although Josie did not particularly look forward to spending time alone with the meddlesome woman, she didn't feel it was necessary for Nathan to suffer her company, too. She decided to offer him a good excuse to leave.

"I thought you were headed outside to speak with Rafe about something," she said, wrinkling her forehead as if she truly did not understand why he was still there.

Nathan's face lit with noticeable relief and he quickly seized the opportunity. "Yes, I was. I still am. I just wanted to be sure you didn't need anything else before I left."

"I'm fine," she assured him, then smiled knowingly. "Besides, if I need anything, I'm certain I can persuade your aunt to get it for me."

"Of course. I'd be glad to help in any way I can," Cynthia responded readily, pressing a smile on her face as she turned to an angle that allowed her to see them both. She glanced first at Josie, then at Nathan. "If you have something you need to do, Nathaniel, don't let *me* stop you."

"I know I should stay and visit, but I do need to talk to Rafe," he agreed with a quick nod, already backing from the room. "It shouldn't take very long. I'll try to get back before you leave."

"Take all the time you need," Cynthia said in a singsong voice, bending forward to pat Josie's arm reassuringly with her left hand while she waved him away with her right. "We'll be just fine."

Nathan glanced at Josie, as if to send her a silent message of thanks, then left.

"Well, my dear, how's your poor ankle?" Cynthia asked as she pulled one of the bedroom chairs closer to the bed and sat down ever so properly on the edge. The high, melodic tone she'd used when speaking with Nathan was gone. A notch of what appeared to be true concern had formed between her eyebrows.

"Much better," Josie told her, her attention focused momentarily on the ridiculous brilliant blue hat Cynthia had selected. With three fat ostrich plumes wafting about over her head, Nathan's aunt reminded her of a pompous peacock. It took quite a mental struggle to keep from laughing. "The swelling is completely gone and I really don't think it would hurt anything at all if I got out of this bed and started walking on it a little. But Nathan still insists I stay off it. He won't even let me remove the bandage yet."

"And he's right. Though it may look and feel much better, you should continue to follow orders and take special care of it," Cynthia agreed. "It's far better to be safe than sorry."

Josie nodded, finding it odd that Cynthia had finally agreed with Nathan on something. A moment of silence followed while Josie tried to think of what else the two of them might talk about. She wanted to think of something that would not encourage Cynthia to spew out any more nonsense about Nathan. She was in no mood to suffer through another argument with the woman, but was at a loss as to what they could talk about.

Finally, for lack of any other ideas, Josie decided on the weather. "My, but the afternoons in East Texas are warm. It's hard for me to believe that it is only May. I can just imagine what it will be like in July."

Cynthia stared at her for a long moment, her gloved hands folded primly in her lap. Finally she said what was foremost on her mind, which had absolutely nothing to do with the unusually warm weather. "I'm so glad to see that you made it safely through the night. You don't know how I've worried about you, especially now that you're injured and can't easily fend for yourself."

"There's no reason to worry about me," Josie tried to assure her. She felt a slow tightening in her stomach, aware Cynthia was about to start in on Nathan again. As tired as she was, she didn't think she could take any more of the woman's silly accusations. She wondered if there was any way to distract her onto another topic of conversation. "I'll be fine."

"I wish I could believe that. I truly wish I could. But, after I made that comment about Nathaniel dropping you down the stairs on your way to dinner, I couldn't get you off my mind I was so worried. Although you don't seem to realize the danger you are in here, I do. I had nightmares all night."

"Nightmares?"

"Yes, I dreamed I heard you screaming out my name as you fell down the stairs. I dreamed I was just outside the house when it happened, but when I rushed in to help, you were already lying in a crumpled heap at the foot of the stairs—exactly like I found Carl several weeks ago. Your back was broken, your face frozen with disbelief and horror."

Josie shuddered at the thought, then forced a reassuring smile. "But, as you can easily see, I'm still very much alive. The fall down those stairs barely hurt me."

Cynthia's eyes widened, aghast. "Then it is true? He did try to throw you down those stairs?"

Josie's stomach felt as if it was made of cold lead when she realized how carelessly she'd spoken. Quickly, she sought to rectify the damage she'd done. "No, he didn't *throw* me down the stairs. But he did slip while carrying me and we both tumbled down the stairs together."

"I knew it," Cynthia said, shaking a gloved finger at Josie with further warning. "Didn't I tell you?"

"But it's not what you think. It was an accident."

"Just like the broken ladder was an accident?" Cynthia asked, tossing her head back and squaring her shoulders defiantly.

399

"No," Josie rushed to answer, recalling that the broken ladder had not been an accident at all. But in the same instant, she realized that although Cynthia didn't know anything about the tampering that had caused the ladder rung to break she would soon come to suspect such if she didn't say something quick. "I mean, yes. It was an accident, just like the broken ladder."

Cynthia's eyes narrowed while she studied the uncertainty in Josie's expression. "There's something you're not telling me, isn't there?"

"No, of course not," Josie lied, wondering how she could possibly get out of the present situation without Cynthia becoming even more suspicious.

"Yes, there is. Something else has happened. Something you are afraid to tell me." She leaned forward and rested her left hand on Josie's wrist. "Please tell me what has happened. I can't help you if I don't know what's going on."

Josie sighed softly, wondering if it might indeed be a wise thing to let someone else know what had happened, someone who was in no way involved. Even Nathan himself had said he'd feel better once he knew someone else had been made aware of their troubles. Plus, it would prove to Cynthia once and for all that Nathan was innocent.

"We had a prowler last night," she finally admitted.

"A prowler? Here?" Cynthia responded with a gasp. Her hand flew to her gaping mouth.

"Yes. And it appears last night was not the first time our prowler has paid us a visit."

Cynthia fell back in her chair and pressed her gloved palms against her cheeks. Her eyes widened as some of the color drained from her face. "Oh, my. What happened?"

Josie recounted the events of the previous night,

ending with the mysterious disappearance of the prowler from the library.

"Was anything valuable stolen?" Cynthia asked in horror.

"Yes. But not from the library. And we don't think it was taken last night. That's why we believe the thief has been in this house before."

"Oh, dear! What did he get?"

"One of the paintings in Carl's studio."

"Oh, no, not one of Carl's paintings. Which one?"

Josie glanced sadly at the sunshine spilling in through her window, for it still hurt to know that painting was gone. There was just something about the little girl and the kitten that had made it special to her. "The one of a little girl playing with a kitten."

"The one Carl painted of you?" Cynthia asked, horrified.

"Me?" Josie turned to face Cynthia again.

"Yes, didn't you know? Didn't your grandmother's letters tell you about that painting?"

"No. But how could Carl possibly have painted a picture of me? He never even met me."

"Your grandmother had a picture of you that she had handled so often it had started to wear out. Worried she wouldn't have anything to remind her of what you looked like after it did finally come apart, she asked Carl to transfer the image to canvas. Carl did, adding touches he thought would make it special—make it seem like you'd finally come to visit. The result of his work was that painting. He finished it just days before she fell ill. He was still carving a frame for it when she died. I'm so sorry to hear it's missing."

Josie's eyes grew wide with wonder as she tried to remember the painting better. She tried to picture the little girl's face in her mind. But, to her dismay, all she could clearly visualize at that moment was the playful yellow kitten in the little girl's lap. Tears of frustration and anger filled her eyes.

"Have you told the sheriff?" Cynthia wanted to know, watching Josie closely while she waited for an answer.

"No. Not yet. As you know, it takes nearly four hours to make a trip into town and back. Nathan is afraid to leave Oakhaven unprotected for that long."

Cynthia looked at her curiously, her forehead wrinkled with disbelief. "And didn't you think that was a little strange?"

"No. Why would I?"

Cynthia's eyebrows pulled inward. "You don't think it a little strange that a painting worth thousands of dollars has disappeared from this house yet Nathaniel hasn't bothered to tell the sheriff?"

"I told you. He's afraid the thief might return while we are gone," Josie explained. Suddenly she realized how suspicious it all must sound to an outsider. "If that happened, we could lose a lot more than the one painting."

Cynthia shook her head skeptically, causing the tall feathers in her hat to flutter in different directions. "And what about the servants? Doesn't he realize they would still be here to protect the place even if you two had to leave?"

"But that's just it. The first robbery probably happened in broad daylight while the servants were all here working away. If we were to leave the place in their hands, there's a very real chance it could happen again."

"The painting disappeared in broad daylight? Are you sure?"

"Reasonably so. Either then or during the early evening while we are both downstairs having dinner."

"What makes you think so?"

"Because, Nathan locks the house for the night at bedtime, and keeps it locked until morning."

Cynthia fell silent while she digested this last bit of information. "And it never once occurred to you to suspect Nathaniel?"

"Of course not. Why would I?"

Cynthia glanced heavenward a moment, then squared her shoulders and looked at Josie straight on. "Because it is very possible he took that painting and sold it himself, then invented all this business about a prowler to help cover his own crime. Which would also explain why he didn't want the sheriff involved. Tell me, did anyone else actually see this prowler?"

"Well, no, but—"

Cynthia was not interested in buts and didn't give her a chance to offer any. "And, by chance, has Nathaniel recently disappeared for any substantial amount of time?"

Josie remembered his trip into town to speak with Jason shortly after her accident. He was gone for hours. "Well, yes, but he—"

"And did anyone actually see him when he left?"

"I'm not sure. I think Shirley may have."

"But then I guess it doesn't really matter if someone saw him leave or not," she muttered, as if thinking aloud. "He could have hidden the painting somewhere where he could double back and pick it up after everyone had watched him leave empty-handed. Or he may have hidden it at the bottom of a wagon and covered it up with something. He's clever enough to have found a way to get it out of here without anyone knowing."

"But why would he do that?" Josie asked, trying to reason with her. "In less than two months, the painting would have been half his anyway."

403

"Half his," Cynthia pointed out. "Don't you see? By taking it now and selling it himself, he doesn't have to share any of that money with you."

Josie did not like the doubts this woman was trying to place in her mind. "Nathan is not like that."

Cynthia pressed her eyes closed and shook her head, clearly dismayed by Josie's relentless determination to defend her nephew. "When will you ever see Nathaniel for what he really is?"

"I already do," Josie told her firmly, angry that her attempt to prove him innocent had gone so completely awry. What did it take to convince this woman? "I see him as a warm, caring person who would never do anything to deliberately harm anyone."

Cynthia's gaze met hers. "How can I make you see how very wrong you are? How can I make you see the very real danger you are in?"

"That's not necessary. I'm no fool. I do know that I'm in danger here," Josie told her. "And I know that danger will continue to exist until we finally catch whoever has been sneaking into the house behind our backs."

"You really believe there was a prowler?"

"Of course I do. And Nathan and I both think we know who it is."

Cynthia leaned forward, her hand at her throat again. "And who might that be?"

"Pearl Beene."

Josie's answer took Cynthia by surprise. "Pearl Beene? Why would you suspect Pearl? No one has even *seen* the woman since the day of your father's funeral."

"It's a long, complicated story, but Nathan thinks she might have taken his father's keys."

"His keys? But I thought Nathaniel found those keys."

"He found a spare set. Carl's personal set is still missing."

"And he's blaming Pearl for having taken them," she surmised, in that I-have-it-all-figured-out voice of hers. "How clever."

Josie felt her anger build to explosive proportions. Clearly Cynthia was prepared to doubt anything and everything Nathan said or did. "He and Jason both think she may have taken them."

"And I suppose they blame her for having killed Carl, too. How very convenient to blame someone who is not around to defend herself."

Josie clenched her hands with frustration as she finally reached the limit of her endurance. "It's no more than you yourself suggested. If I remember correctly, you told both of us how very strange you thought it was that she'd disappeared so suddenly after Carl's funeral. I believe your conclusions were that she was either running directly from the sheriff or from someone else who could link her to the crime."

"You must have misunderstood me. That was what some of the other people around here thought. I then explained that I believed her disappearance was the result of some sort of blackmail. Remember? I explained my theory to both of you. I think she discovered something she shouldn't have and then tried to use that information for her own personal gain. Only the person she tried to blackmail didn't take too kindly to it. I honestly believe the woman is dead."

"That may well be true," Josie conceded, her voice edged with impatience. "Since I never actually knew the woman, I'm in no real position to argue the point."

"Finally!" Cynthia sighed aloud with relief and clasped her hands together. "You are starting to believe me."

"No, not really. I simply don't want to argue with you about something I obviously know so little about. Pearl Beene may indeed be dead. Our prowler may be someone we haven't yet considered. But then again, Pearl may still be alive and planning to plunder us all no matter the risks. I really don't know which is true. But I do know one thing. Nathan has nothing to do with any of it."

Cynthia looked crestfallen. "I wish you would at least try to keep an open mind about this. Until you have absolute proof of who stole that painting, don't eliminate the possibility that Nathaniel may have taken it."

"Guilty until proven innocent?" Josie asked, crossing her arms and looking at her with a raised eyebrow.

"Something like that," Cynthia admitted, her chin thrust forward with haughty defiance. "Until you know for a fact who took that painting, you should suspect everyone."

"Even you?"

Cynthia's eyes widened at such an insult. "No, of course not! How could I have taken that painting?"

"I don't know why you should be so upset. You yourself told me I should suspect *everyone*," she said, finding the shocked expression on Cynthia's face most gratifying. The meddling old woman deserved to suffer a little.

"Well, I never!" she sputtered, rising instantly from her chair.

"Until I have proof, how can I be sure?" Josie said with a thoughtful expression.

"Good day to you, *Miss Leigh*," she said, tossing her shoulders back as she turned to leave, tripping over the chair in her haste.

"And a good day to you, *Miss Garrett*," Josie said,

feeling no regrets for her harsh words as she watched the woman regain her balance, shove the chair aside, then march briskly from the room. As she listened to her booted footsteps clatter rapidly down the stairs, Josie tossed her head back and laughed out loud. Though she knew she would have to apologize to Cynthia eventually for such rude behavior, for now she was delighted by what she'd done.

"A very good day to you indeed, *Miss Garrett.*"

Chapter Twenty-four

Restless, mostly as a result of Cynthia's visit, Josie decided she'd stayed in bed long enough, especially since her ankle wasn't even bothering her anymore. When Nathan failed to return right away, she reached a point in which she could not stand the solitude any longer. She decided to risk his ire and first removed the bandage, then climbed immediately out of bed.

Having grown used to the comfort of wearing no shoes, she didn't bother with either her boots or her slippers. She took just enough time to slip into a thick pair of stockings before hurrying downstairs.

Eager to see Nathan again, having been apart from him for well over two hours and thinking he might be in the library at this time of day, she went there first. When she neared the open door, she heard the low drone of women's voices from inside. Moving closer, she overheard what was being said.

"I tell you, I've had just about enough of him," Ruby muttered.

"With wot we're getting paid, I don't think you 'ave any real reason to be complainin'," Shirley responded in her usual Australian lilt. "No reason at all."

Though Josie abhorred people who eavesdropped, she found herself drawn ever closer to the open doorway.

"Yes, I do. It's Sunday, damn it! We are supposed to have the afternoon to do whatever we want to do. But, no, Mister High Almighty thinks we got nothing better to do than work our fingers to the bone. Who does he think he is? He even has poor Rafe out there in the hot sun painting those fences."

"Maybe 'e doesn't realize it's Sunday," Shirley suggested. "After all, 'e is not a regular churchgoer that one. One day probably seems like any other to 'im."

"Oh, he knows all right. He just doesn't care. All he cares about at the moment is this damned carpet and selling this damned house for all he can get," Ruby said with clear disgust. "He's just like his father."

"You knew 'is father?" Shirley asked, surprised. "You never mentioned that to me."

There was a long pause before Ruby answered. "Well, I didn't exactly know the man, but I heard plenty about him. Everyone around these parts has heard about Carl Garrett. He lived out here in this big house like some big lord with his beautiful mistress at his side, never caring what others thought of him. Only caring about himself and what others could do for him. Exactly like that son of his. Living the good life, with a pretty little mistress to keep him happy and servants to do all his work."

Josie leaned heavily against the wall. Her legs felt suddenly too weak to hold her. *Ruby knew.* Ruby knew she and Nathan had spent the night together and she clearly thought the worst of her for it.

"Mistress? You don't know that!" Shirley admonished. "Shame on you for spreading such petty gossip."

"Don't I know it? How else do you explain that Mr. Garrett's bed was never slept in last night?"

Shirley gasped. " 'Ow do you know that?"

"When I went upstairs earlier to see if Miss Josie needed anything, I found her door closed. When I stepped closer, thinking to knock, I could hear the two of them inside giggling like a couple of schoolchildren. So I peeked over into his room and discovered his bed was still made. And even you will have to admit that man is not exactly the type to bother with his own bed. Why, you know as well as I do what shape that room was in when he finally gave us permission to go in there and clean all that out for him. He hadn't bothered to make his bed in weeks, and you can bet he hasn't bothered to make it since."

"Wot man does?" Shirley responded agreeably. "So, you figure 'e spent the entire night in 'er bed, do you?"

"And a long night it was. Why do you think they never came down for supper and were so late coming down for breakfast?"

"You mean—?"

"That's exactly what I mean."

"But 'ow could they? I mean wot with 'er injured ankle and all."

"It's not her ankle he was interested in."

"Oh my!"

Josie had heard enough. Though she didn't want them to know she had eavesdropped on their conversation, she was ready to bring an immediate stop to the terrible things they were saying about her. With her hands clenched at her sides, she took several steps back, then approached the door again. This time she made enough noise to alert the women to her presence.

Upon entering the room, she glanced at both of them, as if surprised to see them. "What are you two doing in here? Aren't you through yet?"

Shirley looked away, clearly embarrassed, but Ruby met her gaze straight on. Both women sat on the floor with large wooden fans in their hands, waving them low over the carpet.

"Mr. Garrett wants us to be sure we get up all the blood that was in here and that we get this carpet dried before mildew sets in," Ruby explained. "What are *you* doing in here? I thought that doctor said you was to stay in *bed* for a couple of days. Aren't you supposed to stay off that foot and get plenty of rest?"

Aware of the emphasis Ruby had placed on the word "bed," Josie glared at her, mentally snatching her up by that skinny little throat and strangling her until she turned purple. When she responded to what Ruby had said, it was in a barely controlled voice. "My ankle is much better, thank you."

To prove it, she took several solid steps toward them. When she came to a stop, she stood only a few feet away. Looking Ruby squarely in the eye, as if daring her to offer any further comment, she asked, "Have either of you seen Nathan?"

"Not lately," Ruby admitted, glancing toward Shirley, then lifting her face back up to look at Josie. "Last I heard, he was headed out to talk to Rafe. But that was a while ago, not too long before his aunt left out of here in such a . . . hurry. I don't know where he is now."

"Thank you," she told them, then turned to leave. Remembering what they'd said about Nathan earlier, and still very angry because of it, she paused just inside the doorway and glanced back at them. "By the way, I think you should know how very much Nathan appreciates your willingness to work on Sunday afternoon. You should also know that you'll both be well rewarded for your trouble." She'd see to it, if she had to pay the extra wages herself!

As she left the room, she heard Shirley come immediately to Nathan's defense. "See there, 'e does care that we're 'aving to work on a Sunday."

"Humph!" came Ruby's ready response.

Then the room fell silent.

Heading straight for the front parlor, Josie paced restlessly about while she waited for Nathan to return from wherever he'd gone. Having discovered that Ruby and Shirley were both aware Nathan had spent the night in her bedroom bothered her more than she'd thought it would. Yet, what annoyed her the most was not so much the fact that they knew; it was more the disapproving voice Ruby had used when discussing it. Ruby had made it sound so awful when, in truth, what she'd shared with Nathan had turned out to be the most beautiful experience of her life.

But how could she possibly make them see that? What's more, why should she even care what they thought? Why should she care what *anyone* thought? Except Nathan.

But then, she had to wonder, what *did* Nathan think? What *was* his opinion of her after he'd so easily won her affection? And what would she think of herself when the time came for them to leave Oakhaven and go their separate ways? Clearly she was headed for a terrible fall, and yet there was nothing she could do about it.

Or was there? Though it was too late to undo what had already occurred between them, it was not too late to do something that would prevent it from happening again. It was not too late to try to salvage at least a small part of her self-esteem before she ended up much like her grandfather had, bitter and heartbroken.

By the time Nathan entered the house, just as it started to turn dark, Josie had her mind set. She would not allow herself to become emotionally dependent on Nathan. Rather than make matters any worse than they already were, she would bring an abrupt end to *that* part of their relationship, aware if she didn't put a stop to it right then, she would only grow to love him more.

The pleasure she felt in his arms was not worth the eventual price she would have to pay. She did not want to end up like her grandfather. Nathan would have to understand that he was to spend that night, and every night that followed, in his own room asleep in his own bed—alone.

Having heard his footsteps in the hallway as they became steadily louder, she took a deep breath, held it a moment, then called out to him.

"What are you doing downstairs?" he asked after he'd followed the sound of her voice into the front parlor and found her sitting in a small armchair facing an empty fireplace.

"I was tired of lying around in that bed with nothing

412

to do," she told him, trying to smile when she glanced up at him. Her heart fell into a thousand shattered pieces at the mere sight of his handsome face, knowing the painful task that lay ahead. "And my ankle really is much better."

"Oh, yes, I remember," Nathan said, grinning that crooked smile of his as he crossed the room and knelt beside her. "You don't care much for spending your day in bed all alone. I was just about to come upstairs and rectify that situation."

Aware of the implication, Josie looked away. She felt a sharp, piercing pain when she opened her mouth to speak, making her want to put off saying anything at all. Yet she had to speak the words now, before she lost her courage all together. "Nathan, we have to talk."

"Okay," Nathan answered agreeably. A dimple sank playfully into his cheek. "But to tell you the truth, talking is not exactly what I had in mind."

"Well, it's what *I* have in mind," she answered firmly. When she glanced back at him and noticed his confused expression, it felt as if he'd snatched the heart right out of her and left her with a deep, hollow ache. Though she tried her best to put on a brave front, her lower lip trembled.

"Josie, what's wrong? What did my aunt say to you?" His voice was low with concern as he reached up and placed his hands on her cheeks, holding her head steady so she had to face him. Noticing the swollen tear that clung precariously to her lower eyelid, Nathan moved his hand to dab it away with the tip of his thumb, but she pulled back, avoiding his touch.

"Josie? What is it? What's happened? What did my aunt say to you?"

"It doesn't have anything to do with your aunt," she said, looking away again. The argument she'd had with Cynthia seemed so insignificant now. "It has to do with us."

"I don't understand. *What* has to do with us?"

413

Josie didn't know any other way to tell him than to come right out with it. "Nathan, I've had a lot of time to think about the new direction our relationship has taken and I firmly believe only harm can come of it."

"Harm? I still don't understand. What brought on this sudden change of heart?"

Josie couldn't bear to repeat what she'd overheard in the library — not to Nathan. "I told you. I've had time to consider everything thoroughly, and I think we have only complicated matters by allowing ourselves to . . . to . . ." Why did saying it have to be so painful?

"To what? To make love? Are you so ashamed of what we did that you can't even say it?" Nathan asked, pressing his lips against his teeth with sudden anger. His face hardened as he stood, suddenly towering over her. "What we did is not something you should be ashamed of. Not when you consider how we feel about each other."

"Nathan, don't make this harder on me than it already is," she pleaded and closed her eyes against the pain that sliced through her heart, spilling misery throughout her body.

"Don't make it harder on *you?* What about me? Do you think I am totally incapable of any human emotions? Do you think what I feel for you is something I can turn on and off like a water faucet?"

Josie felt one of the tears that had been blinding her slip forlornly down her cheek while she considered his questions. "To tell you the truth, I don't really know how you feel."

"You don't know how I feel?" Nathan shouted, finding her words hard to believe. "After what we've shared?"

"Nathan, the point is that whatever it is we feel for each other and whatever we have shared as a result of those feelings doesn't really matter. What matters is that we bring a stop to it before one of us ends up badly hurt."

"Doesn't matter?" Nathan repeated, so angry now his hands curled into tight fists at his sides and the muscles in his cheeks pumped steadily in and out. "What we feel for each other may not matter to you, but it damn sure matters to me."

"Nathan, think about it. Think about how much harder it will be for us to say goodbye to each other once all this is finally over. And think about the fact I could leave here carrying your child."

Nathan's lips pressed so hard against his clenched teeth that they lost all color. His pale eyes had become dark with rage. "Would that be so awful?"

"Maybe not for you," she said angrily, realizing she had sorely misjudged him. How could anyone be so insensitive?

"But it would be for you," he said, finishing the statement for her. His eyes narrowed into slits of glinting steel. Furious to have learned that she found the idea of bearing his child so revolting, he turned his back to her and stalked away. Then, realizing he still had something to say, he stopped just inside the door, spun around, and glowered at her. "Don't worry. I won't do anything more to complicate your life. From now on, I plan to stay as far away from you as I possibly can and still be in the same house."

"Good," she called after him, so angered by his total lack of understanding that her fingernails dug painful little trenches into her palms. She kept her proud chin thrust forward until his broad shoulders had completely disappeared from her sight. Then, as she heard his heavy footsteps stomp determinedly up the staircase, her face twisted with anguish. How was she ever going to survive those next two months without seeing Nathan?

Much less the rest of her life.

Hoping to hold on to what little pride she had left, Josie did not want Nathan to know she'd been crying and asked that a supper tray be brought to her room. She waited until she'd heard Nathan go downstairs to eat his own supper, then carried her tray outside and ate her meal on the balcony.

She did not bother to light a lamp. The darkness suited her mood perfectly and the peaceful night sounds helped to calm her frayed nerves but did little to soothe her broken heart. Nor did the night bring with it any answers to the painful questions that tumbled helplessly through her mind.

Missing Nathan already, she tried to visualize a happier day, when she would finally be over him, when he would be little more than a faded memory of the past. But it was impossible to believe such a day would ever exist. He'd become too much a part of her. Despite everything, she loved him dearly.

Even after she'd gone to bed and somehow managed to fall asleep, the hollow pain beneath her breast did not go away. She tossed restlessly in her bed. In the dreams that eventually followed, Nathan's image continued to haunt her. There was no escaping him, even in sleep. At every turn, he was there. Sometimes angry with her, his hands curled into fists. At other times, he held his arms out to her, his eyes dark with passion. The images were frighteningly vivid, the emotions painfully real.

In those shifting dreams, Nathan still wanted her. He appeared in dark doorways and chased her through endless corridors, calling out her name. Though she knew she was running for her life, she did not understand why she was so afraid. Deep down, she knew Nathan would never purposely harm her. Yet she continued to run, her heart pounding, her lungs on fire.

Then, suddenly, there were two Nathans coming after her from different directions. Then three. Then four. Josie came awake with a gasp, confused but relieved to find herself in the familiar darkness of her room.

Listening to the rapid rush of her own pulses, she lay perfectly still, staring into the blackness overhead, adjusting to the fact she'd been asleep. It had all been a dream. But her heart continued to pound hard against her chest while she tried to figure out why the dream had been about Nathan and why it had frightened her as much as it did.

While staring questioningly into the darkness trying to reason out her fears, she suddenly detected a movement. It had been little more than a strange shifting of shadows across the room. Curious, she lifted her head off the pillow in time to see the dark shadow move across the faint light filtering through her window. Thinking someone was outside trying to find a way in, she immediately tossed back the covers. She had to warn Nathan.

Not bothering with a robe, or even her slippers, Josie hurried toward the hall door. It was too dark to see, but she had no reason to think anything stood in her way. No reason to slow her steps.

When she neared the wall where she knew the hallway door to be, she reached out, groping blindly for the handle. Suddenly, as her hand came in contact with the door, something grabbed her by the arm. Or *someone*. But who? Nathan? But why would he . . . ?

In the next instance, a gloved hand clamped down over her mouth and Josie knew her captor was not Nathan.

Panic struck her heart as the taste of old leather filled her mouth. She tried to scream, but the hand pressed harder against her mouth and the sound came out muffled. She tried to wrench herself free, but couldn't. The painful grip on her arm held fast. Instinctively, she fell back against her captor, thinking to send them both off balance. But when she did, she found herself suddenly let go. She fell helplessly to the floor. Pain shot through her shoulder, causing her a moment's hesitation while she tried to recover from the blow, giving whoever was in her room enough time to fling the door wide and run out into the hall.

Furious to realize whoever had attacked her was about to escape, unidentified and unharmed, Josie drew in a deep breath, then screamed at the top of her voice.

There was a heavy thud across the hall, followed by rapid footsteps. Nathan's door swung open.

"Josie?" he cried out, his voice filled with panic.

All Josie could see was his shadow as he stepped out into the hallway. "Nathan, she's in the house! She was in my bedroom. Go after her."

Nathan's shadow disappeared as quickly as it had appeared. She heard a confusion of noises come out of Nathan's bedroom before she detected his footsteps hurrying down the hall. By the time she stood, then hastened out into the hallway to light a lamp, he was gone.

She listened to the different sounds downstairs as she hurried toward the studio to see if anything else was stolen. But knowing whoever had attacked her might still be upstairs hiding in one of the bedrooms, or possibly even in the studio itself, she paused long enough to snatch up a tall blue-and-white porcelain pitcher from a small stand in the hall and held it high over her head for protection.

When she tried the latch, she did so with extreme caution, relieved to discover it still locked. With the pitcher still raised in ready defense, she turned and studied the many darkened doorways along the hall. Pearl could be in any of those rooms, hiding, waiting.

Fortified by her anger, she set her gaze on the closest door, listening carefully while she took several cautious steps toward it. But she was distracted from her purpose by the muffled sound of voices below. Excited voices. One was clearly Nathan's, but she was not sure about the other. Thinking he might be in trouble, she forgot about the bedroom and hurried down the stairs to help.

Upon entering the kitchen, she discovered Ruby, Jeanne, and Shirley huddled together in the entrance of the hallway that led back to their rooms, while Nathan went about the area opening doors, toppling tables and tossing chairs aside in an angry search for Pearl.

Because someone had taken time to light one wall lamp and because Jeanne held a large lighted candle in her hand, Josie could see that the three women wore only their nightdresses and robes; yet, except for his missing boots, Nathan was still fully dressed. Had he expected trouble? Had he left a door unbolted or a window open just so someone would discover it and sneak in? Or had one of the women conveniently slipped a bolt back out of place or maybe opened one of the unprotected windows up front? So many questions to consider, yet there was no time for answers.

"You mean to tell me none of you saw or heard anything?" Nathan shouted angrily as he stalked past them, yanked open the door to Jeanne's bedroom, then peered inside.

"Just Miss Josie's scream," Shirley answered in a trembling voice as she moved cautiously around to hide behind Jeanne's right shoulder, keeping the large black woman between herself and Nathan at all times — clearly confused by his anger. Though her eyes were open wide, her mind was muddled enough to cause her to stumble about awkwardly while continuing to try to stay on the opposite side of Jeanne. "Then, only minutes later, we 'eard you downstairs slamming the doors and knocking over the furniture."

"But nothing else? Nothing at all?" he bellowed furiously.

"No, sir. Nothing I can recall."

"Why?" Jeanne dared to ask. "What that ghost done this time?"

"Ghost?" Nathan asked, his voice raised, annoyed that the woman continued to believe in such things. "Will you stop it with the ghost? Someone has been in this house again. I'm certain of it."

The three women looked questioningly at each other as Nathan hurried back toward the kitchen. His gaze swept the room in a futile search for places he might have missed. When he glanced toward the dining-room door, he finally noticed Josie standing there, the porcelain pitcher grasped tightly in her hand, her eyes wide as silver dollars. When he then noticed that the shoulder of her white nightdress was stained with a large patch of blood, his heart froze in midbeat.

"How bad are you hurt?" he asked, forgetting his search as he rushed forward to investigate.

"Hurt?" Josie looked down, puzzled by his reaction, and she, too, noticed the bloodstain covering her upper shoulder and part of the sleeve near the top of her arm. The material had turned dark, glistening red and sticking to her like a second skin. In her sudden state of panic, she hadn't noticed any real injuries. Staring at it curiously, she slipped a hand inside the garment and felt beneath the stained area. There was a deep, sticky gash along the back of her shoulder. But there was no pain. Pulling the material up over her shoulder so she could see the stained area better, she noticed there was a small, jagged tear only a few inches below the shoulder seam.

"I must have cut myself when I fell," she said. Her face twisted into a frown while she tried to figure out what she could have fallen on and why she hadn't noticed any pain."

"How bad is it?"

"Not too bad. I think it's already stopped bleeding," she told him as she dropped the material back into place, ready to dismiss the injury entirely. She was more concerned with the fact someone had been in the house again — and this time had shown the audacity to come right into her room. "Did she get away?"

"Probably, by now," he growled and looked back at the three women still huddled together, looking like frightened children. Aware they were going to be of absolutely no help to either of them, he ordered them back into Jeanne's room, where he demanded they keep an eye on each other until his return. Then he turned back to Josie. "But I intend to find out exactly how she got in here. Someone had to have helped her." He reached for a candle that sat on a nearby work table, then slipped his hand into his pocket for a match. "First, I intend to check each window and every door in this house until I find the one that opens."

"Let me help you look," Josie insisted, reaching for the drawer she knew held more candles. "You check the rooms on the east side of the house while I'll check the ones along the west side."

When she turned her back to him to light the candle she'd found, Nathan's attention was again drawn to the large bloodstain on her nightdress. "No, wait a minute."

Josie glanced back to see what he wanted and was touched by the true concern revealed on his face. "Now, Nathan Garrett, don't you dare try to order me back to my room. I'm just as eager to find out how she got in and out of this house as you are."

"I wasn't ordering you to do anything. I just want you to take this with you," he said, pulling up his shirt and producing a pistol from inside his waistband. "You may need it."

"You don't really think Pearl might still be inside this house, do you?" she asked as she accepted the gun. Her heart sped into rapid motion at the mere thought.

"No, not really. I just don't want to take any more chances. Not where you are concerned."

Josie smiled, touched by his words. "I'll be careful," she promised before leaving the room to help search for an unbolted door or an unlatched window.

Twenty minutes later, after a thorough search of the house both upstairs and down, Nathan called Josie into the library and carefully closed the door.

"Did you find anything?" she asked as she moved across the room to set her candle down on the desk, then turned to face him.

"No. Every window and every door in this house is still bolted shut. That means no one has left this house."

"Then you think she's still in this house?" Josie asked, her eyes darting about the room with renewed alarm.

"If she is, she's a damned good little hider," Nathan said with a slow shake of his head.

"Then maybe she slipped out a window, and whoever is helping her to get in and out managed to latch it back before you were able to get downstairs."

"No, that's not likely. All the windows at the back of the house have screens nailed over them. After all, that's the hottest part of the entire house. And there just wasn't enough time for anyone to have relatched one of the windows in the front part of the house and still get safely back to her room before I arrived in that kitchen. No, I honestly think that whoever was in your room is still in this house."

Josie's eyes widened. "Then you *do* believe she's still here? But where? We've looked everywhere."

Nathan studied the situation further. "I know. That's why I'm starting to believe at last that one of the main troublemakers lives right in this house. There's a possibility Pearl has passed those keys on to someone else, someone we would have no reason to suspect."

"But who?"

"I don't know. All I know is that whoever was in your bedroom had just enough time to get back downstairs and into bed. But not enough time to do anything else."

"I guess that lets Rafe off the hook."

Nathan nodded that he agreed. "And that's also why I feel that I can now safely send him into town to get help."

"You're going to send Rafe to get the sheriff?"

"And the doctor."

Josie was pleased. Cynthia's assumption that Nathan was putting off telling the sheriff because he was actually afraid to had just crumbled into dust.

"I don't need a doctor," she protested, thinking it would be absurd to wake Dr. Harrison at this hour of the night for such a minor injury. "The bleeding has stopped."

"Just the same, I want him to look at it."

Rather than argue with him, knowing his mind was made up, she tilted her head to one side and smiled agreeably. "Whatever you say."

Nathan stared at her a moment, wishing he could go to her but remembering his solemn promise to stay away from her. Though she stood only a few feet away, it felt as if they were worlds apart. How he longed to take her into his arms and hold her close, but he was too afraid she'd misread his intentions and pull away. He couldn't bear another rejection.

"I'm glad you plan to be sensible about this because," he said, smiling, "because, right now, I'd like for you to go back upstairs and lie down. You've lost a lot of blood and I don't want to chance it starting to bleed again."

"What are you going to do?"

"First I plan to go outside and tell Rafe what has happened. I want him to leave for Silver Springs right away. Then I plan to have a little talk with Jeanne, Ruby, and Shirley. I'm hoping that whoever is involved in this will do or say something to give herself away before the sheriff even gets here."

"And if she doesn't?"

"Then we'll just have to wait until she does, won't we?"

Chapter Twenty-five

Everything had occurred so quickly that Josie hadn't yet had the time to wonder why anyone had gone into her bedroom at all. It wasn't until she reached the top of the stairs and saw the door to her room that her curiosity was aroused. What could possibly have lured anyone inside? She owned nothing worth stealing and there certainly weren't any paintings in her room. Even if there once had been, they would have been removed and safely stored in the studio with the rest.

Curiously, Josie hurried toward her room. Now that the entire house had been carefully searched, most of the rooms had been left well lighted, including her own. Though Nathan had been the one to check all the upstairs windows and doors and all the upstairs hiding places, she trusted him to have been thorough in his search and felt perfectly safe entering her room alone.

The first thing she wanted was to find out what she'd fallen on. The nearest piece of furniture would have been a small, straight-legged table with a rounded top, but she didn't remember hearing it crash to the ground beneath her, nor could she recall having set anything on top of it recently that could have been knocked off during the brief struggle before her fall. Yet she had to have landed on something—something with a sharp edge or jutting corner.

Upon entering the door, she glanced immediately at the floor where she'd fallen, surprised to find a bronze

424

metal box lying near the door. It looked to be about a foot wide, possibly sixteen inches long and several inches deep. Bending over, she picked it up to examine it more carefully, finding it far heavier than she'd expected.

The box appeared to be a security box of some sort, meant to keep valuables. It had a small lock on the side and fitted into the bottom was a small cloth-covered panel with raised edges. When she reached inside to touch it, she discovered the cloth was damp. But there were no markings that might identify the owner, nor was there anything else on the floor that might have spilled out. She wondered if whoever had brought the box into her room had hoped to fill it with something worthwhile before leaving the house, possibly jewelry.

Though the only jewelry she'd brought with her to Oakhaven was a small silver bracelet with a tiny hand-engraved locket, Josie was very pleased with herself for having awakened and surprised her intruder before she could get her hands on it — or anything else for that matter. It delighted Josie to think how frustrated the woman must be to have gone to such obvious trouble, almost getting caught in the act — yet ending up with nothing.

Having solved the mystery of her injury to her satisfaction, Josie set the metal box on a nearby table, then crossed the room to the dresser and pulled out a fresh nightgown. She'd considered putting on a regular day dress, knowing she would get no more sleep that night anyway, but realized it would be easier for the doctor to examine her shoulder if she wore a loose-fitting gown.

After removing the ruined gown and tossing it aside, she took time to examine her latest injury more carefully. Turning her back to the mirror, she glanced over her shoulder and saw that the cut was angular in shape but barely two inches wide. Reaching back to touch the wound, she discovered that although it was obviously a deep cut, it was not at all sore. She hoped it would stay that way, but she had her doubts. The area around the opening was already starting to turn red.

As she returned to the bed where she'd left her clean gown, she glanced at the clock to check the time. One o'clock. It would be well after four before Rafe returned with either the sheriff or the doctor. Eager to tell the sheriff everything so he could help them catch Pearl, she dreaded the long wait but realized she had no other choice.

Snatching her white gown off the bed while still deep in dismal thoughts, she lost hold of the material and sighed heavily when it floated to the floor in a rumpled heap. Wondering what else could possibly go wrong before the night was over, she bent down to pick up the gown. When she did, she noticed something move under her bed. *A snake!*

Josie was halfway into the hall before she thought about screaming—and well into Nathan's bedroom and on top of his bed before she decided to stop. When she pressed her hand against her breast to help steady her pounding heart, she became immediately aware she was still naked. Her gown was still on the floor beside her bed.

Hearing Nathan's footsteps bounding up the stairs, she grabbed the first garment she saw and slipped it on. The shirt felt enormous and awkward, but at least it covered the essentials. She was still fumbling with the tiny pearl buttons when she climbed down off his bed then stepped out into the hall. Aware he was headed for her room, she called out his name.

Nathan came to an abrupt halt, confused to find her coming out of his bedroom, dressed in his shirt. And even more confused to see how pale she looked.

"What happened?" he asked, looking every bit as bewildered as he felt.

"There's a snake under my bed," she said in a trembling voice, feeling an incredible urge to throw herself into the safety of his arms.

"A snake?" His eyebrows shot up with surprise. "In your bedroom? What kind of snake?"

Josie's mouth flattened, perplexed by all the questions. "How should I know what kind? A snake is a snake as far as I'm concerned. And I don't particularly like having one under my bed."

"How did it ever get in there?" he asked as he slowly eased over to her door and peered inside. His blue eyes were wide with caution as he stretched his neck first to one side then the other to enable him to see better.

"How should I know how it got in there? All I want to know is how you plan to get it out."

Nathan did not enter the room, but he knelt low to the floor in an attempt to view the dark shadows beneath her bed. "I don't see any snake under there. Maybe you imagined it," he said hopefully as he straightened back up. "It has been a trying day."

"Trying or not, I didn't imagine it." She looked at him expectantly, clearly waiting for him to do something heroic. "Though there's probably less than a foot between the bedfringe and the floor, I saw that snake as plain as I can now see the nose on your face."

Nathan lifted his hand to touch his nose, and frowned. Aware she was waiting for him to take action, he glanced back into the room, then reluctantly stepped inside, glad now that he'd taken the time to put his boots back on after he came back upstairs to check the windows and doors earlier.

"And you're sure you saw it under your bed?"

"Positive."

"But, as you can see, it's not under there now. I wonder where it went," he said as he moved slowly across the room, careful to keep a safe distance between himself and anyplace a snake might hide. When he reached the center of the room, he glanced back over his shoulder at Josie, who stood balanced on one foot just outside the door, her eyes stretched wide. "Do you see it anywhere?"

Josie leaned into the room without actually stepping inside and looked around but saw no sign of the snake. "Maybe it's hiding under my gown," she suggested, nodding toward the crumpled white garment that still lay beside the bed.

Nathan glanced around for a weapon of some sort, preferably something five foot or longer. Finding no such implement, but spying a pink parasol with a two-inch brass tip propped against the wall between the dresser and washstand, he carefully stepped over and snatched it up, brandishing it in his right hand like a sword.

Armed for battle, he turned back around and stepped cautiously toward the bed, his eyes in constant search of any unexpected movement. When he neared the spot where the gown lay, he leaned way over and poked at the motionless garment with the tip of the parasol. The garment jumped but not nearly as high as Nathan did.

"I think I've found it," he said, his voice stretching from a high-pitched yelp down to a low, throaty whisper. *But now what?* He considered stepping on it in an attempt to trap it beneath his boot, but had no way to know how long the snake was. He did not want to take the chance of it striking anywhere above the top of his boot. What he needed was to find some way to imprison the horrible little creature until he could figure out just what to do with it. Looking around for something he could use, his gaze fell across the metal box. Cautiously, he began to back away from the gown, toward the table where Josie had left the box.

"What are you going to do with that?" Josie asked as she watched him pick the box up off the table and peer quizzically at it.

"The way I see it, I've got two choices," he explained. "The first choice is to open this thing up and try to trap the bugger inside. But if that doesn't work, my second choice is to beat the bloody hell out of him with it." He glanced back at the now motionless gown, one eyebrow lowered with concentration, then at the box again. "You don't happen to have a larger one of these, do you?"

Despite the seriousness of the situation, Josie laughed. "No, I'm afraid not."

"Are you sure?"

"That's not even my box. Whoever was in here earlier must have left it behind. That's what I cut my shoulder on when I fell."

Nathan's head jerked up as his gaze met hers. "This isn't your box?" His eyes widened with realization as he reached inside and touched the cloth panel, then raised the box to his nose and sniffed. "That snake did not get in here by accident. It was brought up here deliberately. In this box."

"What?"

"Someone let that snake loose in here on purpose."

Josie's initial feeling of panic was replaced by a sudden burst of anger. "And if it *is* a poisonous snake, that means whoever brought it in here hoped to—" Her eyes stretched wider at the thought. Someone wanted to kill her.

Certain now that they were dealing with a poisonous snake, Nathan became even more cautious. Setting the box on its side only a few feet from the gown, with the hinged lid laid back, he took the pillows off the bed and shaped thick walls on either side, angled toward the box. Then, when he was certain the snake would have nowhere to go but into the box, he picked up the pink parasol again and used it to jerk the gown off the floor.

Once exposed to the light, the snake, which he could see now was a small brown copperhead and indeed poisonous, did exactly what it was supposed to do and slithered immediately into the box.

With his lips pressed together in concentration, Nathan carefully bent forward until he was close enough to flip the lid closed with the tip of the parasol. He heard the snake come to life inside the box and stayed back until he was sure it would not force the lid open acciden-

429

tally. Even so, he waited until the snake was completely silent again before daring to get close enough to actually pick up the box.

Holding it well away from his body with his thumbs firmly pressed down on the lid, he carried the box outside and set it down in the far corner of the balcony. Then, as an added precaution, he turned one of the wrought-iron tables upside down and rested it on top. Feeling the problem was finally solved, he returned to Josie's side and, with a dramatic wave of his arm, pronounced the bedroom officially free of all harm.

"How do you know?" she asked, glancing apprehensively at the floor as she stepped gingerly into the room. "How do you know there weren't two snakes in that box?"

Nathan's gaze darted about the room. "Two snakes?"

"Or three," she suggested, and stopped just a few feet inside the door.

"Three snakes?" Nothing moved but the blue of his eyes while he continued to scan the lower areas of her bedroom.

"I can tell you right now, I'm not sleeping in here tonight," she said, already having turned and on her way out.

"I don't blame you. I'll get someone to put fresh linens on another bed for you."

"By someone, do you mean one of those three women downstairs?" she asked, glancing back at him pointedly. "One of the very people suspected to have brought that snake up here in the first place? No, thank you. I'd rather prepare my own bed."

"But I don't want you doing anything that might start that wound to bleeding again. Why don't you just sleep in my bed?"

"And where are *you* going to sleep?" she asked cautiously, her heart making a perplexing little leap against her breast.

"Sleep? I don't have any intention of going back to

430

sleep," he said with a slow shake of his head, as if that should have been understood. "I do plan to stay in the same room with you, though. Until we've caught whoever it is who's been causing all the trouble around here, I'm not letting you out of my sight. And I don't care what you have to say about it."

Josie felt comforted by his concern. "After everything that's happened tonight, I have nothing to say to that but thank you."

Nathan released the heavy breath he'd held. "Good. As stubborn as you can sometimes be, I was afraid you'd try to put up some sort of argument."

"Stubborn?" she repeated, tossing her shoulders back, not at all certain she should let him get away with calling her that.

"If not stubborn, then certainly opinionated," he conceded, then glanced down at her attire and smiled approvingly. "I must say, I do like the way my shirt looks on you. By any chance is that what you plan to sleep in tonight?"

"Sleep? Like you, I really doubt I'll be getting any more sleep tonight," Josie said as she gazed up into the shining depths of his blue eyes. She shifted nervously. Now that all the earlier commotion was behind them, she had time to consider that they were alone. She also had time to remember that she wore absolutely nothing underneath his shirt. Her skin tingled with sudden awareness, making her feel a strange contrast of warm and cold.

"Josie, I want so very much to hold you right now." His voice was filled with emotion as he took a tentative step toward her, wondering if she would back away or accept his comforting embrace.

"And I want so much to be held by you," she admitted, blinking back a sudden rush of tears as she ran willingly into his arms. She pressed her eyes closed as his arms came around her and held her close. "Nathan, what am I going to do?"

Having fallen so deeply and so irreversibly in love with him, how was she ever going to live without him?

"For now, you're going to go into my room and lie down while I go back downstairs for a minute," he told her, pulling gently away. Though he'd prefer to stand there and hold her close for the rest of the night, he had responsibilities to look after. He would not rest easy until he knew they were both safe again.

"But I thought you said you weren't going to let me out of your sight," she reminded him, glancing up at him quizzically.

Nathan looked at her with a raised brow. "I'm glad to know none of this has affected your memory." He then smiled and admitted, "I'll only be gone a few minutes. I just want to make sure everything is okay downstairs. Do you think you can possibly stay out of trouble until then?"

"Possibly—if, before you leave, you'll go back into my room and get that pistol for me. I left it on top of my dresser."

"In there with all those snakes?" he asked, clearly teasing her, then pulled away and bravely entered her room.

When he returned minutes later, he not only had the pistol, but carried a neatly folded nightgown as well. "Although I personally like the way you look in that shirt, I figured it might be a little awkward trying to explain to the doctor how you came to be in my clothes so I brought you this."

"That's not the one the snake hid under, is it?" Her nose wrinkled at the thought.

"No. I found this one in that drawer you'd left open," he assured her. "You can slip into it while I'm downstairs. But don't take too long, because if I were to come back upstairs and catch you undressed, I can't promise that I'd be able to keep my hands off you."

For a moment, Josie considered intentionally being without clothes when he returned, but quickly realized

432

the foolishness of such an idea and cast it aside. Now was not the time to let her emotions overrule her head. Not only was there still that unknown danger to consider, there was also her future happiness to keep in mind. That much had not changed. She was going to have a hard enough time trying to forget him as it was.

Chapter Twenty-six

Rafe returned shortly after four o'clock. With him were the doctor, the sheriff, and Jason Haught. The sheriff, who was a tall, burly man named William Mott, waited with Jason in the library while Nathan led the doctor to Josie.

Knowing Dr. Harrison would not allow him to stay in the room during the examination, and not trusting any of his servants enough to ask for their help, he waited long enough to be sure the doctor would not need anything before returning downstairs to have a talk with the other two.

"Rafe told us that someone broke into the house and tried to hurt Josie," Jason stated, his expression grim. "He also said that this is not the first time someone has broken into the house. What exactly has been going on out here and why haven't you sent word to me about it?"

Nathan began at the beginning, explaining to them everything he knew, up to and including the part about the snake. "At first, I thought someone was just trying to scare her away — scare us both away. But now I honestly think someone is trying to kill her."

"Yet make it look like an accident," Jason put in, nodding that he fully agreed.

"But who?" William Mott wanted to know. "Who holds that sort of grudge against her?"

"I don't think it has anything to do with a grudge," Jason said, rubbing his chin thoughtfully. "I think it probably has to do with Carl Garrett's will."

"I don't understand. What is killing Josie Leigh going to accomplish for anybody?" Sheriff Mott asked.

"The same thing that scaring her off would do," Jason pointed out. "I think it is because she was not so easily frightened that her life is now in danger."

"Me, too," Nathan put in quickly. "I think that whoever sabotaged that ladder had hoped the fall would injure her so badly she'd have to be carried into town and put under a doctor's care. That person probably hoped I'd then decide to stay in town, too, at least until I was sure she would be all right."

"What good would that do?" the sheriff asked, still not understanding.

"It would get us both out of the way, at least long enough to steal a wagonload of Father's paintings and possibly some of the silver serving pieces he has."

"I agree," Jason said. "After having stolen that one painting and no doubt discovering just what Carl's paintings are worth, I imagine —"

Jason's explanation was cut short by a light knock at the door.

"She's fine," the doctor said as he stepped inside. Instantly, he noticed the tension in the room. "What's wrong?"

"Plenty," Nathan said, his mind busy with all that had been said thus far.

"Tell him about it later," William said in a gruff voice, then turned to the doctor, "Would it be all right if we had a little talk with your patient?"

"I see no reason why not," Dr. Harrison said, stepping back out of the way. Not really understanding what was going on, but aware of everyone's serious expressions, he followed the others upstairs.

Jason's eyebrows rose questioningly when instead of heading toward Josie's bedroom, Nathan led them directly to his own. He glanced back at the others to see if they thought the arrangement a little odd, but said noth-

435

ing while Nathan knocked and asked if they could come in.

"Yes, I'm decent," Josie responded, watching them curiously as they filed into the room one by one.

"Jason?" she asked, surprised to see his face among the others. "What are you doing here?"

"William came by and told me there was some sort of trouble out here and asked me to come along," Jason explained. "I've sure hated to hear about all that's been going on."

"Ma'am," the sheriff interrupted, quickly taking his hat off and holding it between his hands while he averted his gaze to the floor. Though Josie was fully covered by one of Nathan's robes and had pulled the bedcovers up to her shoulders, he clearly felt uncomfortable looking at her. "I'm sorry to bother you like this, but I have a few questions I'd like to ask you about what happened."

"What do you want to know?" Josie asked, glancing from one to the other, aware that the only person who dared look directly at her was Nathan, and he seemed reluctant to do so.

The sheriff glanced at the window, where the sky was just starting to turn a pale, dusty pink along the distant horizon. "Nathan has told us what happened here tonight, and he also told us some of the things that have happened during the past few days. I'd like to know if you can remember anything that might help us figure out just who's behind it all. He said you had a little tussle with the person. Did you happen to get a glimpse of a face?"

"I wish I had, but it was way too dark. All I can tell you is that she was wearing a leather glove on her right hand and was either barefoot or wearing very lightweight slippers because I didn't hear any footsteps when she fled down the hall."

"If it was so dark, how do you know it was a woman who attacked you?" the sheriff wanted to know, reaching up to scratch his balding head.

Josie thought about that for a moment. "I don't know.

A hunch, I guess. Maybe it could have been a man. But then again, after checking all the doors and windows and finding none of them unlocked, Nathan and I realized whoever had been in my room was still in the house. Therefore, it had to be one of the three women who work for him."

"I don't know about that," Jason said, frowning while he studied the situation fully.

"Who else could it have been?" she asked. "Nathan was downstairs within seconds after it happened. It had to have been one of the housekeepers. They were the only other people in the house at that time."

"There's something that just doesn't make sense about all this. I don't know why, but I have a feeling that it wasn't one of the housekeepers," Jason said, then fell thoughtfully silent while he thought more about it. Finally, he took a deep breath and shrugged. "But then again, I've been wrong before."

"Where are these housekeepers?" the sheriff wanted to know. "I'd like to have a talk with them, too, if you don't mind."

"They're downstairs in Jeanne's room," Nathan said. "By keeping them all together like that, I figured it would be less likely the guilty one would try to make a break for it. And if whoever put that snake in Josie's room is indeed working for someone else, I felt it would be harder for her to get a message out."

"Using the other two as watch dogs," the sheriff commented and nodded approvingly. "Pretty clever idea. Now show me where they are."

One by one, in the same order the men had entered her room, they left, leaving Josie behind feeling undeniably frustrated. Aware she could not simply lie in bed resting while the others tried to solve the mystery of who'd attacked her, Josie waited less than a minute before flinging back the covers and following them. Because she was in her stocking feet, she managed to do so without making a sound and was standing out in the

437

hallway listening to the sheriff question the three house-keepers when a knock at the back door startled her nearly out of her skin. She didn't have time to jump back out of the way and hide before Nathan came charging out of the room to see who was at the door.

"What are you doing out of bed?" he demanded to know as he came to a sudden stop in the hall, staring quizzically at her less-than-appropriate attire.

"Listening," she admitted with a defiant toss of her head that let him know it would do no good to order her back upstairs to bed.

"Dressed like that?"

"My clothing has yet to affect my hearing," she stated bluntly.

"You know that's not what I —" he started to say, but a second, more persistent knock at the door interrupted his train of thought. Turning away from her, aware it would be a waste of time and energy to argue with her, he tossed his hands into the air and headed toward the door. "Coming," he called out as he entered the kitchen.

Knowing Nathan was right about her clothing, and also knowing the other men might come out of Jeanne's room at any moment to see who'd come to the back door at such an early hour, Josie remembered the dirty-laundry basket and hurried to put on yesterday's clothes. Not yet knowing where she might change, she snatched up the clothing from the basket, which was kept in the kitchen, behind a worktable, out of sight until the time came to do the laundry. Spotting the cellar door partially open, she hurried inside and down the stairs, then dressed in the darkness.

When she emerged again, fully dressed except for shoes, she found all four men standing in a semicircle in front of Rafe. Nathan held a piece of crumpled paper in his hands, frowning while he quickly scanned the message. When he finished, his expression went from disbelief to hardened anger. "Where did you find this?"

"Like I said. It was on my bunk when I went back in to

change shirts. I'd have found it sooner, but I'd decided to unsaddle my horse and curry him first."

"What does it say?" the sheriff asked, studying the back of the paper as if hoping to catch a glimpse of the writing on the other side.

"It says, if Josie values her life at all, she will leave Oakhaven while she still can," Nathan said, thrusting the paper at the sheriff. "If she doesn't leave right away, the danger will only get worse."

"Here, let me see that," Jason said, reaching out to intercept the note before the sheriff had a firm grip on it. His brows drew together while he quickly glanced over the message. "Maybe it would be best if she did leave. She can ride back into town with me."

"I'm not going anywhere," Josie said as she stepped father into the room, letting her presence be known.

Everyone looked at her with surprise.

"What are you doing out of bed?" Dr. Harrison wanted to know as he crossed his arms to show his displeasure.

"Trying to find out what's going on around here," she told him with a determined shake of her head.

"Rafe found a note on his bunk—" Nathan started to explain.

"I know. I heard everything. I also heard what Jason had to say about it, but I want you all to know that I'm not going anywhere."

"But you are clearly in danger here," Jason pointed out, studying her expression with a raised brow. "Didn't last night tell you anything?"

"So is Nathan in danger. But I don't hear you suggesting that he leave," she pointed out.

"Now that you mention it, it might not be a bad idea if the both of you left. No inheritance is worth risking your lives."

"*This* inheritance is," Josie said resolutely, stamping her stocking foot on the floor for emphasis.

Nathan lifted his hand as if he intended to argue the point, but let it drop to his side again as he nodded agreeably. "She stays. We both do."

"But what about the note?" the sheriff wanted to know. "Whoever wrote that means business."

"And I think it's safe to assume that this note was not written by one of your housekeepers. With the three watching over each other like they are, there's no way one of them could have slipped out long enough to plant that note out in the barn," Jason pointed out. "Not unless all three of them are in on it, which is highly unlikely."

Nathan ran his hand through his hair as he thought about it. "You're right. And if whoever planted this note is the same person who attacked Josie earlier, that person obviously knows this house better than we do. Well enough to be able to get in and out without using either the doors or the windows."

"Which leads us back to your first suspicion," the sheriff said, nodding. "It has to be your father's house-keeper."

"Not necessarily," Jason said, staring idly into space. "We have to keep our minds open to all possibilities."

"Like what?" Sheriff Mott wanted to know, leaning forward to hear what Jason had to say. "You sound like you suspect something you haven't told us about yet."

"I suspect several things, actually. Like I said, we have to keep our minds open to all possibilities."

"You sound as if you know the culprit's identity."

"I don't want to say just yet. I could be wrong on all counts. Dead wrong. But I do have an idea that I think will force this person, whoever it is, to unwittingly expose him or herself. I'll admit it's a dangerous plan, but I think it will work."

"I'm willing to try anything," Nathan said. "What is this plan?"

"To speed things up a little. To put a little pressure on whoever is out there trying to run you both off. Make that person think time is running out. Maybe, by doing that, we can make them panic into doing something unintentional."

"How?"

"Until now it's been clear that the will is not going to be read anytime soon, and time has not been of any concern. But what if I started spreading rumors around town that I plan to read Carl's will immediately — say, sometime tomorrow. Then, whoever wants you two out of here just might react with such haste, he or she won't take the time to really think their actions through."

"And I could stay out here and help protect the two of you until something does happen," Sheriff Mott said, rubbing his chin thoughtfully.

"No, if you did that, then whoever we are trying to trick might realize it's all a trap and stay away. I'm afraid Nathan and Josie will have to face the danger alone."

Nathan frowned. "Maybe it would be better if Josie wasn't here after all. It might be best if you did take her back into town with you and keep her hidden away until everything is safe. We could pretend her injuries are so serious that the doctor decided to keep her under observation for a few days."

"But what about the inheritance?" Josie reminded him. "If I'm not back here by nightfall, we'll lose the inheritance by default."

"I think Jason was right about that," Nathan said as he studied her determined expression. "No inheritance is worth risking your life."

"Oh, but it's perfectly all right for you to risk yours," she surmised, placing her hands on her hips to show what she thought of that.

"That's different. I'm a man. You're a woman."

"How perceptive. But you really should add that I'm a woman who plans to stay right here and see this thing through," she said, narrowing her eyes as she glared up at him. "Whatever danger there is, we will face it together."

Jason and Sheriff Mott exchanged startled glances while Dr. Harrison shook his head and cocked a grin to one side. "Might as well agree to let her stay. There's never any point arguing with a woman in love."

"Love?" Jason and William responded in chorus, their eyes wide as they turned to stare at the doctor curiously.

"Love?" Nathan asked, his voice trailing barely a second behind the others. He looked at Josie questioningly, only to find her staring at him with her arms now firmly crossed and her chin thrust forward at a stubborn angle.

"My advice to you is to accept the fact that she's staying and prepare yourselves for the worst," Dr. Harrison continued. "I'll leave you plenty of medical supplies in case one of you should somehow get injured, but I'm like Jason, I think anyone else's presence might cause whoever wants to harm the two of you to have second thoughts. And you sure don't want that."

"That's right. You'll have to do this alone. But I'll tell everyone that I plan to read that will early tomorrow morning. That way, whoever you are dealing with here will have to do something tonight."

"You're wrong. They won't have to do it all alone," Rafe said, crossing his arms in a show of support. "Although it might look a little fishy for me to actually be in the house with them, I'll be right outside, doing my regular chores but with my eyes wide open and my gun fully loaded."

"Then it's all set," Josie said. "Nathan and I will pretend nothing out of the ordinary has happened while you three start spreading the rumor that Carl's will is going to be read first thing tomorrow morning."

"What about the housekeepers?" the sheriff asked. "Do you plan to tell them what's going on?"

"No, I'm still not convinced that all three of them are completely innocent. I think the less they know, the better."

"What do you plan to tell them about last night?"

"The truth, minus a few facts. Since they haven't been told about the snake, I'll leave that part out and tell them instead that I thought someone had broken into the house again so I sent for the sheriff. They are bound to have that much figured out anyway. But I'll also tell them

442

there's nothing to really worry about, that Josie was still half asleep when it happened and must have imagined the whole thing. That way, if one of them is in some way involved with whoever left that note on Rafe's bunk, the message will get out that I'm not that concerned about the incident. I'll pretend that Josie overreacted to a bad dream and explain that her injury was probably the result of having slipped and fallen while running blindly in the dark."

"Meanwhile, we'll be getting the word out that the will is to be read tomorrow," Jason said as he reached out to pat Nathan's shoulder encouragingly.

"I'll do the same," Nathan added. "Just in case one of my housekeepers is involved in this, I'll be sure and tell them to expect you for lunch tomorrow *after the reading of Father's will.*"

"And I'll alert Cynthia. It would look a little odd if we claimed to be planning to read the will and didn't invite her to be there," Jason suggested.

"That's a good idea. I'll tell Jeanne to expect both you and Cynthia for lunch tomorrow."

"I guess it's settled then. Who knows, by this time tomorrow, if everything goes according to plan, all your troubles should already be behind you."

"Tell you what," the sheriff piped in. "Just to be on the safe side, I'll make up some excuse to leave town about dark. I'll be hiding somewhere down the road. If something happens, just send Rafe toward town. I'll see him when he passes by. That way, I should be able to get here within the hour."

"Just be careful not to let anyone see you lurking around," Jason warned as the three men headed outside. "If someone smells a trap, no telling what will happen."

Chapter Twenty-seven

In an effort to make the day seem like any other, Nathan quickly searched Josie's bedroom for another snake. When he found none, he left her alone in her room to rest while he disposed of the hapless snake. When he returned to the house he told Jeanne to expect guests for lunch the next day and why, then went to the barn to feed the stock.

Before leaving the house, he made sure Josie had the pistol hidden well within reach. He also placed his rifle where he could get to it easily should the need arise. Though he really did not expect anything to happen until nightfall, he did not want to take any chances.

The day passed uneventfully to Nathan's relief yet frustration. Though he dreaded the danger that lay ahead, the suspense of having to wait was making him edgy. He was ready for Pearl to make her move and be done with it so they could all continue with their lives.

By nightfall, he was jumpy as a cat on the take. Every little noise set his pulses racing. Afraid he could not go on pretending to be unaware of any danger much longer, he decided to make his excuses and retire early. By nine o'clock, he'd locked the house and was headed upstairs when he heard a carriage pull up into the drive.

Surprised by the noise and thinking it odd that the culprit would be so bold as to drive right up to his house, he hurried back down the stairs and into the darkened parlor where he could look out one of the windows without being seen. Peering cautiously through the lace curtains, he felt a strong mixture of relief and annoyance when he discovered the carriage belonged to his aunt and that she was already being helped down by her driver.

Wondering what she could possibly want at such an hour, he headed immediately for the door, reaching it just moments after she'd knocked.

"Aunt Cynthia? What are you doing here?" he asked as soon as he'd unlocked the door and opened it for her.

"I was on my way in from town and wanted to stop by and see that everything is all right," Cynthia said, gazing curiously past him into the darkened house. Only one light burned in the hallway. "Were you going to bed already? Why, it's barely nine o'clock."

"I'm tired," he told her. "I've had a long day and have an even longer one ahead of me tomorrow. Besides, Josie fell and hurt herself last night and has to stay in bed for a few more days which gives me no one to talk to."

"Another accident?" Cynthia asked, clearly skeptical as she brushed passed him. She lifted her right hand to remove her gloves, then thought better of it and left them as they were.

"Yes," he sighed wearily. "Another accident. Seems she had a bad dream, thought someone was chasing after her. She slipped in her bedroom while trying to escape some invisible demon she'd dreamed up and fell against a metal box."

"How badly was she hurt?" Cynthia studied his expression, as if trying to read beyond his words.

"Not too badly. But enough the doctor has ordered she stay in bed a few more days."

"Is that so? Is she going to be able to come down for the reading of the will tomorrow?" Cynthia wanted to know, glancing toward the darkened stairs at the far end of the entrance hall.

Nathan felt a sudden surge of his pulses to know that Jason had indeed gotten the word out about the will. Now, if only Pearl had somehow caught wind of it. "I see

445

Jason did get a message to you about the will in time."

"He sent someone out this morning, but because I was a little surprised to hear it was going to be so soon, I went immediately into town to see about it. After all, you'd told me it was going to be at least three months from the date of your arrival. Carl hasn't even been dead that long."

"And what did he tell you?" Nathan felt the muscles around his stomach tighten as he wondered if Jason had somehow managed to convince her that the reading of the will was legitimate or if he'd had to let her in on the whole thing.

"He told me he'd decided to hurry things along because Josie wanted to go home and he felt that she'd stayed long enough to satisfy Carl's reasons for having requested that she live here for a while. Seems the three months you told me about was not a set length of time, just a suggested time. He's decided that if you both stay here until the reading of the will tomorrow that Carl's wishes will have been met and whatever is in that will can be revealed."

"Yes," Nathan said quickly, thinking Jason had handled the situation very well. "That's the way he explained it to us, too."

"And is Josie going to be able to hear Jason read the will?"

"Yes, I think she should be able to come downstairs long enough for that. If not, I'll ask Jason to go upstairs and read it there. After all, if Josie is to inherit half of everything, she really should be present when the thing is read."

Cynthia's eyes were wide and thoughtful while she studied him for a long moment. "Yes, I agree. Everyone mentioned in the will should be present when it is read. Until tomorrow, then."

"Until tomorrow," he agreed, following her outside and standing on the front step until she had safely returned to her carriage.

Having already locked the rest of the house, Nathan quickly relocked the front door then went straight to his room and closed the door. He produced enough noise to make it sound as if he'd gone to bed, then slipped quietly out onto the balcony and into Josie's room, where he planned to stay until morning.

Because they did not want to alert anyone to Nathan's whereabouts, neither spoke aloud. Instead, Nathan moved about in his stocking feet and conveyed any messages by hand signs or by silently mouthing the words. Though neither planned to sleep, Josie was dressed in a soft white nightdress and Nathan wore one of his father's flannel nightshirts with a pair of rolled-up trousers underneath. That way, if either of them had to get out of bed and go downstairs for any reason, it would look as if they'd indeed gone on to bed.

By ten o'clock, Josie had turned out the lamp and the two of them lay quietly in the dark, Josie beneath her bedcovers and Nathan stretched out on top. The pistol lay on the bed between them, where Josie could easily find it, and the rifle sat across Nathan's lap. Occasionally, despite the darkness, he sensed her growing restlessness and reached out into the darkness to find her hand and squeeze it reassuringly.

"Did you lock Jeanne, Shirley, and Ruby in their rooms like Rafe suggested?" she asked softly, after several moments of silence.

"No, after I thought more about it, I decided not to. Although it would keep them from interfering like Rafe said, I was afraid it might backfire. If one of them is indeed helping Pearl get in and out, they need to be free to do so. Besides, Pearl is smart enough to know that I'd locked those doors because I was on to her."

"I see," Josie said, then fell silent again.

As the night wore on, every little creak and groan of the house seemed grossly magnified, causing one or both of them to jump. Hours crept by at an incredibly slow pace with nothing more eventful happening than a sudden gust of wind pushing against the window screen. Then, finally, they heard a noise that was different from the usual night sounds. It sounded like a door creaking off in the distance.

"Did you hear that?" Josie asked, her voice but a breathless whisper as her hand flew to her throat.

Nathan nodded that he had, but, realizing she could not see him clearly enough to be sure of his head movement, he whispered softly, "Yes. It came from downstairs."

Quietly, he slipped out of bed, his rifle in his right hand. Needlessly, he motioned for Josie to be quiet with his left hand while he moved slowly toward the door. He pressed himself against the wall beside the entrance while he waited for another sound.

Sucking in a deep breath, Josie picked up the pistol and carefully resituated herself in bed until she was sitting at a better angle. She had watched Nathan's black form slowly cross the room and become lost in the shadows beyond. Listening for another sound, one that could not be attributed to Nathan or the brisk night wind, she, too, waited for whatever was to happen next.

For several minutes there was silence. Finally, Nathan could stand it no longer and he carefully eased the bedroom door open and stepped out into the hall. Having detected no movement, he was on his way to the staircase when he heard footsteps—rapid footsteps—coming up the stairs. Quickly, he swung himself into a darkened doorway and hoped that his white nightshirt would not reflect enough light to give his location away.

His heart pounded with such force through the rigid muscles in his body he could barely hear the footsteps anymore when the dark shape first appeared at the top of the stairs. His lungs burned with the need to draw a long, hard breath, but he was afraid to breathe afraid of the sound it might make. He waited motionless until the shape hurried past him on its way to Josie's bedroom.

Finding the door partially open, the shadow did not

hesitate before entering the room. Nathan was only a few steps behind.

"Hold it right there," he called out as he stepped inside in time to see the shadow hovering over Josie's bed.

The sound of the match as it scraped the side of a lamp filled the darkness with startling clarity. Seconds later, as Josie touched the match against the raised wick, there was enough light to finally see who had entered Josie's room.

"Ruby?" The strain in Josie voice revealed her shock. "You?"

"Yes, it's me," Ruby answered, glancing fearfully at the pistol in Josie's hand, then back at the rifle in Nathan's. Both weapons were pointed directly at her heart. "I—I came up here to tell you that there's somebody downstairs trying to get in this house—may already be in this house. First, I heard him moving around out near the back porch, then I heard him rattling the cellar door. While I was on my way through the dining room to come tell you, I thought I heard a door open somewhere behind me."

Josie studied the fear on Ruby's face, wondering if the reaction was because she'd been caught or because there really was someone else in the house. When she glanced at Nathan, she could tell he was asking himself the same questions.

"Keep her here," he said, nodding at Ruby as he backed sideways out of the room. "I'll go downstairs and investigate."

"Ruby, sit down," Josie said, indicating a nearby chair. "Until we get this cleared up, I don't want you to leave that chair for any reason."

"Yes, ma'am," Ruby said dutifully, her gaze frozen on the pistol in Josie's hands as she reached her hand back and felt for the chair behind her.

Worried that Nathan might find more trouble than he'd bargained for downstairs, Josie quietly slipped out of bed and stepped closer to the door so she could listen.

Though she started across the room with the pistol still aimed in Ruby's direction, as she began to detect unusual sounds below the pistol slowly lowered to her side.

She bent forward through the doorway and glanced toward the darkened stairway, wondering what the sounds meant. Was Nathan all right? Would calling out his name to find out endanger him in any way? Fear tightened around her heart as she moved farther into the hallway, her attention fully focused on the sounds below.

Unaware Ruby had gotten up out of her chair and followed her out into the hallway, she jumped several inches when she felt the woman's hand lie gently on her shoulder. "Ruby!" she gasped in a strident whisper. "I thought I told you to stay in that chair."

"You did, but I had to come out here and see what was going on," she said, her voice filled with concern as she, too, studied the dark shadows at the end of the hall. "I don't know who broke into this house, or why, but I don't mind admitting that I'm scared to death. What if they hurt Mr. Garrett, then come up here and try to hurt us, too? There's a lot of meanness in this world. There's no telling what they'll do to us."

They? For the first time, Josie considered that there might be more than one person downstairs waiting for Nathan. She turned to look at Ruby, her eyes accusing. "Did you lead him into a trap? How many people are down there?"

"I didn't lead nobody nowhere. And I have no idea how many people are down there. I didn't stick around long enough to find out. I just hope Shirley and Jeanne are all right."

Josie was torn between what she'd been told to do and what she wanted to do. Though Nathan had ordered her to keep Ruby upstairs, she desperately wanted to be downstairs where she might be of some help to him.

"Come on, let's go," she finally said, motioning toward the stairs with the pistol.

"Not me," Ruby said, her eyes stretched wide. "You go

on down there if you want, but I'm staying right here."

"I can't leave you here," Josie protested, growing more frustrated by the moment.

"Oh yes you can," Ruby said, with a resolute shake of her head. "Because I sure as hell ain't going down there. No telling what's waiting for us."

"But I've got a gun pointed at you. You have to go down there with me," she tried to reason with her.

"You might as well shoot me now, 'cause I ain't going down there," Ruby said, still shaking her head adamantly.

"Fine, stay here. But don't you dare try anything," she finally said, too eager to see if Nathan was all right to wait any longer.

"I'll go back and sit in that chair if it'll make you feel any better. Just you be careful," Ruby warned her, then disappeared immediately into Josie's bedroom.

Knowing Ruby was still a suspect and should not be left alone, but at the same time too worried about Nathan to stay with her any longer, Josie went against her better judgment and hurried toward the stairs. Descending quickly into the blackness, she listened for any sounds that might alert her to where the danger lay. As her foot touched the main floor, she heard noises in the library and, with her pistol held in readiness, went to investigate.

Because there were no lights, all Josie could see inside the library was a solitary shadow moving about the room. With her pistol clutched firmly in her hands, cocked and ready to fire, she called out Nathan by name.

"What the hell are you doing down here?" Nathan's voice returned, verifying that the shadow was his. "Where's Ruby?"

"Upstairs in my bedroom," she answered softly, not wanting her voice to carry as she stepped inside. "What have you found out? Is there someone else in this house?"

"I don't know. I've got a feeling there is, but I just can't be sure."

"Do you want me to call for Rafe?"

"Not yet. But I do want you to go back upstairs and keep your eye on Ruby."

Having seen that Nathan was all right, and realizing that the noises she'd heard had probably been made by him, Josie agreed to go back upstairs. "But you'd better call me if you need any help."

"I promise. Just get upstairs."

Moments later, when Josie appeared in her bedroom doorway again, Ruby sat in the chair just like she'd promised, facing the hall with wide, frightened eyes.

"Good, you're still here," Josie commented as she entered the room. "I was afraid that when I came back up I'd find you had gone."

Ruby looked up at her for a moment, then away again, as if studying something that lay just a few feet behind Josie. When Josie turned to see what had the woman's attention, she gasped. Out of the shadow directly behind the bedroom door stepped Cynthia, a small derringer gripped in her hand.

"Not a word out of you," Cynthia said. Her voice was so low Josie had almost not heard her, but the warning behind it was clear. "Just put that revolver down, young lady, and do exactly as you are told."

"What are you doing here?" Josie asked, despite the warning to be quiet as she slowly knelt to the floor and placed the gun at her feet.

"I told you, not a word," she repeated, again in a soft but firm voice as she waved the derringer in front of her. "Just keep quiet and step out onto the balcony." She glanced then at Ruby, who had yet to move anything but her eyeballs. "You, too, out onto the balcony."

When neither Josie nor Ruby moved to fulfill her demands, she clenched her teeth and took a step forward. Her eyes glowed with dark fury as she pointed the derringer right into Ruby's frightened face. "Now!"

Slowly Ruby rose from the chair and headed for the balcony door, all the while keeping a cautious eye on

Cynthia. Reluctantly, Josie followed.

"What do you plan to do with us?" Josie asked as soon as the three of them were outside. A cold wave of apprehension sifted over her.

"I told you to keep quiet. Or have you decided to alert Nathaniel to my whereabouts? I'll gladly shoot him for you, if that's what you really want," Cynthia said, waving both the derringer and the revolver she'd stopped to pick up where it lay on the floor.

Josie snapped her mouth shut and shook her head adamantly. That was not at all what she wanted.

"Good, then I shouldn't have any more trouble out of you," Cynthia commented as she tucked the revolver under her arm long enough to pull the door closed behind her. All the while she kept the smaller pistol pointed at Josie's breast. After she finished closing the door and had stepped toward them, a demonic smile stretched her thin lips wide across her narrow face. "Now, if you two will kindly climb up onto the railing there, I'd be most grateful."

Ruby's eyes darted from the railing to the derringer, then back to the railing. Finally, she chose to take her chances with the railing and slowly climbed up into a chair, then out onto the railing itself, which stood about waist high. She put her hand against the stone wall for balance while she waited for what was to happen next.

"You, too," Cynthia said, moving closer as she reached for the revolver again. "On the railing. Now! Or have you changed your mind about Nathaniel? Maybe you'd like to call him up here after all. That way I could have the pleasure of shooting him with one of his own guns."

"You ain't going to make us jump off here are you?" Ruby asked fearfully, dividing her attention between the gravel walkway below and the two guns in Cynthia's hands.

"Well, I would rather it looked like an accident of some sort, but if you'd prefer to be shot, so be it," Cynthia said, still smiling as she raised the derringer and again aimed it at Ruby's head. "I can always make it look like Josie or Nathaniel shot you thinking you were a prowler."

"But why me? I ain't never done nothing to you," Ruby pleaded, her hands trembling as she tried to keep her balance on the narrow railing.

"No, and you never will," Cynthia commented, then suddenly stepped forward and pushed Ruby off the railing, startling the woman so completely she didn't scream until she struck the ground. Then it was as if the force of the fall had pushed the air past her vocal cords.

"You next, my dear," Cynthia said, not even glancing over the side to see Ruby sprawled on the graveled walkway below. "Up on that railing."

"You can't really expect to get away with this," Josie said, hoping to somehow make her think her actions through more clearly. Pressing her hands protectively over her pounding heart, she began slowly backing away. "You can't possibly believe that you can get away with killing us all."

"I can, and I will." Cynthia said calmly, then motioned toward the railing with the derringer. "It's your turn. Get up there."

"Why are you doing this?"

"Why?" Cynthia repeated as if she couldn't believe Josie was quite so naive. "Because if I don't kill you tonight, and Jason really does read that will tomorrow, I'll never be able to get my hands on everything that should be mine. I just can't take any more chances. Once the will has been read and Jason agrees that all the requirements have been met, you will legally become half owner of Carl's estate, and Nathan will get the other half—and that's not fair. What's even less fair is that although I could eventually get Nathan's half from him, being his next of kin, I could never hope to get your half from you."

Glancing at the lighted windows beyond Cynthia's left shoulder, Josie caught a glimpse of movement inside her bedroom. Her heart froze when she realized Nathan was inside her room, probably unaware of the danger that lurked just outside the door. Hoping to distract Cynthia and alert Nathan to her whereabouts at the same time, she asked a question she felt certain would get a reaction from her. "And why do you feel that's not fair?"

"Because I'm the one who deserves to have it all, not you. And certainly not Nathan. Now get up there."

After stepping up into the same chair Ruby had used, Josie glanced back through the windows again and noticed Nathan was no longer in her room. She wondered if he'd heard them talking and was already on his way through his own room to approach Cynthia from behind or if he'd gone back downstairs looking for her there. Her frantic questions were answered only moments later when she detected a slight movement at Nathan's door.

455

Chapter Twenty-eight

Wanting to keep Cynthia distracted while Nathan eased out onto the balcony, Josie teetered precariously on the chair with one foot on the railing. Acting as if she was about to do exactly what she'd been told, she glanced back at Cynthia. "I'll jump. But not until you tell me how you managed to get in and out of the house, even when it was locked."

Cynthia chuckled. "I'm the one who took Carl's keys, and I therefore had a key to that padlock on the cellar door, which is the only door Carl never bothered to put inside-security bolts on. I guess he'd neglected to do so because holly had grown up all around it, and it was never used. He may have forgotten the door even existed. But I knew it was there. And as soon as Nathaniel and Pearl had both left, I pushed away the holly and made sure that key still worked. I've been using it to get in and out ever since. That's how I was able to sneak back inside and spread the spoonful of butter on the stairs so Nathan would be sure and slip when he carried you down to supper. It's also how I got inside to let that snake loose in your room, and earlier to search the library for Carl's will."

"Why did you think the will was in the library?"

"The way Jason kept finding reasons not to read the will, and wouldn't even let me see the thing, I began to think he didn't have a copy of the will at all. And if he didn't have a copy of the will, then there was only one other place I knew of where it might be—in Carl's library. Besides, I wanted to get my hands on one of Carl's pistols just in case it ever came to this."

A tight knot formed in Josie's chest as she realized the fall had not been an accident at all, but a carefully planned attempt to harm her—harm them both. And the gun had been taken out of the library for the same purpose. "So you sneaked in through the cellar door again and again. Is that also how you got the painting out of the house without us ever knowing it? You carried it out through the cellar?"

"No. It was pretty heavy and I was afraid I'd make too much noise trying to carry it down those steep, narrow steps, even though it was in the middle of the night and everyone was sound asleep. So, instead, I wrapped the painting in blankets to muffle any noise, made a rope harness for it, then lowered it from the window down to where Rafe was waiting."

"Rafe?" Josie asked, surprised, then glanced back over her shoulder toward the barn, wondering if it could be true.

"That's right. Rafe works for me. That's why he hasn't come running yet. Fact is, he's guarding the house right now, making sure no one goes in or out except me."

Josie glanced up in time to see the astonished expression on Nathan's face as he moved into the dim light that glowed through her windows. Her heart froze the moment she realized he intended to speak.

"Rafe is in on this?" Nathan asked, clearly unwilling to believe it.

Cynthia let out a startled gasp as she spun around only to find Nathan's rifle already pointed at her.

"Nathaniel!" she cried out as she brought her right hand around and fired the derringer once in Nathan's direction, striking him in the upper shoulder only a split second before he pulled the trigger on his rifle.

457

A scream slipped past Josie's lips when she saw Nathan stumble backward.

"Rafe!" Cynthia called out for help as she dropped the now useless derringer and stepped back. A dark patch of blood formed where Nathan's bullet had struck her, just inches above her right breast. "Rafe get up here."

Aware Rafe was already on his way, Josie made a move for the revolver in Cynthia's left hand, only to find the woman had second-guessed her. Seconds before she'd reached her destination, Cynthia had managed to transfer the revolver to her right hand and had quickly pointed it at her.

Wincing with pain, Nathan had already raised his rifle in preparation to take a second shot, but hesitated when he realized Cynthia had clear aim at Josie.

"There now, that's better. And now that you understand the seriousness of the situation, I advise you to toss that rifle over the railing before I lose my temper and decide to shoot a hole right through her," Cynthia said, cocking the hammer back on the pistol to prove she meant business. Rafe's footsteps could be heard inside the house in the silence that followed.

Nathan studied the situation only a moment longer before doing exactly what he'd been told. He cringed at the sound of the weapon as it clattered to the ground, then opened his eyes wide the moment he heard another sound below. The sound of a window opening.

"There she is. She's been hurt. I told you I heard her scream." It was Jeanne's voice followed immediately by the sounds of footsteps on the front veranda. "Ruby? What happened? Are you all right?"

"Has she been shot?" Shirley asked fearfully as she joined Jeanne out in the yard.

"No, not that I can tell. But she won't wake up. Go get Mr. Garrett so we can carry her inside. Tell him we also heard gunshots."

"No, don't go back inside," Nathan shouted out. "I already know about Ruby and the gunshots. Go get help instead. Hurry!"

"Rafe, get them," Cynthia cried out, stepping over to the banister and watching in horrified disbelief as Jeanne and Shirley took off running in different directions, their nightgowns flapping behind them. Angrily, she raised Nathan's pistol and fired twice at each one. "Rafe, don't let them get away. The sheriff may have heard the gunshots and already be on his way. We can't leave any witnesses."

Rafe's footsteps fell silent in the house, as if he was undecided what to do, then quickly he turned around and headed the other way, back down the stairs.

Aware that Rafe was no longer an immediate threat, Nathan made a lunge for the pistol just as Cynthia turned back around to face him. As his hand closed around the barrel, the pistol went off again. The bullet barely missed his leg and struck the balcony floor. He felt the hot metal searing into the tender flesh of his hand, but he refused to let go and continued trying to twist the weapon out of her grasp, amazed at her strength. The uncanny strength of a madwoman.

"Only one bullet left," he warned her as he managed to get his other hand on the gun, wanting to try to wrench it out of her grasp again. "Not enough to kill both of us." Finally, he broke the weapon out of her hands just as Josie grabbed her by the arm and slung her to the floor.

"And it is not enough for you to kill both of us," Cynthia said defiantly. "Use that bullet to kill me and you won't have one to protect yourself against Rafe."

"I'll go down and get the rifle," Josie said, aware Cynthia spoke the truth.

"No, stay here. Rafe could come back at any moment. Besides, after a fall like that, I doubt that rifle works."

"Then I'll go get more bullets for the revolver," she offered. "Where are they?"

Nathan ran his hand across his face, remembering exactly what he'd done with the last of his bullets. "Rafe has them. He told me this afternoon he was down to his last two bullets and asked if I had any more. I gave the box to him, thinking he'd be using them to help protect us."

"So you are indeed down to one bullet," Cynthia cautioned him. "And you don't dare use it to kill me."

"I don't have any intention of killing you," Nathan told her. "Unless, of course, I have to."

"You just might have to," Cynthia said as she pushed herself up off the floor and stood proudly, though wavering slightly before him. Her legs had grown steadily weaker from the loss of blood. "Because I'm not giving up until I get what's rightfully mine."

"And just what do you think is rightfully yours?" he asked. A deep shudder passed through him when he noticed the eerie way she now stared at him—eyes wide, never blinking.

"Carl's estate should be mine, not yours. I'm the one who looked after him all those years, not you. I'm the one who spent all my time making sure he was happy and well taken care of. But did he appreciate anything I did for him? Did he care that I was sacrificing my own life just to help make his a little happier? Not at all. Instead, he arranged to leave me with virtually nothing. Oh, sure, he planned to see to it I had a place to live and enough money to get by, but he wouldn't even let me have ownership of my own house, said I was too irresponsible. Me! Irresponsible? So he fixed it so I wouldn't be able to sell my own house should I want to, nor could I pass it along to my children if I ever decided to get married and have a family. Unless, by some impossible chance, it turned out that you and Josie didn't want the place enough to live here for a little

460

while, I was to end up with nothing. *Nothing,* for all those years of sacrifice."

Remembering how Jason had told him that Cynthia was not yet aware of the terms in the will, Nathan's eyes narrowed. "How do you know all that?"

"Carl told me," she admitted. "He told me all about his new will the night he died."

"You talked with him that night?"

"Talked with him? I'm the one who killed him."

Nathan felt as if someone had struck him hard against the stomach with a board. For a moment, he could hardy breathe. "You killed my father."

"Sort of."

"How do you sort of kill someone?" Anger spread through him like a cold mist.

"It was an accident. I'd come by to ask him to loan me some money so I could get new drapes for my drawing room, but he refused. He told me I was too much of a spendthrift and claimed I had no sense of money. He then told me about his new will and how he hoped to give everything to you and Annabelle's grand-daughter. I got angry when he tried to turn away from me to go downstairs, so angry that I shoved him side-ways as hard as I could. Somehow, he stumbled forward instead and fell down the stairs."

Not ready to believe what he'd heard, Nathan sank back against a table for support while he slowly digested that last bit of information. "And then you took his keys and made up some wild story about having found him already dead."

"Of course I did," Cynthia said with a sharp toss of her head that caused her a moment of dizziness. "I told you. I didn't mean for him to fall. I only wanted to make him turn back around and face me, but I wasn't sure I could convince the sheriff of that so I pretended I knew nothing about it at all. It was better that way."

"Better for you, I suppose," Josie said as she moved to

stand beside Nathan and offer her support. The blood that had formed along his shirtfront worried her. Much more loss and he would start to grow weak, if he hadn't already.

"You stay out of this!" Cynthia hissed, cutting her gaze to Josie. Her eyes blackened with a resurgence of anger. "You don't even belong here. Neither does he for that matter. After all, where was he after his father married your grandmother? They tried to get him to come visit, but he wouldn't. He refused to have anything more to do with them. Never even wrote them letters. I never cared much for Annabelle, either, but at least I kept in touch with Carl during that time. I even came to visit a few times. And after Annabelle proved gracious enough to die only a couple of years into the marriage, who do you think came forward to help him through the sorrow? Me! But did Carl appreciate everything I did for him? Did he appreciate all the sacrifices I made? Not at all! Instead, he decided to give everything to a son who didn't even care enough to write a letter and a young woman he'd never even met."

Cynthia had a wild look when she began slowly walking toward Nathan, as if she no longer cared if he used his last bullet on her or not. "You didn't even try to contact him after that woman finally died. Not once. But I came immediately and took care of him day and night. I saw him through his grief. I helped him resume his life. Yet he rewarded me for all that by deciding to give you two the first chance at getting Oakhaven."

"I wasn't even aware of Annabelle's death for almost a year afterward," Nathan responded feebly, knowing how that alone showed what a poor son he'd been. He'd had so little contact with his father during the past twelve years, he wasn't even aware when his second wife had died.

"But when you did find out she was dead, you didn't even bother to send your condolences, nor did you try to contact him again," she bit out accusingly as she continued to advance toward him with wide, empty eyes.

"I was afraid to," he admitted, remembering that he'd felt it was too late for anything like that. They had grown too far apart to ever hope for reconciliation. Still, he suffered incredible pangs of guilt because, deep down, he knew that what Cynthia had just accused him of was the truth. He really didn't deserve any of his father's inheritance.

Suddenly, he realized that was what had been bothering him all along. His father had decided to give him an opportunity to inherit half of everything he'd owned, yet in no way did he deserve it. The only one who really deserved to inherit anything was Josie. She'd never been given the opportunity to know his father or her grandmother and therefore nothing could possibly have been expected from her by either of them during any part of their lives.

"You don't have any right to come here and try to take everything away from me," Cynthia said, jarring him loose from his thoughts. "And I'm not going to let you get away with it."

Having said that, she made a wild leap for the gun, moving purely from the strength of her own black rage. Nathan was able to react quickly enough to raise the weapon out of her reach, yet he did nothing to stop her from pelting his chest repeatedly with her fists. In a way, he felt he deserved it.

"Stop it," Josie cried out, moving forward to intervene until a voice from below caught her attention.

"Miss Garrett? You still up there?" Rafe had returned. He stood out in the yard calling up to her.

"Yes, I'm still here," Cynthia shouted angrily at him, stopping her assault long enough to glance over the railing and see Rafe's solitary figure staring up at her.

"I think we'd both better get out of here, Miss Garrett. Both those women got away from me and are probably on their way to find help. And if the sheriff did hide out somewhere along the main road like he said he would, then he's bound to have heard those gunshots. He's probably halfway here by now."

"If he was out on the main road, that means we still have a few minutes. Get up here. Nathan still has a gun, but it only has one bullet left. There's no way he can get both of us. Get up here and pick him off through one of the windows."

Nathan stared at her with a puzzled expression, unable to believe any of this was happening. It all seemed like a bad dream. He spun about, looking for a place where Josie could hide.

One bullet might not offer Nathan much of an advantage in Cynthia's mind, but it must have been enough to give Rafe second thoughts.

"I can't do that."

"But why not?" Cynthia cried out with disbelief, clutching the railing for support. Her determination was clearly still strong, but her physical strength was slowly ebbing with the gradual but constant outflow of blood.

"I can't just come up there and shoot someone. Helping you steal something that's rightfully yours is one thing, but killing someone for no reason is something else entirely. I don't want no part of it. You do your own killing."

"You coward," Cynthia screamed, leaning over the railing and shaking her fist at him. Again, she seemed to find subhuman strength within the dark realms of her own uncontrollable rage. "You yellow-livered coward! You're the one with a gun. Get up here and kill this bastard right now."

"I can't do it. I just can't," Rafe tried to explain.

The clamoring sound of horses in the distance caught everyone's attention. Rafe turned to face the

464

noise only a moment before he took off running toward the barn. Seconds later, he'd mounted a horse and rode off in the opposite direction just as hard as he could.

"Coward!" Cynthia called after him as she made another wild leap for the pistol in Nathan's hand, this time catching him off guard, for he had not thought she had enough strength left in her. The gun clattered to the floor between them.

Josie and Cynthia dove for it at the same moment, but Josie was too far away. Cynthia got there first. Smiling victoriously, she came up with the pistol in both hands, aimed immediately off into the darkness, and fired. Her eyes were black with cold fury when she turned to Nathan and asked, "Did I get him? Did I get the bloody coward?"

Rather than tell her she hadn't even come close, he eased the now empty gun from her grasp and nodded, fighting his own dizziness and pain. "You got him. Right square in the back, you got him."

Subdued over the thought of having at least gotten even with Rafe, Cynthia went downstairs peacefully with Nathan and Josie to await the sheriff's arrival. By the time they reached the parlor, she'd lost what was left of her strength and had to be helped the last part of the way.

To Nathan's relief, the sheriff had two deputies with him when he rode up into the yard just minutes later. After he quickly explained what had happened, the two deputies took off in the same direction Rafe had ridden while the sheriff dismounted, leaving his horse untethered, then followed Nathan to where Ruby still lay, twisted and bent.

"What a horrible way to die," he said morosely, shaking his head as he knelt beside her body. Slowly, he removed his hat and held it in both hands. "Does she have any next of kin I should notify?"

"I really don't know. You'll have to ask Jason about

465

that," Nathan said as he, too, knelt beside Ruby's body. Slowly, he unbuttoned his shirt, then draped it over her face and shoulders, carefully tucking the bloodied area out of sight. Quietly, he blinked back his tears and smiled fondly. "Such a cantankerous old woman. Always saying exactly what was on her mind."

"I'll send a wagon back for her first thing come daylight," Sheriff Mott promised, then rose to go inside.

Nathan grimaced when he, too, tried to stand. He found that he almost did not have the strength to get back to his feet. Clutching his shoulder with his uninjured hand, he discovered he was still bleeding, though not as profusely as before. Slowly, he turned to where Josie and Cynthia waited.

When they entered the parlor they found Cynthia lying on a sofa and Josie quietly administering to her wound.

Glancing up when she heard the footsteps in the doorway, Cynthia greeted the sheriff with a polite smile. "I guess you're here to arrest me," she said in a relaxed tone, as if she was discussing nothing more important than the weather.

"Yes, I'm afraid I have to, ma'am," Sheriff Mott said as he stepped forward and took her hand. Alerted by the outward calm of her voice and the glazed look in her eyes that the woman had lost all hold on reality, he glanced curiously at Nathan while he continued to talk to Cynthia in a soothing voice. "I just hope you understand why."

"Of course I understand. I did a naughty thing and I must be punished. But I am so pleased to have such a handsome escort."

"Thank you, ma'am," he said, glancing up at Nathan with his heavy brow drawn, showing how concerned he was about her condition. "Nathan, I'm going to need to borrow a wagon to get her into town."

466

"No, please," Cynthia interrupted. "My buggy is not far from here. If you don't mind, I'd rather we ride in it. Besides, I'll need it first thing in the morning. That's when Jason plans to read Carl's will, you know."

"Yes, ma'am, I know. Just show me where your buggy is," he said, looking worriedly at the blood staining her blouse as he carefully lifted her into his strong arms. "Do you think you can stand for me to carry you that far?"

"Of course. I'm fine," she claimed, then offered him a pleasant smile. "It's nice that you are so concerned."

"Need any help, Sheriff?" Nathan asked, taking a step forward.

"Just get the door," the sheriff told him. "She's not very heavy."

After opening the front door, Nathan and Josie followed the two outside and watched as the sheriff walked out into the moonlit yard with Cynthia still clutched in his arms. They headed off toward the nearest woods, where she must have left her buggy. The sheriff paused just long enough to whistle for his horse, but continued across the yard while the animal trotted in his direction.

As soon as the three were out of their sight, Nathan turned to Josie and pulled her into his arms. He held her close for several minutes before succumbing to the pulsating pain in his shoulder and letting go. Grimacing, he braved a quick glance downward to see just how badly he'd been injured.

His last thought before the dark gray haze drifted over him was that pain or no pain, it felt wonderful to be holding Josie in his arms.

Chapter Twenty-nine

The headstone read: Ruby Waters. Born March 25, 1812, died May 18, 1875. She was buried beside her sister shortly after noon on Thursday, March 20, in a small cemetery only twelve miles from Oakhaven.

Because Nathan was still feverish, slipping in and out of delirium, Josie did not attend the graveside services but allowed Jeanne and Shirley to borrow Nathan's wagon so they could go. She sat alone at his bedside as he slept — peacefully for the moment. His fever was down, but he was still a very sick and weak man. She hoped he would awaken soon and stay awake long enough to get more of Jeanne's broth down. Dr. Harrison felt that the most important thing for him at the moment was to get as much rest and nourishment as possible.

Josie, too, was in sore need of sleep, but she'd refused to leave Nathan's bedside for more than a few minutes at a time. His waking moments were so few she did not want to chance missing a single one. Whenever her fatigue became so great it overpowered her determination to stay awake, she curled up on the small sofa in his room and dozed.

She was dozing when a fly buzzing just inches over Nathan's head startled him awake. He was momentarily confused to find himself tucked away in bed during the middle of the day, but he quickly remembered why he was there.

"What time is it?" he asked when he glanced up and found Josie seated only a few feet away, unaware she was asleep.

Josie awoke with a start, blinking at him as she adjusted to the fact he was awake again and this time talking. Her heart soared as she quickly assessed the marked improvement in his health. Though the doctor had assured her he would recover, she had nevertheless worried something would go wrong.

"It's almost two o'clock," she said after a quick glance at the clock.

Nathan's lips pursed into a frown while he digested that bit of information. "Now, tell me what day it is."

"It's Thursday," she said, grinning when that seemed to make his expression even more perplexed. Quickly, she swung her legs around and brushed some of the wrinkles from her mint-green skirt as she sat up straight.

"Thursday? What happened to Wednesday?"

"It followed Tuesday right on out of here," she said, laughing lightly as she stood and crossed the room. "Do you remember Tuesday?"

"Vaguely. I remember getting shot and I remember watching the sheriff take Cynthia away. I also remember waking up much later and having you shove a bowl of hot broth in my face. That was Tuesday, wasn't it?"

"No, the broth was on Wednesday. Do you also recall that you ate very, very little of that broth?"

"It wasn't all that great," he muttered, twisting his face into a thoughtful frown while he tried to push himself into a sitting position. He winced at the pain in his shoulder and glanced immediately at the fresh white bandage. "I see the doc's been here."

"Twice a day since you were shot," she told him as she reached out to touch first his forehead then his unshaven cheek with her wrist. "Good, your fever is still down. I'll go downstairs and warm up some more broth."

"Why more broth? Why can't I have a big juicy steak with lots of potatoes and corn?" he asked, licking his lips at the mere thought of it. "After all, I haven't really eaten in days."

"Because there's no one here to cook it. And all Jeanne left for you was the broth the doctor had instructed she make."

"Left for me? Where is Jeanne?"

"I let her go with Shirley to Ruby's funeral," she explained. Her smile faded as another wave of sadness swept over her. "They both wanted to go and I saw no reason why they shouldn't."

"Oh." Nathan nodded that he understood, then fell silent for a moment. Finally, he asked, "Did they ever catch Rafe?"

"Yes, that same morning. The sheriff has him in jail."

"And Aunt Cynthia?"

"Still in jail."

Nathan stared up at the ceiling for several minutes before glancing back at Josie. The muscles in his jaw flexed in and out, revealing the torment of his thoughts. "You know, as crazy as Aunt Cynthia was, she was right about one thing. I don't deserve to inherit any of Father's estate."

"Don't be silly, of course you do. You're his son." Josie knelt beside the bed, her expression puzzled.

"Some son," he muttered, shaking his head sadly, looking again at the ceiling. "Aunt Cynthia was right. I barely knew the man, nor did I try very hard to get to know him. After Mother died, I did what I could to forget him. I tried to put him out of my life entirely. I was still too angry with him for what all he'd done — for all the misery he'd caused my mother. And now I think, I was even a little jealous of him, because no matter how badly he hurt her, Mother continued to love him with all her heart."

470

"That's understandable," Josie said as she reached out and took his hand in hers. She ached to comfort him in some way. "And, obviously, your father did not hold those feelings against you, either."

"But he should have. He never should have included me in his will. I don't deserve it."

But Josie did. Nathan knew Josie deserved to have it all. That's why he planned to stay on at Oakhaven until the three months were completed, at which time the will could officially be read and the estate finally settled. Then, as soon as Jason had declared them the legal owners, Nathan intended to sign his half of everything over to her. If she wanted, she could stay at Oakhaven forever. Or she could sell it and return to her friends in Cypress Mill a very rich woman. He would support either decision—whichever would make her happier, for that was all that mattered, that Josie be happy.

Unknown to Nathan, Josie was toying with similar thoughts as she headed downstairs to warm his broth—only her intention was for Nathan to be the sole owner. Having realized just how deeply she loved him, she wanted to give Nathan her half, feeling that he did indeed deserve it. The inheritance itself was never really important to her anyway. Just knowing her grandmother had loved her enough to want her to share something of her life was enough for her.

All that truly mattered to Josie now was Nathan's happiness. All she would ask of him would be enough money to get back Cypress Mill. Having realized she had no real place in his life, and knowing he would be too busy trying to see to settling the estate to have much time for her anyway, she felt it would be better for everyone if she left Oakhaven just as soon as they'd signed the papers that would make everything legally Nathan's. Though it hurt to know she only had a few weeks left to be with him, she felt certain her decision to

471

leave right away was the best for all concerned.

Because July 10, the earliest possible date the will could be read, fell on a Saturday and Jason's plans were to read the document that very afternoon, Josie was forced to alter her plans to leave Oakhaven immediately following the reading. With no train transportation offered on Sundays and the last train headed east due to depart shortly after five that afternoon, she had little choice but to remain until the following Monday. Therefore, when Jason arrived shortly before three to proceed with the reading of Carl's will and get the necessary papers signed, she hadn't yet started to pack. Her plans were to wait and pack everything Sunday afternoon. For now, she tried not to think about it, tried not to dwell on the pain that filled her heart.

"I hope you don't mind that I'm a little early," Jason said, smiling at Josie as he handed Shirley his hat and quickly divested himself of his lightweight summer coat. "But I'd like to get this over with and be on my way back to town as quickly as possible. I've got a dozen things that I need to get done."

"That's fine. Nathan's already in the library," she told him, indicating they should join him by a wide sweep of her hand. Fact was, Nathan had been in the library for hours, sitting in his father's chair, staring idly into space.

"He is? Good. Then I see no reason why we can't get on with it," he commented, patting the side of the small valise he'd brought with him. "I've got everything I need right here."

The ache in Josie's heart tightened painfully as she slowly led Jason down the hall toward the open door. By the time they'd entered and found Nathan still seated, still staring idly off into space, the hurt inside Josie reached unbearable proportions. How she dreaded

472

leaving on Monday. But she knew she could not stay. Having to watch while Nathan sold all of his father's belongings to total strangers would only add to her misery. No, it was best she leave before that happened.

"As you both probably already know, this will is dated only days before Carl's death," Jason began as he took the desk chair that Nathan had quickly vacated and offered to him. "And it is written in his own hand, which I'm afraid makes it a little difficult to read."

Nathan, who had crossed the room to stand beside Josie, nodded that he understood. He smiled fondly as he pulled a couple of upholstered chairs closer to the desk. "I've seen his handwriting."

"Then you'll bear with me while I try to read this to you as best I can," Jason said, glancing up to make sure they both were seated, ready for him to begin. When no one said anything to forestall the proceedings, he adjusted his eyeglasses just so and began reading.

Sinking back in his chair, Nathan's expression revealed none of the emotions that tore at him as his father's own words were read aloud. Sitting perfectly still, with one hand pressed against his temple, he listened carefully to every word.

Josie, too, tried not to reveal the painful emotions that swelled up inside her for Nathan's sake, but when Jason reached the passage that explained why he'd chosen the two of them to inherit everything, the tears spilled with a will of their own.

"Nathan, my son, I want you to know how very much I love you," Jason read, pausing only long enough to glance up and see how Nathan and Josie were responding. Though he was fully aware of their pain and felt deeply sorry for them both, he continued to read. "Son, I also want you to know that I fully understand why you were so reluctant to let me be a part of your life, especially after my marriage to Annabelle. Although I regret the way things turned out between us, I do understand why, and want you to know I probably would have reacted the same way had I found myself in similar circumstances. After all, I was never a good father to you."

Nathan closed his eyes to the bitter anguish that gripped him, but he continued to listen while Jason read on. "I hope that by having met, and by having lived with Josie Leigh, who is so very much like her wonderful grandmother, you will have in some way come to better understand why my Annabelle was so important to me. Important enough to make me take the chance of alienating my only son forever. And I hope that Josie, too, better understands why her grandmother was willing to leave her family behind. If not, there are several letters her grandmother wrote to her through the years. Jason Haught knows about them and has been asked to present them to her upon my death. Maybe after she's read them, she'll better understand the true depth of our love."

"Although there is no doubt in my mind that the two of you have indeed fulfilled my three-month request, since I know it is in both your natures to meet any challenge that comes your way, I feel I should make alternate provisions for my estate should one of you have decided it not worth the trouble. Should that have happened, my sister, Cynthia Garrett, is to be given outright title to the house she lives in and to the twenty acres that surround it, as well as five thousand dollars with which to live on. But the rest of my estate is to be sold in auction and the proceeds divided between the Hudson River School of Art in New York and the Southern Conservatory of Arts in Atlanta."

"However, I do feel these alternate provisions will prove unnecessary, because I am certain you two have met the challenge and are entitled to the properties listed at the beginning of this document. I want you to know it pleases me to think of my son living at

Oakhaven, even if only for a few months. I just hope he has found the same happiness I found there and plans to stay, filling it once again with love and laughter. I also hope that Josie Leigh will be the one to share in that love and laughter, because it was always my and Annabelle's wish that the two of you meet one day. Having kept up with you both in the best ways we could, we always felt certain you two would find yourselves meant for each other in much the same way Annabelle and I were. But even if that is not the case, I do wish you both well. And I hope that whatever you decide to do with Oakhaven will bring both of you the happiness you deserve."

Nathan stirred in his chair, thinking that was the end of his father's will, but when Jason did not look up, he realized there was more.

"And, although I have no right to ask this of you, I do have one last request."

Nathan looked questioningly at Josie, whose eyes were riveted on the paper in Jason's hand and whose hands tightly gripped the folds of her pale gray skirt. He wondered what sort of favor his father could possibly ask of them.

"Nathan, Josie, I would like for you to give living at Oakhaven three more months, knowing what you now know. I in no way will demand it of you, because whether you decide to stay or leave, Oakhaven is now yours to do with what you want. It is just a last request from a man who hopes you'll give Oakhaven every opportunity to grow on you, to become a part of you as it did me. Other than that, I have only one last thing to say, and that is that I love you both, especially you, Nathan. I am proud to call you my son."

Nathan pressed his eyes closed and did not open them again until he heard the faint rustling of paper that meant Jason was indeed finished. When he glanced at Josie again, there were tears in his eyes.

Slowly, he stood and waited to see what her reaction would be.

With a strong mixture of tangled emotions spilling from her heart, Josie flung herself immediately into his arms. "Oh, Nathan. What are we going to do?"

Nathan's arms closed tightly around her as he pressed his damp cheek into her hair. His father's will had opened his eyes to so many things. "I'm going to ask Jason to leave us alone for a moment so we can discuss this."

"Of course. Take all the time you want. I'll wait out in the hall," Jason said, leaving his papers scattered across the desk in his haste to leave the room.

Still holding Josie close, he waited until Jason had closed the door behind him before asking the question that had been bothering him for weeks now. "Josie, there's something I have to ask you. Something I have to know."

"What is it?" Josie asked, pulling back just enough to be able to look into his eyes. The tears that lingered there tore at her heart.

"It has to do with something Dr. Harrison said."

"What?" she asked, trying to remember what that might be. Her heart froze in midbeat as she wondered if it had anything to do with Nathan's health. Were the two of them keeping something from her? "What did Dr. Harrison tell you?"

Nathan studied her beautiful upturned face for a long moment while working up the courage to answer her. He realized he would be leaving himself wide open for another rejection, but he had to know the truth. "A few weeks back, when Dr. Harrison bluntly announced that you were a woman in love, you never attempted to deny it. Why is that?"

"Because he spoke the truth. I *am* a woman in love," she said, tilting her head while she waited for a response, hoping against hope it would be a favorable

476

one.

Nathan drew in a long breath and held it before finally adding, "Yet he seemed to think you're in love with *me*."

"I am in love with you."

The beginnings of a smile formed on his lips. "But if that's true, why were you so insistent that we not make love again? Why the big speech to keep me at arm's length?"

"Because I didn't want to end up bitter and heartbroken like my grandfather," she admitted honestly.

"You mean your decision to bring a stop to everything that was happening between us wasn't because you suddenly realized you didn't love me quite enough?"

"Of course not. Nathan, I'll always love you with all my heart."

Blinking as he thought more about it, he asked, "Then, the thought of having my children doesn't repulse you?"

"Not in the least." She smiled—an odd contrast to the tears still in her eyes.

"Not even a little?" he asked, wanting to be sure.

"No, not even a little."

He glanced at her with a cautiously raised brow. "Okay, then prove it."

"How? By staying here with you for another three months?" she asked, knowing he would want to do that for his father's sake.

"No, by staying here with me for the rest of our lives. Marry me, Josie," he said, gently placing his hands on her cheeks so he could study her expression better. "I want you to be my wife."

"Your wife? Isn't that a little sudden?"

"Not really. To tell you the truth, I had already planned to ask you to marry me weeks ago, but that was before you let me know how you felt about me, and about having my children."

"But I only said those things because I didn't want to end up alone and heartbroken, much less unmarried and pregnant. Your child would have been a constant and painful reminder of what I thought could never be."

"But it *can* be, if you'll just agree to marry me."

"What about Twin Oaks and your life there?"

Nathan continued to cradle her face with his hands as he looked deep into her eyes. "Don't you understand? My life is here now with you." And to prove it, he crushed her against him in a fiercely passionate, almost painful embrace, but when his lips came down to possess hers, his kiss was tender, full of promise and love.

"How about if we leave it up to a friendly game of chance?" he asked, smiling down at her with a devilish glimmer in his blue eyes as he pulled erect again but continued to hold her in his arms. "If you win, you can go your own way, just as you'd always planned. If I win, you marry me just as soon as we can arrange for a proper wedding. How about it? I know where there's a deck of cards. I can go get them right this minute."

"There's no reason to bother," she said as she slipped her arms around his neck and pulled him down for yet another kiss. "You win."

And so did she.

Author's Notes

Though some people might complain that a relationship that started from nothing more than a recklessly made wager between strangers (like Nathan's and Josie's) is a little too far-fetched to be believable, let me assure you it is not. My own marriage to Bobby Edward Alsobrook—which is nineteen years strong now—can clearly attest to that.

If asked about the outcome of such a careless wager, made on a cold Friday night in November, 1968, Bobby Alsobrook will grin and readily admit, "It may have been only a small, fifty-cent bet between strangers during a local high school football game, but it was the costliest bet I ever lost." Poor Bobby, he's been paying the price ever since.

GET YOUR VERY OWN
ZEBRA
BIG MOUTH BOX
...PERFECT FOR THE
LITTLE THINGS
YOU LOVE!

The Zebra Big Mouth Box is the perfect little place you need to keep all the things that always seem to disappear. Loose buttons, needle and thread, pins and snaps, jewelry, odds and ends...all need a place for you to get them when you want them.

Just put them in the Big Mouth!

Zebra has imported these beautiful boxes from Sri Lanka. Each box is hand-crafted and painted exclusively for Zebra in this Indian Ocean paradise. Each box is only $12.95 plus $1.25 for postage and handling. To get your very own ZEBRA BIG MOUTH box or to give one to a friend enclose your check for the above amount with your name and address and send it to:

ZEBRA BIG MOUTH BOX
Dept. 101
475 Park Avenue South
New York, New York 10016

New York residents add applicable sales tax.
Allow 4-6 weeks for delivery!